YOUNG SHADOW

FANTAGRAPHICS BOOKS INC.
7563 LAKE CITY WAY NE
SEATTLE, WASHINGTON, 98115
WWW.FANTAGRAPHICS.COM

EDITOR / ASSOCIATE PUBLISHER: ERIC REYNOLDS
BOOK DESIGN: BEN SEARS
PRODUCTION: PAUL BARESH & COVEY
PUBLISHER: GARY GROTH

ISBN 978-1-68396-412-4
LIBRARY OF CONGRESS CONTROL NUMBER 2020942335

FIRST PRINTING: APRIL 2021
PRINTED IN CHINA

PLUS WORLD

FANTAGRAPHICS

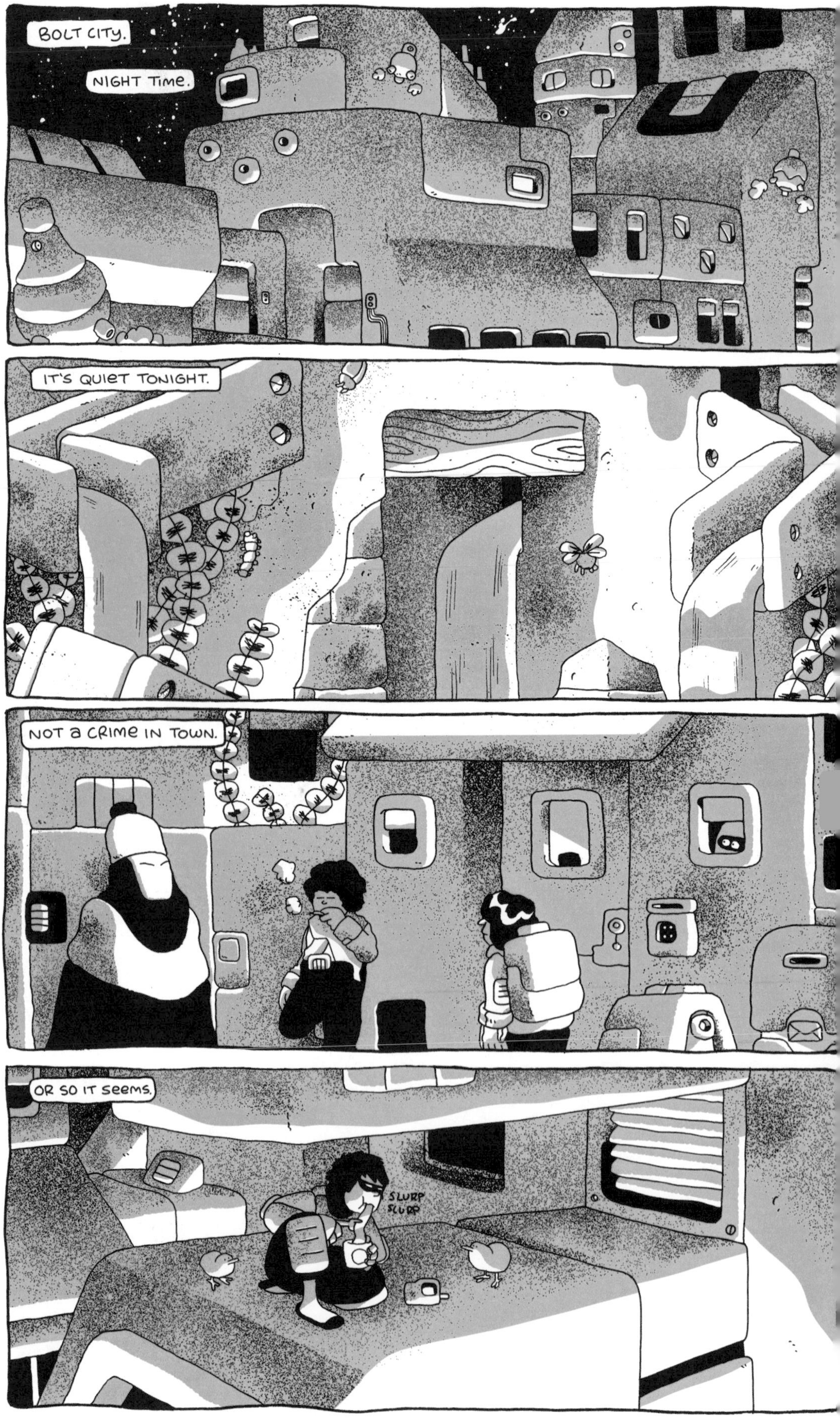
BOLT CITY.
NIGHT TIME.
IT'S QUIET TONIGHT.
NOT A CRIME IN TOWN.
OR SO IT SEEMS.
SLURP SLURP

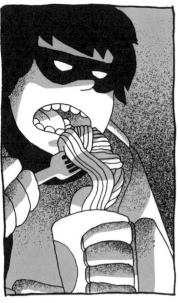

SLOW TONIGHT.

GLUG GLUG

GOOD STUFF.

BIP

BLIP

RING RING

HOLD ON, I'M COMING!

GRETA'S LANTERN GROTTO, WHAT CAN I DO FOR YOU?

HEY, IT'S ME.

SEEN ANYTHING SUSPICIOUS TONIGHT?

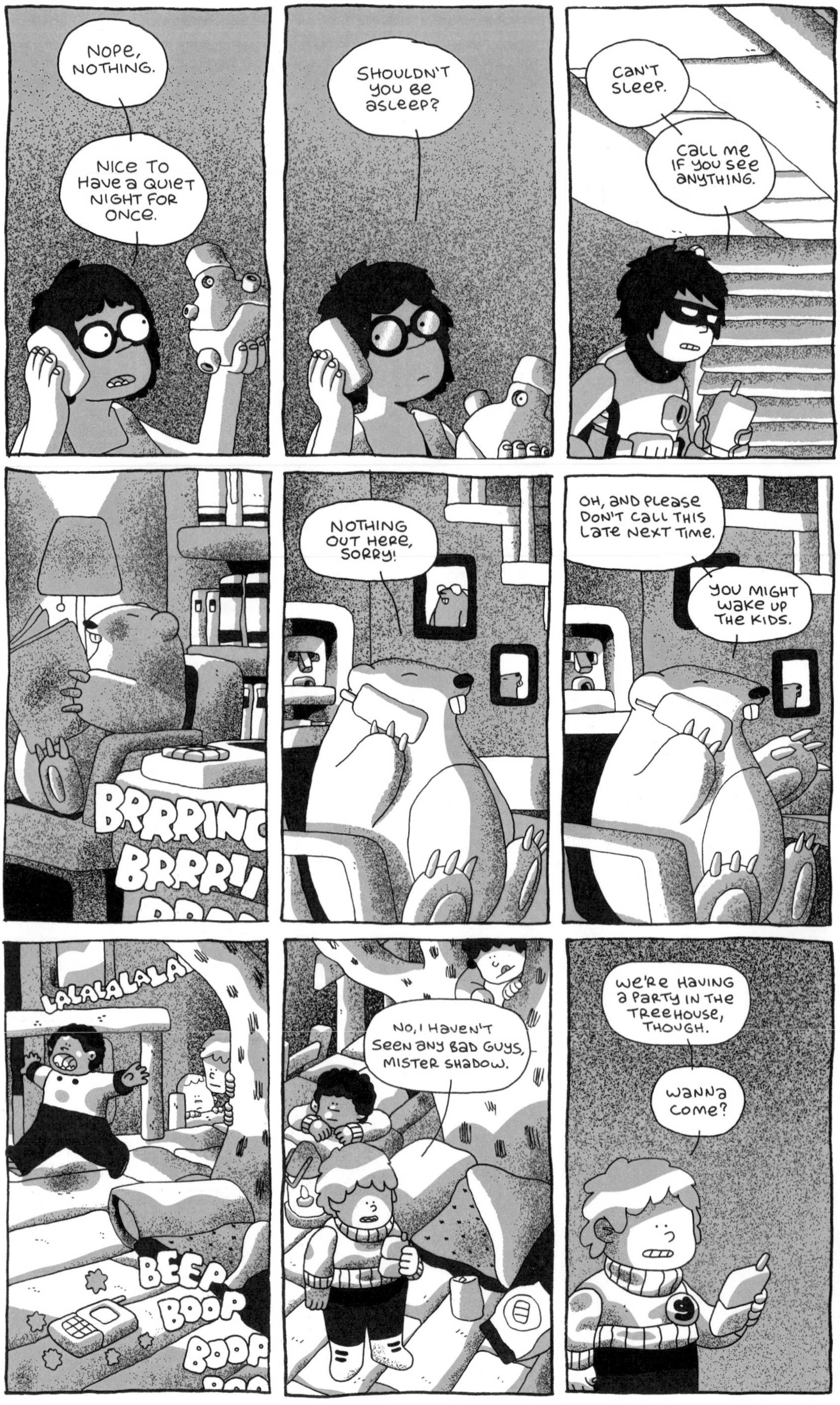
NOPE, NOTHING.
NICE TO HAVE A QUIET NIGHT FOR ONCE.
SHOULDN'T YOU BE ASLEEP?
CAN'T SLEEP.
CALL ME IF YOU SEE ANYTHING.
BRRRING
NOTHING OUT HERE, SORRY!
OH, AND PLEASE DON'T CALL THIS LATE NEXT TIME.
YOU MIGHT WAKE UP THE KIDS.
LALALALALA
BEEP
BOOP
NO, I HAVEN'T SEEN ANY BAD GUYS, MISTER SHADOW.
WE'RE HAVING A PARTY IN THE TREEHOUSE, THOUGH.
WANNA COME?

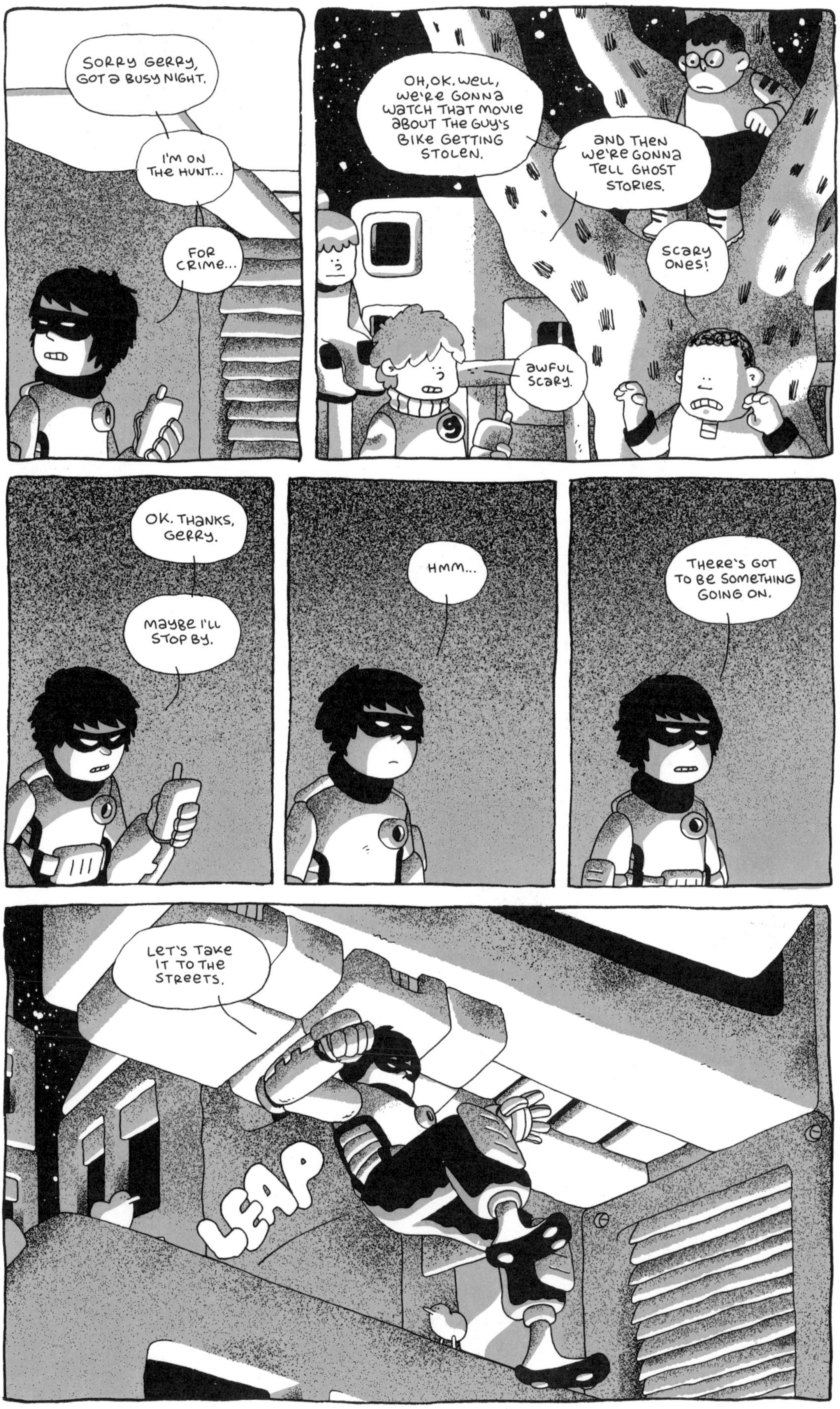
SORRY GERRY, GOT A BUSY NIGHT.
I'M ON THE HUNT...
FOR CRIME...
OH, OK, WELL, WE'RE GONNA WATCH THAT MOVIE ABOUT THE GUY'S BIKE GETTING STOLEN.
AND THEN WE'RE GONNA TELL GHOST STORIES.
SCARY ONES!
AWFUL SCARY.
OK. THANKS, GERRY.
MAYBE I'LL STOP BY.
HMM...
THERE'S GOT TO BE SOMETHING GOING ON.
LET'S TAKE IT TO THE STREETS.
LEAP

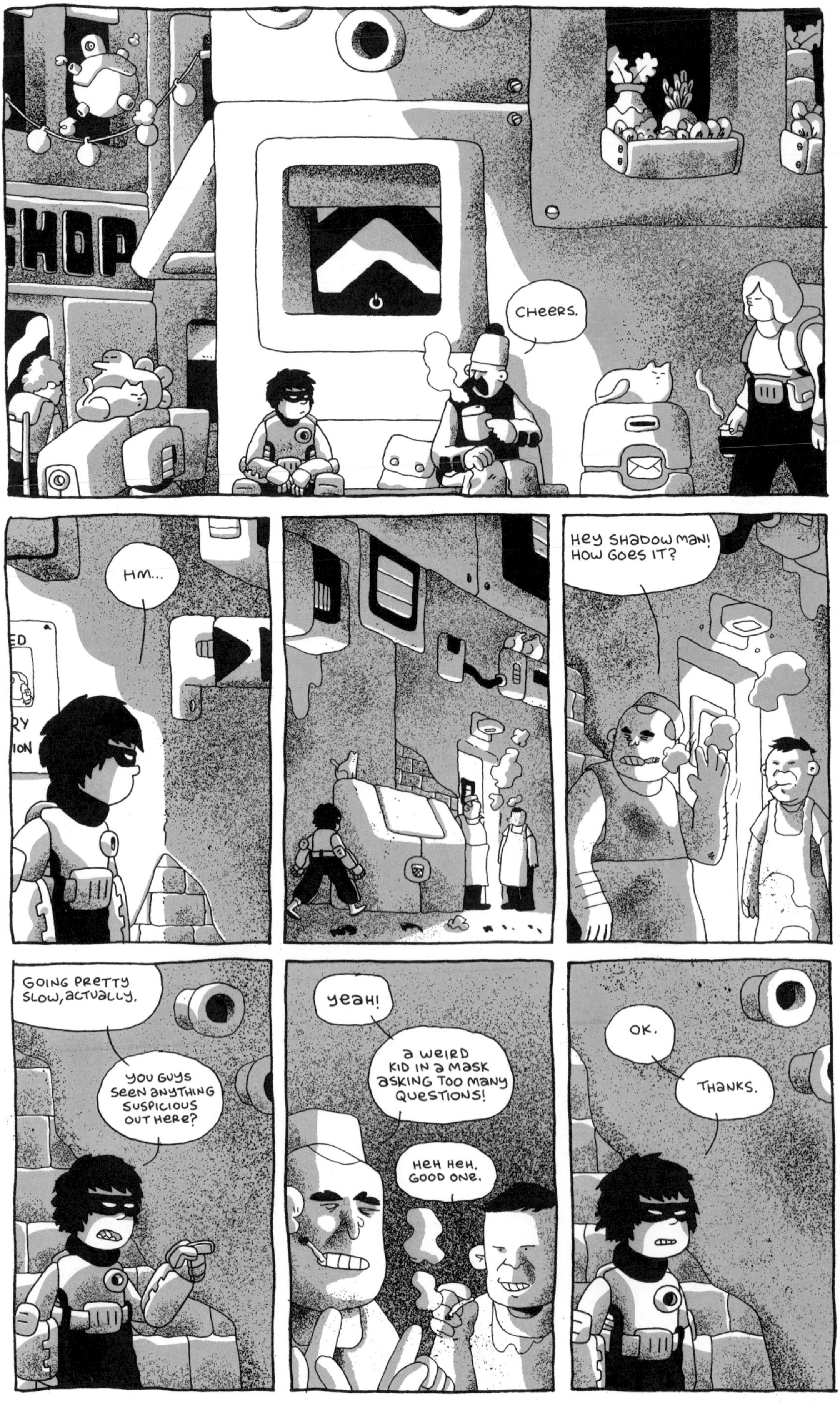

SHOP
CHEERS.
HM...
HEY SHADOW MAN! HOW GOES IT?
GOING PRETTY SLOW, ACTUALLY.
YOU GUYS SEEN ANYTHING SUSPICIOUS OUT HERE?
YEAH!
A WEIRD KID IN A MASK ASKING TOO MANY QUESTIONS!
HEH HEH. GOOD ONE.
OK.
THANKS.

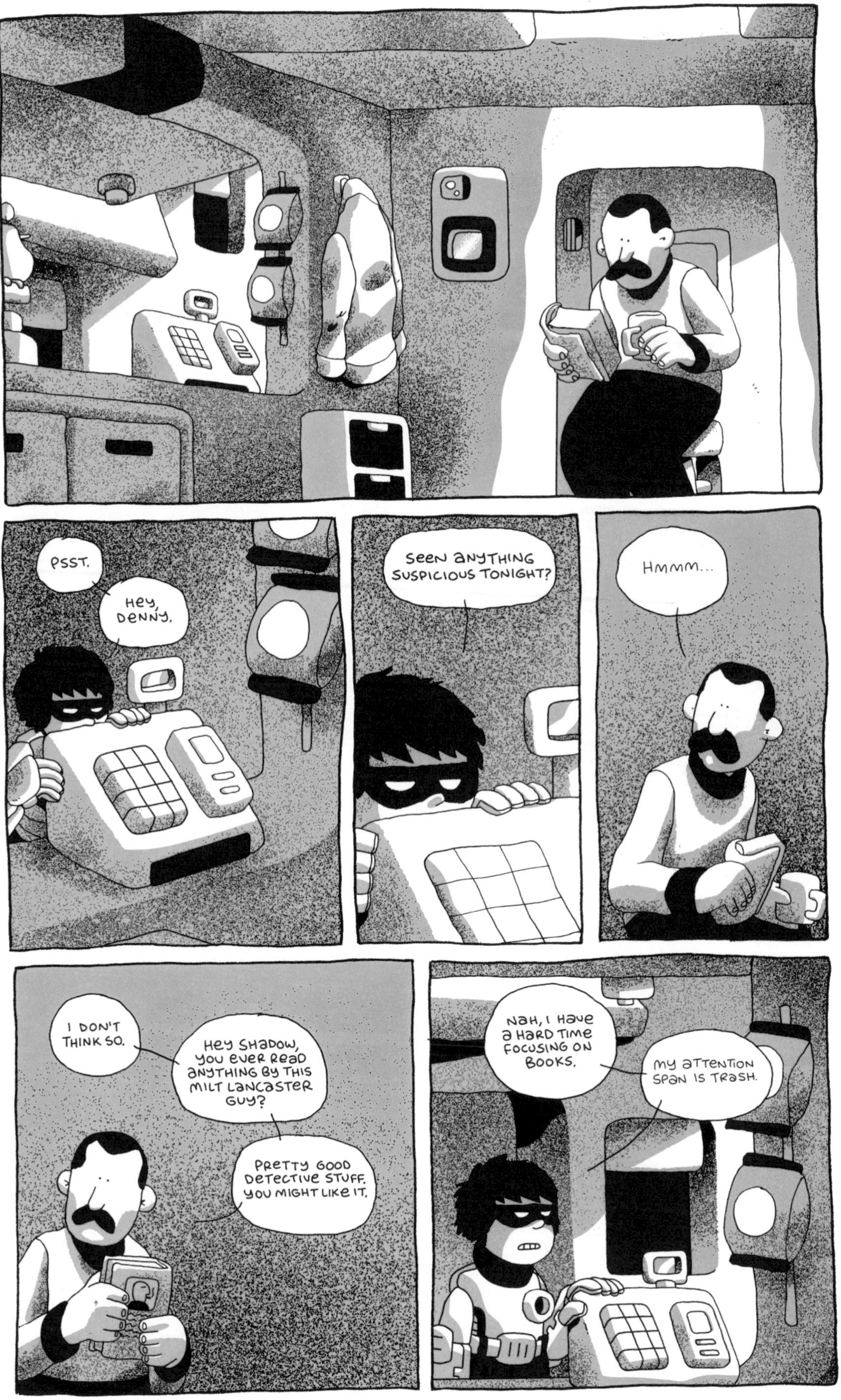
PSST.
Hey, DENNY.
SEEN ANYTHING SUSPICIOUS TONIGHT?
HMMM...
I DON'T THINK SO.
Hey SHADOW, YOU EVER READ ANYTHING BY THIS MILT LANCASTER GUY?
PRETTY GOOD DETECTIVE STUFF. YOU MIGHT LIKE IT.
NAH, I HAVE A HARD TIME FOCUSING ON BOOKS.
MY ATTENTION SPAN IS TRASH.

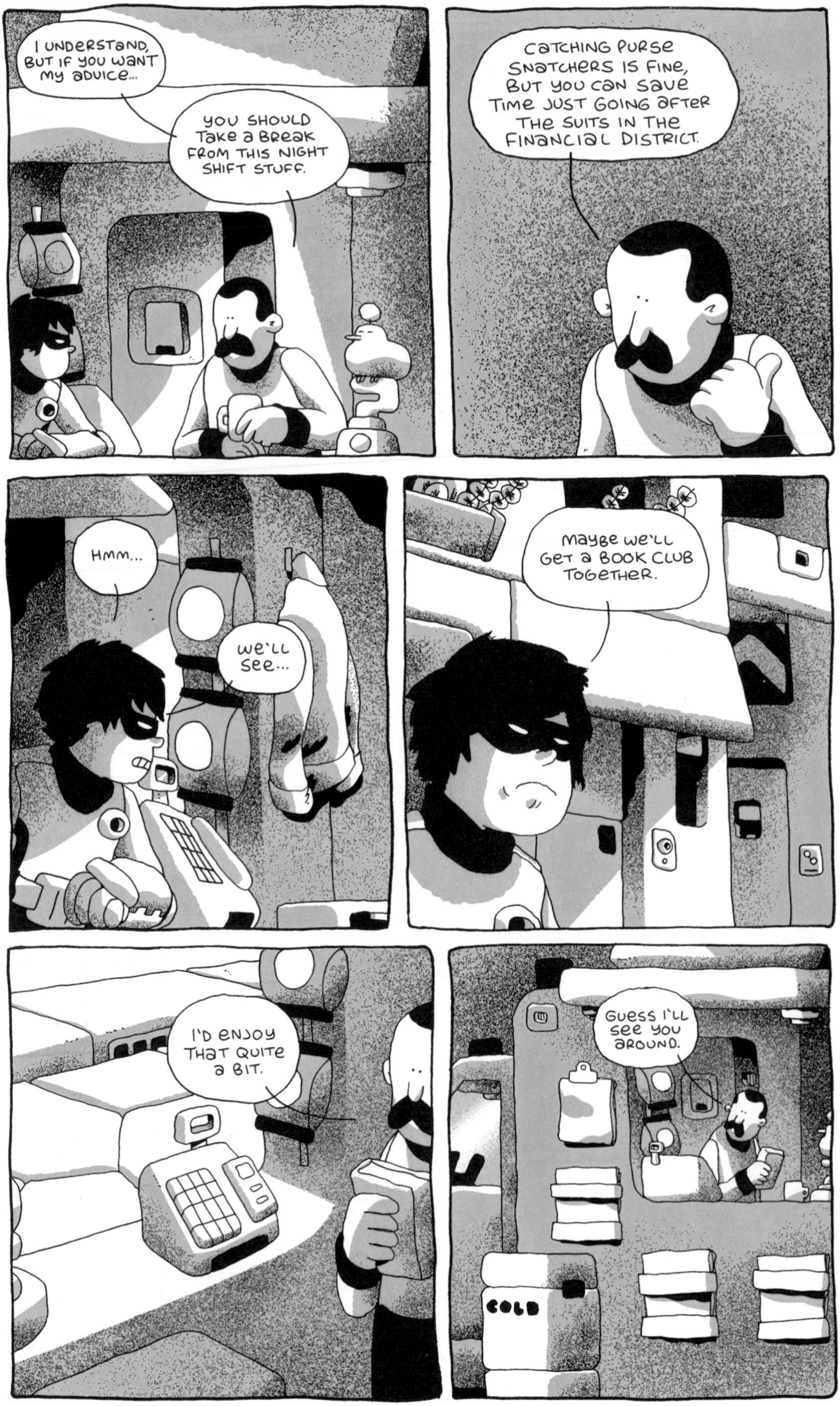
I UNDERSTAND, BUT IF YOU WANT MY ADVICE...
YOU SHOULD TAKE A BREAK FROM THIS NIGHT SHIFT STUFF.
CATCHING PURSE SNATCHERS IS FINE, BUT YOU CAN SAVE TIME JUST GOING AFTER THE SUITS IN THE FINANCIAL DISTRICT.
HMM...
WE'LL SEE...
MAYBE WE'LL GET A BOOK CLUB TOGETHER.
I'D ENJOY THAT QUITE A BIT.
GUESS I'LL SEE YOU AROUND.
COLD

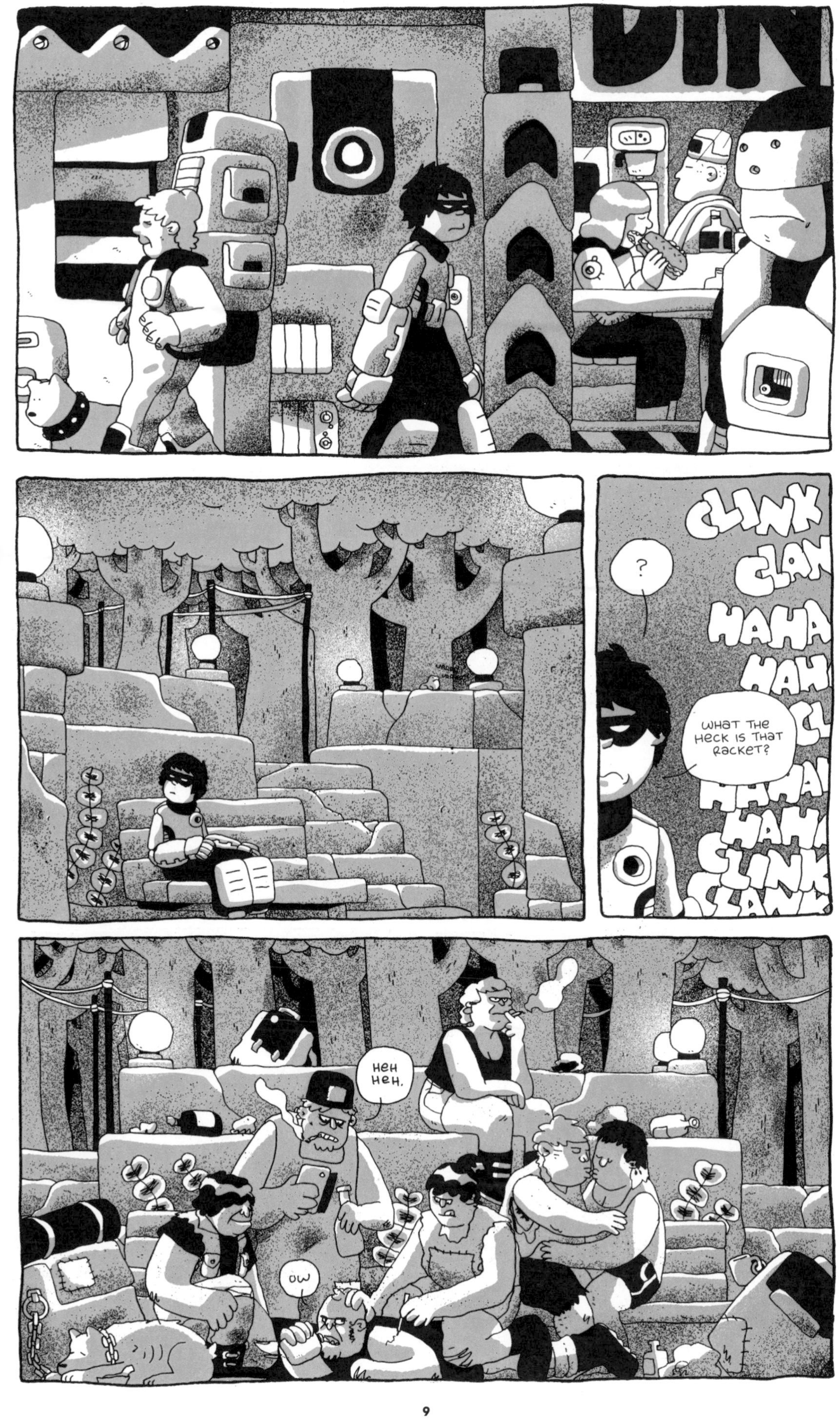
CLINK
?
WHAT THE HECK IS THAT RACKET?
CLINK
HEH HEH.
OW

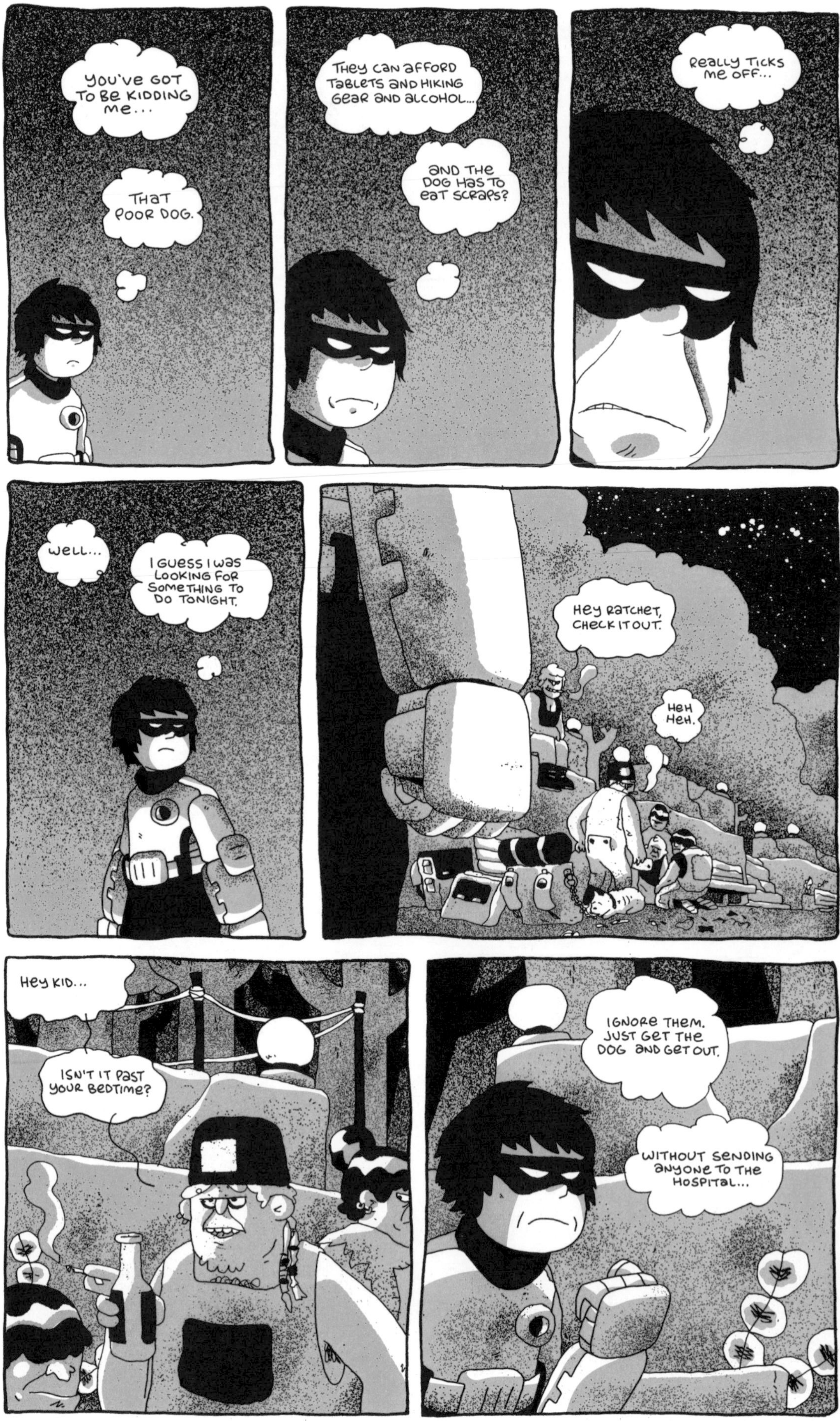
You've got to be kidding me...
That poor dog.
They can afford tablets and hiking gear and alcohol...
And the dog has to eat scraps?
Really ticks me off...
Well...
I guess I was looking for something to do tonight.
Hey Ratchet, check it out.
Heh heh.
Hey kid...
Isn't it past your bedtime?
Ignore them. Just get the dog and get out.
Without sending anyone to the hospital...

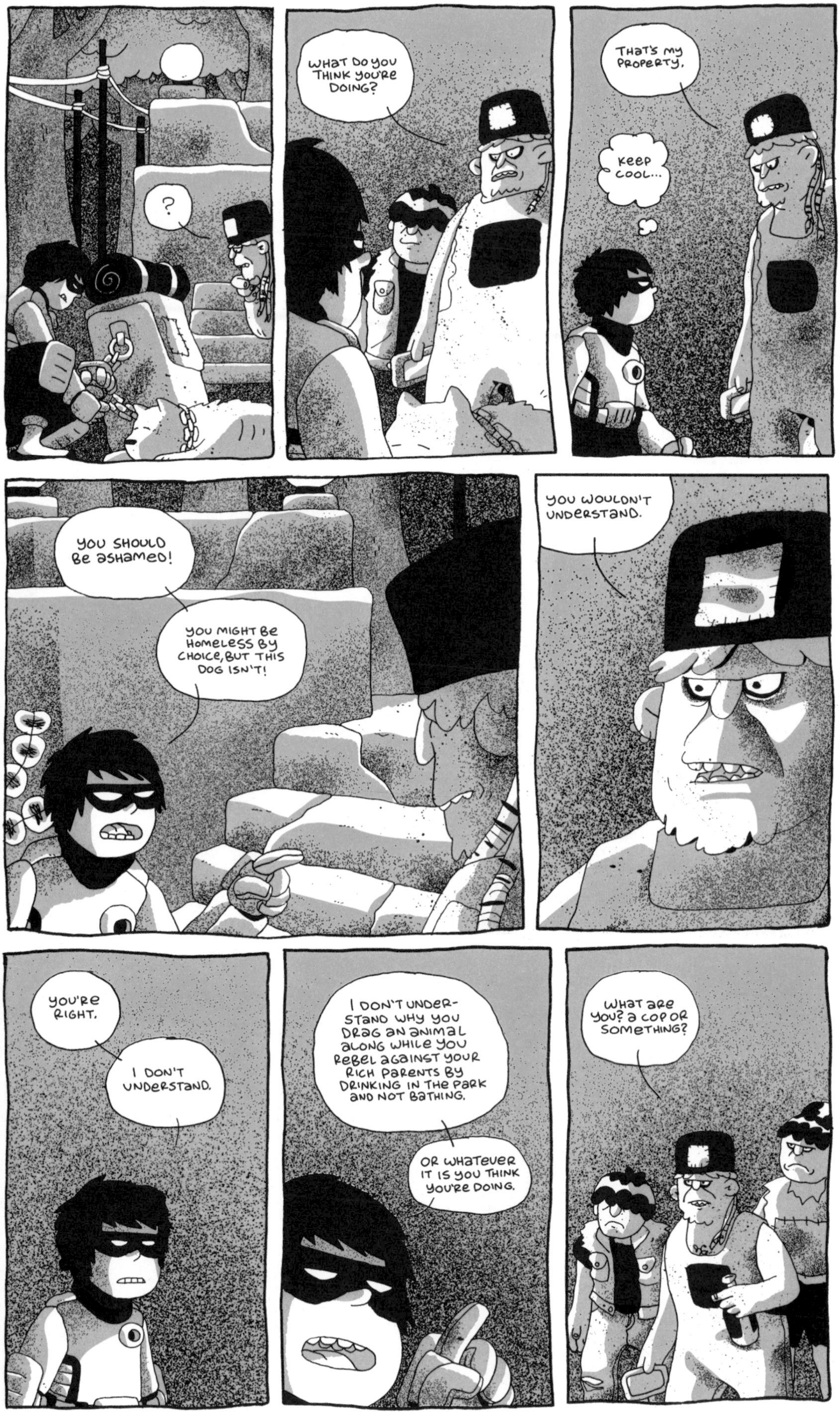
?
WHAT DO YOU THINK YOU'RE DOING?
THAT'S MY PROPERTY.
KEEP COOL...
YOU SHOULD BE ASHAMED!
YOU MIGHT BE HOMELESS BY CHOICE, BUT THIS DOG ISN'T!
YOU WOULDN'T UNDERSTAND.
YOU'RE RIGHT.
I DON'T UNDERSTAND.
I DON'T UNDERSTAND WHY YOU DRAG AN ANIMAL ALONG WHILE YOU REBEL AGAINST YOUR RICH PARENTS BY DRINKING IN THE PARK AND NOT BATHING.
OR WHATEVER IT IS YOU THINK YOU'RE DOING.
WHAT ARE YOU? A COP OR SOMETHING?

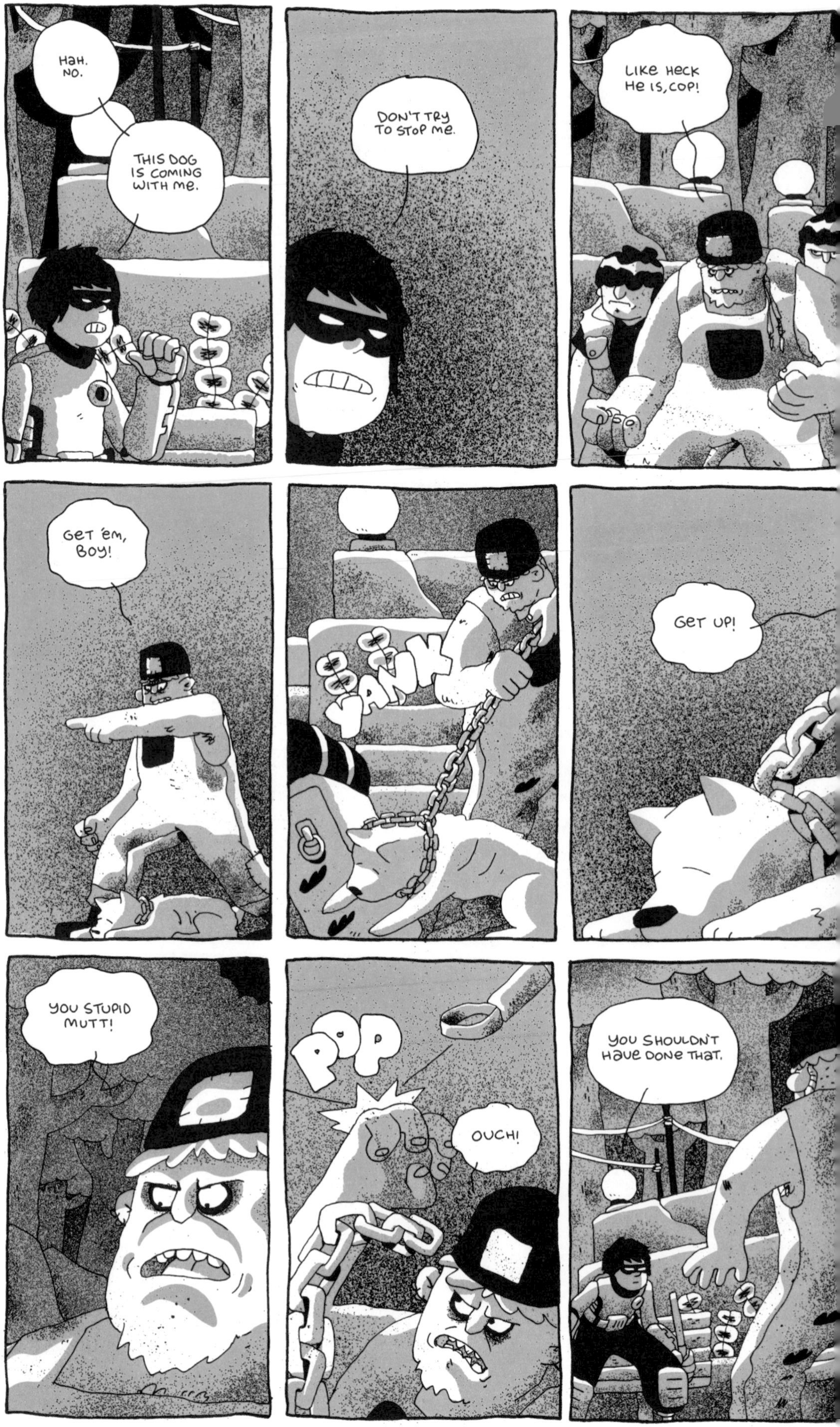
HAH. NO.
THIS DOG IS COMING WITH ME.
DON'T TRY TO STOP ME.
LIKE HECK HE IS, COP!
GET 'EM, BOY!
YANK
GET UP!
YOU STUPID MUTT!
POP
OUCH!
YOU SHOULDN'T HAVE DONE THAT.

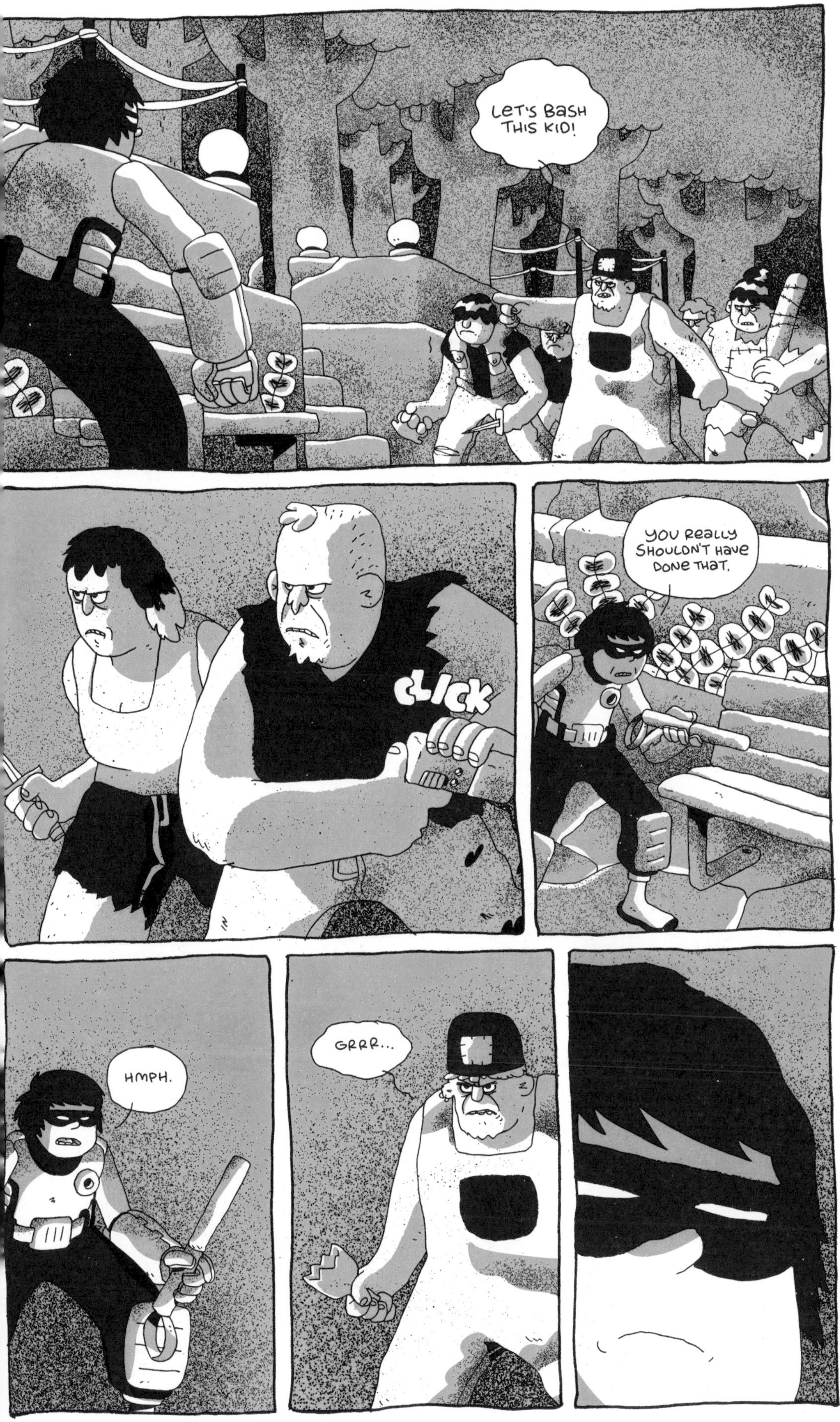
LET'S BASH THIS KID!
CLICK
YOU REALLY SHOULDN'T HAVE DONE THAT.
HMPH.
GRRR...

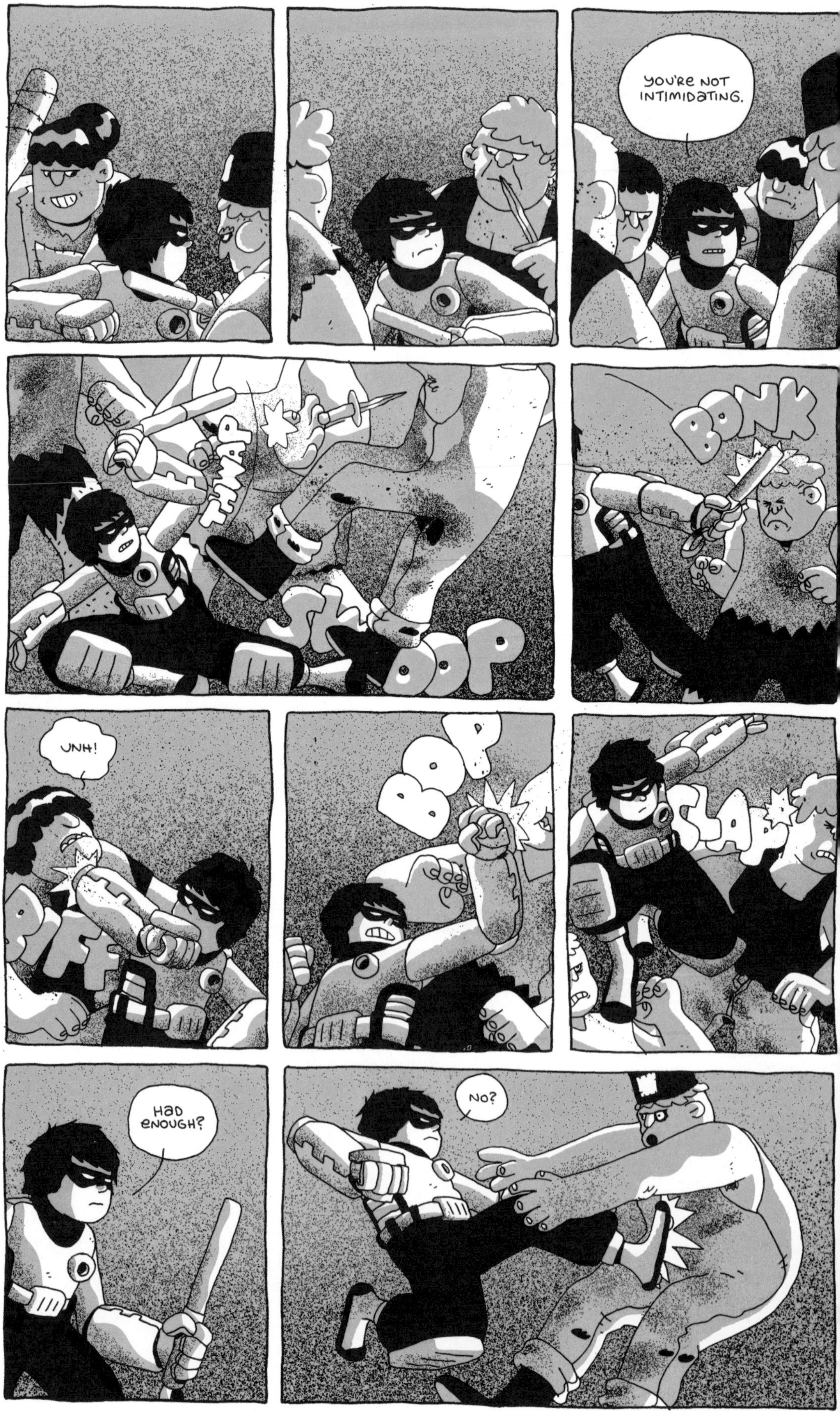
YOU'RE NOT INTIMIDATING.
THWAP
SHOOP
BONK
UNH!
BIFF
BOP
SLAP
HAD ENOUGH?
NO?

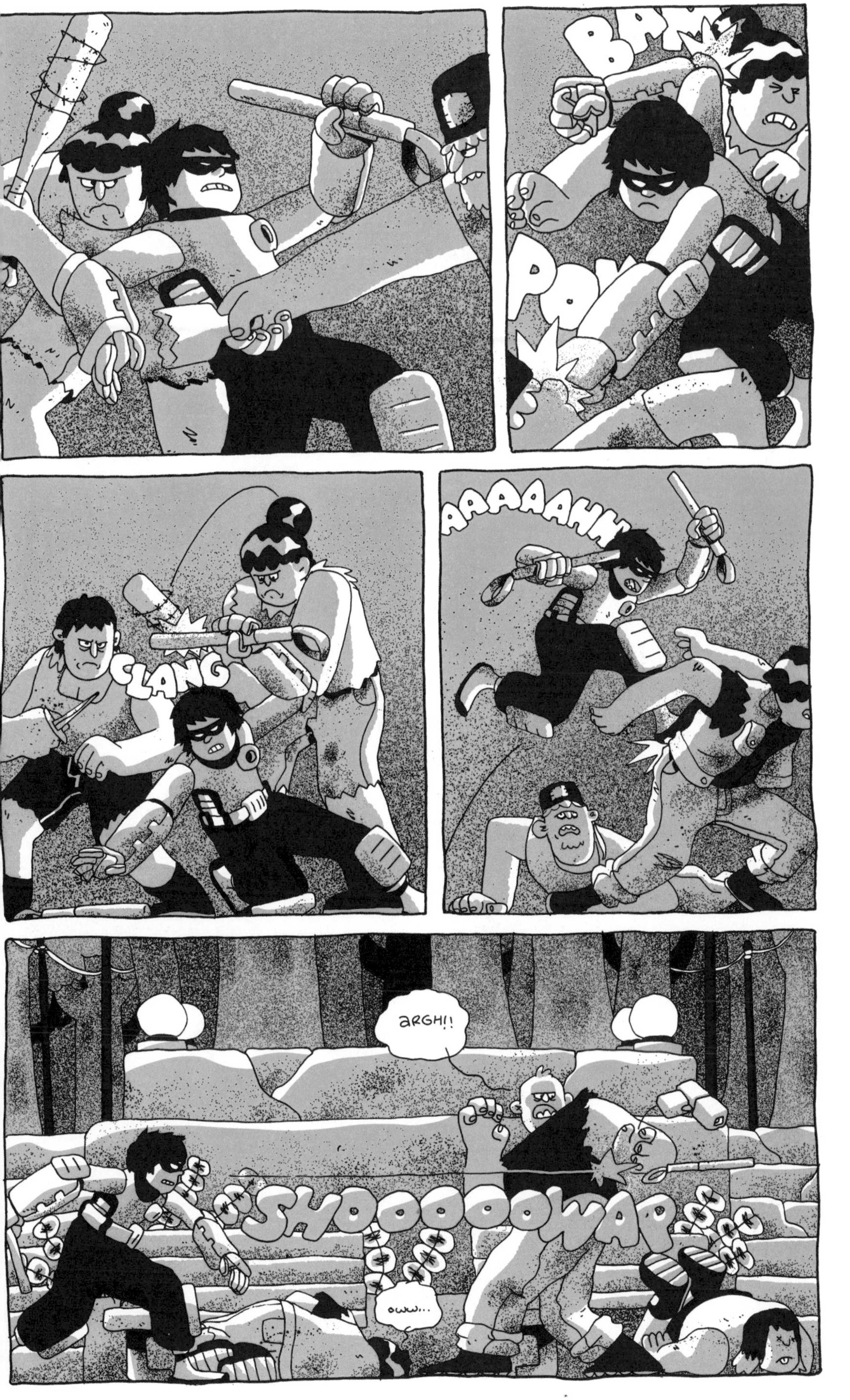
CLANG
AAAAAHH
ARGH!!
SHOOOOOWAP
oww...

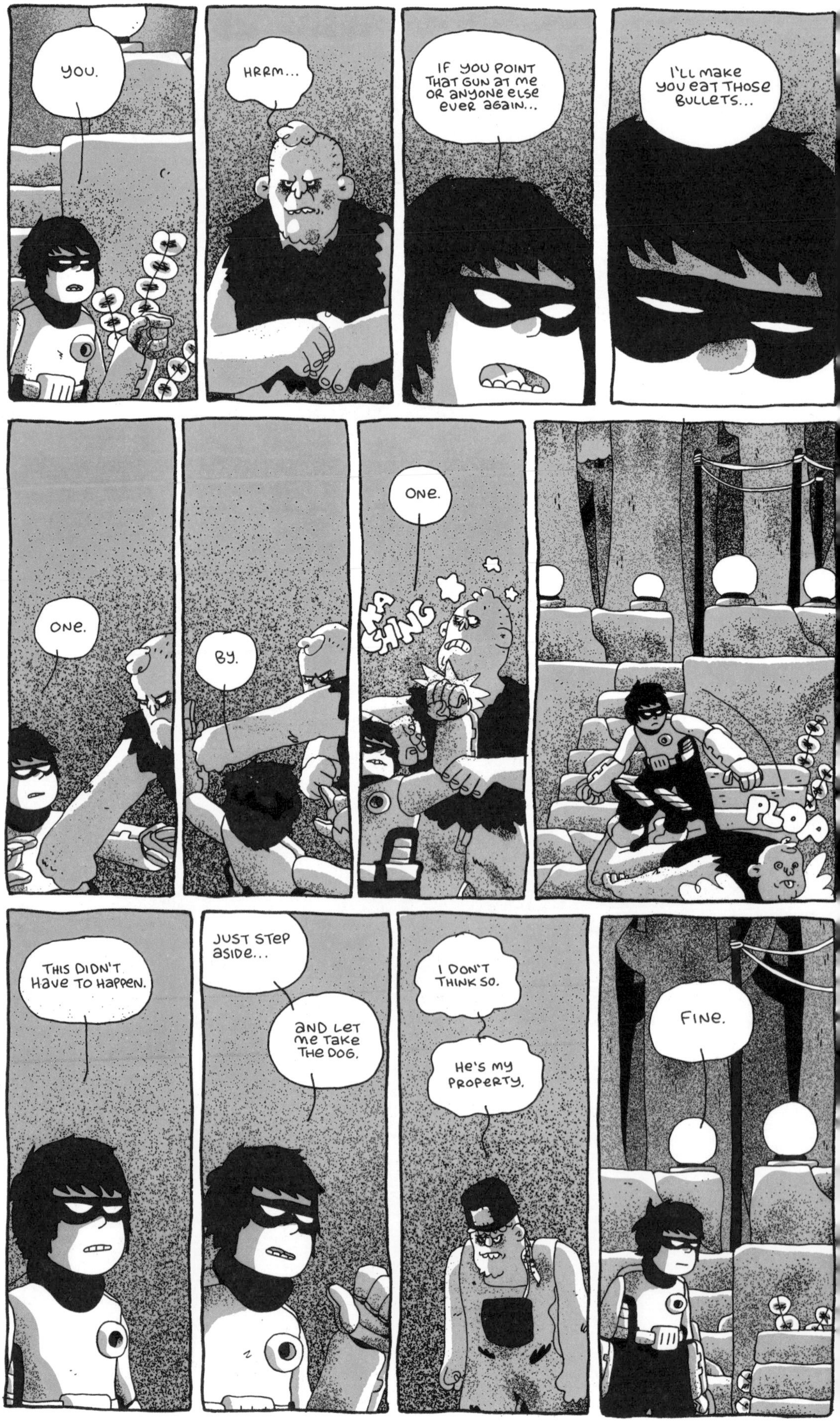
YOU.
HRRM...
IF YOU POINT THAT GUN AT ME OR ANYONE ELSE EVER AGAIN...
I'LL MAKE YOU EAT THOSE BULLETS...
ONE.
BY.
ONE.
KA CHING
PLOP
THIS DIDN'T HAVE TO HAPPEN.
JUST STEP ASIDE...
AND LET ME TAKE THE DOG.
I DON'T THINK SO.
HE'S MY PROPERTY.
FINE.

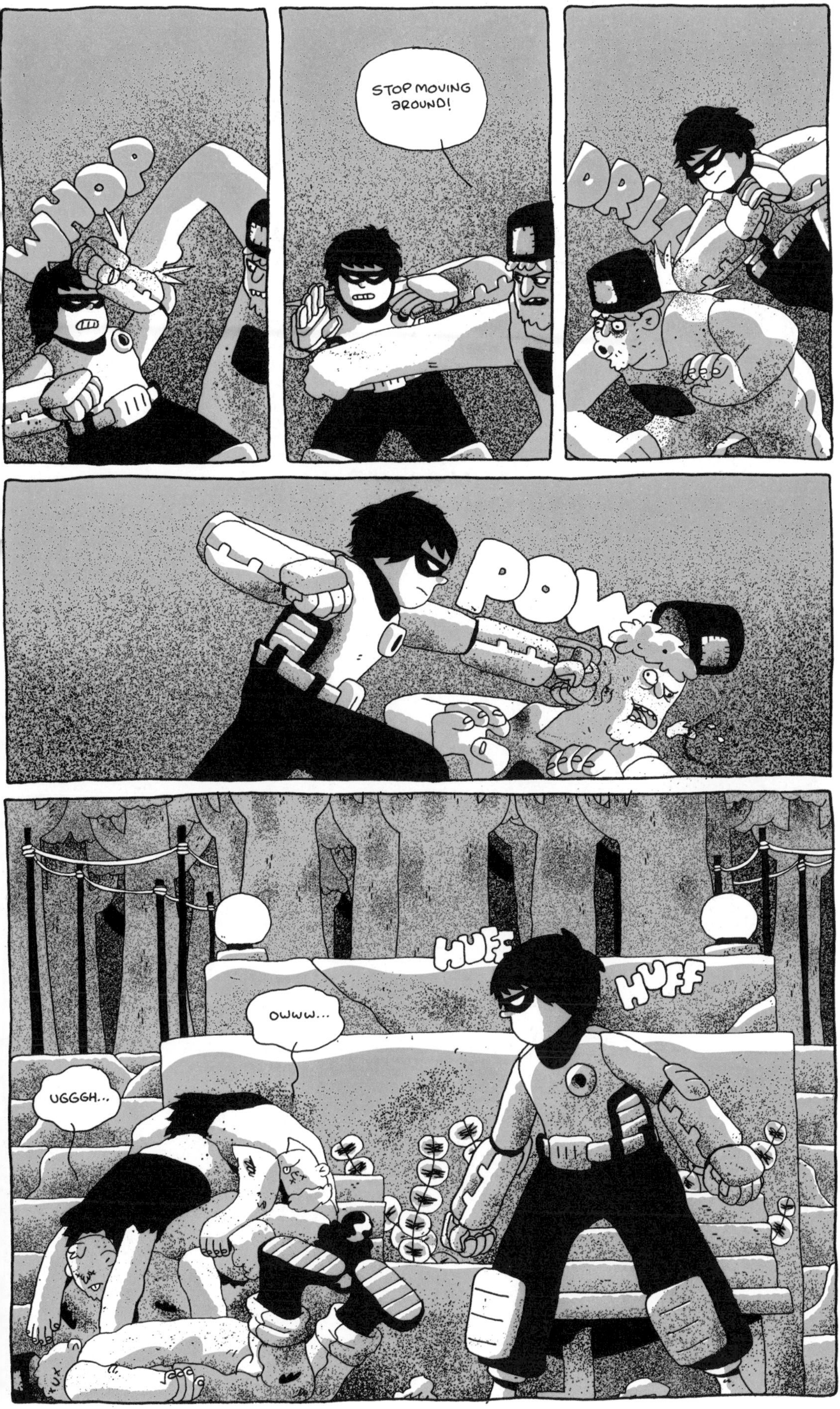
WHOP
STOP MOVING AROUND!
DRILL
POW
HUFF
HUFF
OWWW...
UGGGH...

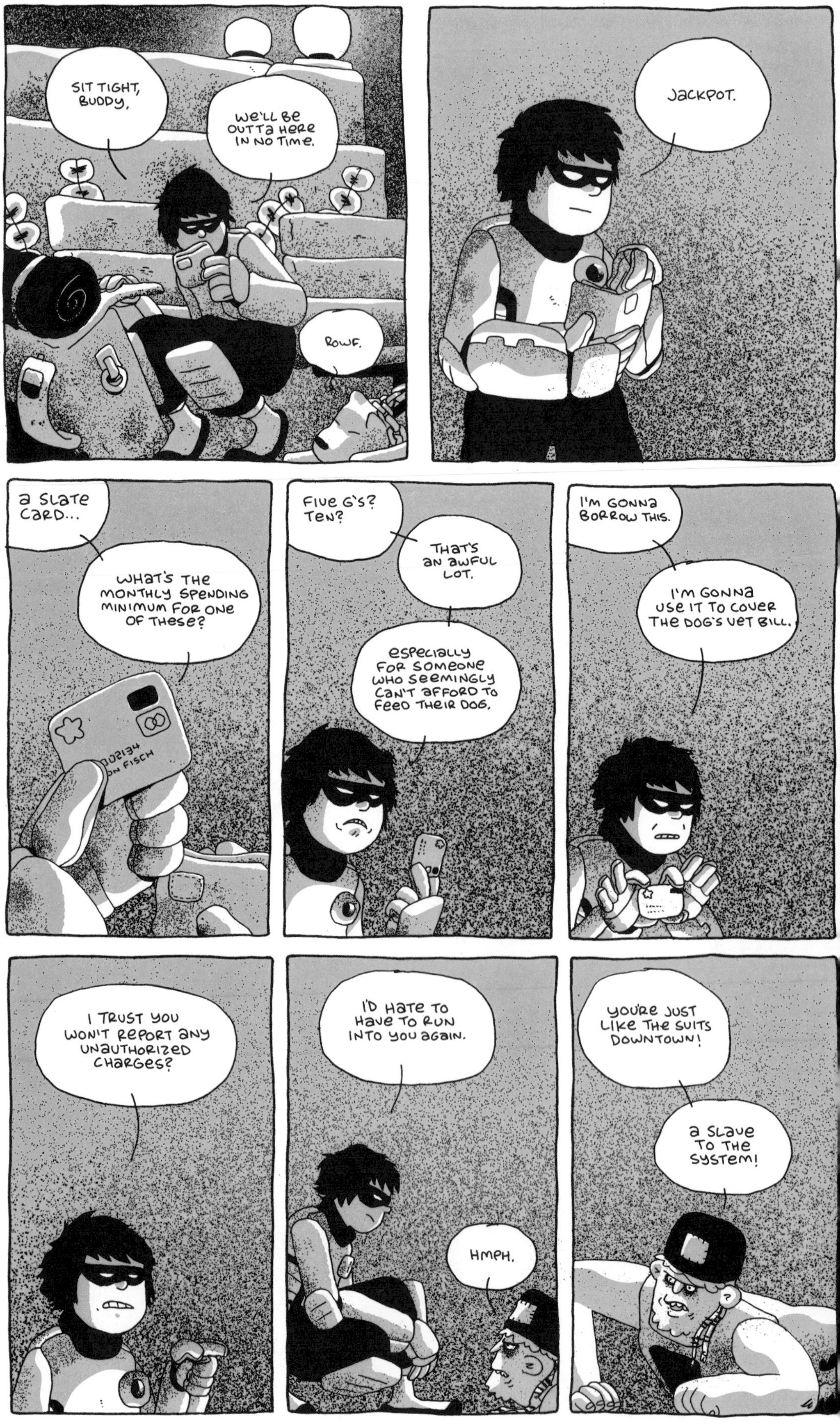
SIT TIGHT, BUDDY,
WE'LL BE OUTTA HERE IN NO TIME.
ROWF.
JACKPOT.
A SLATE CARD...
WHAT'S THE MONTHLY SPENDING MINIMUM FOR ONE OF THESE?
FIVE G'S? TEN?
THAT'S AN AWFUL LOT.
ESPECIALLY FOR SOMEONE WHO SEEMINGLY CAN'T AFFORD TO FEED THEIR DOG.
I'M GONNA BORROW THIS.
I'M GONNA USE IT TO COVER THE DOG'S VET BILL.
I TRUST YOU WON'T REPORT ANY UNAUTHORIZED CHARGES?
I'D HATE TO HAVE TO RUN INTO YOU AGAIN.
HMPH.
YOU'RE JUST LIKE THE SUITS DOWNTOWN!
A SLAVE TO THE SYSTEM!

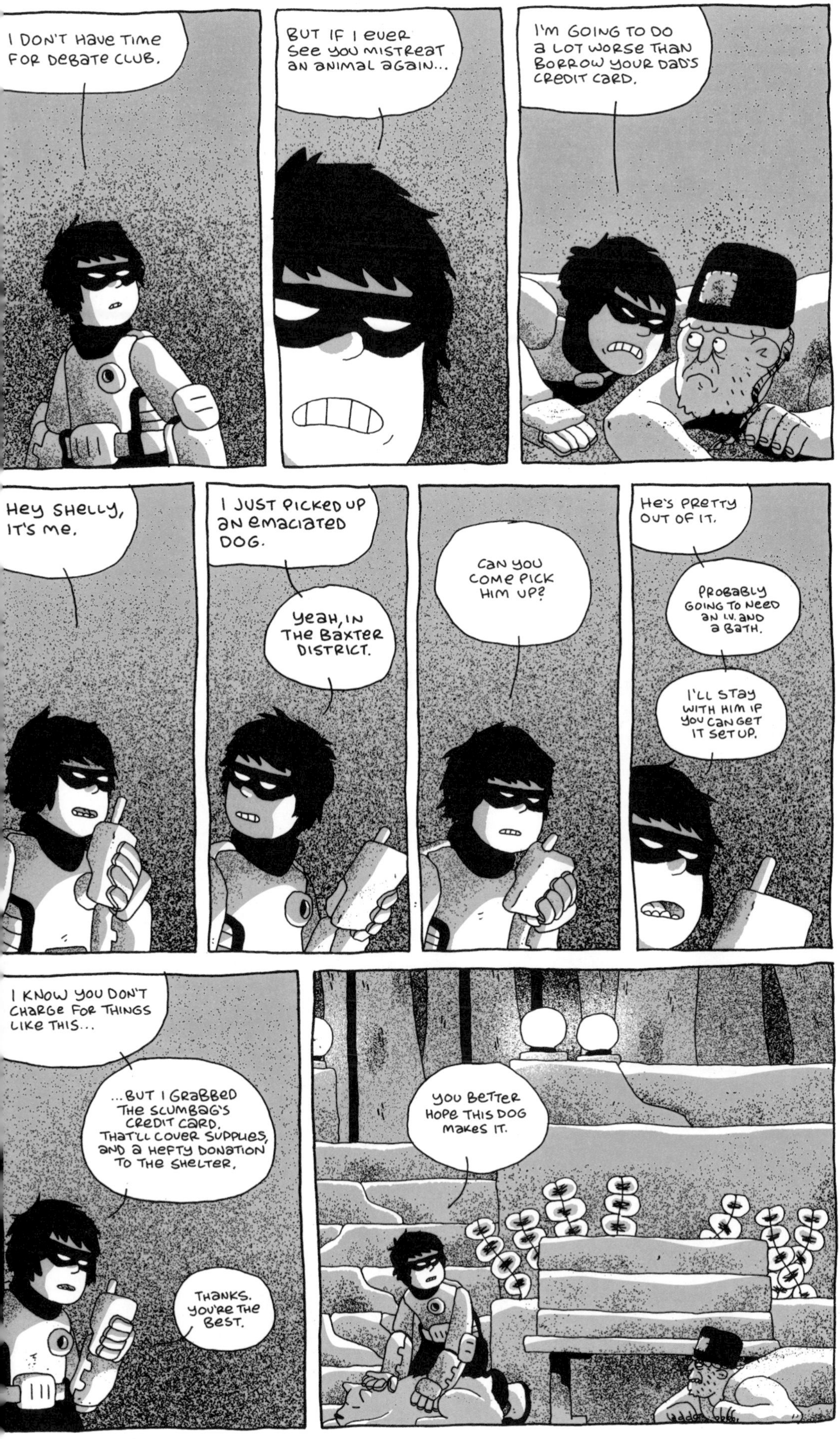
I DON'T HAVE TIME FOR DEBATE CLUB.
BUT IF I EVER SEE YOU MISTREAT AN ANIMAL AGAIN...
I'M GOING TO DO A LOT WORSE THAN BORROW YOUR DAD'S CREDIT CARD.
HEY SHELLY, IT'S ME.
I JUST PICKED UP AN EMACIATED DOG.
YEAH, IN THE BAXTER DISTRICT.
CAN YOU COME PICK HIM UP?
HE'S PRETTY OUT OF IT.
PROBABLY GOING TO NEED AN I.V. AND A BATH.
I'LL STAY WITH HIM IF YOU CAN GET IT SET UP.
I KNOW YOU DON'T CHARGE FOR THINGS LIKE THIS...
...BUT I GRABBED THE SCUMBAG'S CREDIT CARD. THAT'LL COVER SUPPLIES, AND A HEFTY DONATION TO THE SHELTER.
THANKS. YOU'RE THE BEST.
YOU BETTER HOPE THIS DOG MAKES IT.

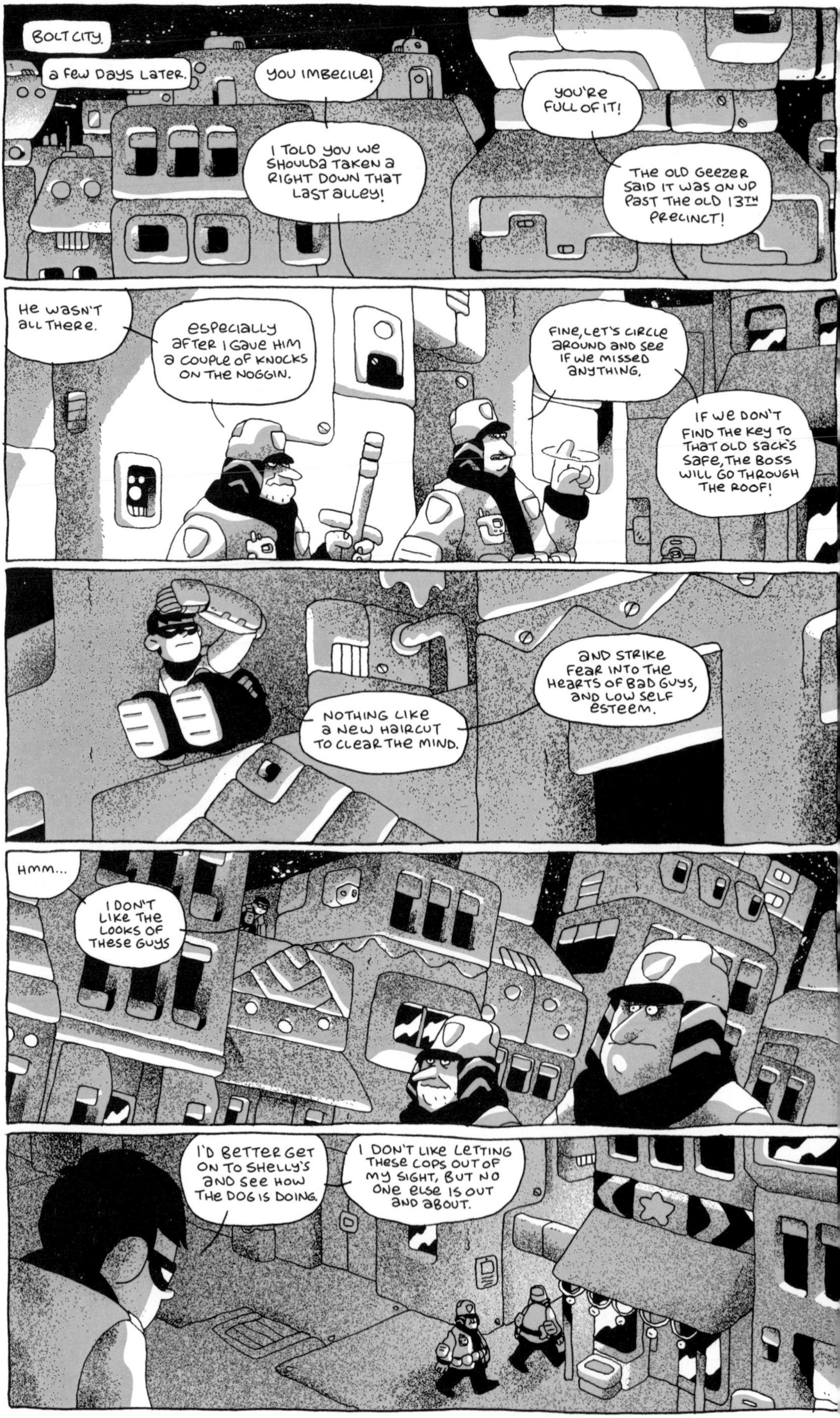
BOLT CITY.
a few Days Later.
YOU IMBECILE!
I TOLD YOU WE SHOULDA TAKEN A RIGHT DOWN THAT LAST ALLEY!
YOU'RE FULL OF IT!
THE OLD GEEZER SAID IT WAS ON UP PAST THE OLD 13TH PRECINCT!
He WASN'T ALL THERE.
ESPECIALLY AFTER I GAVE HIM A COUPLE OF KNOCKS ON THE NOGGIN.
FINE, LET'S CIRCLE AROUND AND SEE IF WE MISSED ANYTHING.
IF WE DON'T FIND THE KEY TO THAT OLD SACK'S SAFE, THE BOSS WILL GO THROUGH THE ROOF!
NOTHING LIKE A NEW HAIRCUT TO CLEAR THE MIND.
AND STRIKE FEAR INTO THE HEARTS OF BAD GUYS, AND LOW SELF ESTEEM.
HMM...
I DON'T LIKE THE LOOKS OF THESE GUYS
I'D BETTER GET ON TO SHELLY'S AND SEE HOW THE DOG IS DOING.
I DON'T LIKE LETTING THESE COPS OUT OF MY SIGHT, BUT NO ONE ELSE IS OUT AND ABOUT.

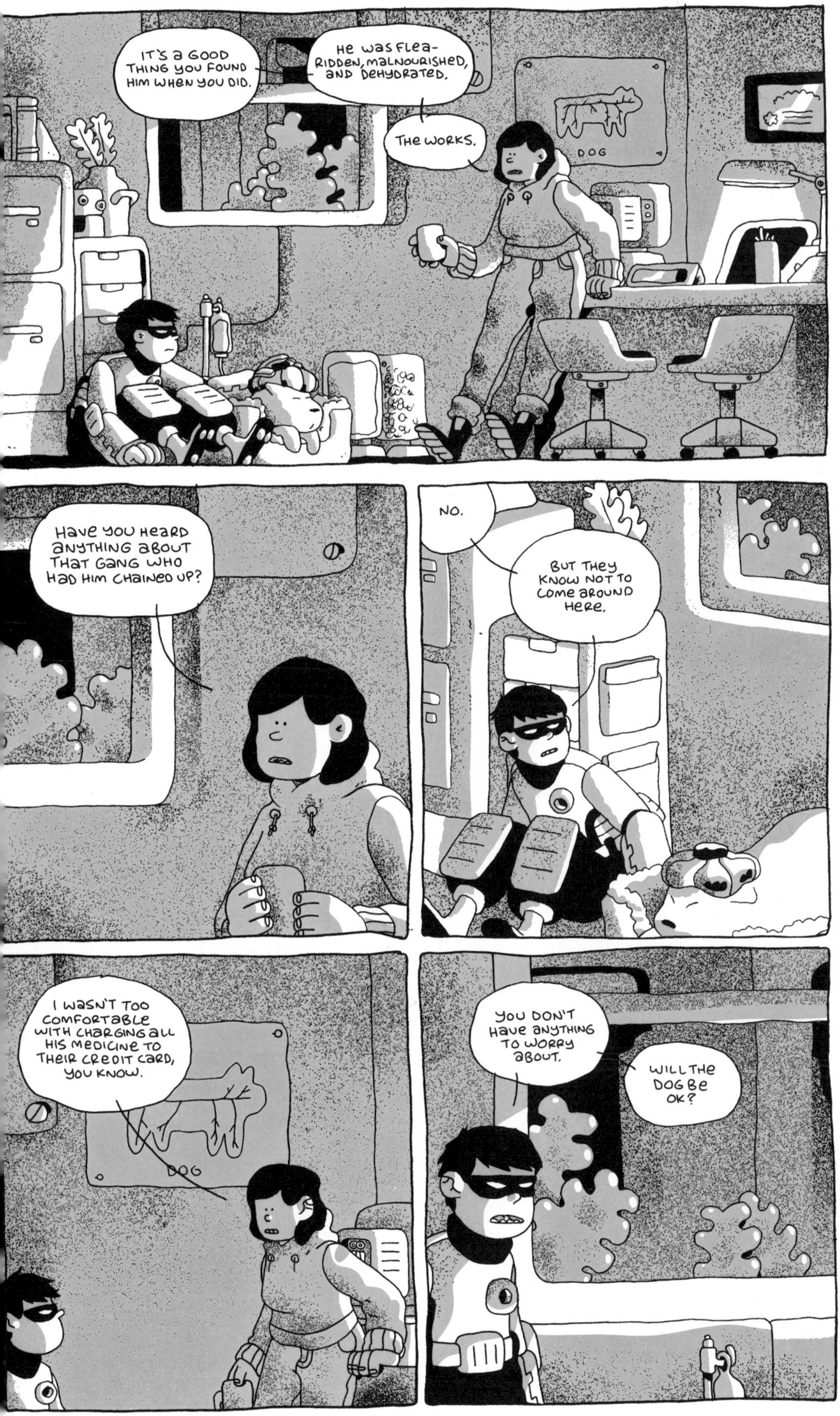
IT'S A GOOD THING YOU FOUND HIM WHEN YOU DID.
HE WAS FLEA-RIDDEN, MALNOURISHED, AND DEHYDRATED.
THE WORKS.
DOG
HAVE YOU HEARD ANYTHING ABOUT THAT GANG WHO HAD HIM CHAINED UP?
NO.
BUT THEY KNOW NOT TO COME AROUND HERE.
I WASN'T TOO COMFORTABLE WITH CHARGING ALL HIS MEDICINE TO THEIR CREDIT CARD, YOU KNOW.
DOG
YOU DON'T HAVE ANYTHING TO WORRY ABOUT.
WILL THE DOG BE OK?

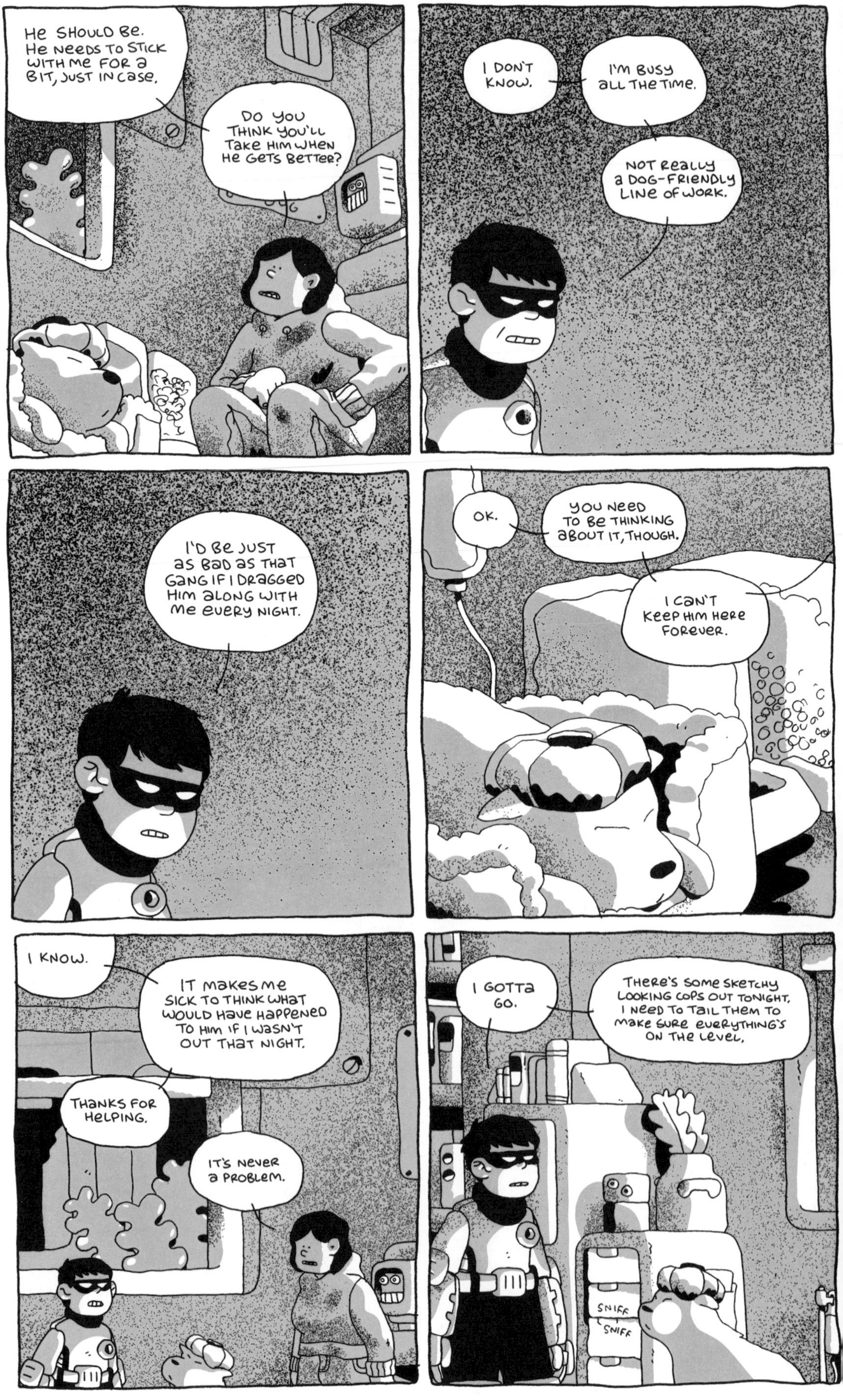
He SHOULD Be. He NEEDS TO STICK WITH Me FOR a BIT, JUST IN case.
DO YOU THINK YOU'LL TaKe HIM WHEN He GeTS BETTER?
I DON'T KNOW.
I'M BUSY aLL THE TIME.
NOT ReaLLY a DOG-FRIENDLY LINe OF WORK.
I'D Be JUST aS BaD aS THaT GaNG IF I DRaGGED HIM aLONG WITH Me eveRY NIGHT.
OK.
YOU NeeD TO Be THINKING aBOUT IT, THOUGH.
I caN'T KeeP HIM HeRe FOReveR.
I KNOW.
IT MaKeS Me SICK TO THINK WHaT WOULD Have HaPPeNeD TO HIM IF I WaSN'T OUT THaT NIGHT.
THaNKS FOR HeLPING.
IT'S Never a PROBLeM.
I GOTTa GO.
THeRe'S SOMe SKeTCHY LOOKING COPS OUT TONIGHT. I NeeD TO TaIL THeM TO MaKe SURe eveRYTHING'S ON THe LeveL.
SNIFF
SNIFF

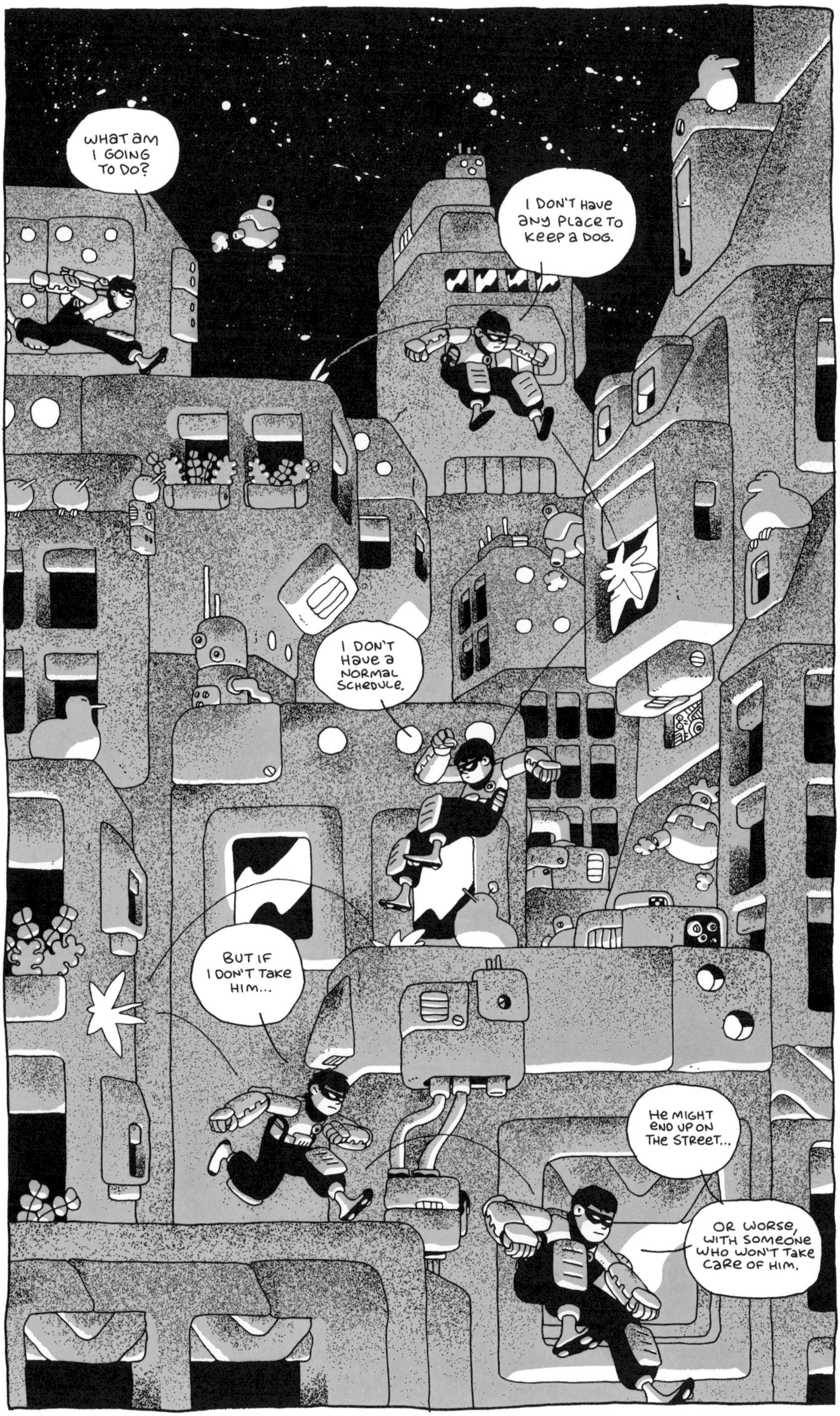
WHAT AM I GOING TO DO?
I DON'T HAVE ANY PLACE TO KEEP A DOG.
I DON'T HAVE A NORMAL SCHEDULE.
BUT IF I DON'T TAKE HIM...
HE MIGHT END UP ON THE STREET...
OR WORSE, WITH SOMEONE WHO WON'T TAKE CARE OF HIM.

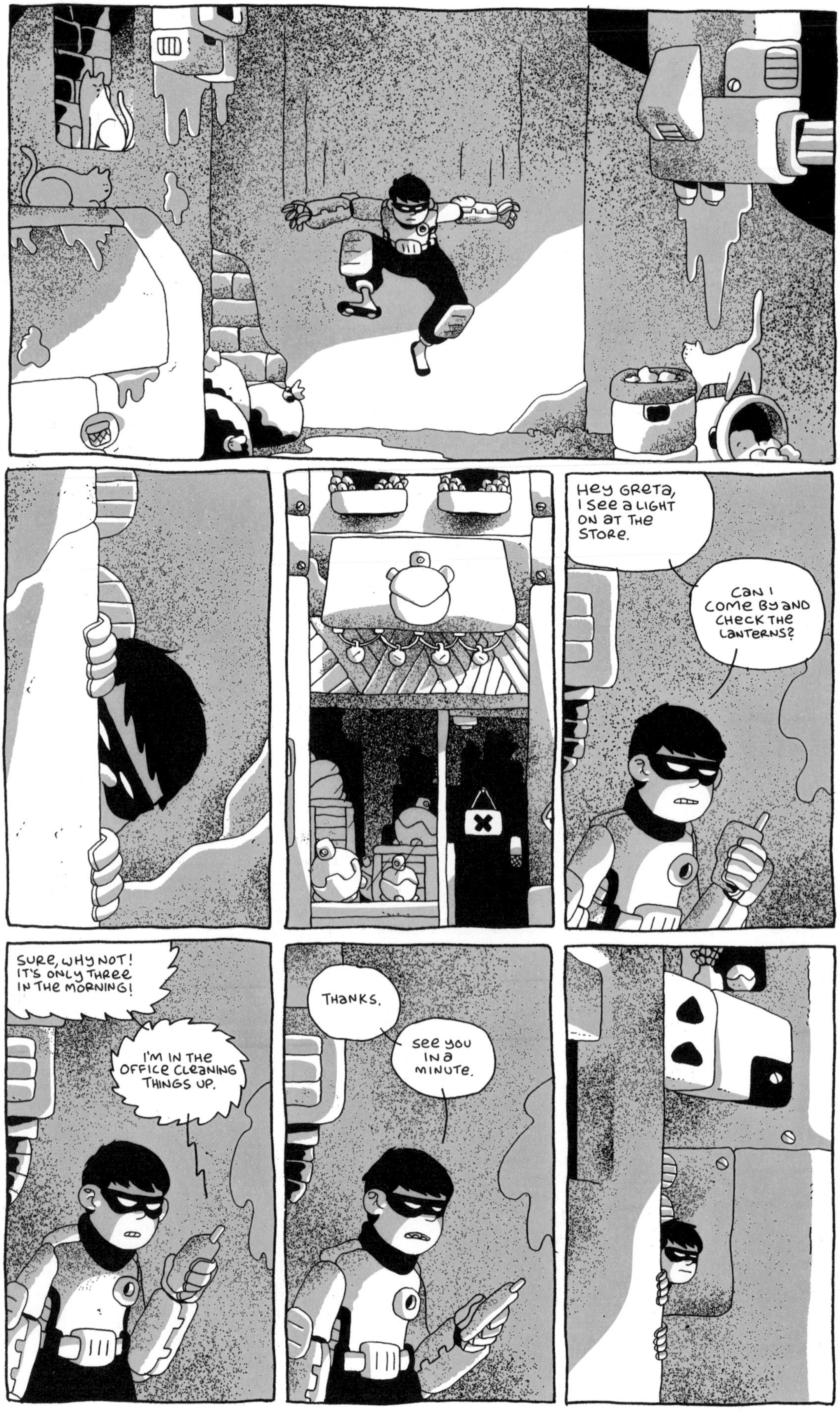

Hey Greta, I see a light on at the store.
Can I come by and check the lanterns?
Sure, why not! It's only three in the morning!
I'm in the office cleaning things up.
Thanks.
See you in a minute.

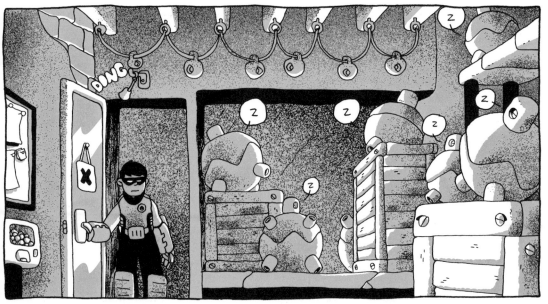

HEY BUDDY...

YOU SEEN ANY MEAN-LOOKING COPS AROUND HERE TONIGHT?

PLOOF

HM...

WHAT ABOUT YOU GUYS?

ANYTHING?

PLOOF

PLOOF

NO COPS AT ALL...

OLD TOWN IS USUALLY LOUSY WITH THEM THIS TIME OF NIGHT.

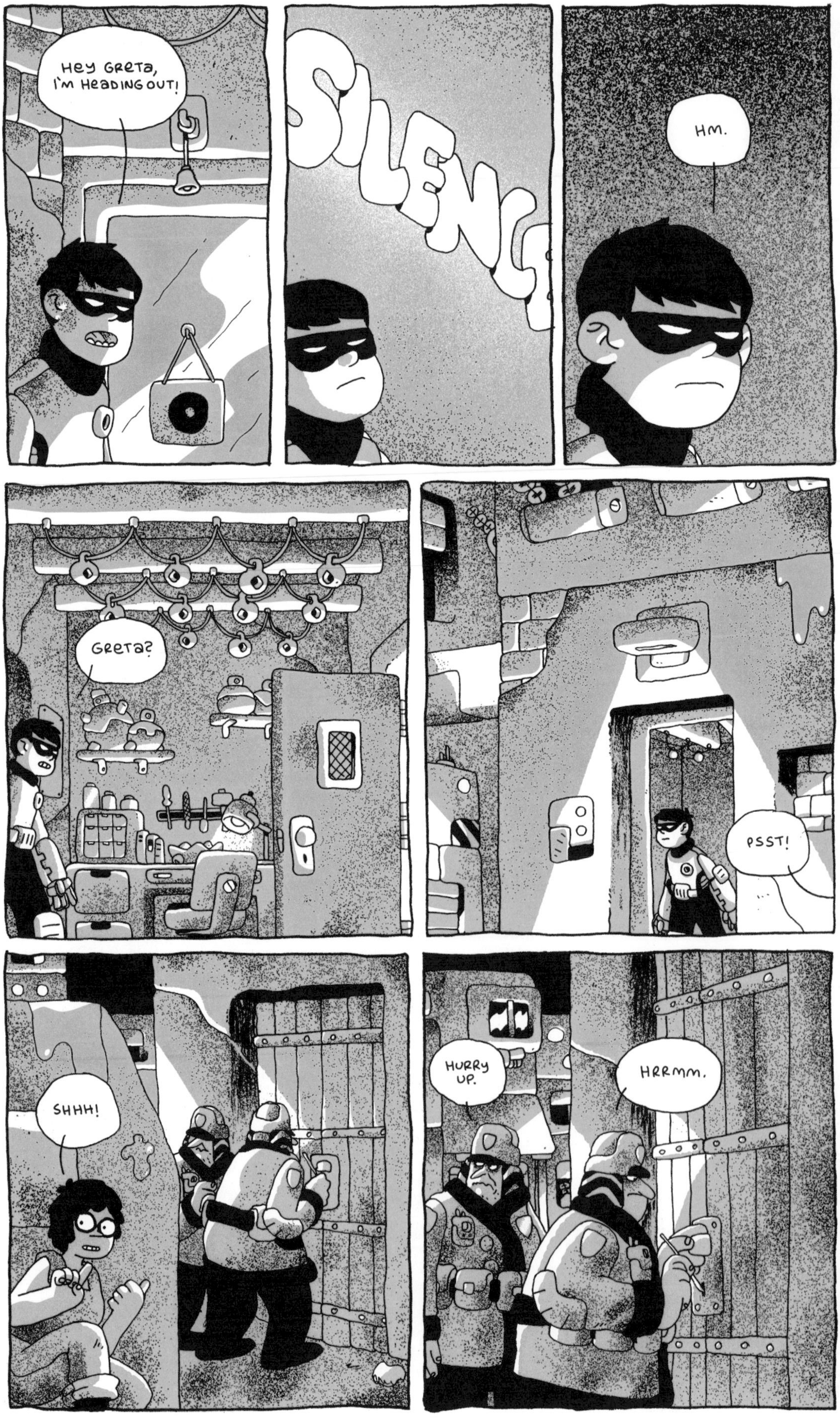

Hey Greta, I'm heading out!
SILENCE
HM.
GRETA?
PSST!
SHHH!
HURRY UP.
HRRMM.

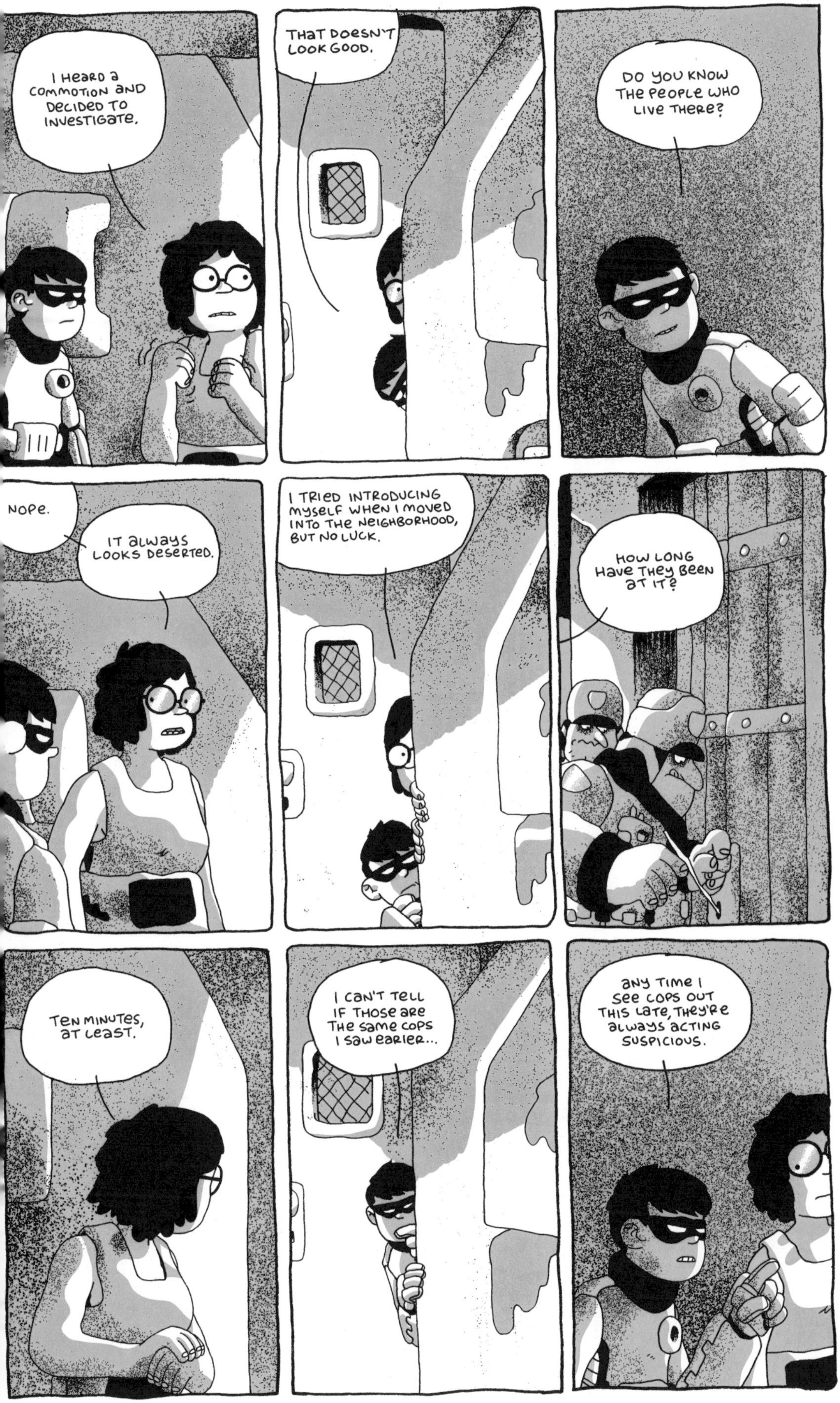

I HEARD A COMMOTION AND DECIDED TO INVESTIGATE.
THAT DOESN'T LOOK GOOD.
DO YOU KNOW THE PEOPLE WHO LIVE THERE?
NOPE.
IT ALWAYS LOOKS DESERTED.
I TRIED INTRODUCING MYSELF WHEN I MOVED INTO THE NEIGHBORHOOD, BUT NO LUCK.
HOW LONG HAVE THEY BEEN AT IT?
TEN MINUTES, AT LEAST.
I CAN'T TELL IF THOSE ARE THE SAME COPS I SAW EARLIER...
ANY TIME I SEE COPS OUT THIS LATE, THEY'RE ALWAYS ACTING SUSPICIOUS.

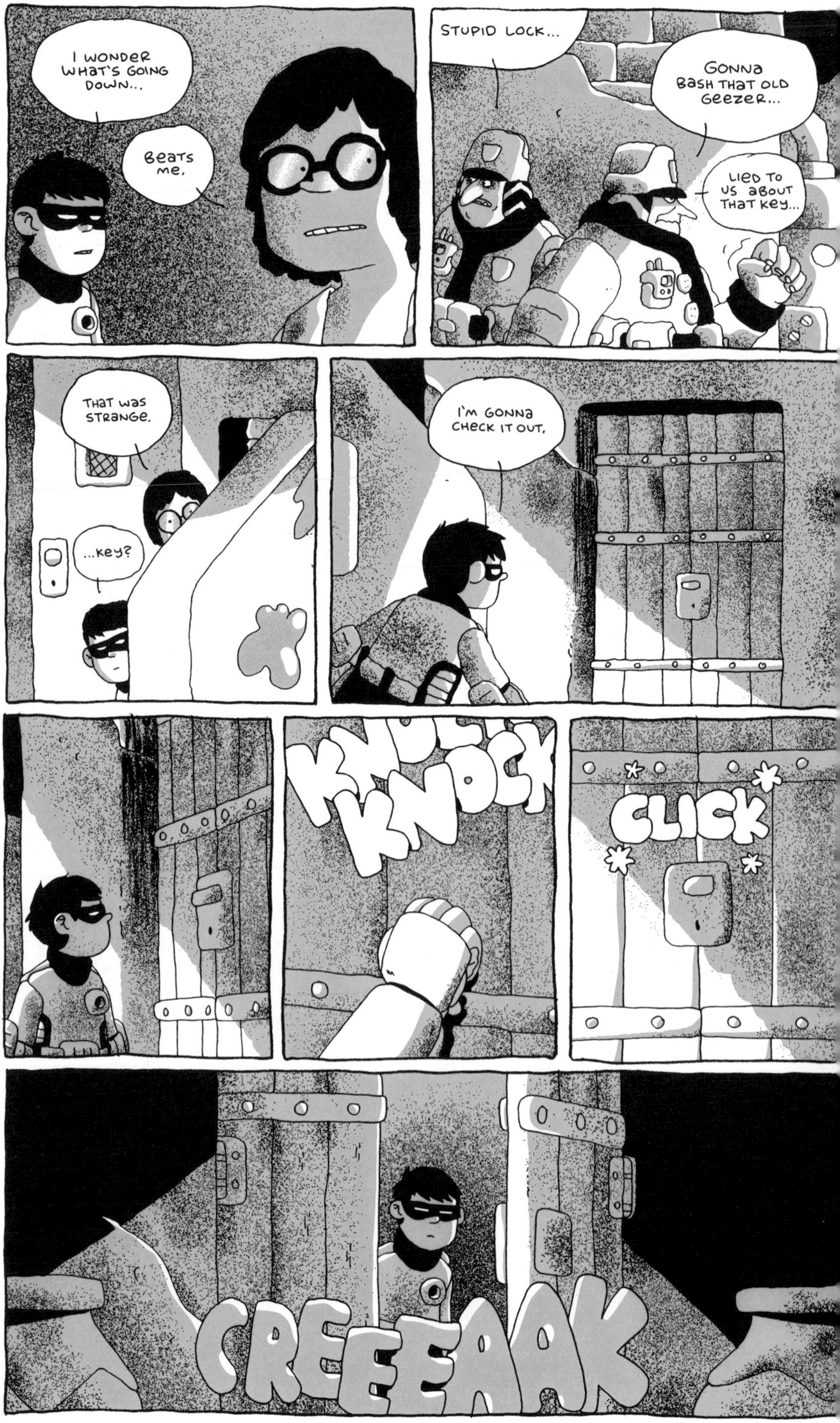
I WONDER WHAT'S GOING DOWN...
Beats me.
STUPID LOCK...
GONNa BASH THAT OLD GEEZER...
LIeD TO US aBOUT THAT key...
THAT was STRANGE.
...key?
I'M GONNa CHECK IT OUT.
KNOCK KNOCK
CLICK
CREEEAAK

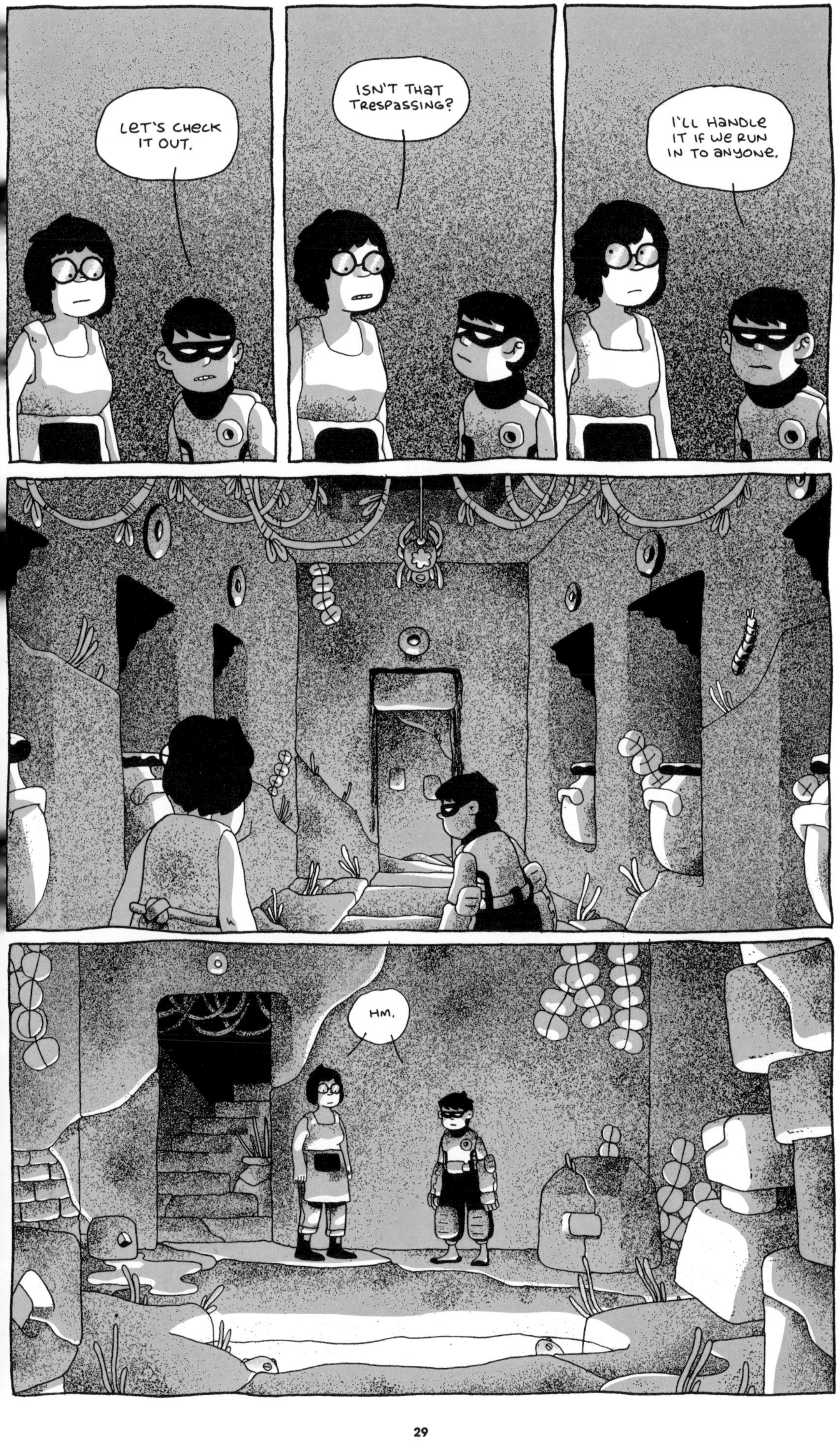
LET'S CHECK IT OUT.
ISN'T THAT TRESPASSING?
I'LL HANDLE IT IF WE RUN IN TO ANYONE.
HM.

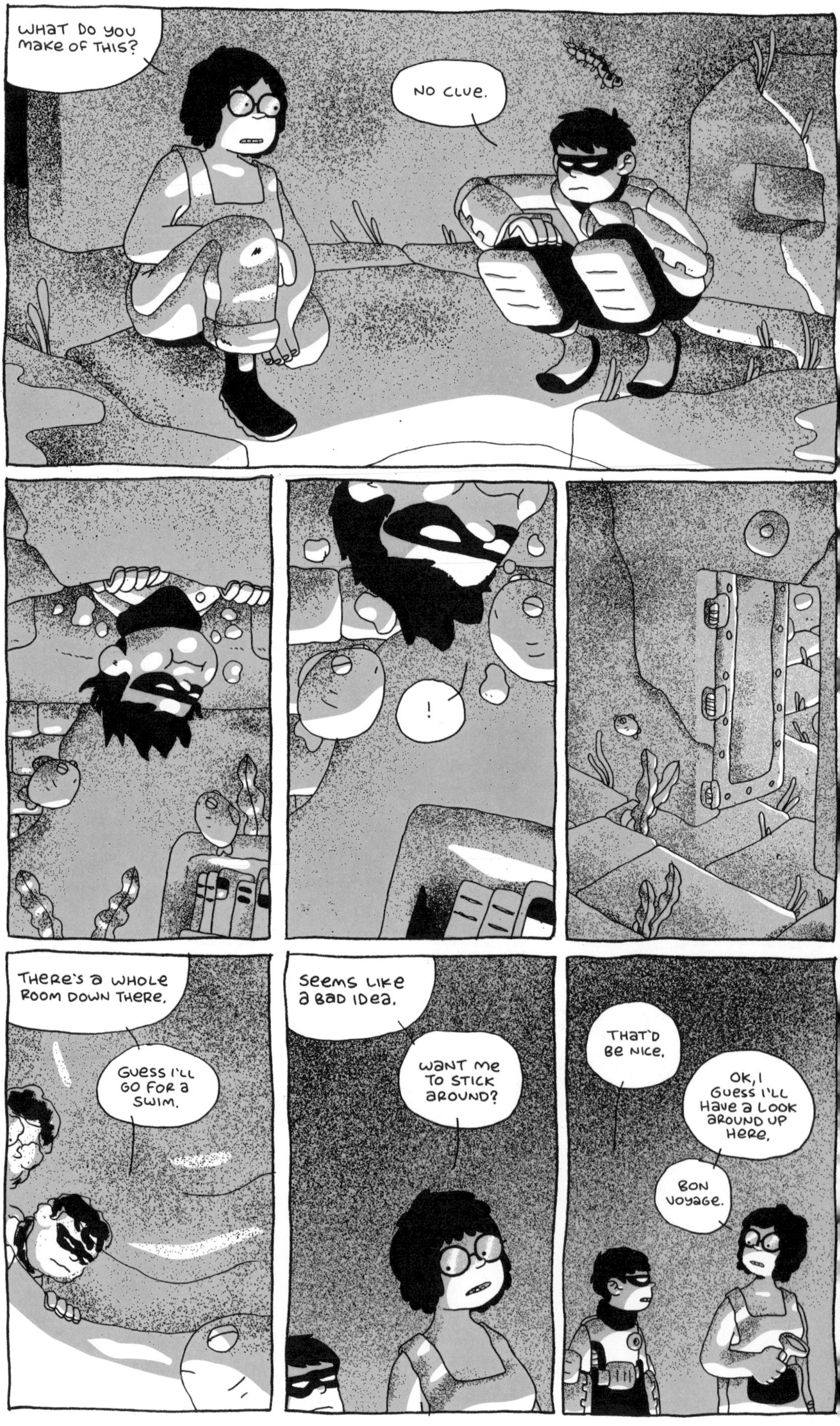
WHAT DO YOU MAKE OF THIS?
NO CLUE.
!
THERE'S A WHOLE ROOM DOWN THERE.
GUESS I'LL GO FOR A SWIM.
SEEMS LIKE A BAD IDEA.
WANT ME TO STICK AROUND?
THAT'D BE NICE.
OK, I GUESS I'LL HAVE A LOOK AROUND UP HERE.
BON VOYAGE.

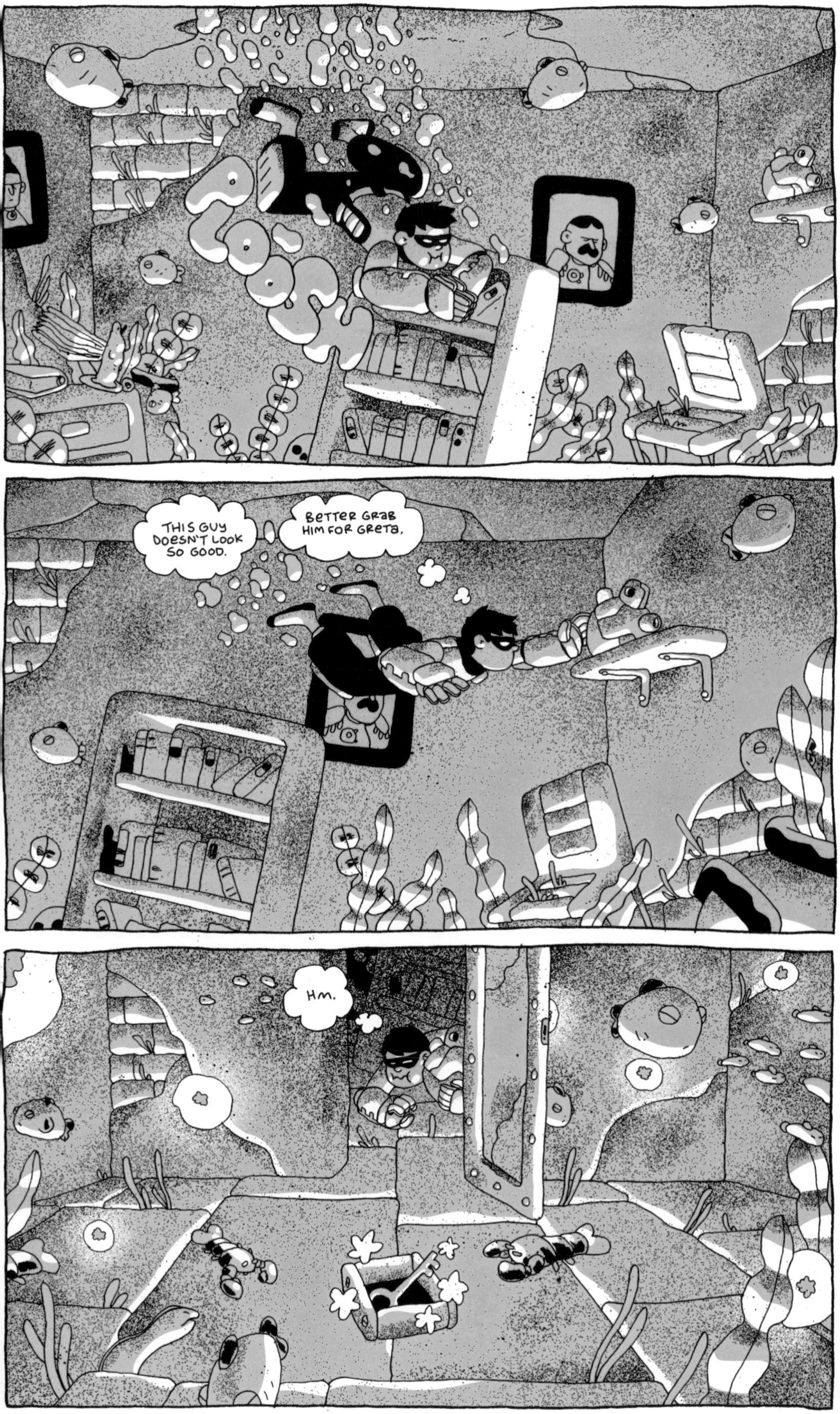
PLOOSH
THIS GUY DOESN'T LOOK SO GOOD.
BETTER GRAB HIM FOR GRETA.
HM.

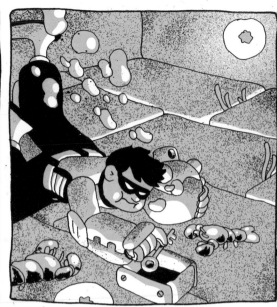

THOSE COPS ARE LOOKING FOR YOU.

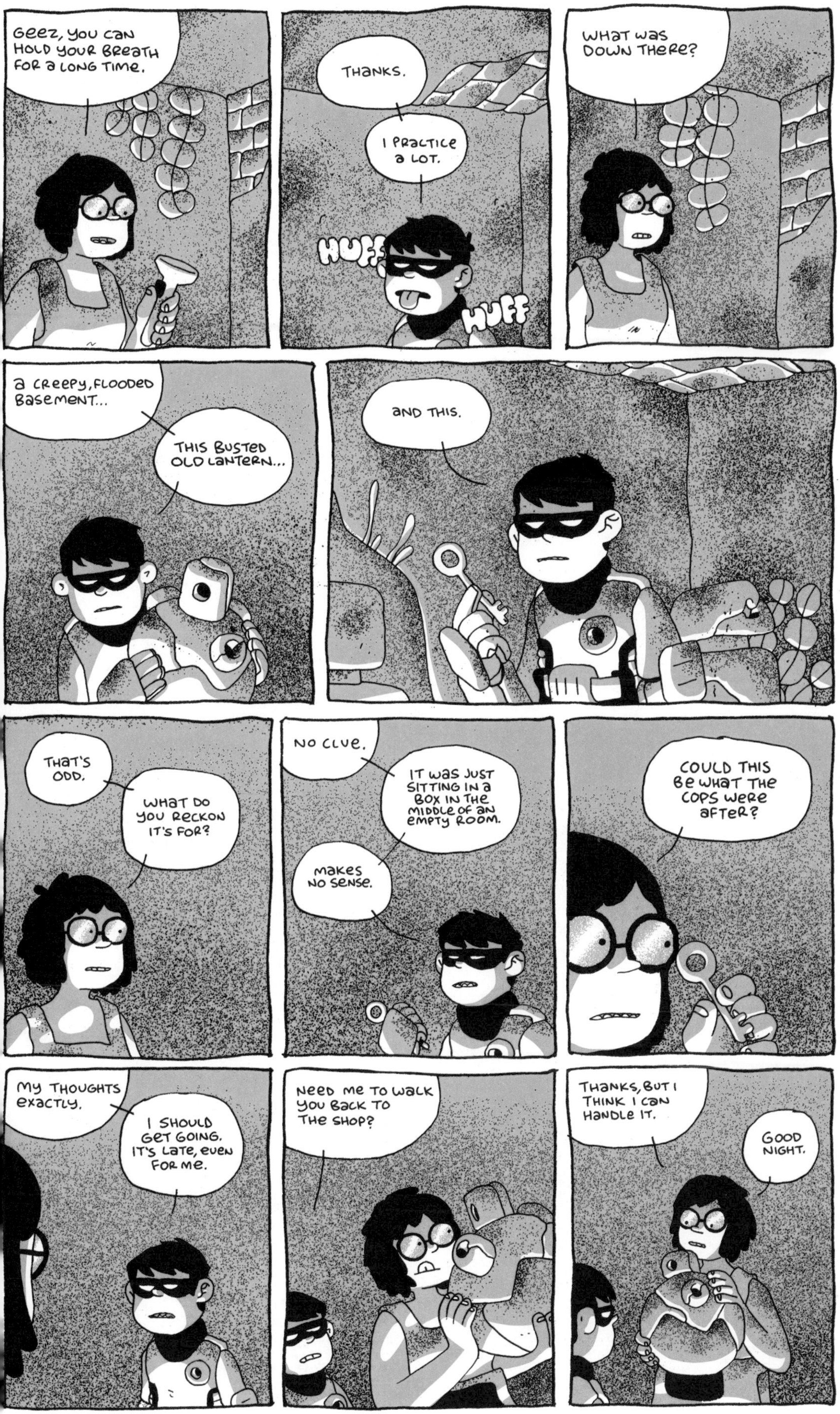
GEEZ, YOU CAN HOLD YOUR BREATH FOR A LONG TIME.
THANKS.
I PRACTICE A LOT.
HUFF
HUFF
WHAT WAS DOWN THERE?
A CREEPY, FLOODED BASEMENT...
THIS BUSTED OLD LANTERN...
AND THIS.
THAT'S ODD.
WHAT DO YOU RECKON IT'S FOR?
NO CLUE.
IT WAS JUST SITTING IN A BOX IN THE MIDDLE OF AN EMPTY ROOM.
MAKES NO SENSE.
COULD THIS BE WHAT THE COPS WERE AFTER?
MY THOUGHTS EXACTLY.
I SHOULD GET GOING. IT'S LATE, EVEN FOR ME.
NEED ME TO WALK YOU BACK TO THE SHOP?
THANKS, BUT I THINK I CAN HANDLE IT.
GOOD NIGHT.

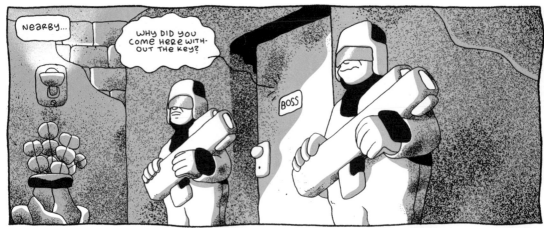

NEARBY...

WHY DID YOU COME HERE WITHOUT THE KEY?

BOSS

WELL, UM, SIR... THE OLD MAN GAVE US BAD DIRECTIONS. HE—

NOT GOOD ENOUGH.

THAT OLD SACK IS WEAK, AND HE STILL PULLED A FAST ONE ON YOU.

VERY SORRY, SIR!

WE'LL GO OUT LOOKING AGAIN TOMORROW.

WE'LL FIND IT THEN, HONEST.

YOU SHOULD HAVE FOUND IT TONIGHT.

I WANT WHAT'S IN THAT SAFE. I WON'T TOLERATE ANY MORE INCOMPETENCE!

THAT "YOUNG SHADOW" HAS BEEN CAUSING PROBLEMS FOR MY LOWER RANKING ASSOCIATES...

YOU FALL INTO THAT CATEGORY.

DON'T LET HIM INTERFERE AGAIN.

YES SIR!

GOOD.

NOW GET LOST.

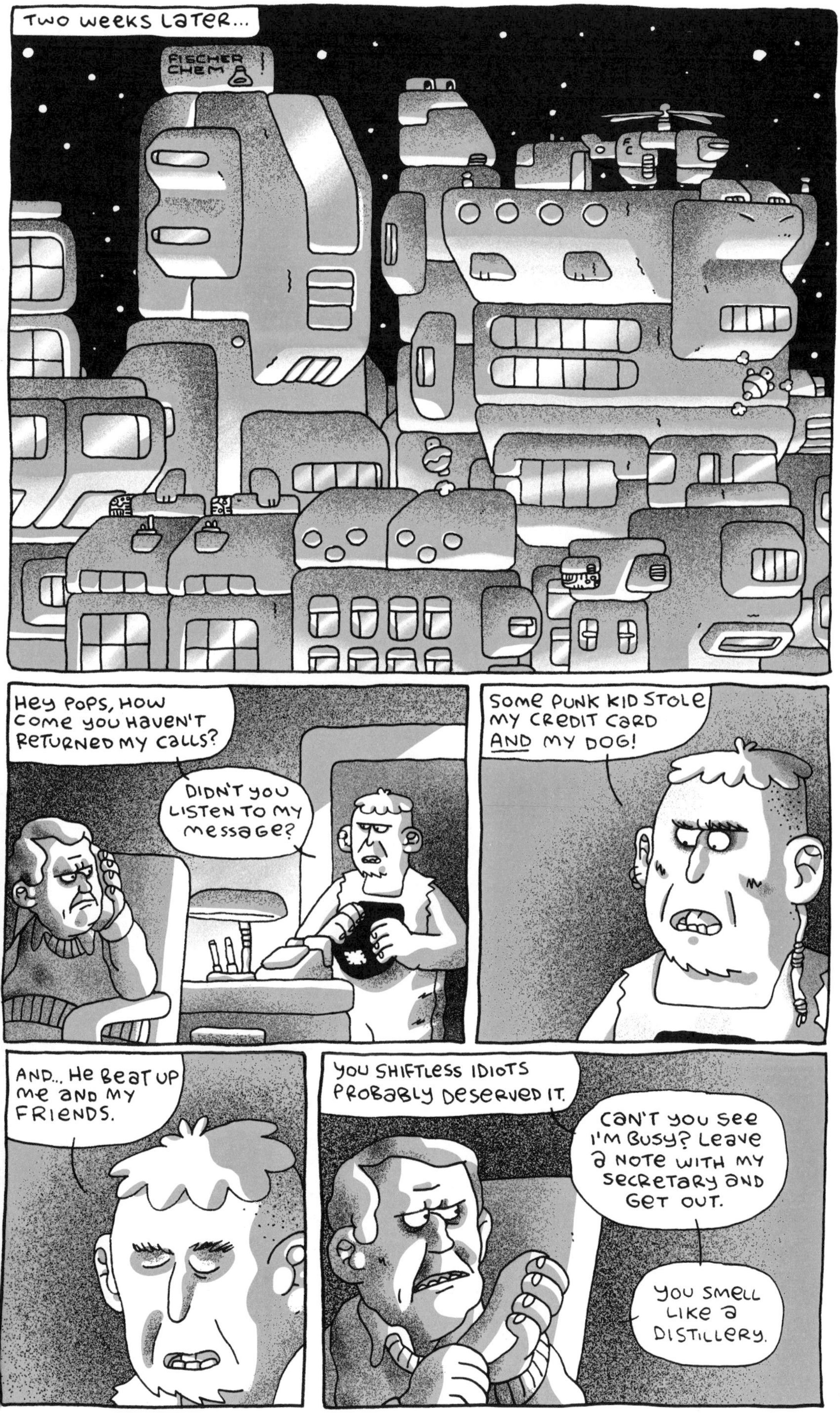
TWO WEEKS LATER...
FISCHER CHEM
HEY POPS, HOW COME YOU HAVEN'T RETURNED MY CALLS?
DIDN'T YOU LISTEN TO MY MESSAGE?
SOME PUNK KID STOLE MY CREDIT CARD AND MY DOG!
AND... HE BEAT UP ME AND MY FRIENDS.
YOU SHIFTLESS IDIOTS PROBABLY DESERVED IT.
CAN'T YOU SEE I'M BUSY? LEAVE A NOTE WITH MY SECRETARY AND GET OUT.
YOU SMELL LIKE A DISTILLERY.

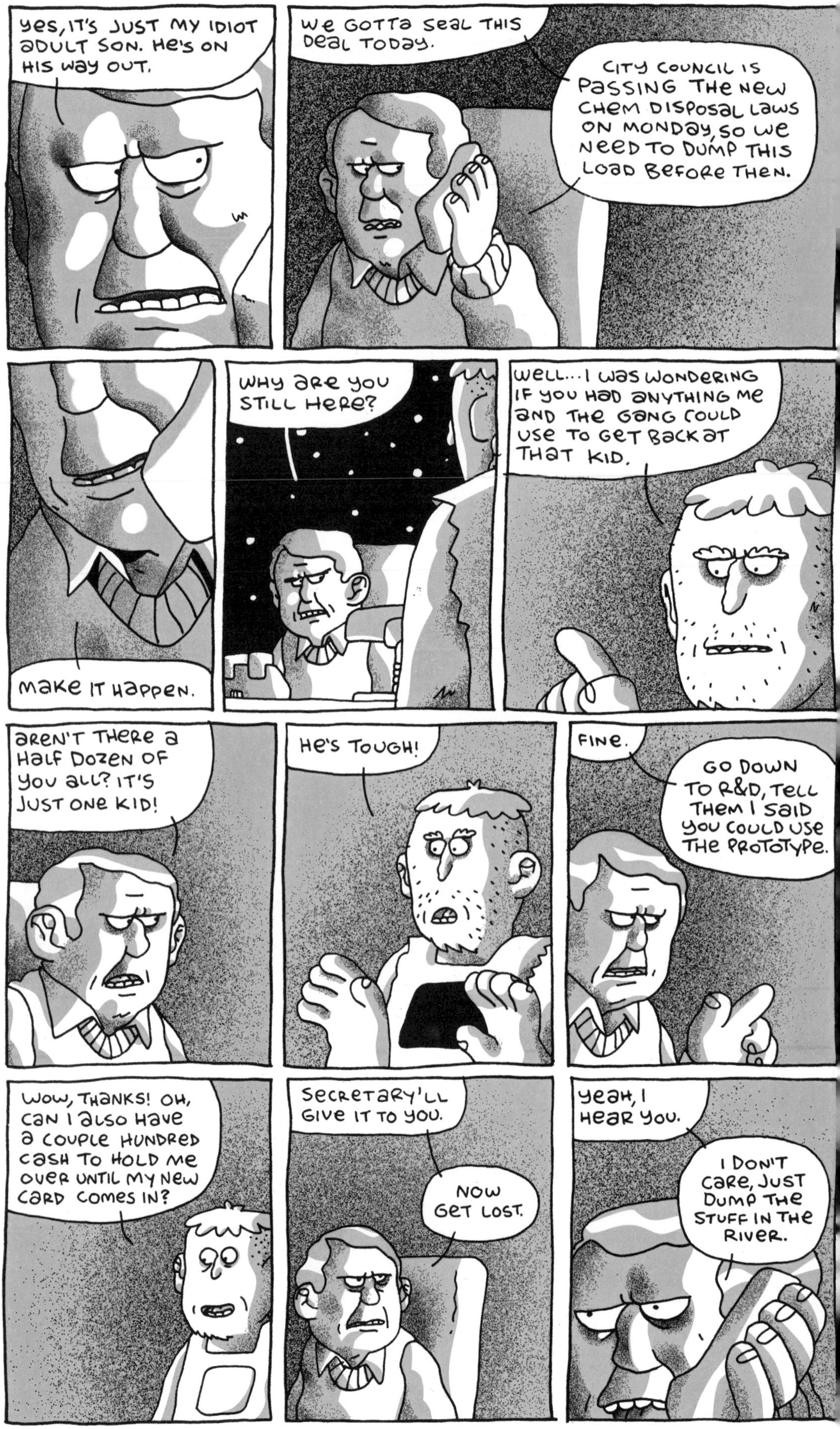
yes, IT'S JUST MY IDIOT ADULT SON. He'S ON HIS WAY OUT.
We GOTTA SeAL THIS DeAL TODAY.
CITY COUNCIL IS PASSING THE NEW CHEM DISPOSAL LAWS ON MONDAY, SO WE NEED TO DUMP THIS LOAD BEFORE THEN.
MAKE IT HAPPEN.
WHY ARE YOU STILL HERE?
WELL... I WAS WONDERING IF YOU HAD ANYTHING ME AND THE GANG COULD USE TO GET BACK AT THAT KID.
AREN'T THERE A HALF DOZEN OF YOU ALL? IT'S JUST ONE KID!
He'S TOUGH!
FINE.
GO DOWN TO R&D, TELL THEM I SAID YOU COULD USE THE PROTOTYPE.
WOW, THANKS! OH, CAN I ALSO HAVE A COUPLE HUNDRED CASH TO HOLD ME OVER UNTIL MY NEW CARD COMES IN?
SECRETARY'LL GIVE IT TO YOU.
NOW GET LOST.
YeAH, I HeAR YOU.
I DON'T CARE, JUST DUMP THE STUFF IN THE RIVER.

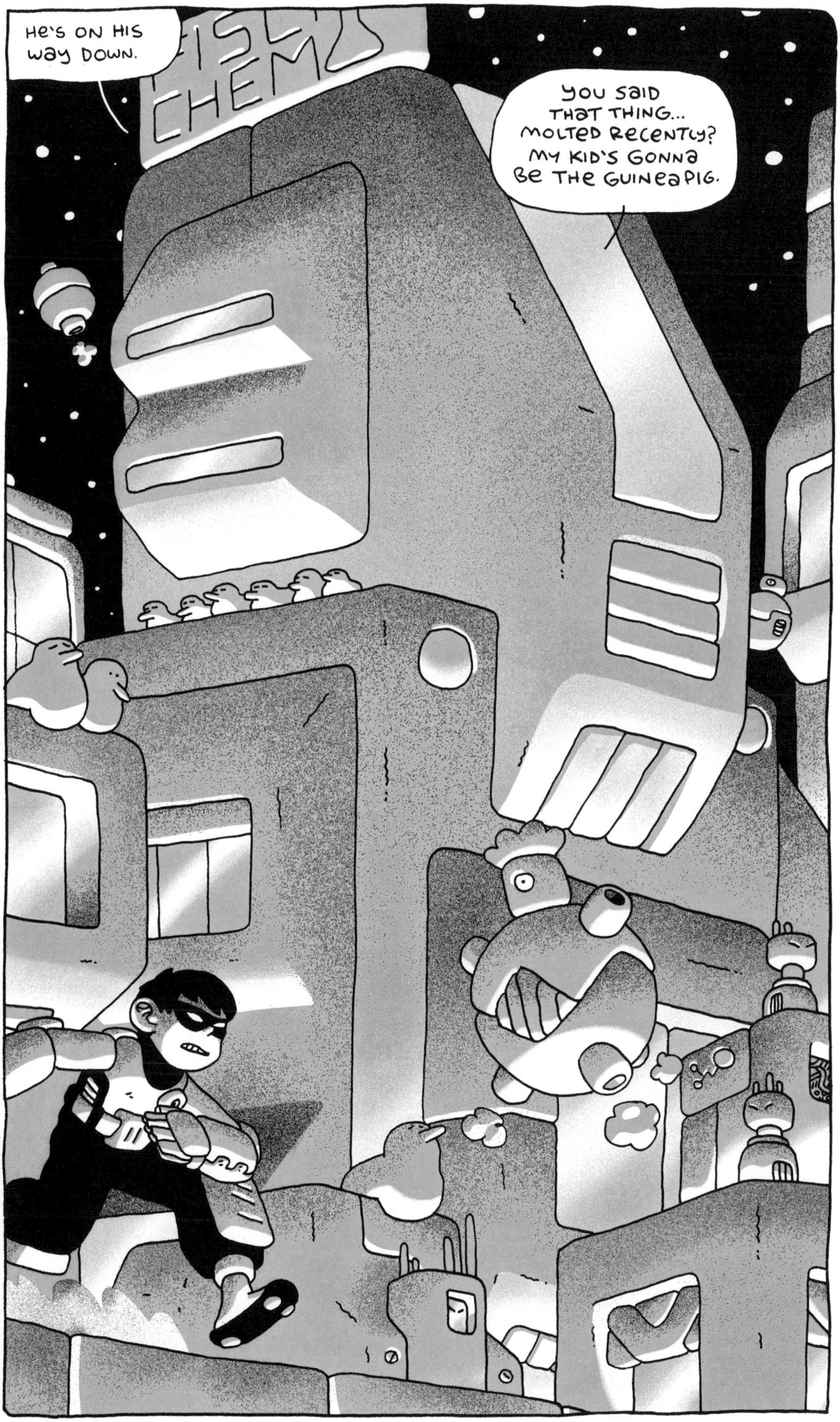
HE'S ON HIS WAY DOWN.
YOU SAID THAT THING... MOLTED RECENTLY? MY KID'S GONNA BE THE GUINEA PIG.

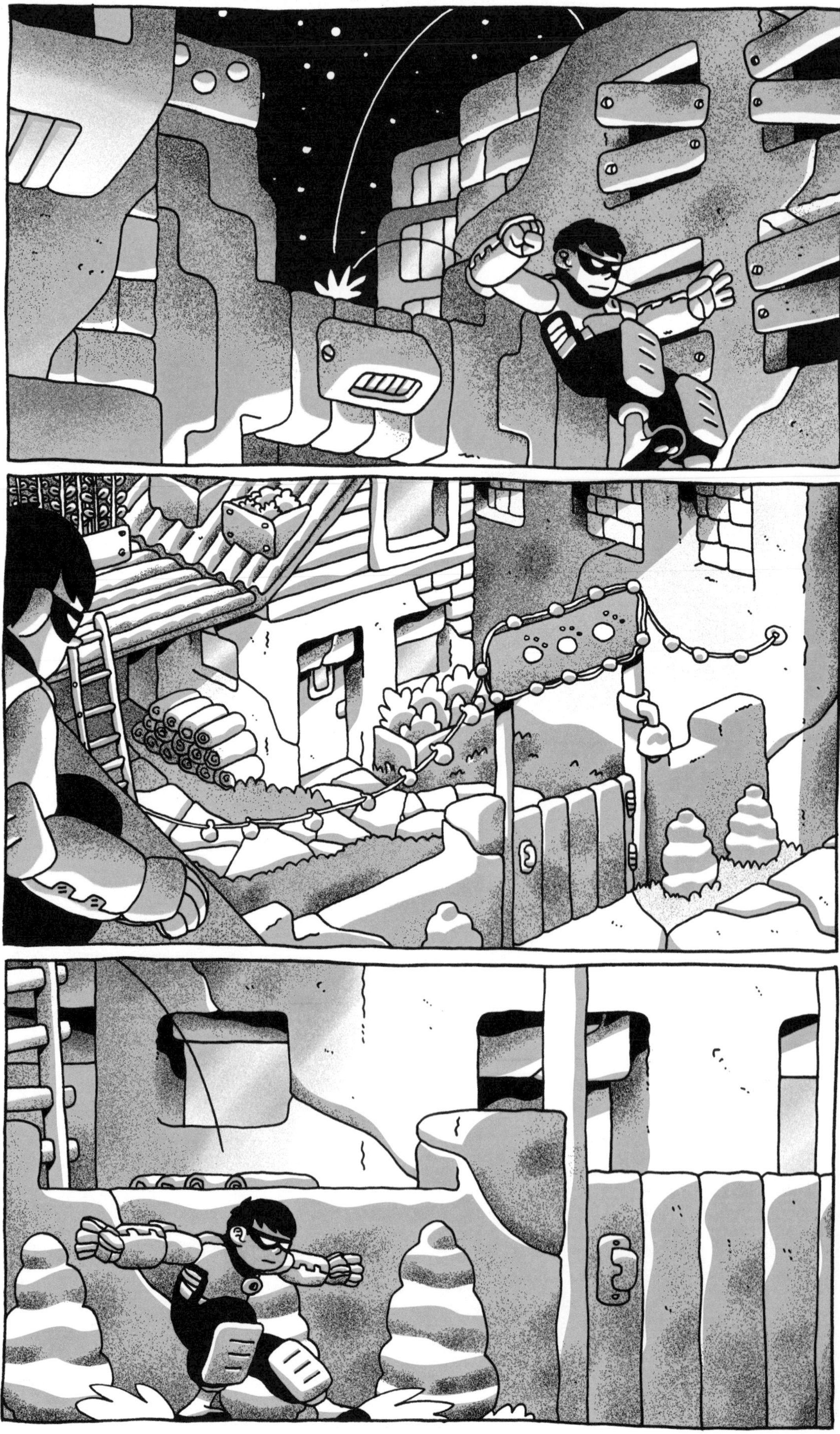

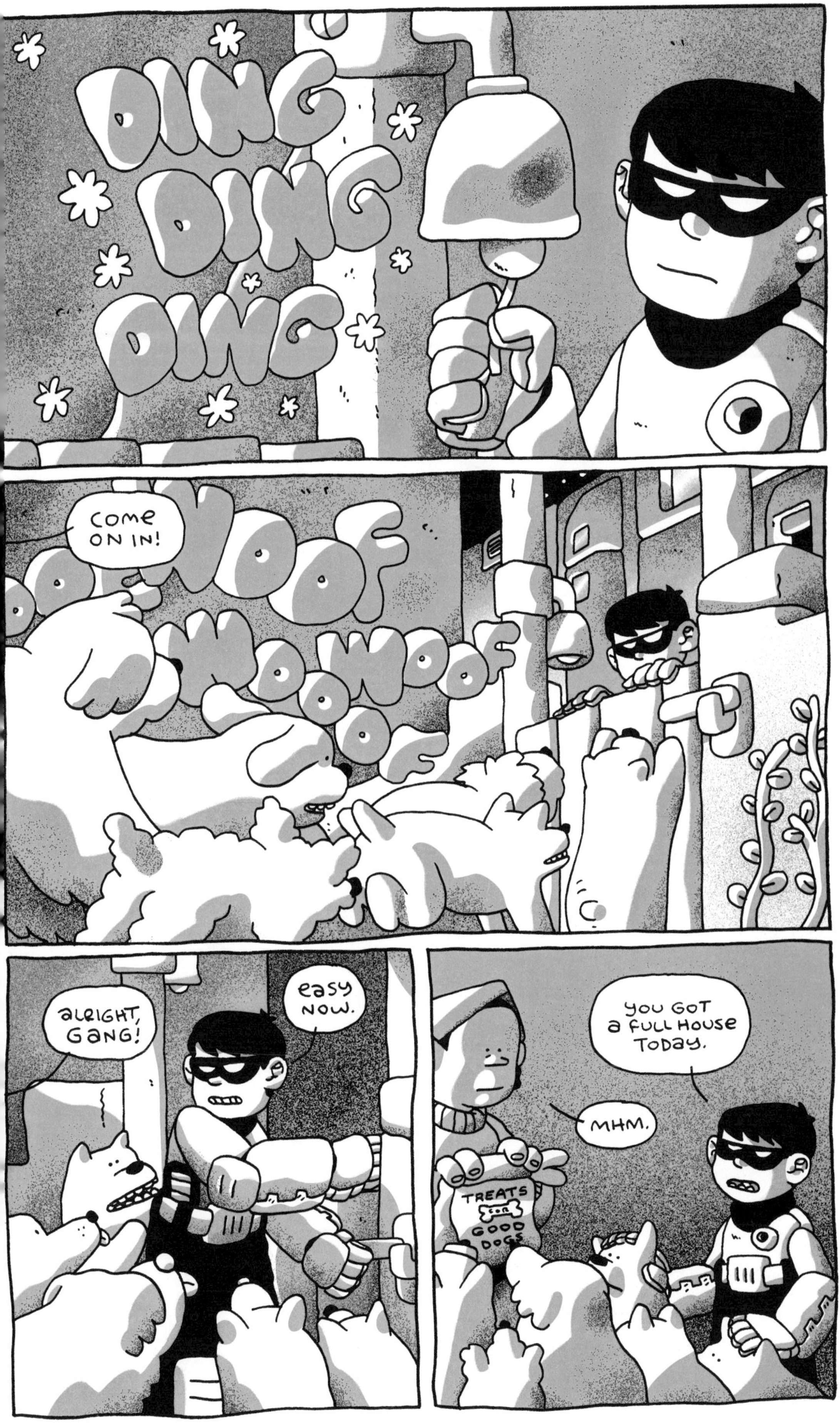
DING
DING
DING
COME ON IN!
WOOF
WOOF
WOOF
ALRIGHT, GANG!
EASY NOW.
YOU GOT A FULL HOUSE TODAY.
MHM.
TREATS FOR GOOD DOGS

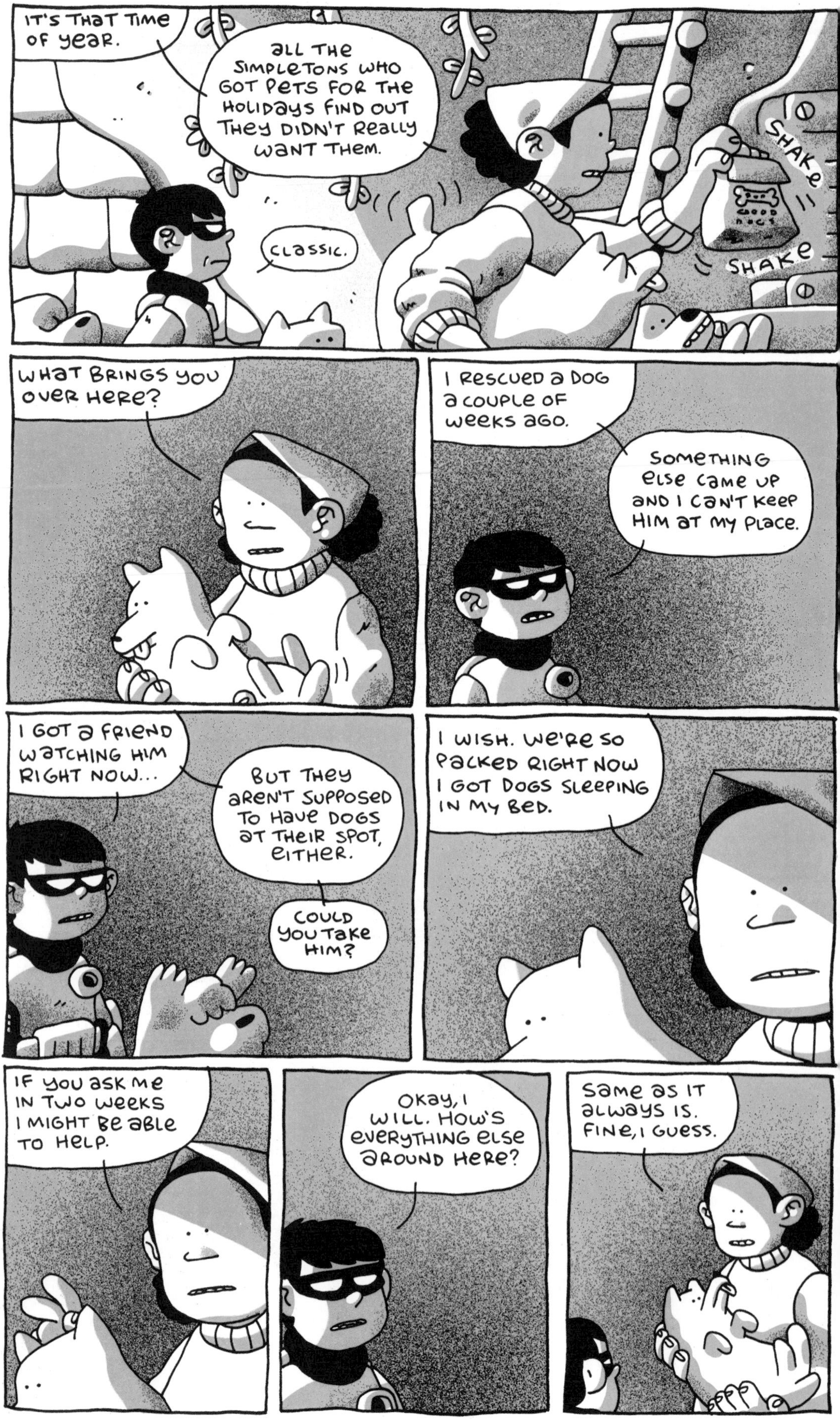
IT'S THAT TIME OF YEAR.
ALL THE SIMPLETONS WHO GOT PETS FOR THE HOLIDAYS FIND OUT THEY DIDN'T REALLY WANT THEM.
CLASSIC.
SHAKE
SHAKE
GOOD DOGS
WHAT BRINGS YOU OVER HERE?
I RESCUED A DOG A COUPLE OF WEEKS AGO.
SOMETHING ELSE CAME UP AND I CAN'T KEEP HIM AT MY PLACE.
I GOT A FRIEND WATCHING HIM RIGHT NOW...
BUT THEY AREN'T SUPPOSED TO HAVE DOGS AT THEIR SPOT, EITHER.
COULD YOU TAKE HIM?
I WISH. WE'RE SO PACKED RIGHT NOW I GOT DOGS SLEEPING IN MY BED.
IF YOU ASK ME IN TWO WEEKS I MIGHT BE ABLE TO HELP.
OKAY, I WILL. HOW'S EVERYTHING ELSE AROUND HERE?
SAME AS IT ALWAYS IS. FINE, I GUESS.

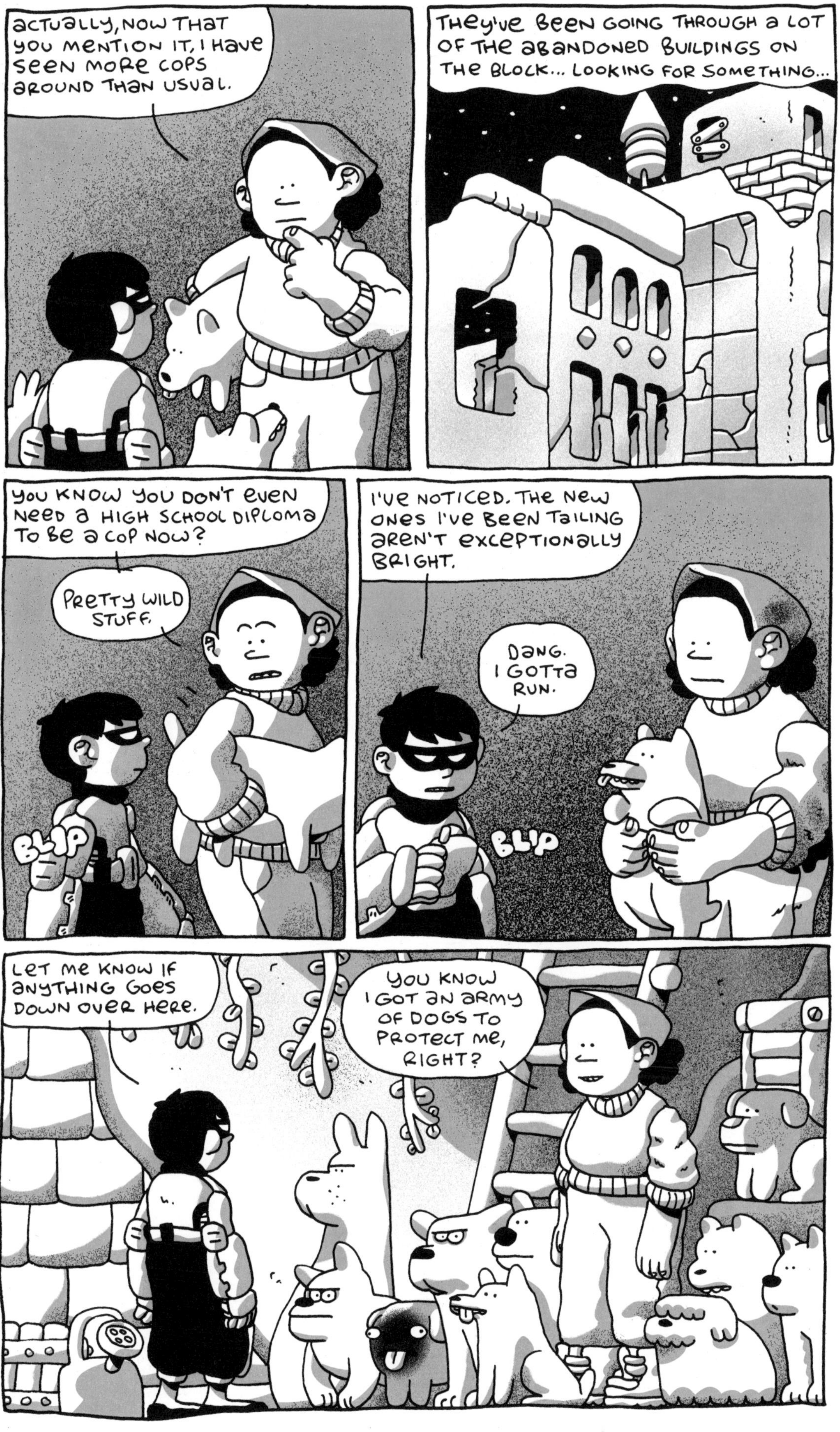
ACTUALLY, NOW THAT YOU MENTION IT, I HAVE SEEN MORE COPS AROUND THAN USUAL.
THEY'VE BEEN GOING THROUGH A LOT OF THE ABANDONED BUILDINGS ON THE BLOCK... LOOKING FOR SOMETHING...
YOU KNOW YOU DON'T EVEN NEED A HIGH SCHOOL DIPLOMA TO BE A COP NOW?
PRETTY WILD STUFF.
BLIP
I'VE NOTICED. THE NEW ONES I'VE BEEN TAILING AREN'T EXCEPTIONALLY BRIGHT.
DANG. I GOTTA RUN.
BLIP
LET ME KNOW IF ANYTHING GOES DOWN OVER HERE.
YOU KNOW I GOT AN ARMY OF DOGS TO PROTECT ME, RIGHT?

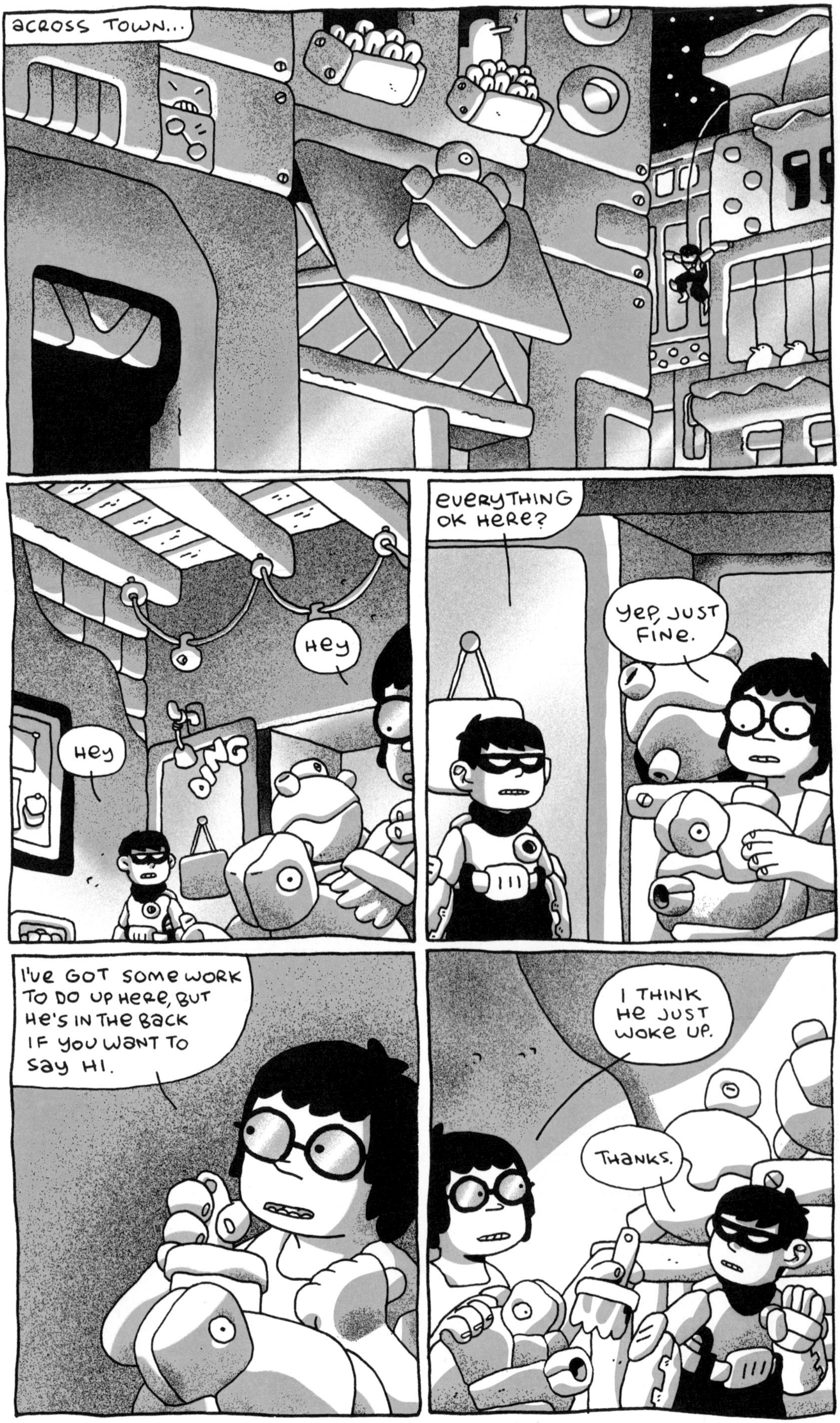
across town...
hey
hey
DING
everything ok here?
yep, just fine.
I've got some work to do up here, but he's in the back if you want to say hi.
I think he just woke up.
Thanks.

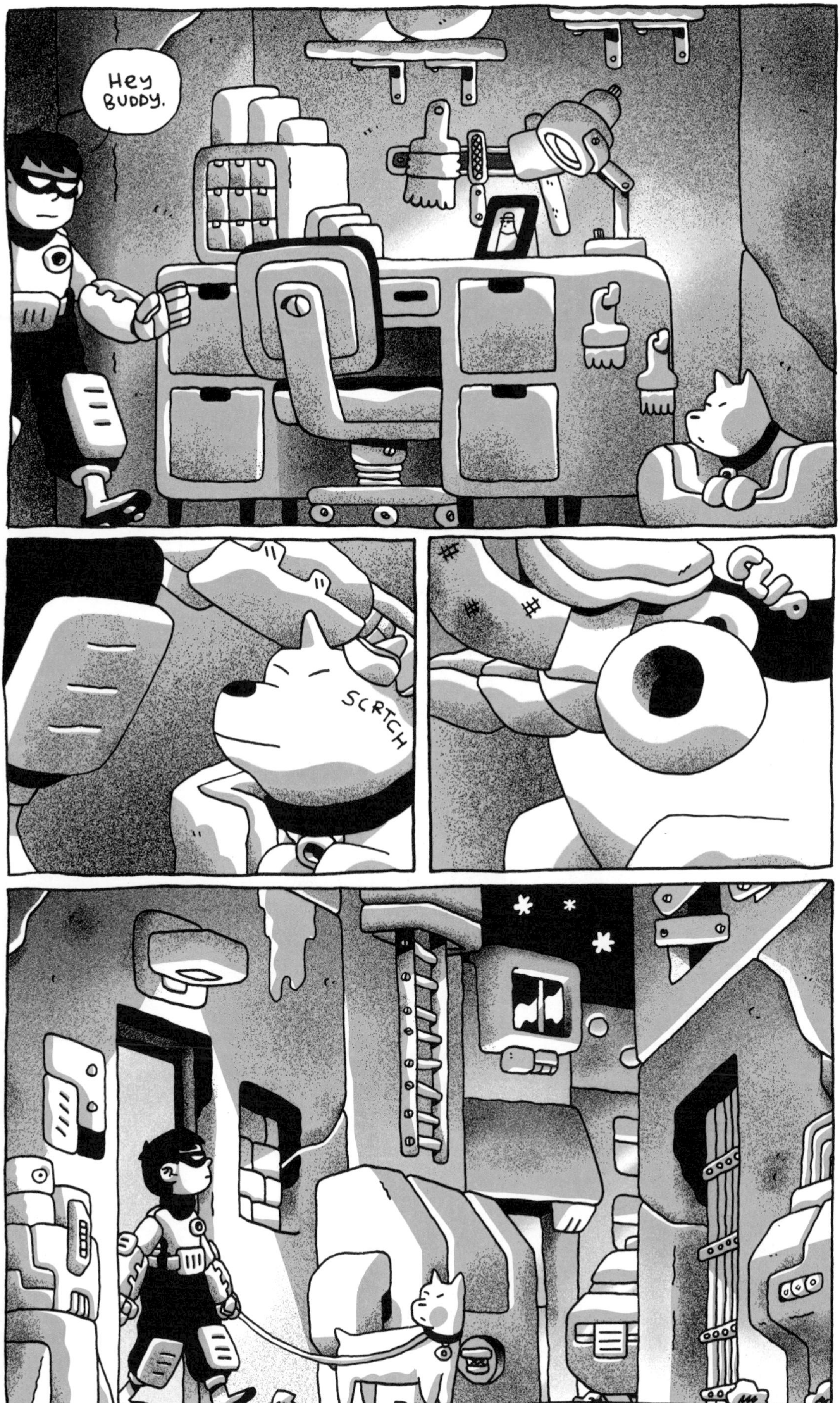
Hey
BUDDY.
SCRTCH
CLIP

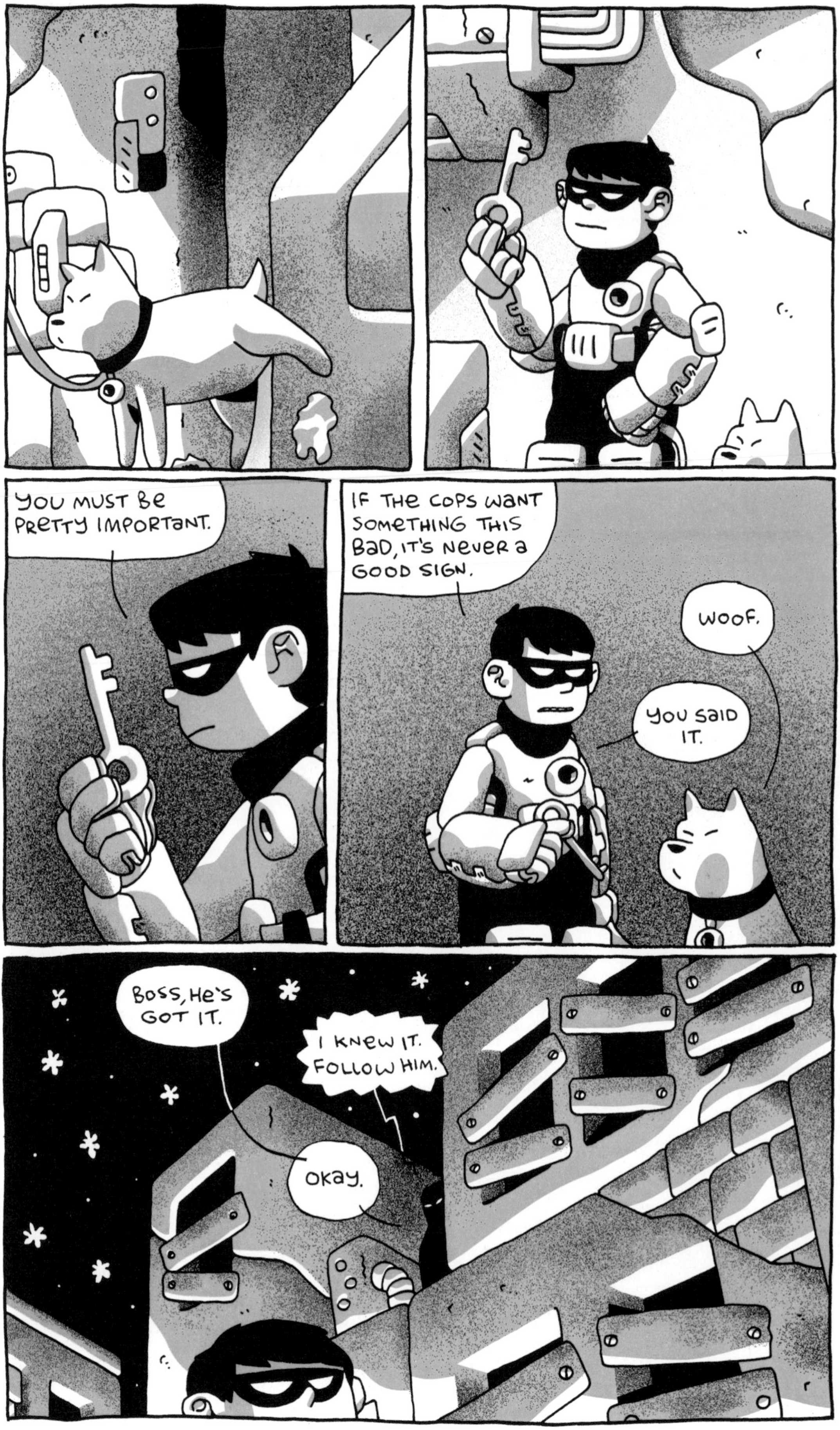
YOU MUST BE PRETTY IMPORTANT.
IF THE COPS WANT SOMETHING THIS BAD, IT'S NEVER A GOOD SIGN.
WOOF.
YOU SAID IT.
BOSS, HE'S GOT IT.
I KNEW IT. FOLLOW HIM.
OKAY.

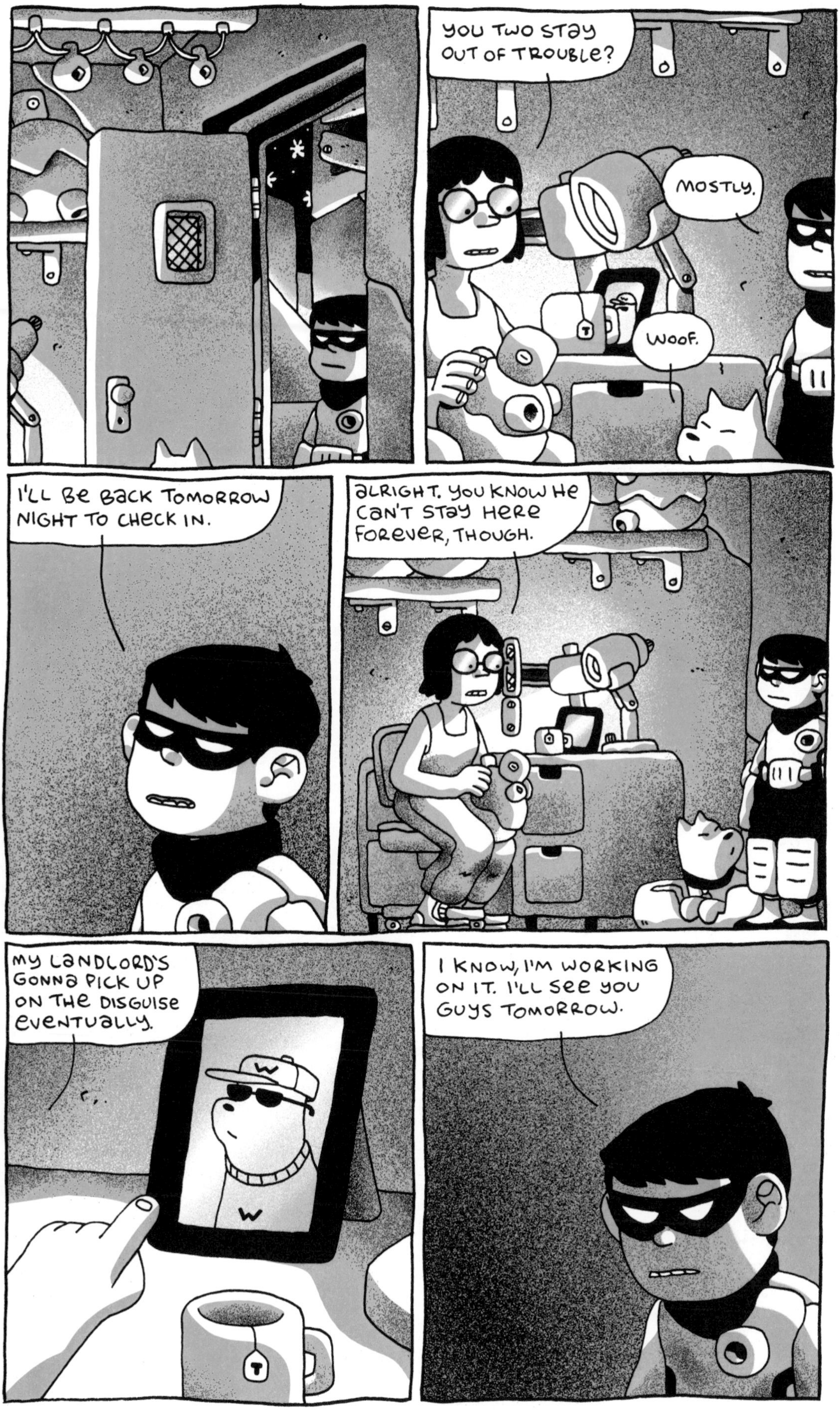
YOU TWO STAY OUT OF TROUBLE?
MOSTLY.
WOOF.
I'LL BE BACK TOMORROW NIGHT TO CHECK IN.
ALRIGHT. YOU KNOW HE CAN'T STAY HERE FOREVER, THOUGH.
MY LANDLORD'S GONNA PICK UP ON THE DISGUISE EVENTUALLY.
I KNOW, I'M WORKING ON IT. I'LL SEE YOU GUYS TOMORROW.

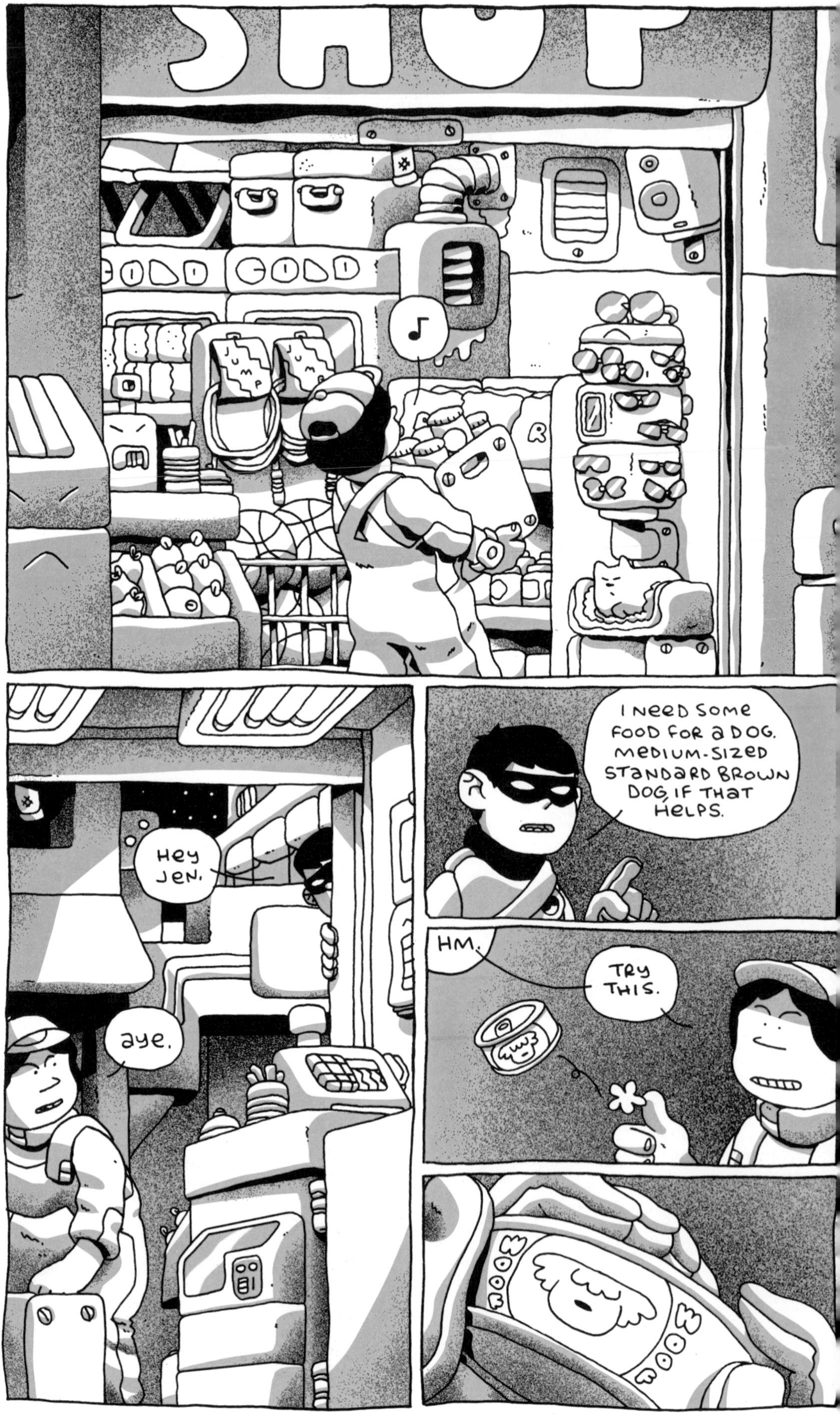
SHOP
JUMP
JUMP
Hey Jen.
aye.
I need some food for a dog. Medium-sized standard brown dog, if that helps.
HM.
TRY THIS.
WOOF
WOOF

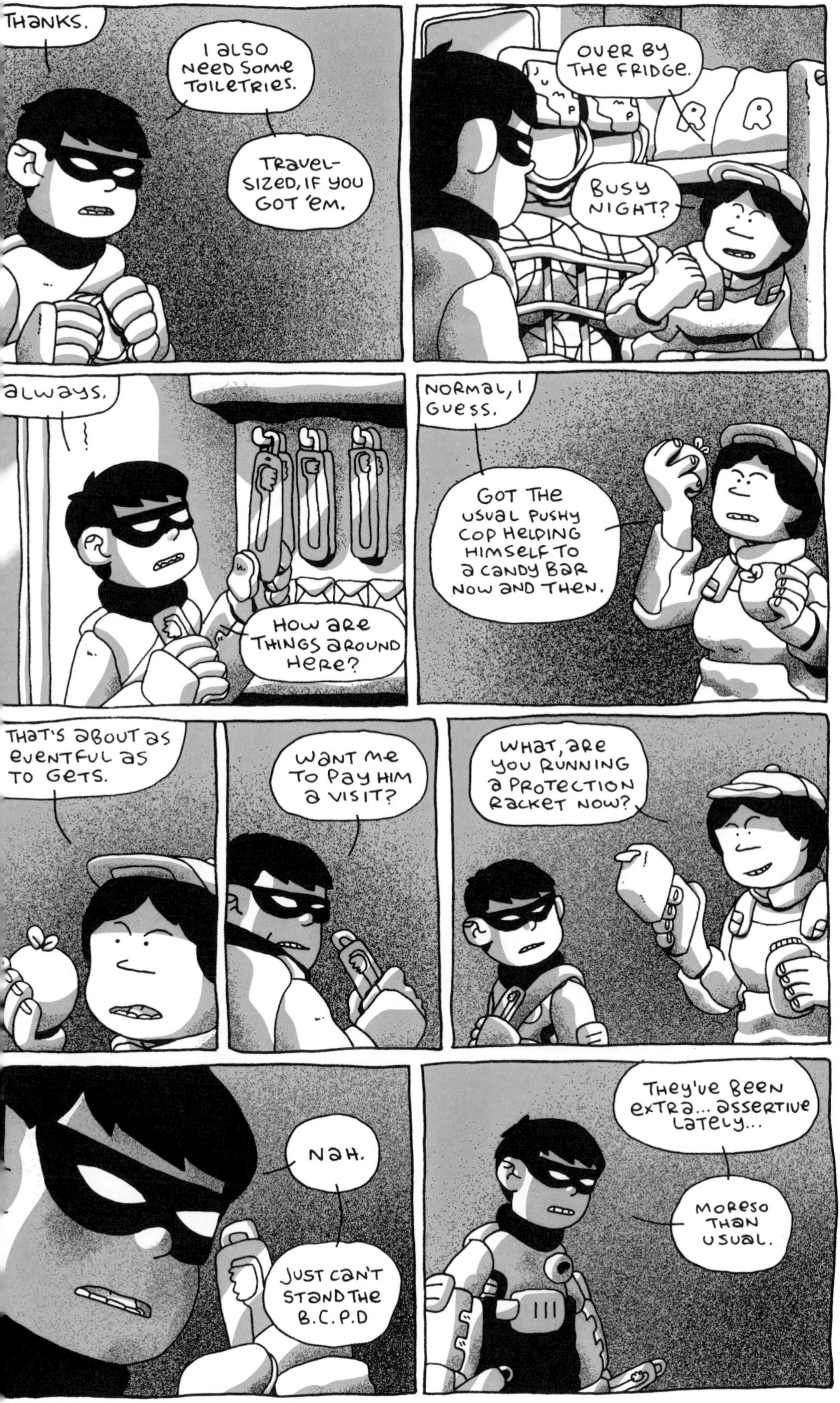
THANKS.
I ALSO NEED SOME TOILETRIES.
TRAVEL-SIZED, IF YOU GOT 'EM.
OVER BY THE FRIDGE.
BUSY NIGHT?
ALWAYS.
HOW ARE THINGS AROUND HERE?
NORMAL, I GUESS.
GOT THE USUAL PUSHY COP HELPING HIMSELF TO A CANDY BAR NOW AND THEN.
THAT'S ABOUT AS EVENTFUL AS TO GETS.
WANT ME TO PAY HIM A VISIT?
WHAT, ARE YOU RUNNING A PROTECTION RACKET NOW?
NAH.
JUST CAN'T STAND THE B.C.P.D
THEY'VE BEEN EXTRA... ASSERTIVE LATELY...
MORESO THAN USUAL.

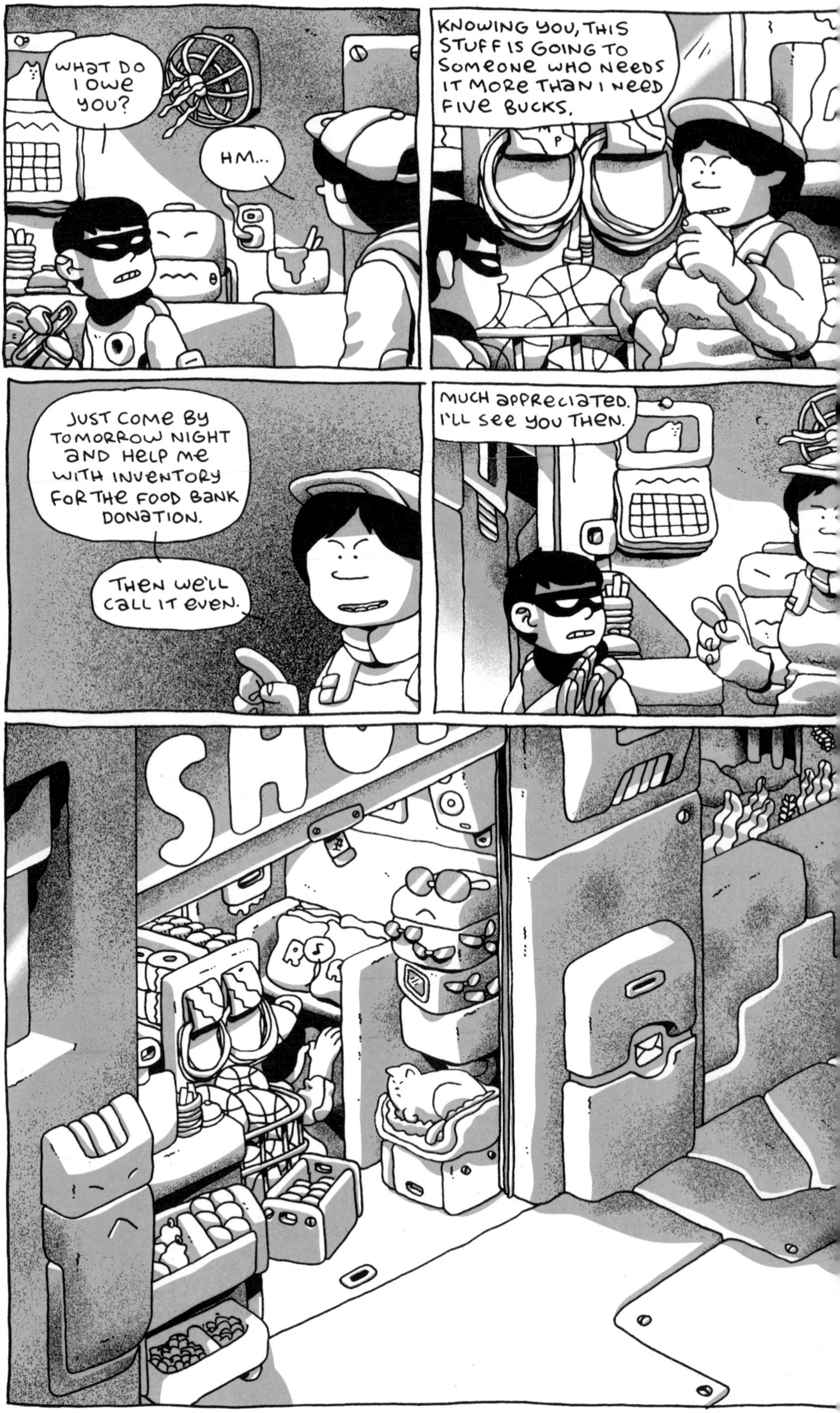

WHAT DO I OWE YOU?
HM...
KNOWING YOU, THIS STUFF IS GOING TO SOMEONE WHO NEEDS IT MORE THAN I NEED FIVE BUCKS.
JUST COME BY TOMORROW NIGHT AND HELP ME WITH INVENTORY FOR THE FOOD BANK DONATION.
THEN WE'LL CALL IT EVEN.
MUCH APPRECIATED. I'LL SEE YOU THEN.

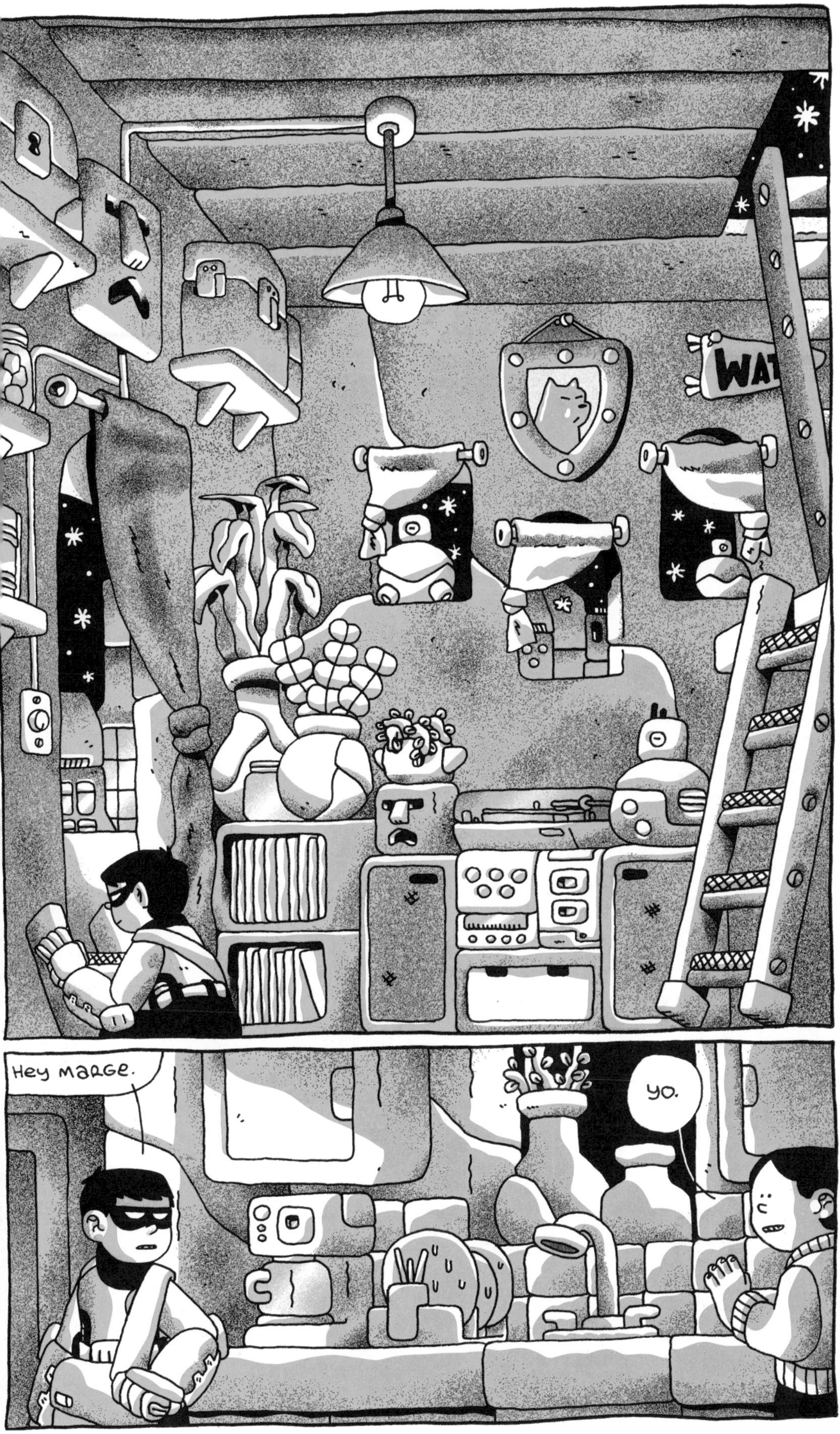
Hey MARGE.
YO.

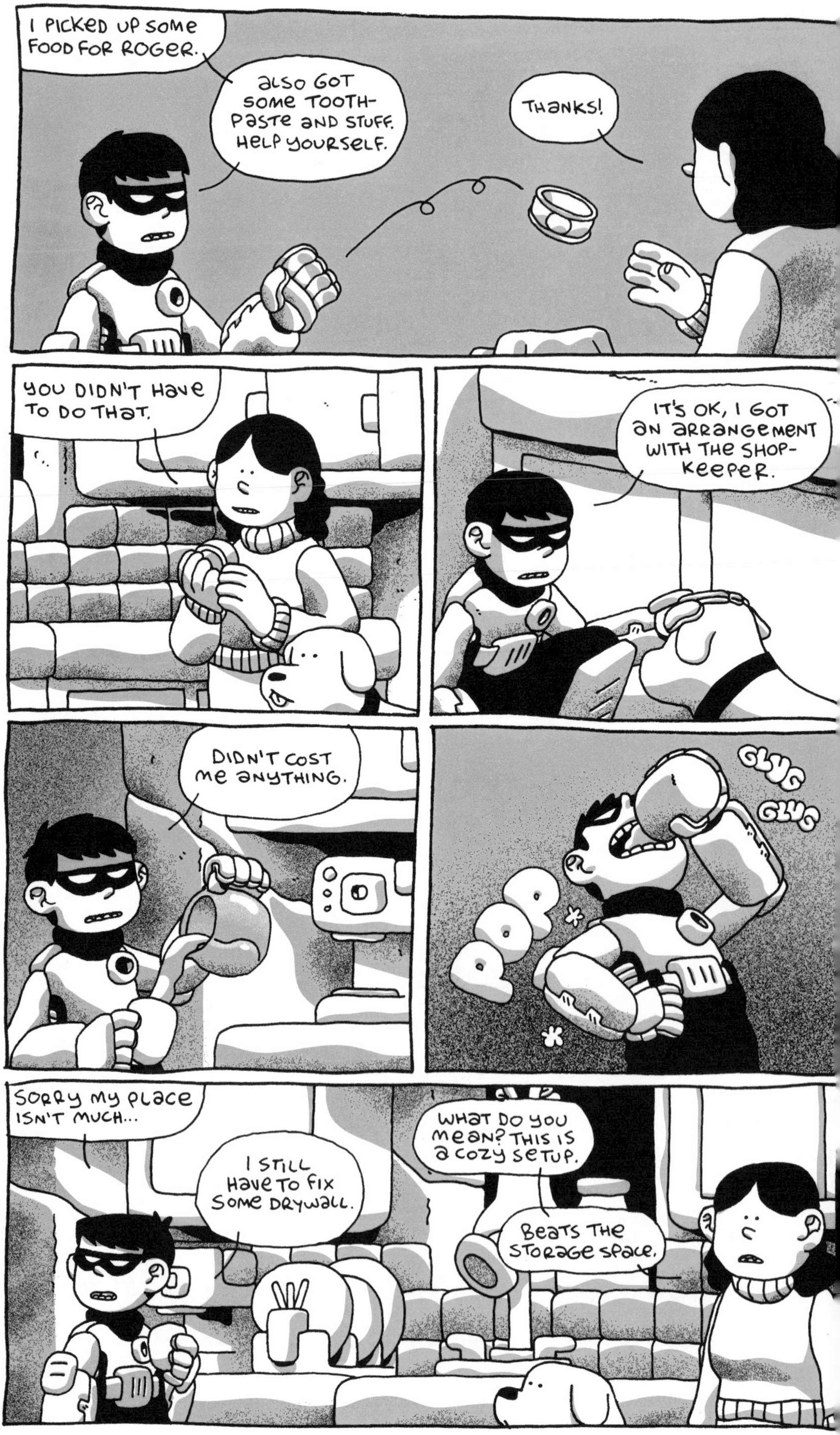
I PICKED UP SOME FOOD FOR ROGER.
ALSO GOT SOME TOOTH-PASTE AND STUFF. HELP YOURSELF.
THANKS!
YOU DIDN'T HAVE TO DO THAT.
IT'S OK, I GOT AN ARRANGEMENT WITH THE SHOP-KEEPER.
DIDN'T COST ME ANYTHING.
GLUG
GLUG
POP
SORRY MY PLACE ISN'T MUCH...
I STILL HAVE TO FIX SOME DRYWALL.
WHAT DO YOU MEAN? THIS IS A COZY SETUP.
BEATS THE STORAGE SPACE.

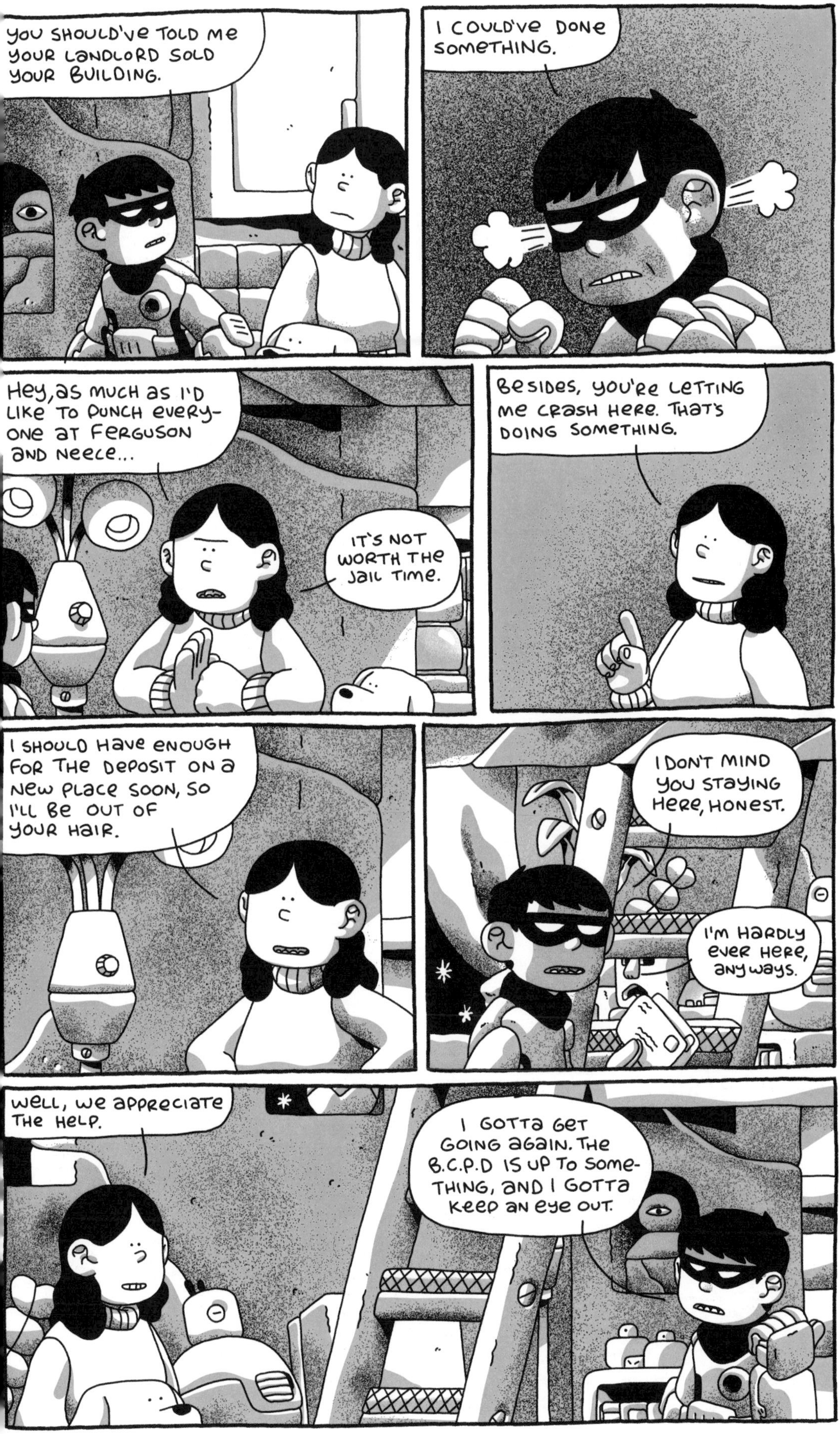
YOU SHOULD'VE TOLD ME YOUR LANDLORD SOLD YOUR BUILDING.
I COULD'VE DONE SOMETHING.
HEY, AS MUCH AS I'D LIKE TO PUNCH EVERY-ONE AT FERGUSON AND NEECE...
IT'S NOT WORTH THE JAIL TIME.
BESIDES, YOU'RE LETTING ME CRASH HERE. THAT'S DOING SOMETHING.
I SHOULD HAVE ENOUGH FOR THE DEPOSIT ON A NEW PLACE SOON, SO I'LL BE OUT OF YOUR HAIR.
I DON'T MIND YOU STAYING HERE, HONEST.
I'M HARDLY EVER HERE, ANYWAYS.
WELL, WE APPRECIATE THE HELP.
I GOTTA GET GOING AGAIN. THE B.C.P.D IS UP TO SOME-THING, AND I GOTTA KEEP AN EYE OUT.

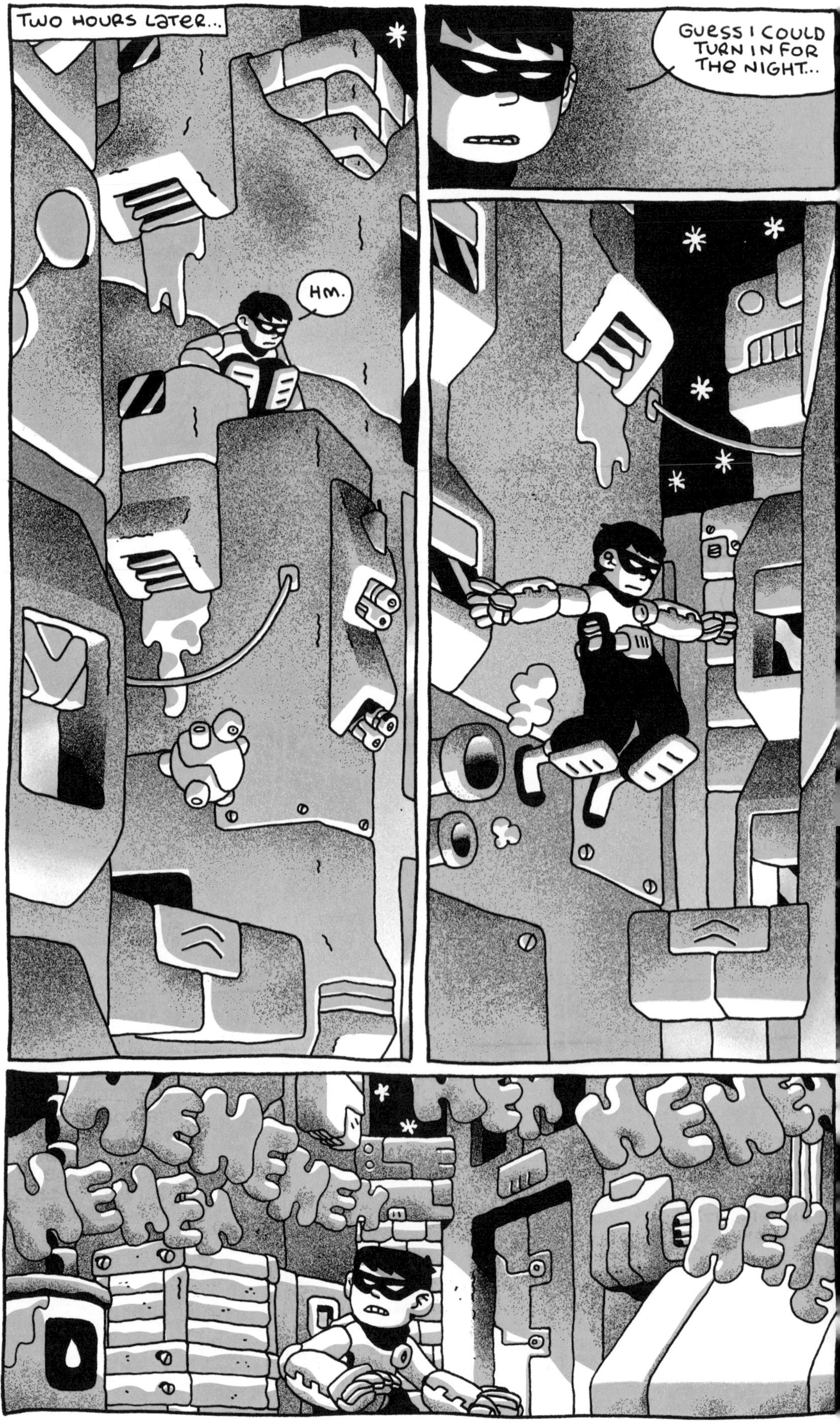
TWO HOURS LATER...
HM.
GUESS I COULD TURN IN FOR THE NIGHT...

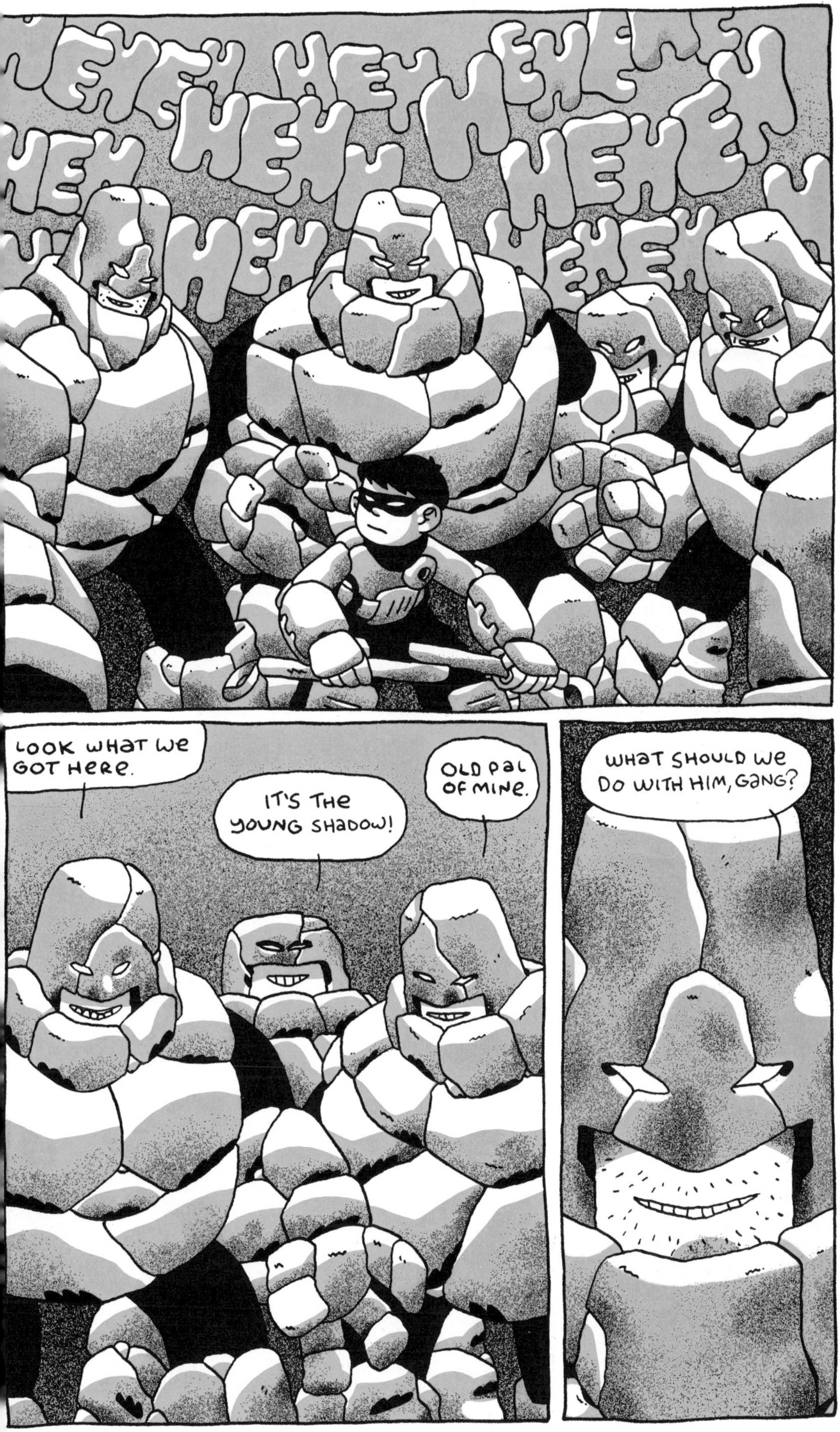

LOOK WHAT WE GOT HERE.
IT'S THE YOUNG SHADOW!
OLD PAL OF MINE.
WHAT SHOULD WE DO WITH HIM, GANG?

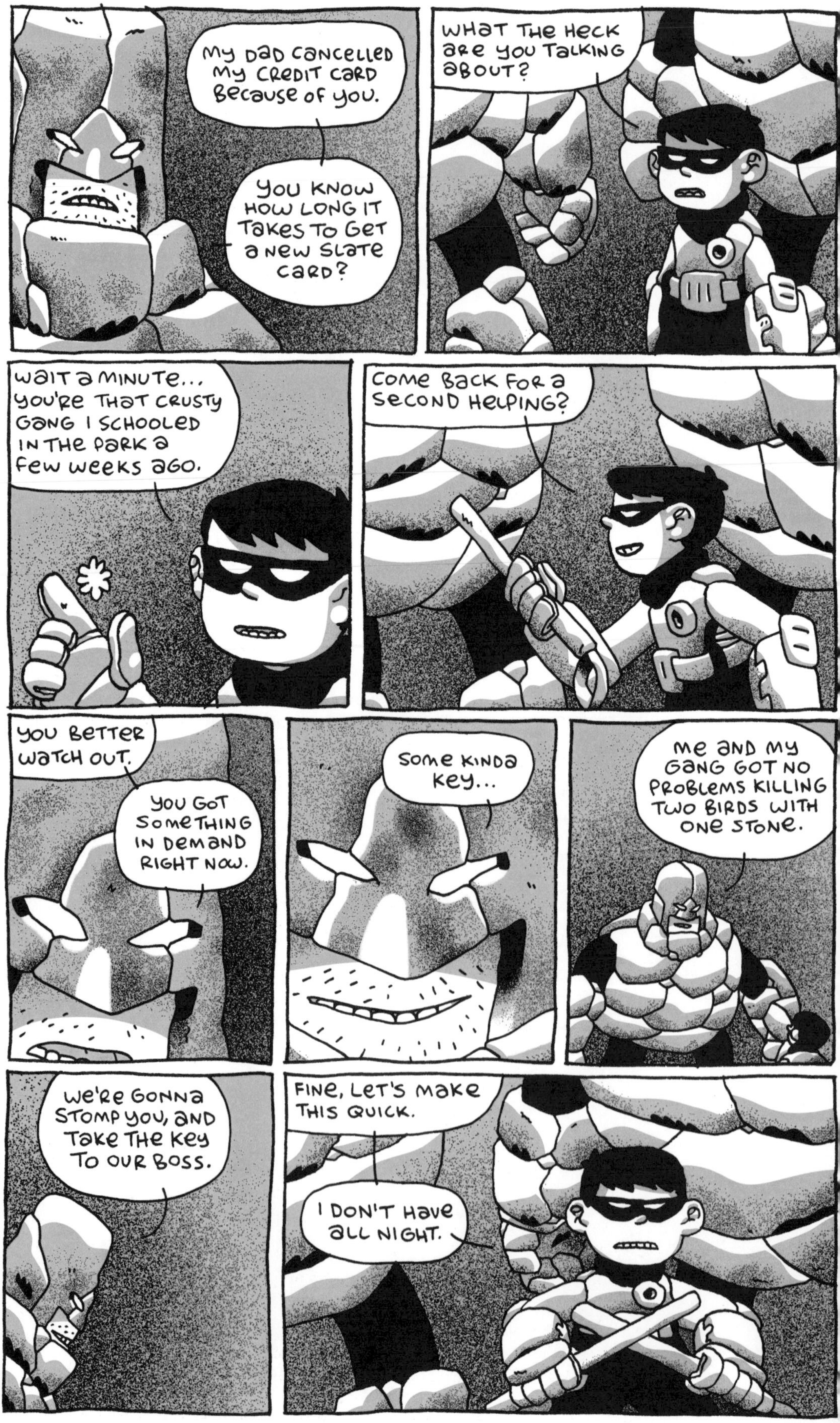
My dad cancelled my credit card because of you.
You know how long it takes to get a new slate card?
What the heck are you talking about?
Wait a minute... you're that crusty gang I schooled in the park a few weeks ago.
Come back for a second helping?
You better watch out.
You got something in demand right now.
Some kinda key...
Me and my gang got no problems killing two birds with one stone.
We're gonna stomp you, and take the key to our boss.
Fine, let's make this quick.
I don't have all night.

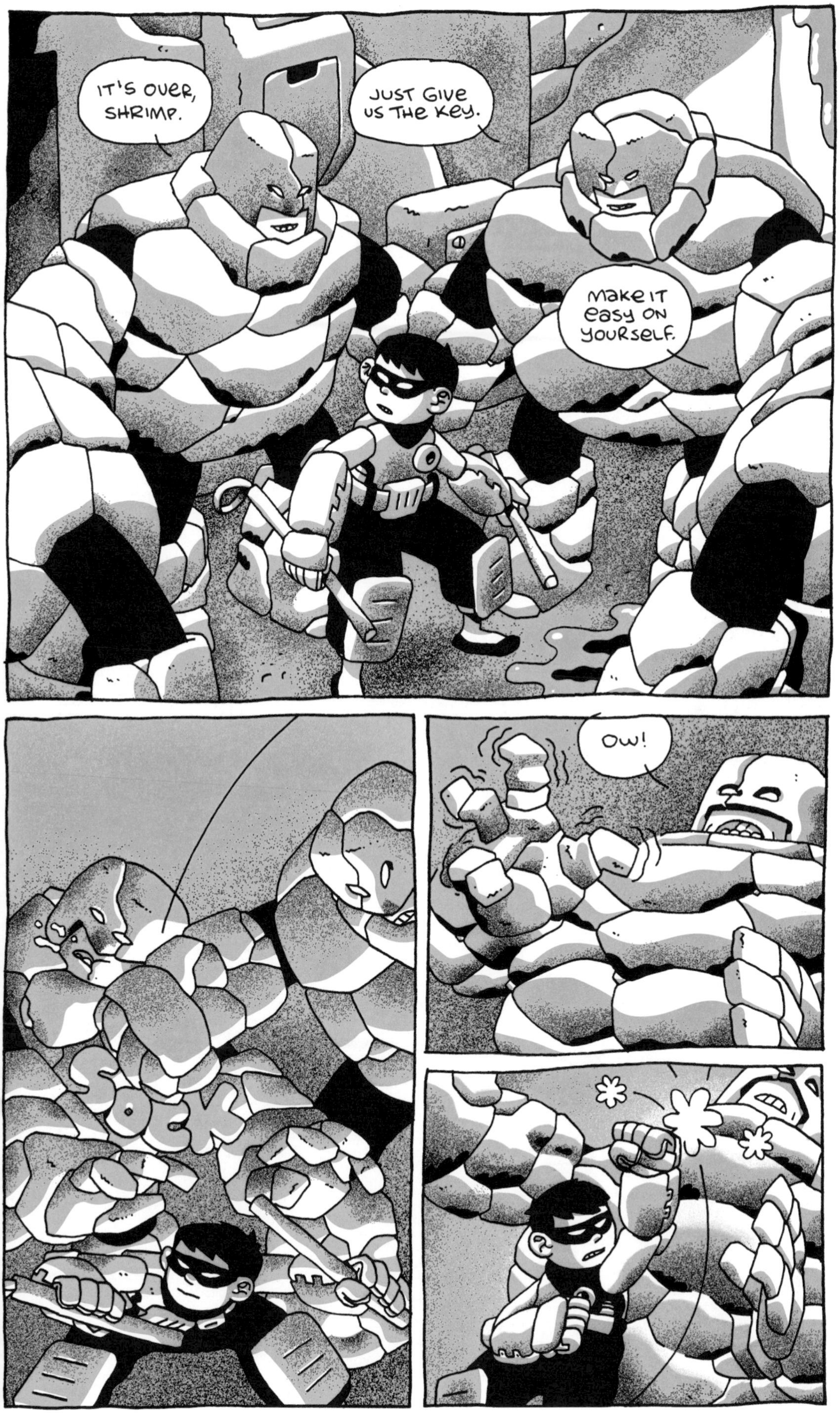
IT'S OVER, SHRIMP.
JUST GIVE US THE KEY.
MAKE IT EASY ON YOURSELF.
SOCK
OW!

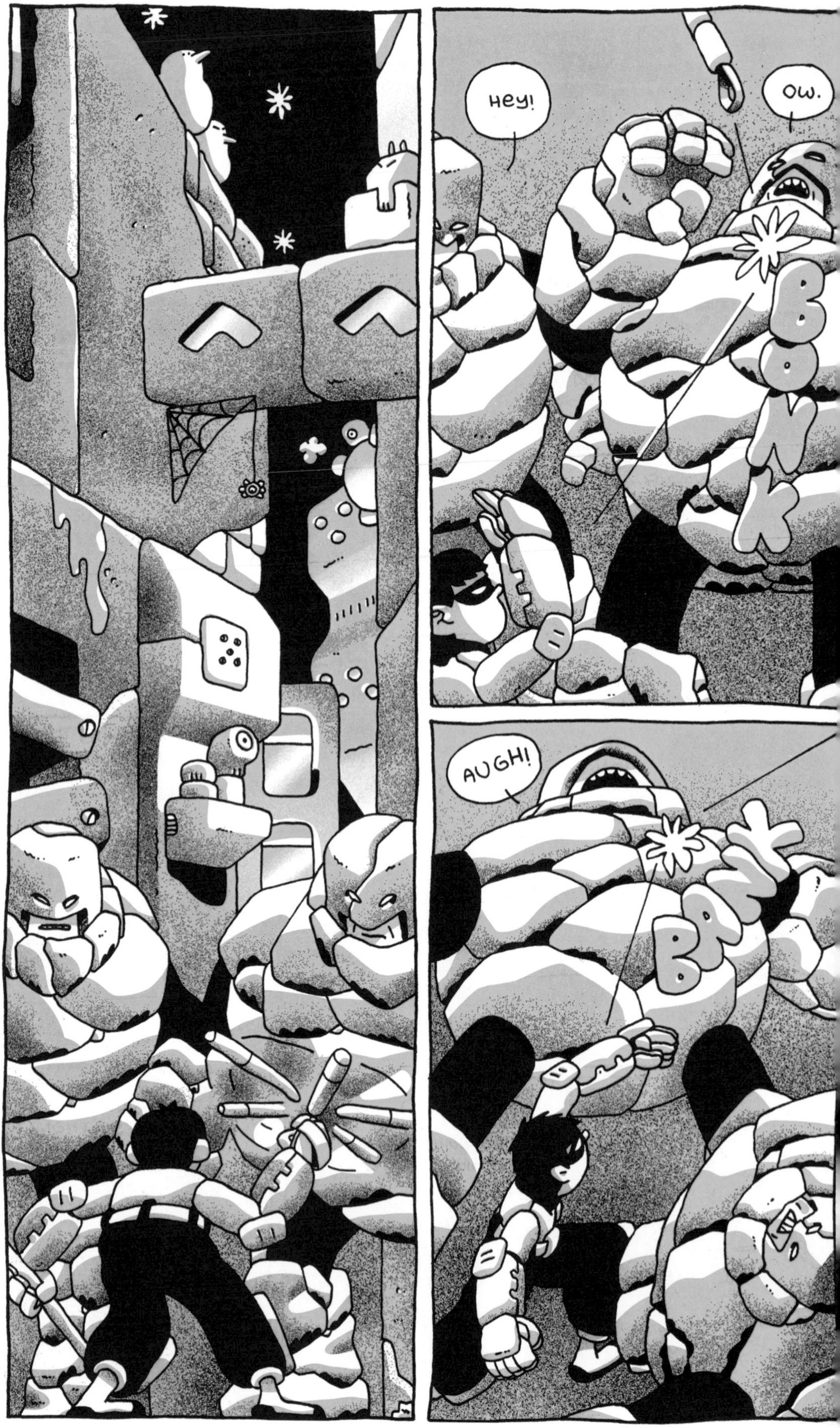
HEY!
OW.
BONK
AUGH!
BANK

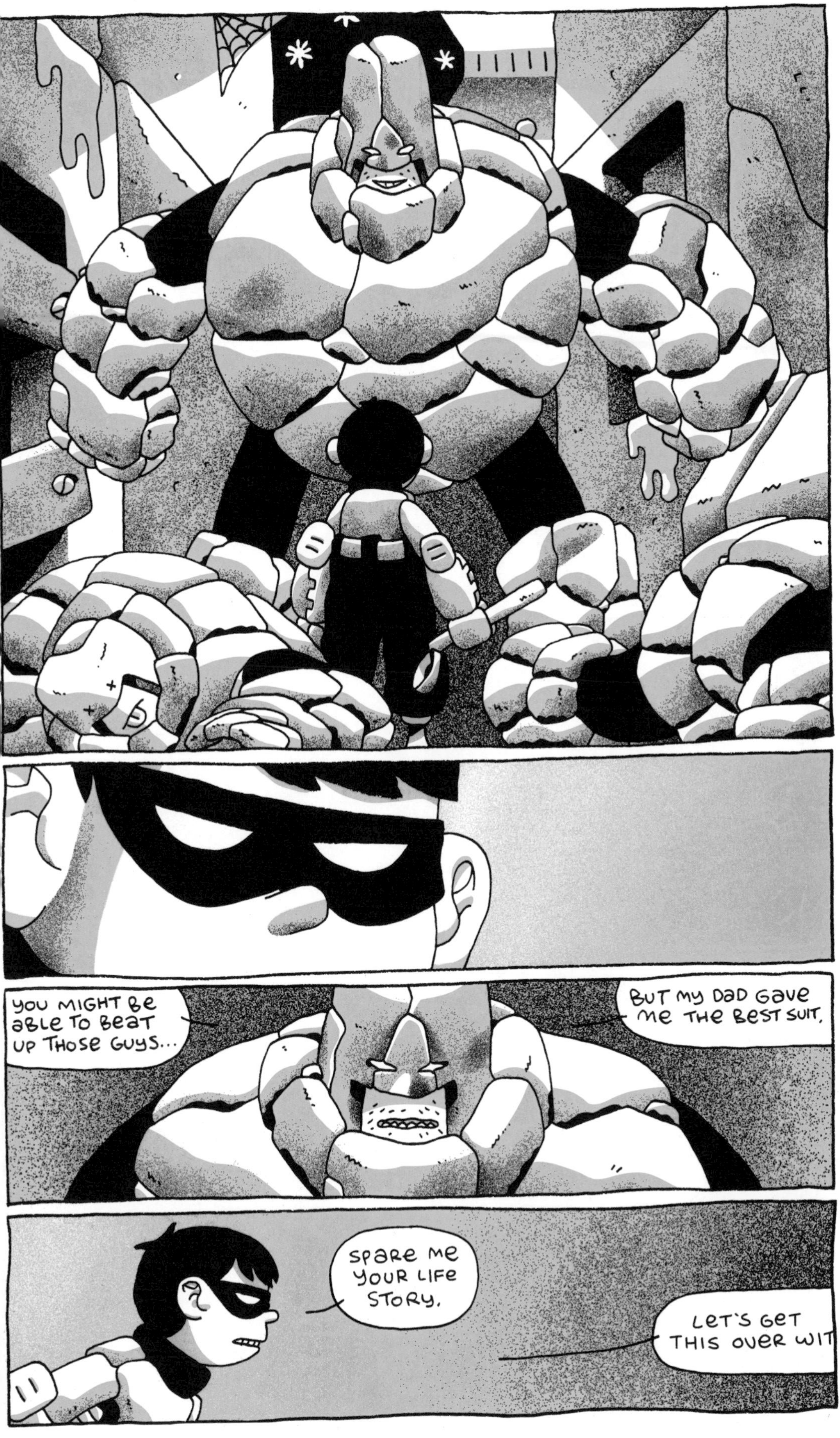
YOU MIGHT BE ABLE TO BEAT UP THOSE GUYS...
BUT MY DAD GAVE ME THE BEST SUIT,
SPARE ME YOUR LIFE STORY,
LET'S GET THIS OVER WIT

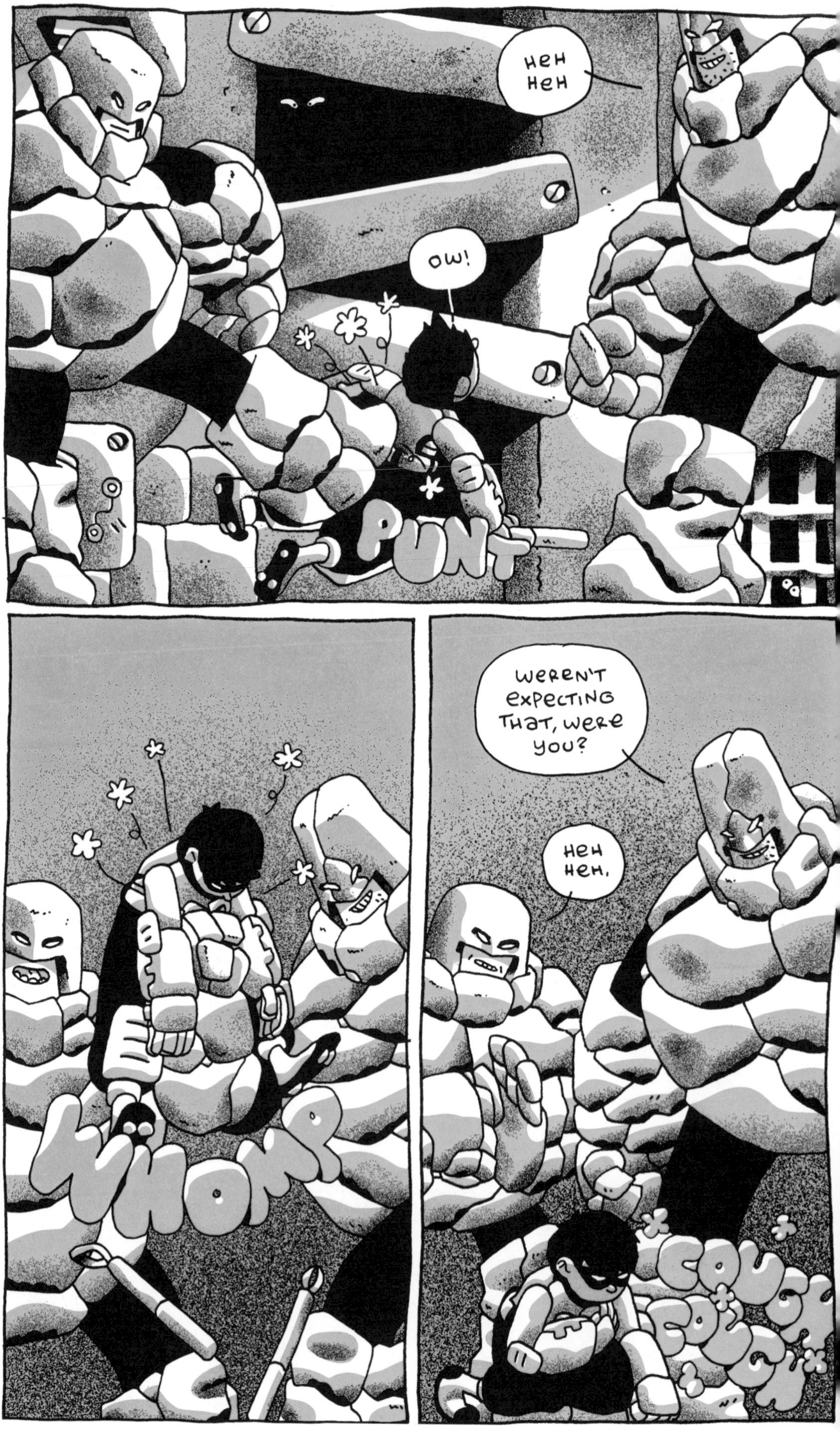
HEH HEH
OW!
PUNT
WHOMP
WEREN'T EXPECTING THAT, WERE YOU?
HEH HEH.
COUGH COUGH

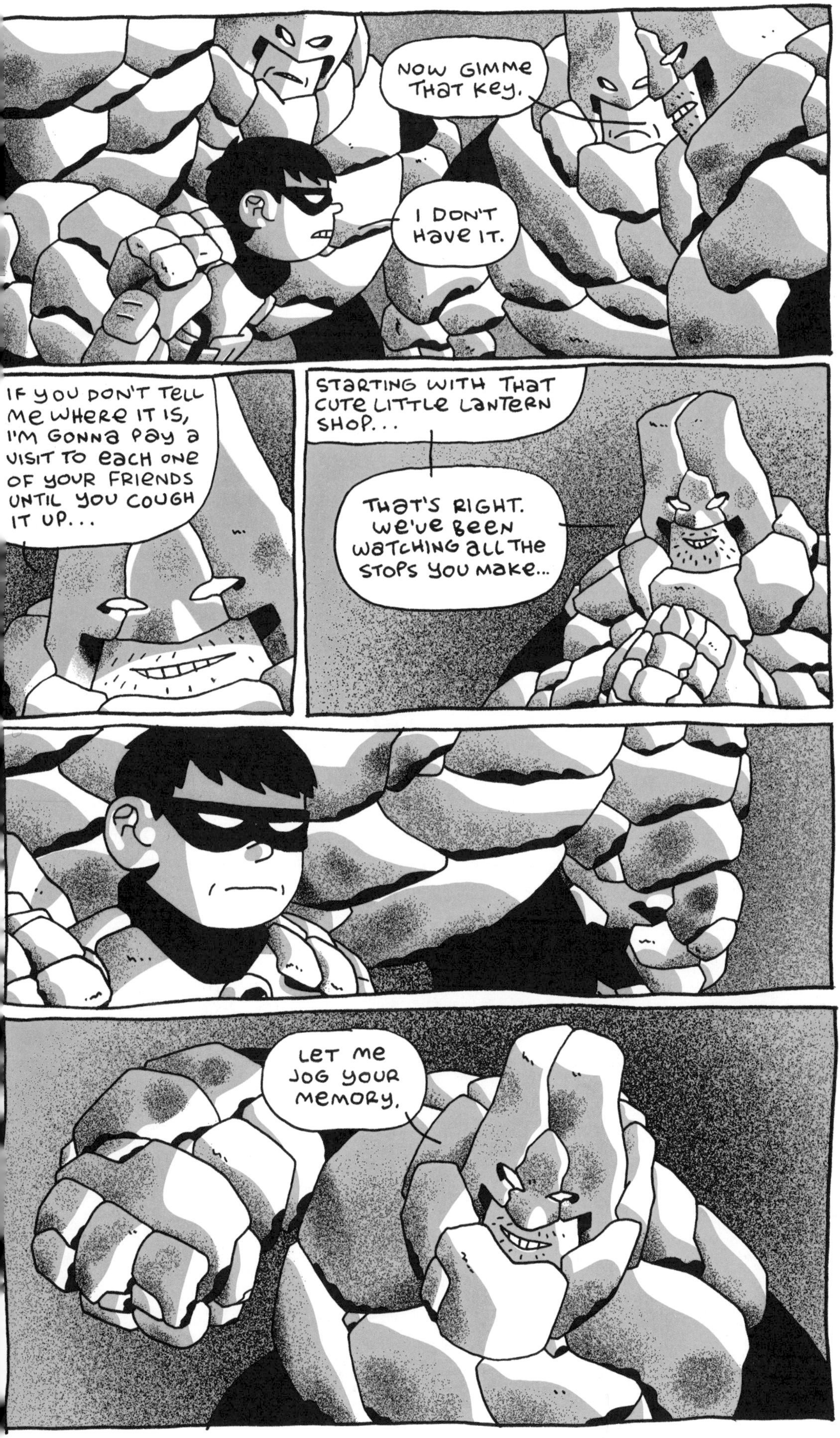

NOW GIMME THAT KEY.
I DON'T HAVE IT.
IF YOU DON'T TELL ME WHERE IT IS, I'M GONNA PAY A VISIT TO EACH ONE OF YOUR FRIENDS UNTIL YOU COUGH IT UP...
STARTING WITH THAT CUTE LITTLE LANTERN SHOP...
THAT'S RIGHT. WE'VE BEEN WATCHING ALL THE STOPS YOU MAKE...
LET ME JOG YOUR MEMORY.

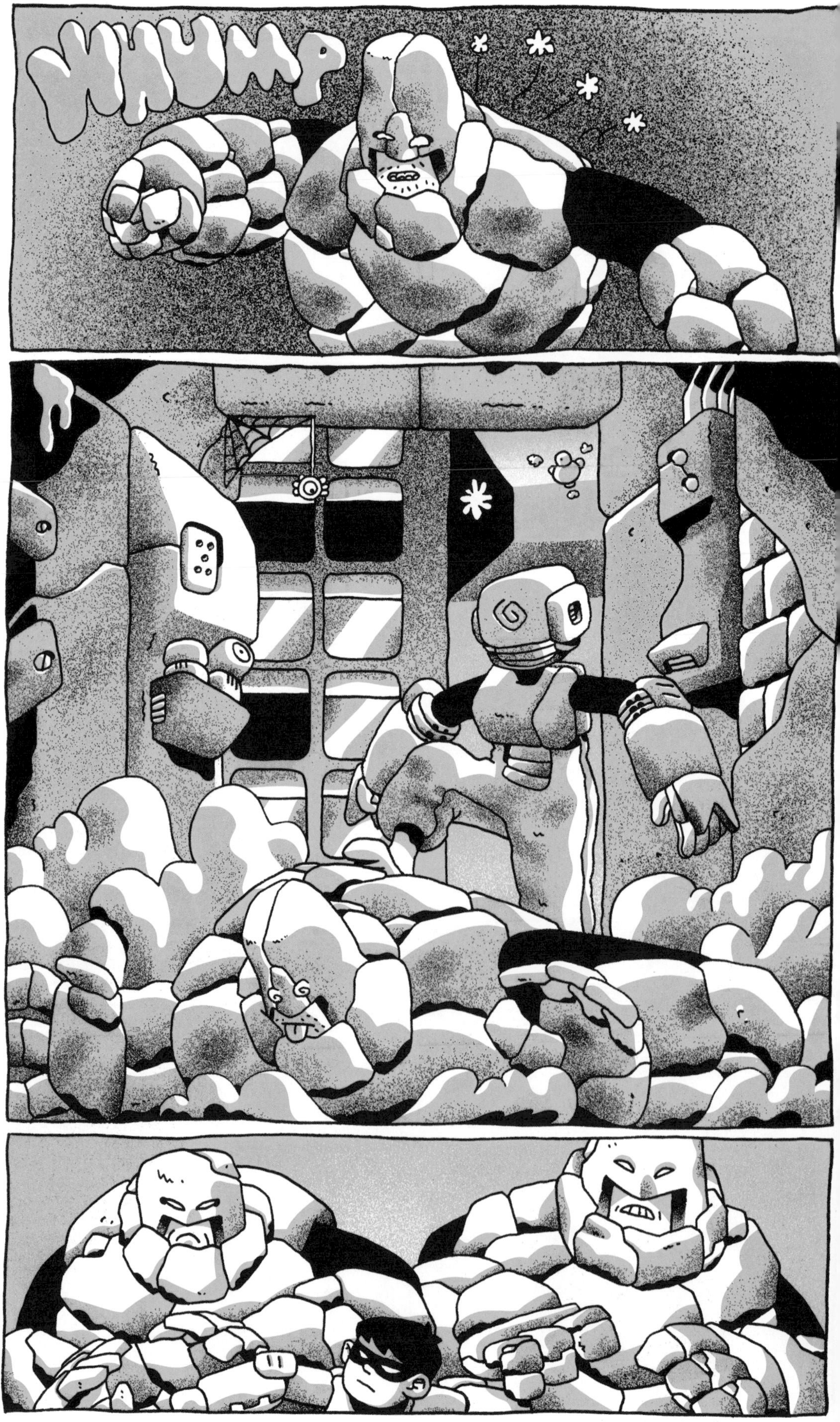
WHUMP

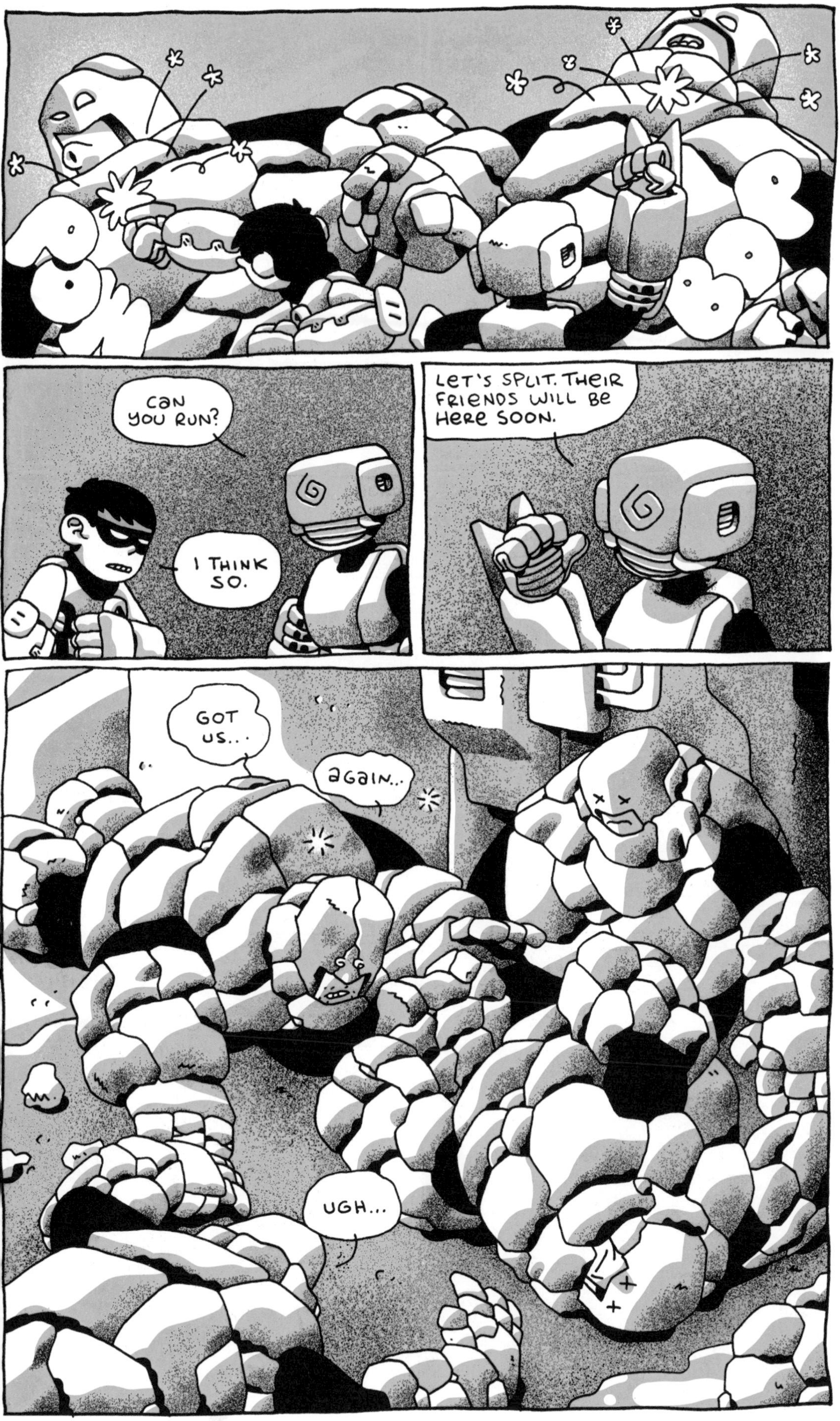
CAN YOU RUN?
I THINK SO.
LET'S SPLIT. THEIR FRIENDS WILL BE HERE SOON.
GOT US...
AGAIN...
UGH...

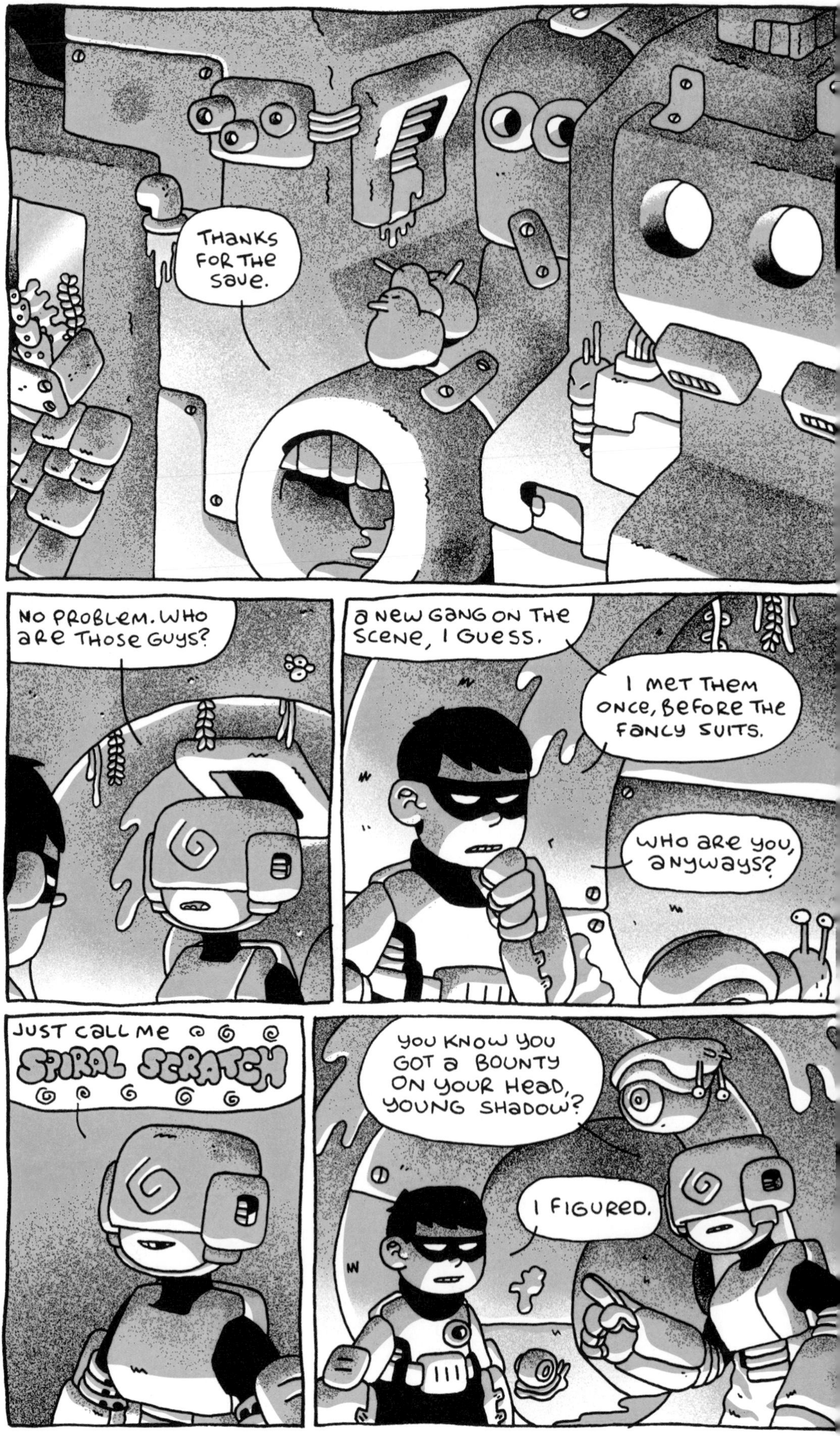
THANKS FOR THE SAVE.
NO PROBLEM. WHO ARE THOSE GUYS?
A NEW GANG ON THE SCENE, I GUESS.
I MET THEM ONCE, BEFORE THE FANCY SUITS.
WHO ARE YOU, ANYWAYS?
JUST CALL ME SPIRAL SCRATCH
YOU KNOW YOU GOT A BOUNTY ON YOUR HEAD, YOUNG SHADOW?
I FIGURED.

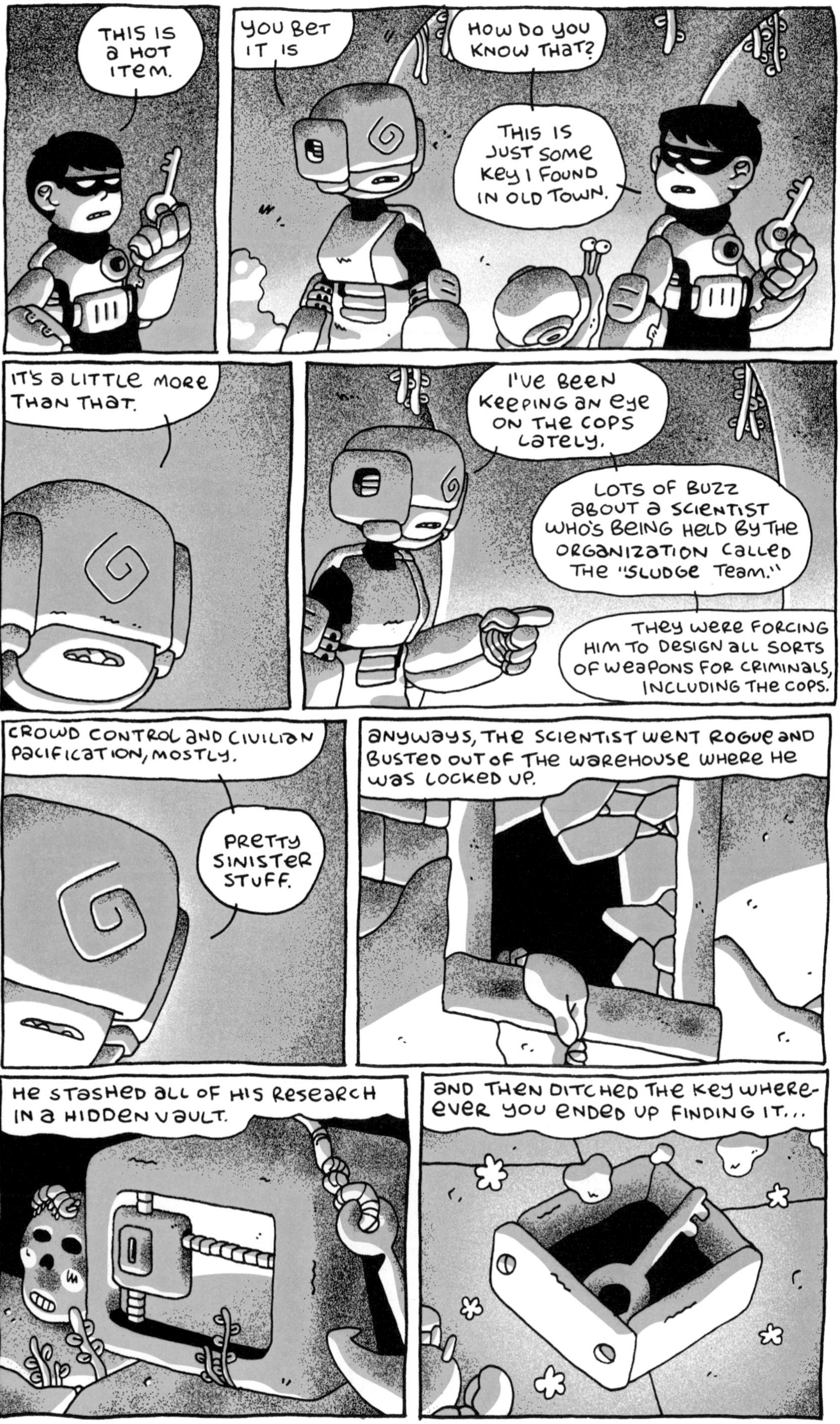
THIS IS a HOT ITEM.
YOU BET IT IS
HOW DO YOU KNOW THAT?
THIS IS JUST SOME KEY I FOUND IN OLD TOWN.
IT'S a LITTLE MORE THAN THAT.
I'VE BEEN KEEPING AN EYE ON THE COPS LATELY.
LOTS OF BUZZ ABOUT A SCIENTIST WHO'S BEING HELD BY THE ORGANIZATION CALLED THE "SLUDGE TEAM."
THEY WERE FORCING HIM TO DESIGN ALL SORTS OF WEAPONS FOR CRIMINALS, INCLUDING THE COPS.
CROWD CONTROL AND CIVILIAN PACIFICATION, MOSTLY.
PRETTY SINISTER STUFF.
ANYWAYS, THE SCIENTIST WENT ROGUE AND BUSTED OUT OF THE WAREHOUSE WHERE HE WAS LOCKED UP.
HE STASHED ALL OF HIS RESEARCH IN A HIDDEN VAULT.
AND THEN DITCHED THE KEY WHEREEVER YOU ENDED UP FINDING IT...

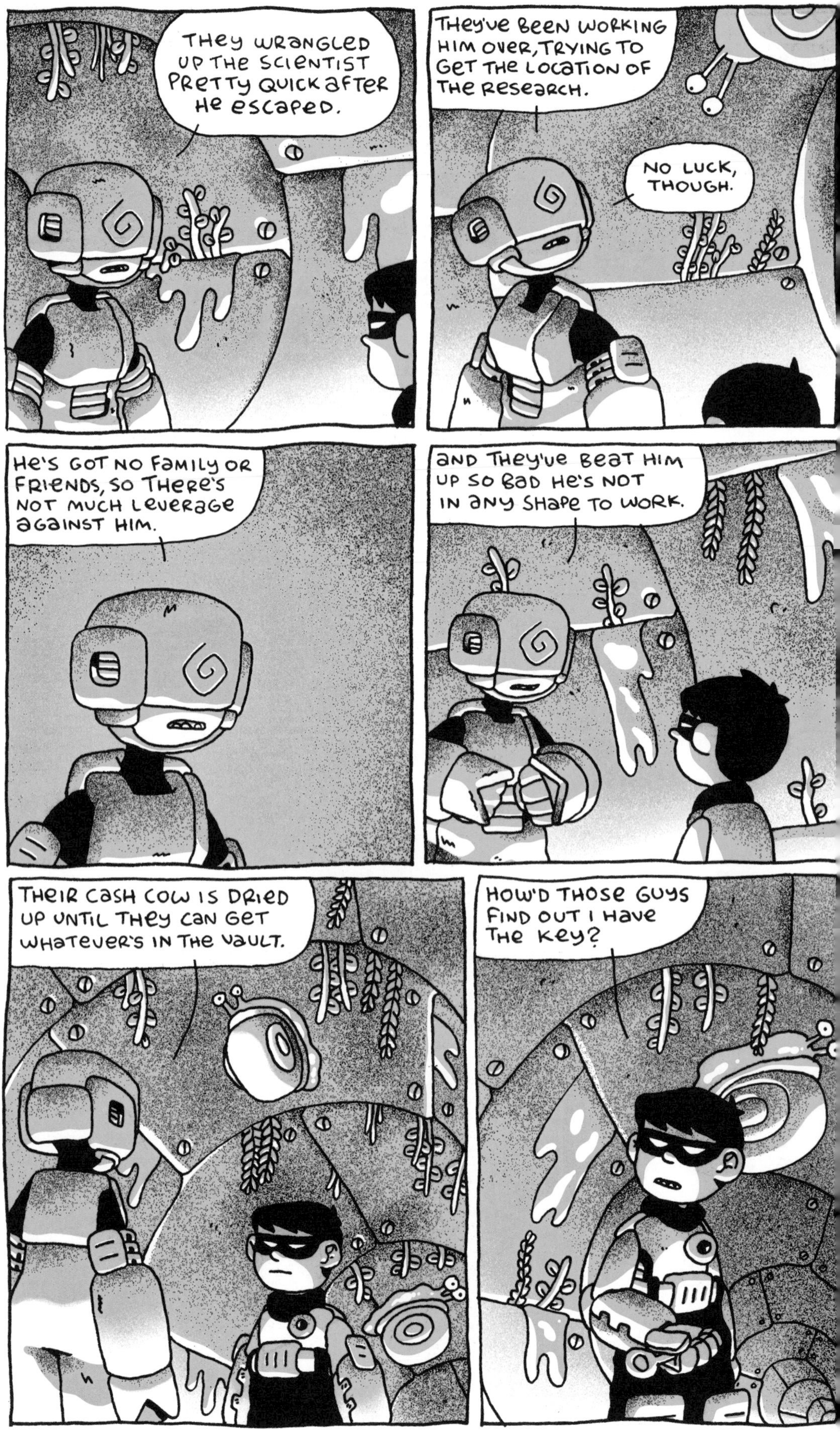
They wrangled up the scientist pretty quick after he escaped.
They've been working him over, trying to get the location of the research.
No luck, though.
He's got no family or friends, so there's not much leverage against him.
And they've beat him up so bad he's not in any shape to work.
Their cash cow is dried up until they can get whatever's in the vault.
How'd those guys find out I have the key?

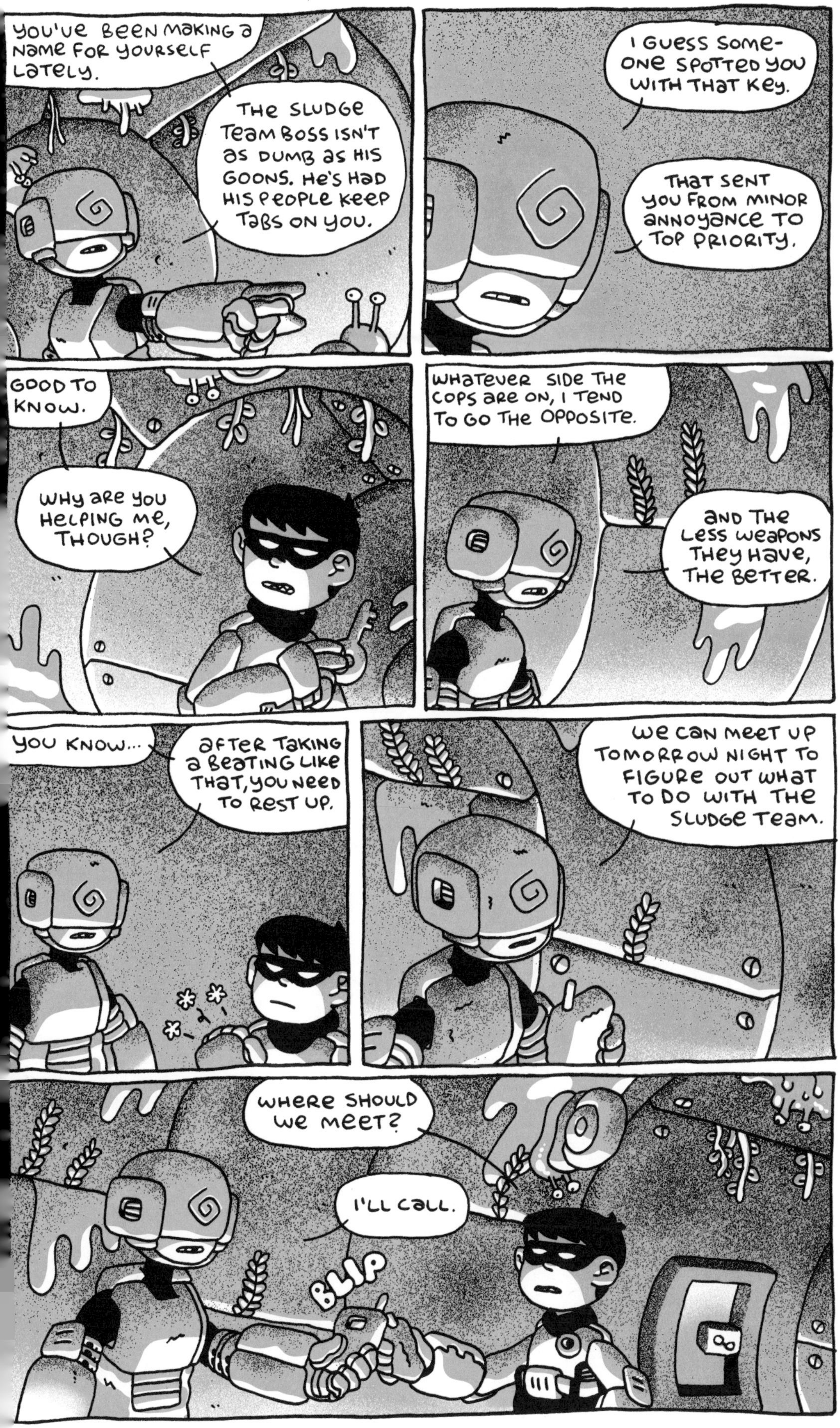
You've been making a name for yourself lately.
The Sludge Team boss isn't as dumb as his goons. He's had his people keep tabs on you.
I guess some-one spotted you with that key.
That sent you from minor annoyance to top priority.
Good to know.
Why are you helping me, though?
Whatever side the cops are on, I tend to go the opposite.
And the less weapons they have, the better.
You know...
After taking a beating like that, you need to rest up.
We can meet up tomorrow night to figure out what to do with the Sludge Team.
Where should we meet?
I'll call.
BLIP

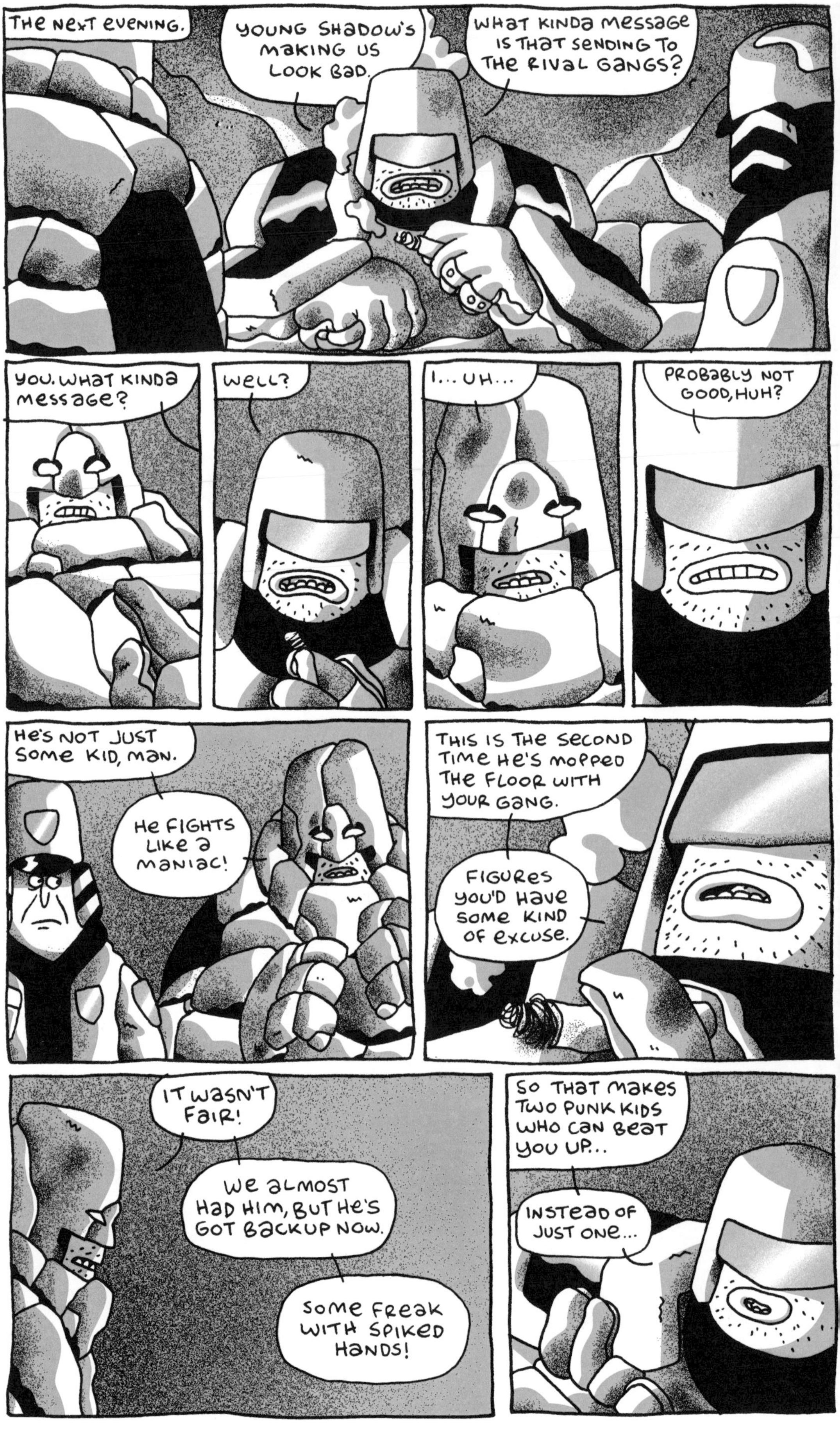
THE NEXT EVENING.
YOUNG SHADOW'S MAKING US LOOK BAD.
WHAT KINDA MESSAGE IS THAT SENDING TO THE RIVAL GANGS?
YOU. WHAT KINDA MESSAGE?
WELL?
I... UH...
PROBABLY NOT GOOD, HUH?
HE'S NOT JUST SOME KID, MAN.
HE FIGHTS LIKE A MANIAC!
THIS IS THE SECOND TIME HE'S MOPPED THE FLOOR WITH YOUR GANG.
FIGURES YOU'D HAVE SOME KIND OF EXCUSE.
IT WASN'T FAIR!
WE ALMOST HAD HIM, BUT HE'S GOT BACKUP NOW.
SOME FREAK WITH SPIKED HANDS!
SO THAT MAKES TWO PUNK KIDS WHO CAN BEAT YOU UP...
INSTEAD OF JUST ONE...

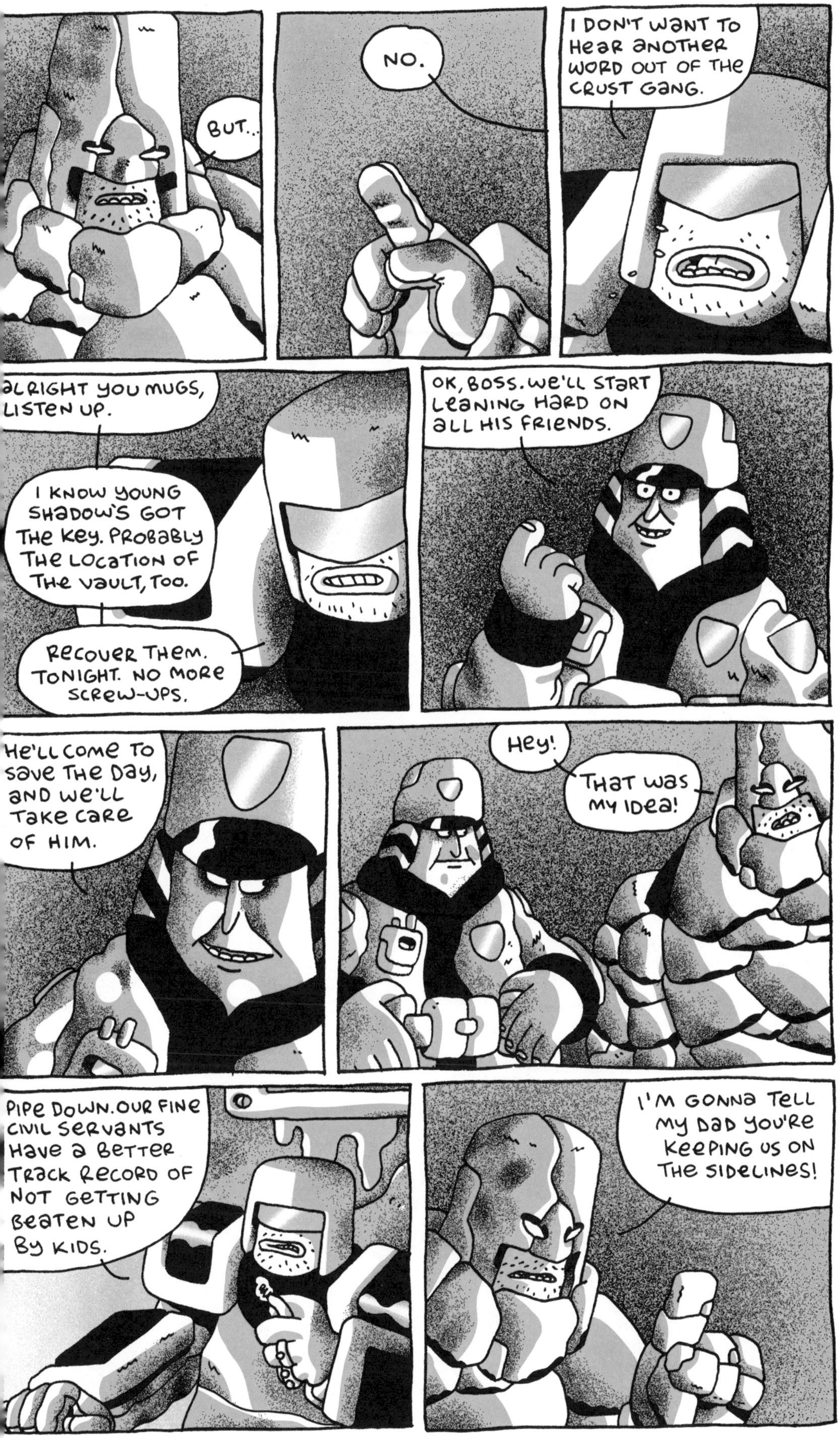

BUT...
NO.
I DON'T WANT TO HEAR ANOTHER WORD OUT OF THE CRUST GANG.
ALRIGHT YOU MUGS, LISTEN UP.
I KNOW YOUNG SHADOW'S GOT THE KEY. PROBABLY THE LOCATION OF THE VAULT, TOO.
RECOVER THEM. TONIGHT. NO MORE SCREW-UPS.
OK, BOSS. WE'LL START LEANING HARD ON ALL HIS FRIENDS.
HE'LL COME TO SAVE THE DAY, AND WE'LL TAKE CARE OF HIM.
HEY!
THAT WAS MY IDEA!
PIPE DOWN. OUR FINE CIVIL SERVANTS HAVE A BETTER TRACK RECORD OF NOT GETTING BEATEN UP BY KIDS.
I'M GONNA TELL MY DAD YOU'RE KEEPING US ON THE SIDELINES!

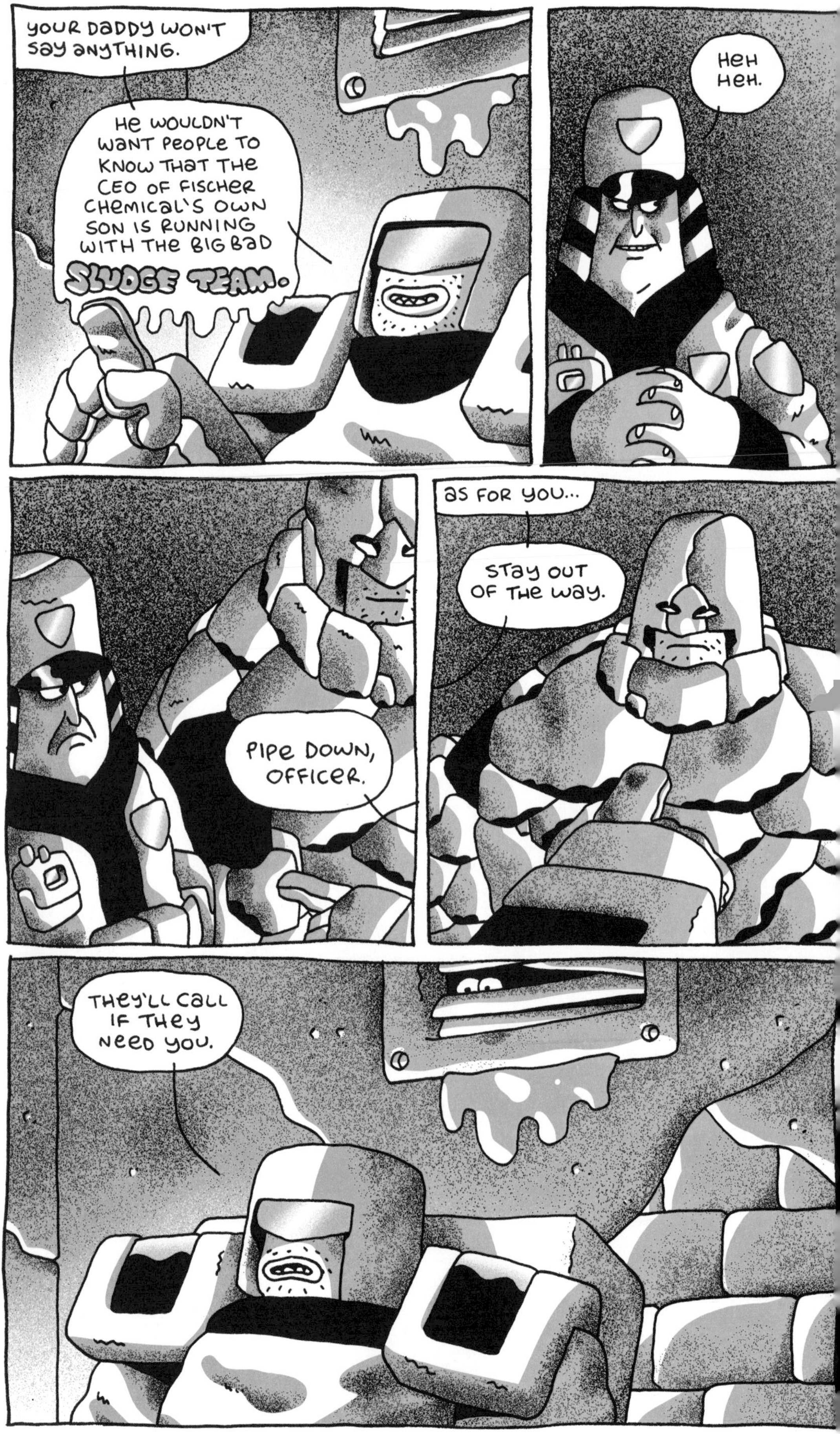
YOUR DADDY WON'T SAY ANYTHING.
HE WOULDN'T WANT PEOPLE TO KNOW THAT THE CEO OF FISCHER CHEMICAL'S OWN SON IS RUNNING WITH THE BIG BAD SLUDGE TEAM.
HEH HEH.
PIPE DOWN, OFFICER.
AS FOR YOU...
STAY OUT OF THE WAY.
THEY'LL CALL IF THEY NEED YOU.

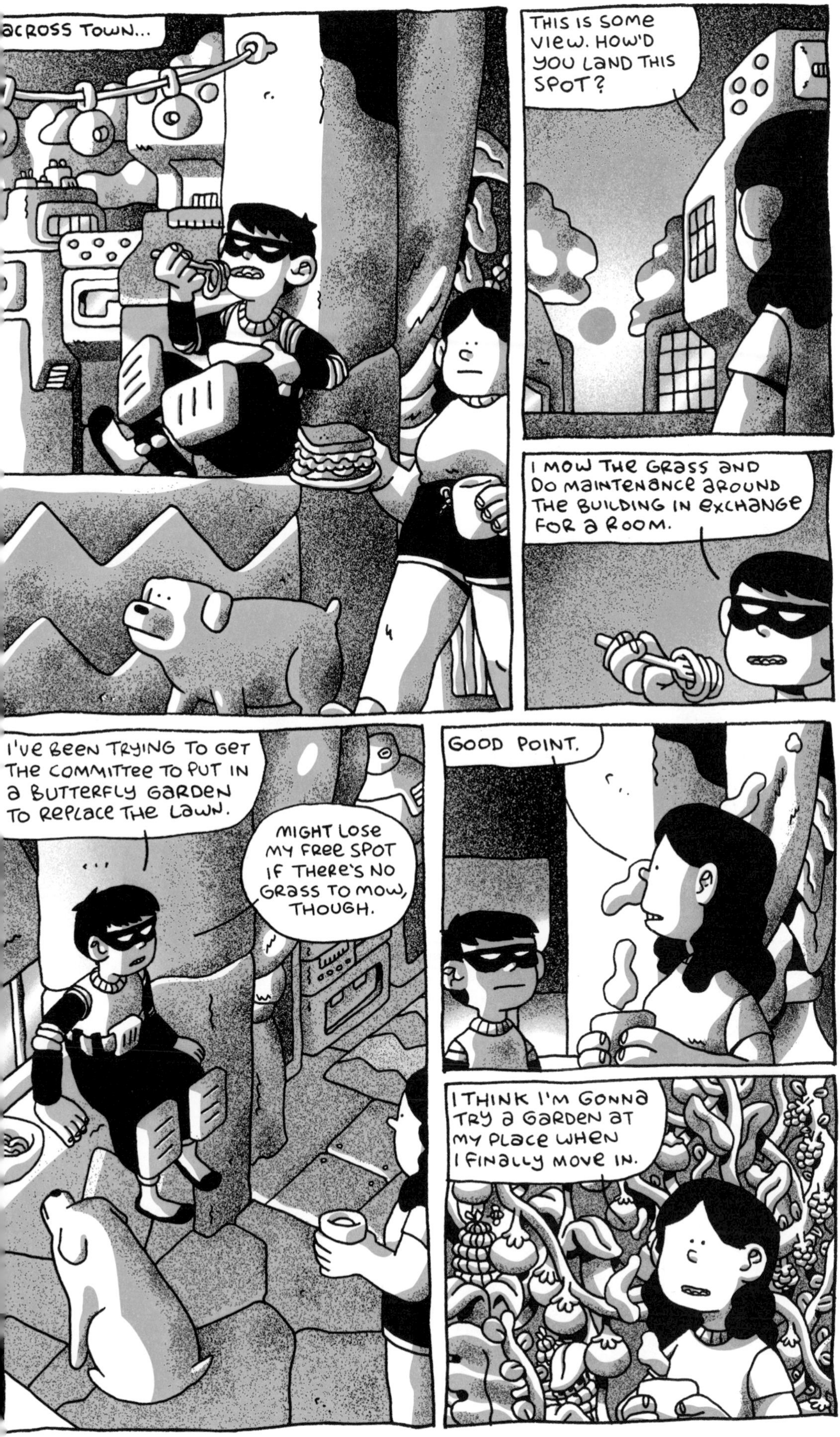
ACROSS TOWN...
THIS IS SOME VIEW. HOW'D YOU LAND THIS SPOT?
I MOW THE GRASS AND DO MAINTENANCE AROUND THE BUILDING IN EXCHANGE FOR A ROOM.
I'VE BEEN TRYING TO GET THE COMMITTEE TO PUT IN A BUTTERFLY GARDEN TO REPLACE THE LAWN.
...
MIGHT LOSE MY FREE SPOT IF THERE'S NO GRASS TO MOW, THOUGH.
GOOD POINT.
I THINK I'M GONNA TRY A GARDEN AT MY PLACE WHEN I FINALLY MOVE IN.

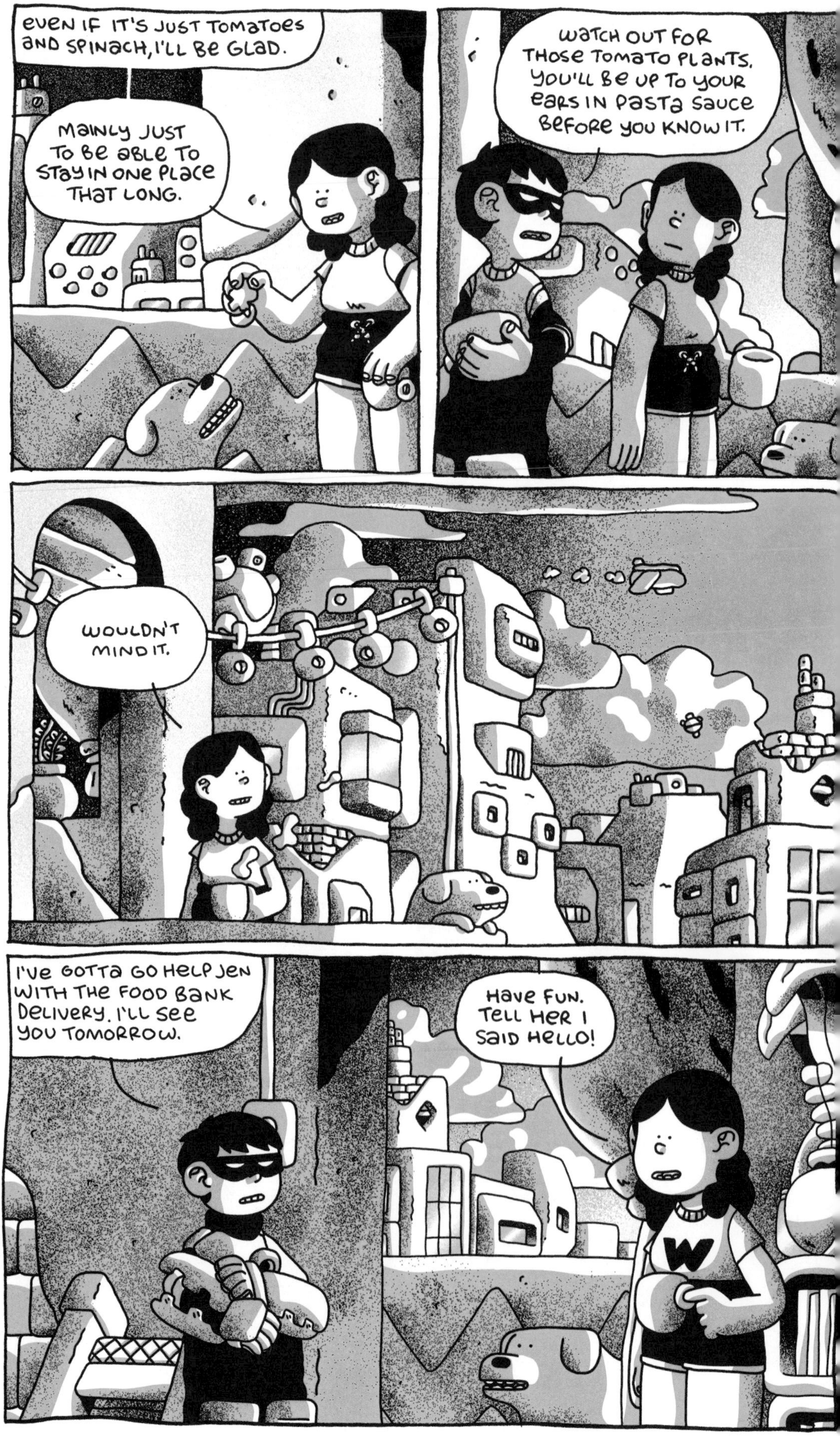

EVEN IF IT'S JUST TOMATOES AND SPINACH, I'LL BE GLAD.
MAINLY JUST TO BE ABLE TO STAY IN ONE PLACE THAT LONG.
WATCH OUT FOR THOSE TOMATO PLANTS. YOU'LL BE UP TO YOUR EARS IN PASTA SAUCE BEFORE YOU KNOW IT.
WOULDN'T MIND IT.
I'VE GOTTA GO HELP JEN WITH THE FOOD BANK DELIVERY. I'LL SEE YOU TOMORROW.
HAVE FUN. TELL HER I SAID HELLO!

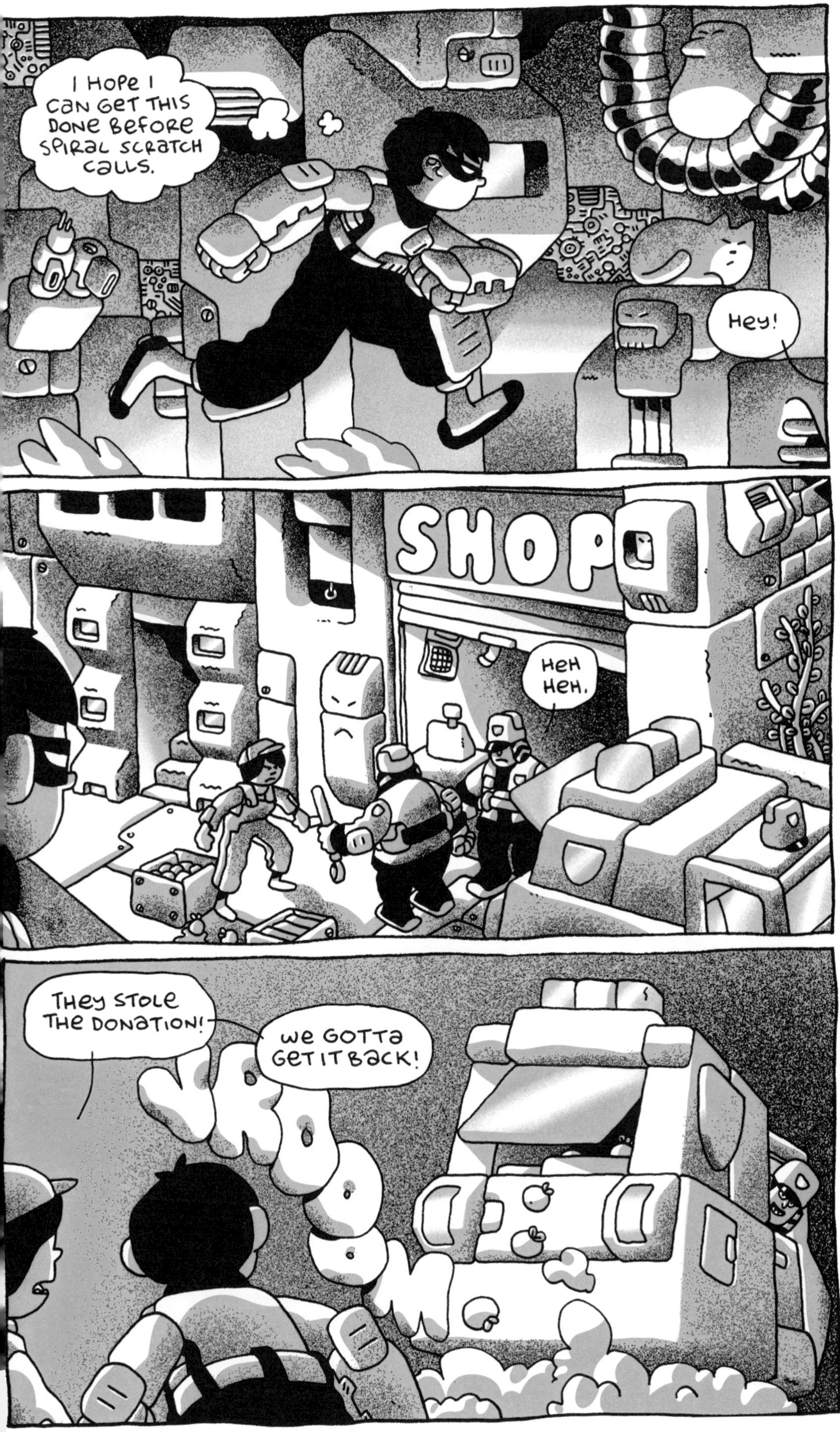
I HOPE I CAN GET THIS DONE BEFORE SPIRAL SCRATCH CALLS.
HEY!
SHOP
HEH HEH.
THEY STOLE THE DONATION!
WE GOTTA GET IT BACK!

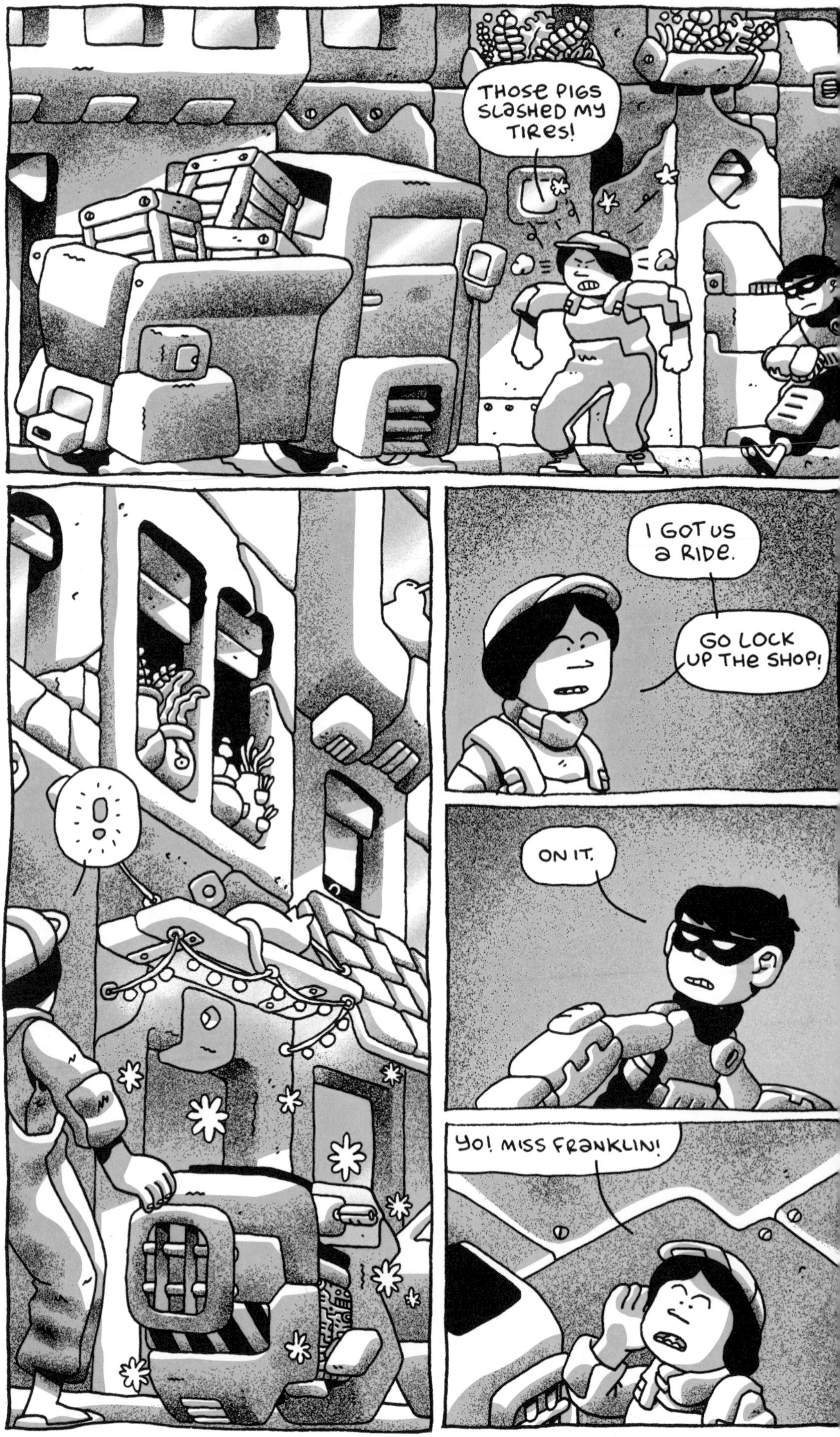
THOSE PIGS SLASHED MY TIRES!
I GOT US A RIDE.
GO LOCK UP THE SHOP!
ON IT.
!
YO! MISS FRANKLIN!

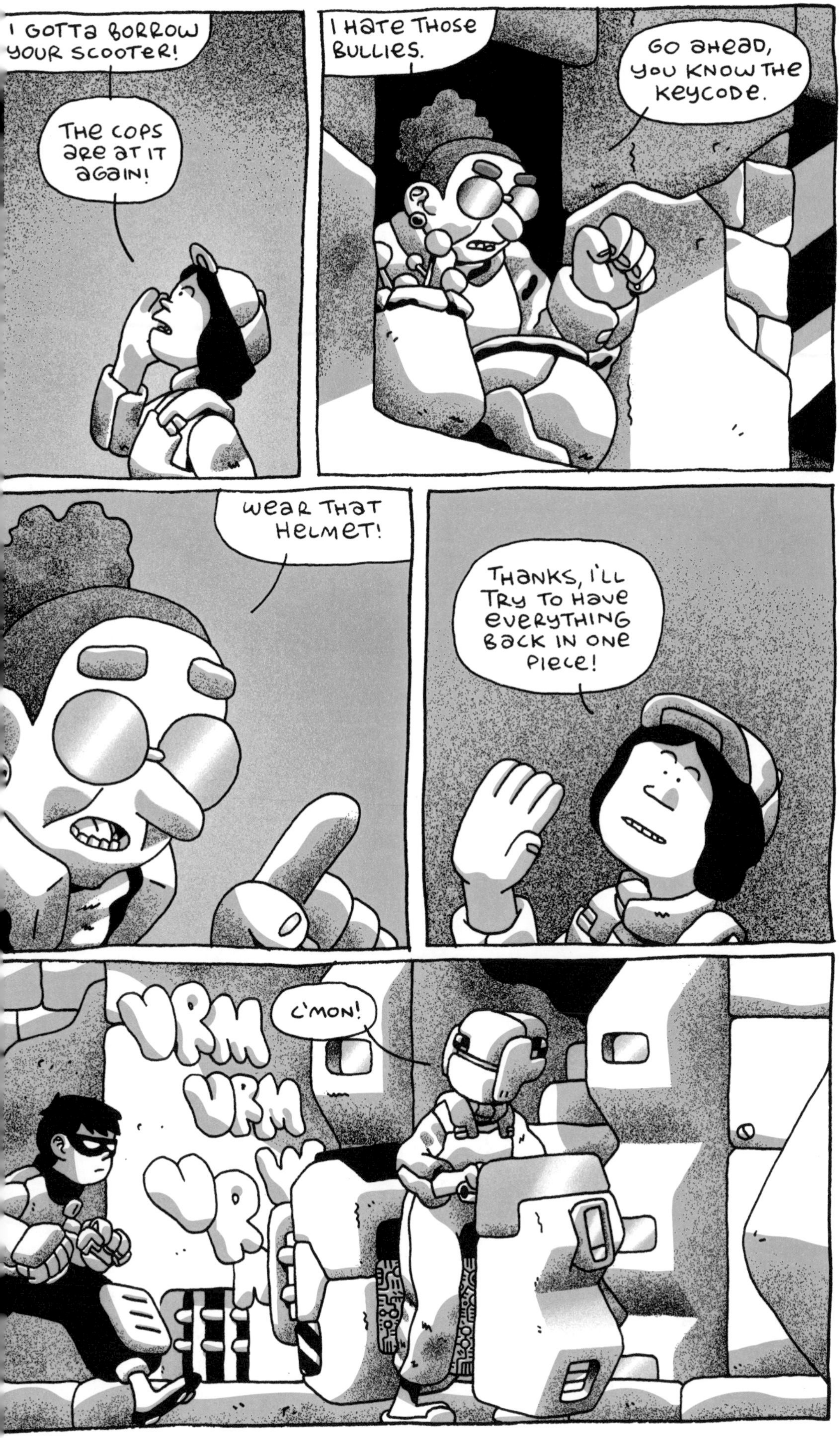
I GOTTA BORROW YOUR SCOOTER!
THE COPS ARE AT IT AGAIN!
I HATE THOSE BULLIES.
GO AHEAD, YOU KNOW THE KEYCODE.
WEAR THAT HELMET!
THANKS, I'LL TRY TO HAVE EVERYTHING BACK IN ONE PIECE!
VRM VRM VRW
C'MON!

GERRY, I NEED A LOCATION ON A POLICE TRUCK.

SURE THING, GIMME A MINUTE.

ANYBODY IN SMOKE TOWN SEEN ANY CRAZY COPS SPEEDING AROUND?

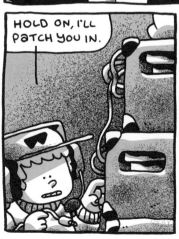

HOLD ON, I'LL PATCH YOU IN.

GO AHEAD.

I SAW 'EM JUST NOW! HEADED TOWARDS THE OLD TOLL BRIDGE!

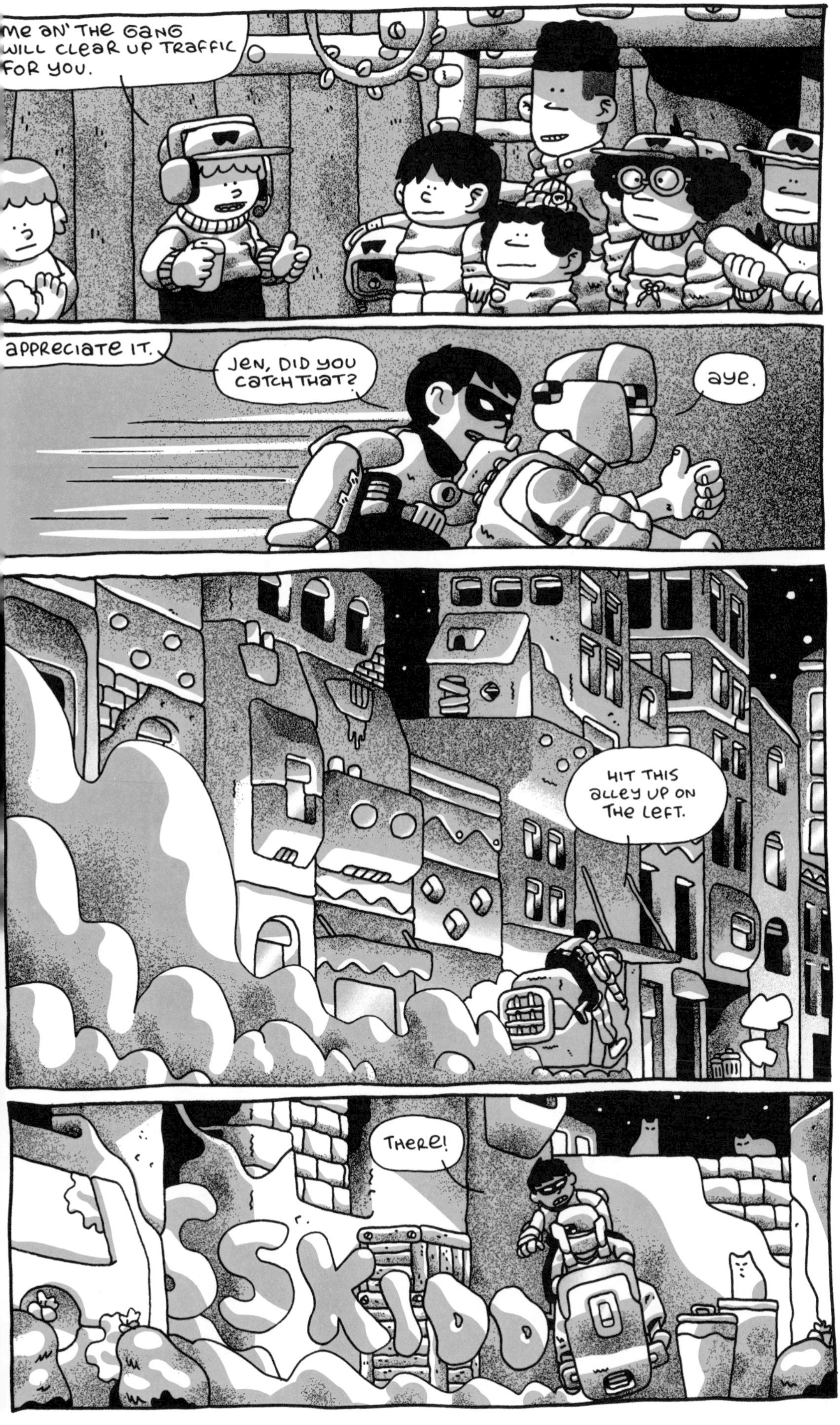
ME AN' THE GANG WILL CLEAR UP TRAFFIC FOR YOU.
APPRECIATE IT.
JEN, DID YOU CATCH THAT?
AYE.
HIT THIS ALLEY UP ON THE LEFT.
THERE!
SKIDOO

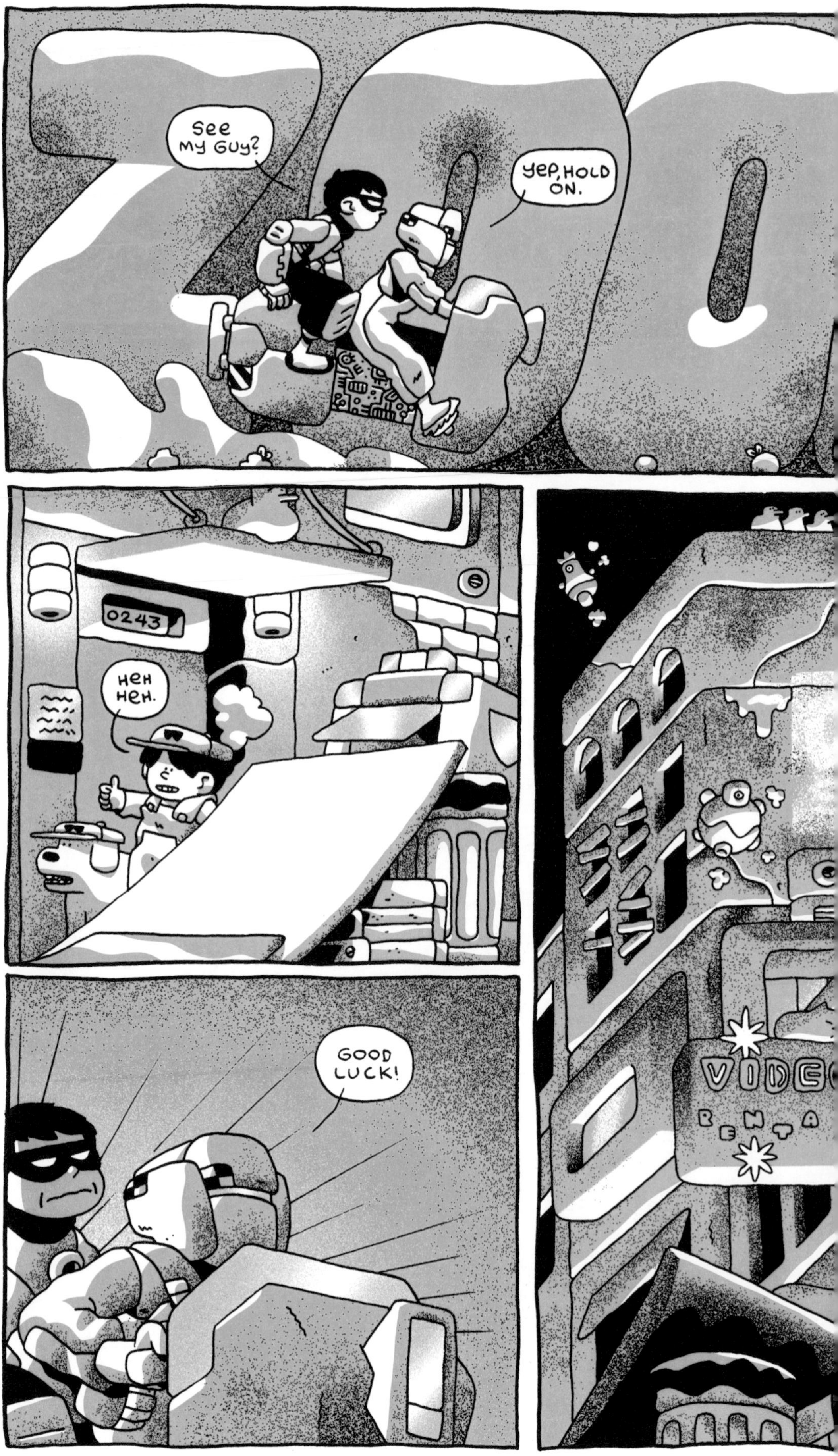
SEE MY GUY?
YEP, HOLD ON.
0243
HEH HEH.
GOOD LUCK!
VIDEO
RENTA

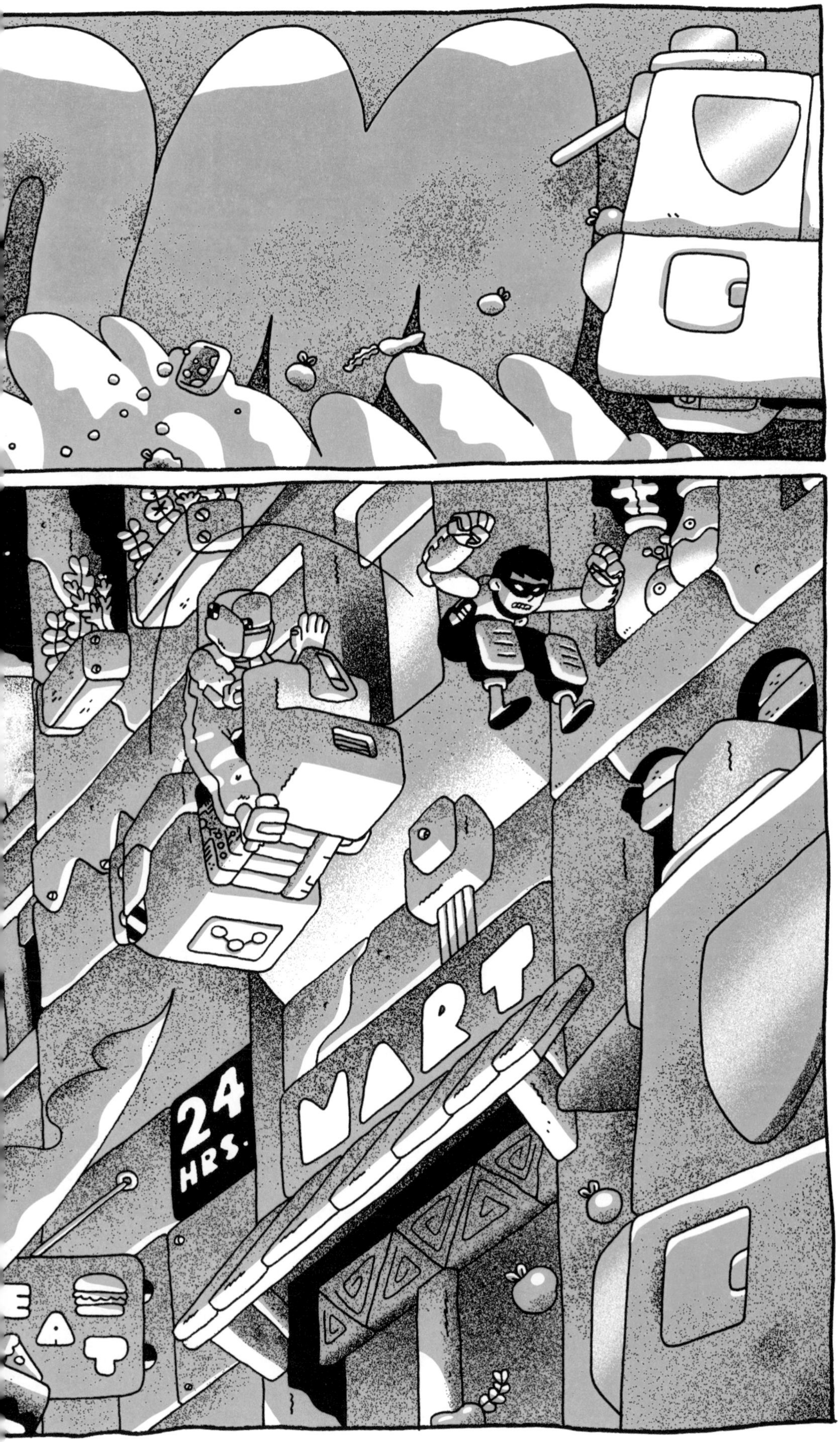
24 HRS.
MART
EAT

SNAP
UH OH.
CREEEEEAK
DON'T CARE FOR THIS.
AAAUG

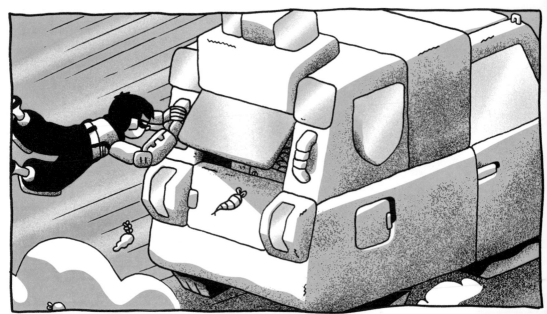

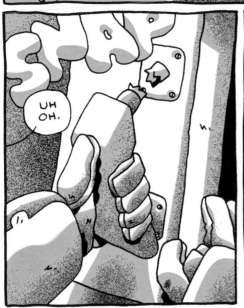

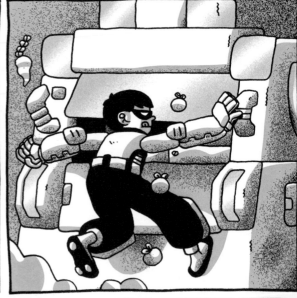

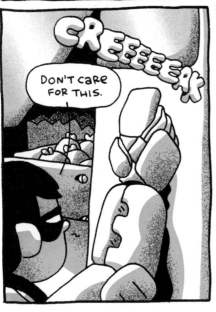

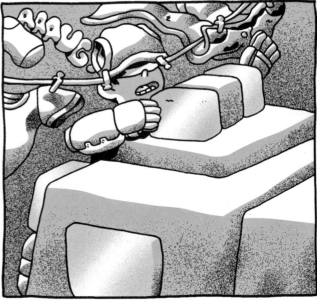

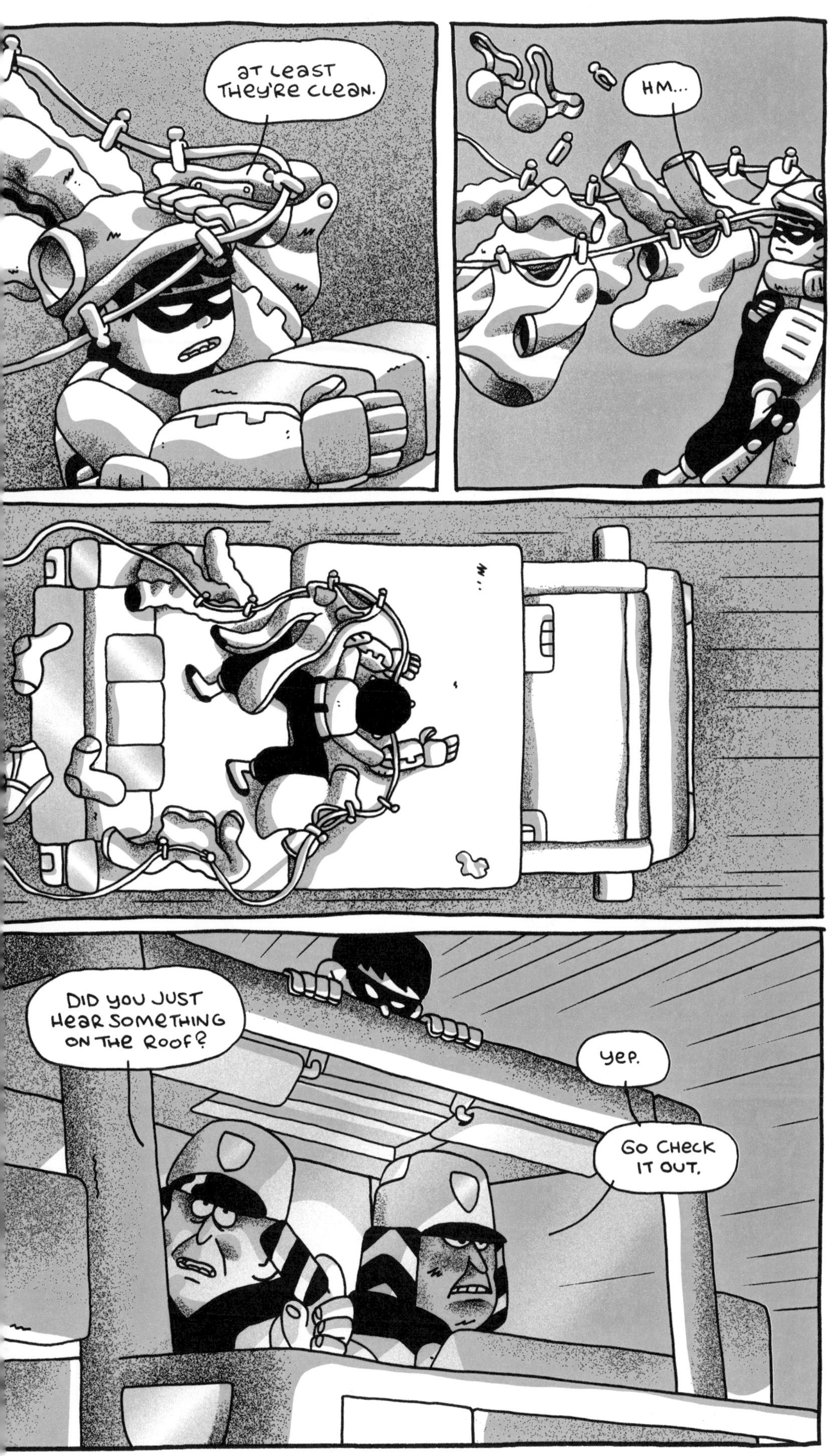
AT LEAST THEY'RE CLEAN.
HM...
DID YOU JUST HEAR SOMETHING ON THE ROOF?
YEP.
GO CHECK IT OUT.

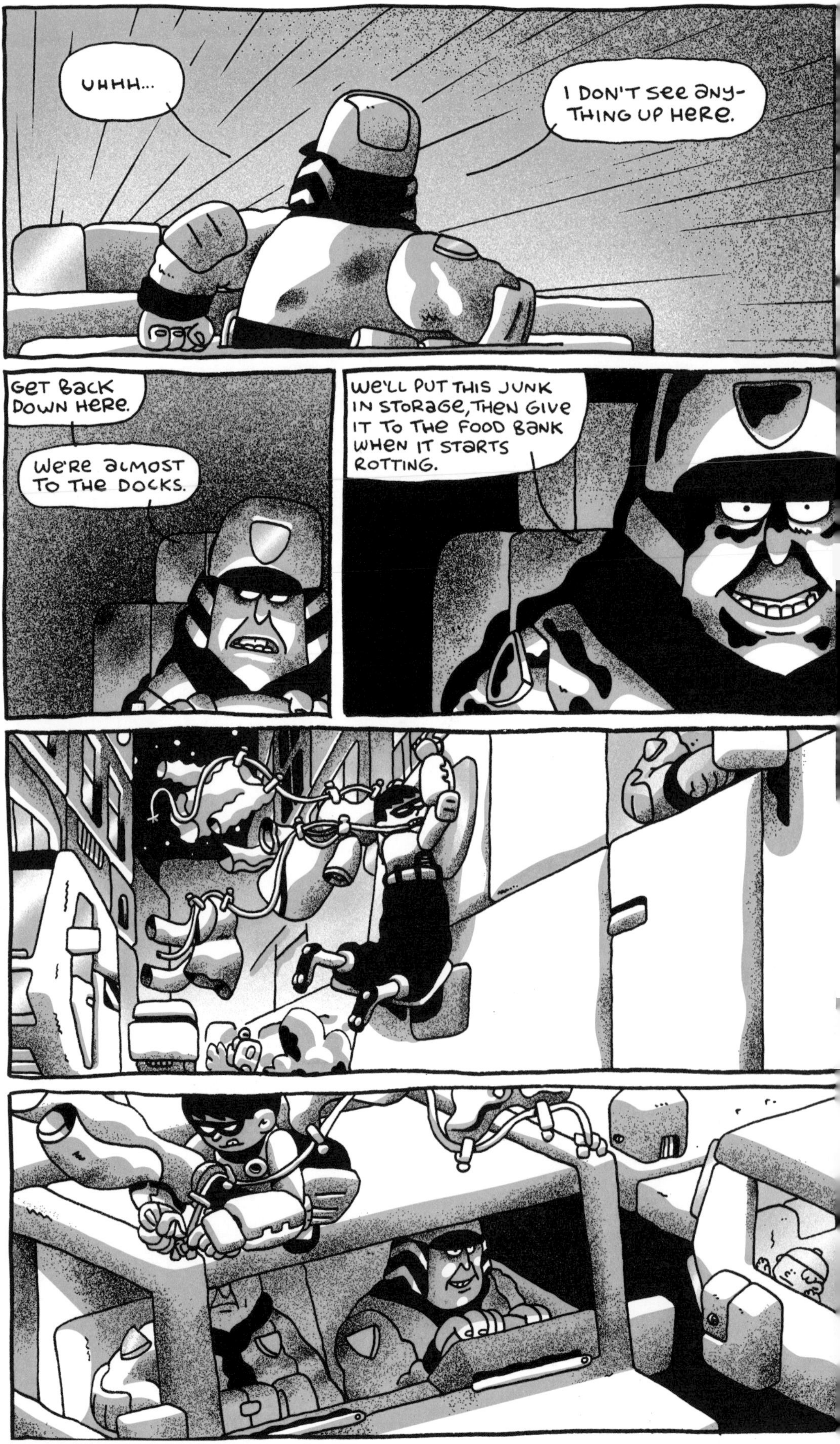
UHHH...
I DON'T SEE ANY-THING UP HERE.
GET BACK DOWN HERE.
WE'RE ALMOST TO THE DOCKS.
WE'LL PUT THIS JUNK IN STORAGE, THEN GIVE IT TO THE FOOD BANK WHEN IT STARTS ROTTING.

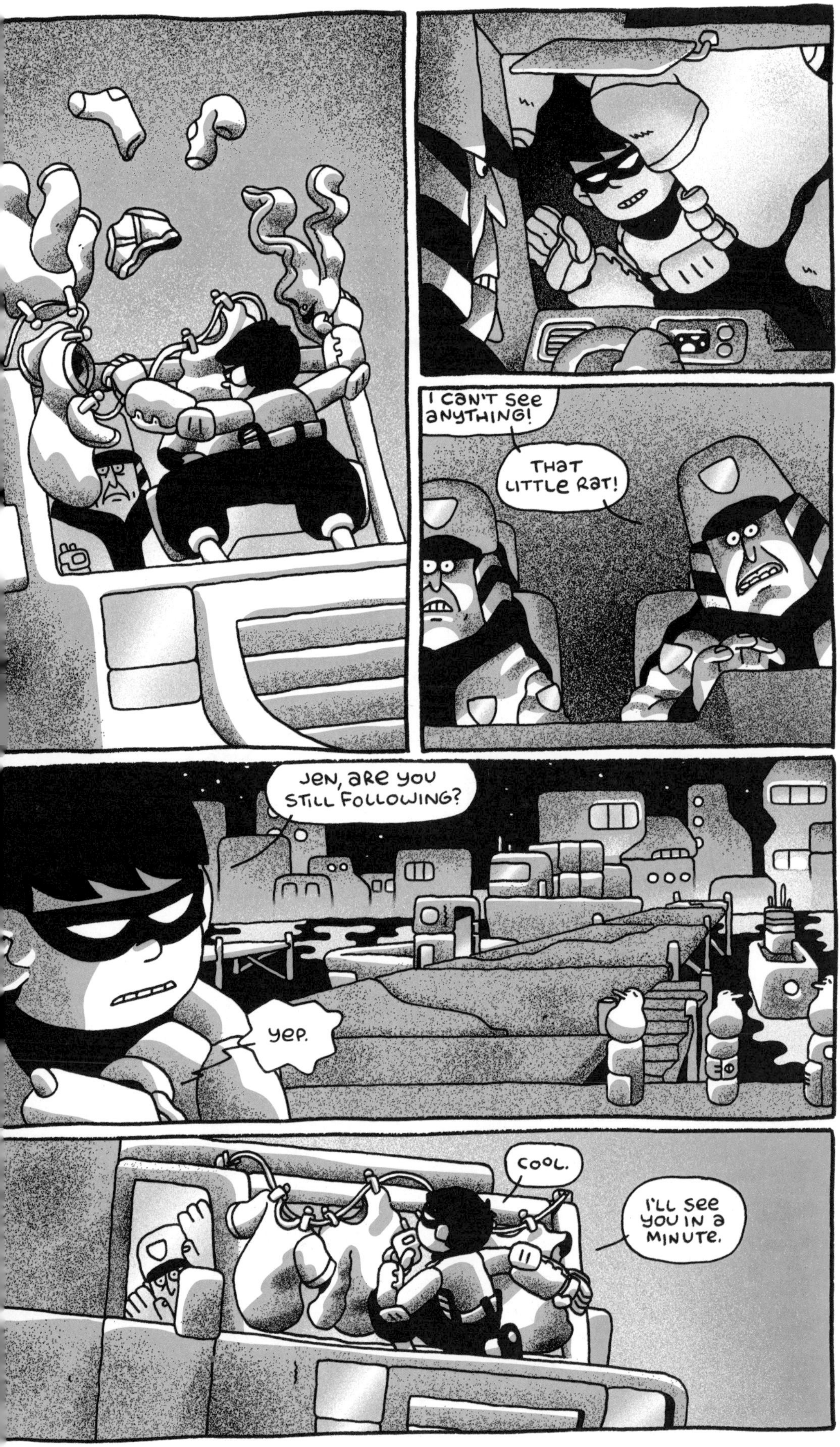
I CAN'T SEE ANYTHING!
THAT LITTLE RAT!
JEN, ARE YOU STILL FOLLOWING?
YEP.
COOL.
I'LL SEE YOU IN A MINUTE.

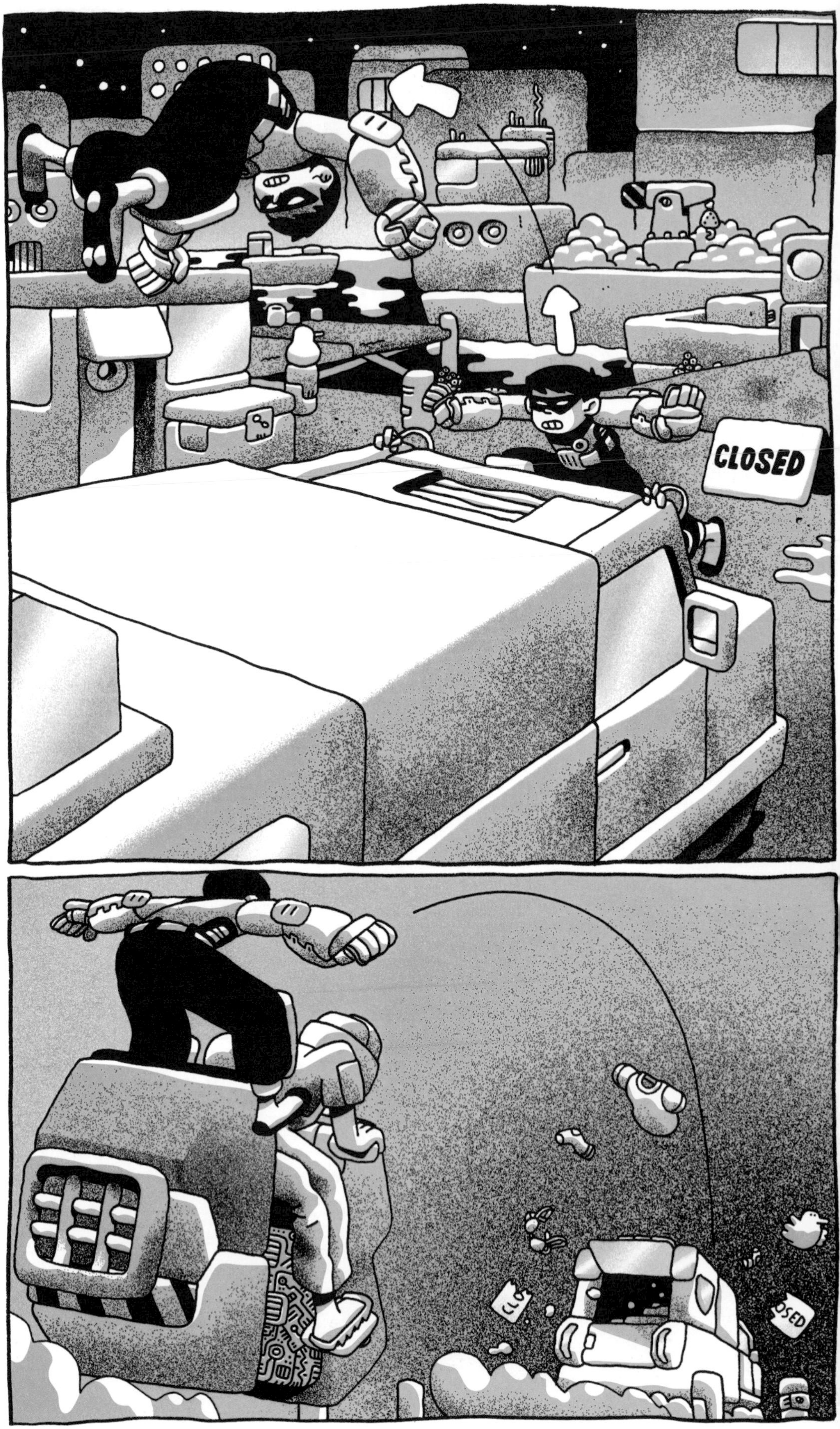
CLOSED

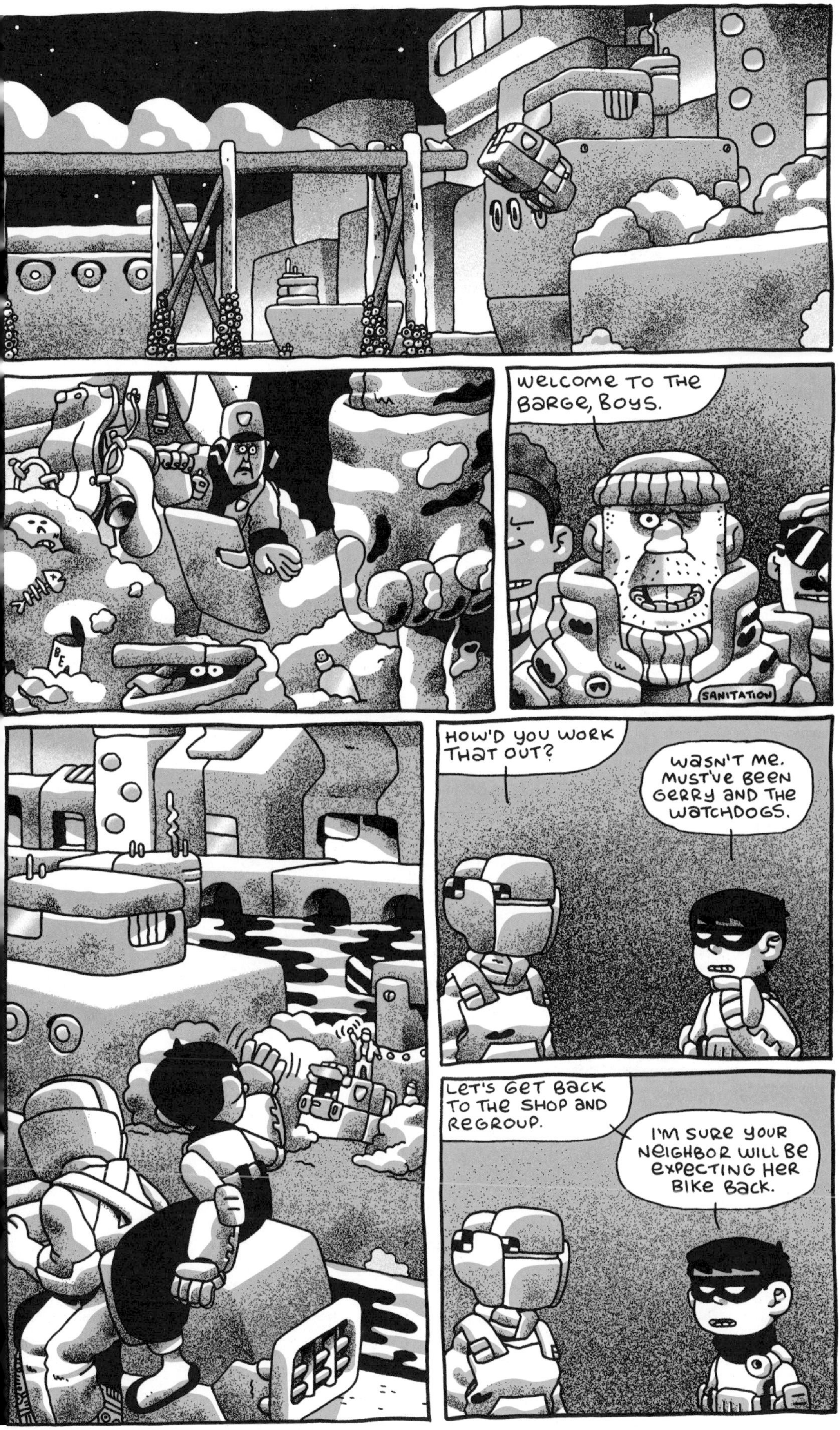
WELCOME TO THE BARGE, BOYS.
SANITATION
HOW'D YOU WORK THAT OUT?
WASN'T ME. MUST'VE BEEN GERRY AND THE WATCHDOGS.
LET'S GET BACK TO THE SHOP AND REGROUP.
I'M SURE YOUR NEIGHBOR WILL BE EXPECTING HER BIKE BACK.

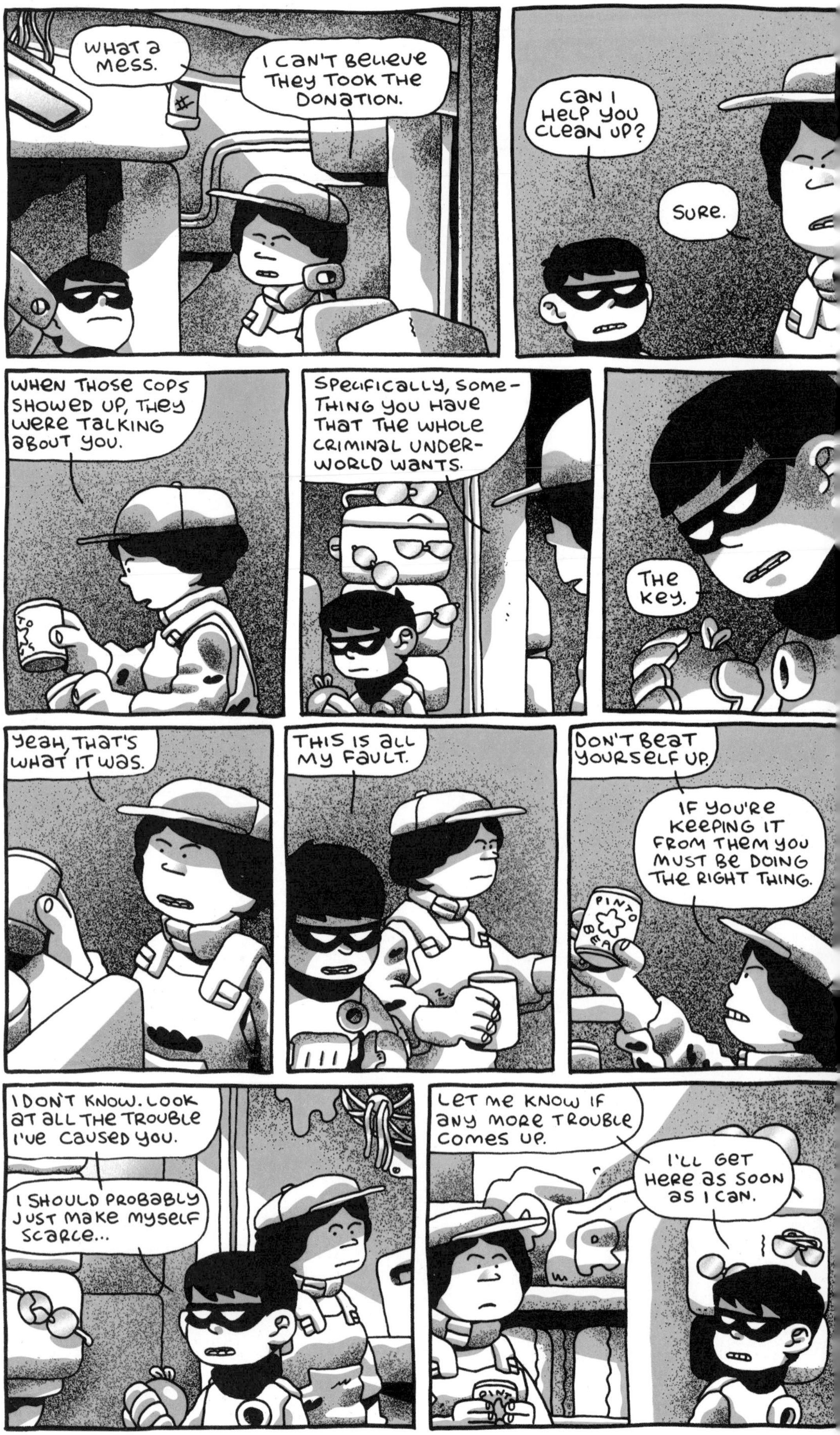
WHAT a MESS.
I CAN'T BELIEVE THEY TOOK THE DONATION.
CAN I HELP YOU CLEAN UP?
SURE.
WHEN THOSE COPS SHOWED UP, THEY WERE TALKING ABOUT YOU.
SPECIFICALLY, SOME-THING YOU HAVE THAT THE WHOLE CRIMINAL UNDER-WORLD WANTS.
THE KEY.
YEAH, THAT'S WHAT IT WAS.
THIS IS ALL MY FAULT.
DON'T BEAT YOURSELF UP.
IF YOU'RE KEEPING IT FROM THEM YOU MUST BE DOING THE RIGHT THING.
PINTO BEA
I DON'T KNOW. LOOK AT ALL THE TROUBLE I'VE CAUSED YOU.
I SHOULD PROBABLY JUST MAKE MYSELF SCARCE...
LET ME KNOW IF ANY MORE TROUBLE COMES UP.
I'LL GET HERE AS SOON AS I CAN.

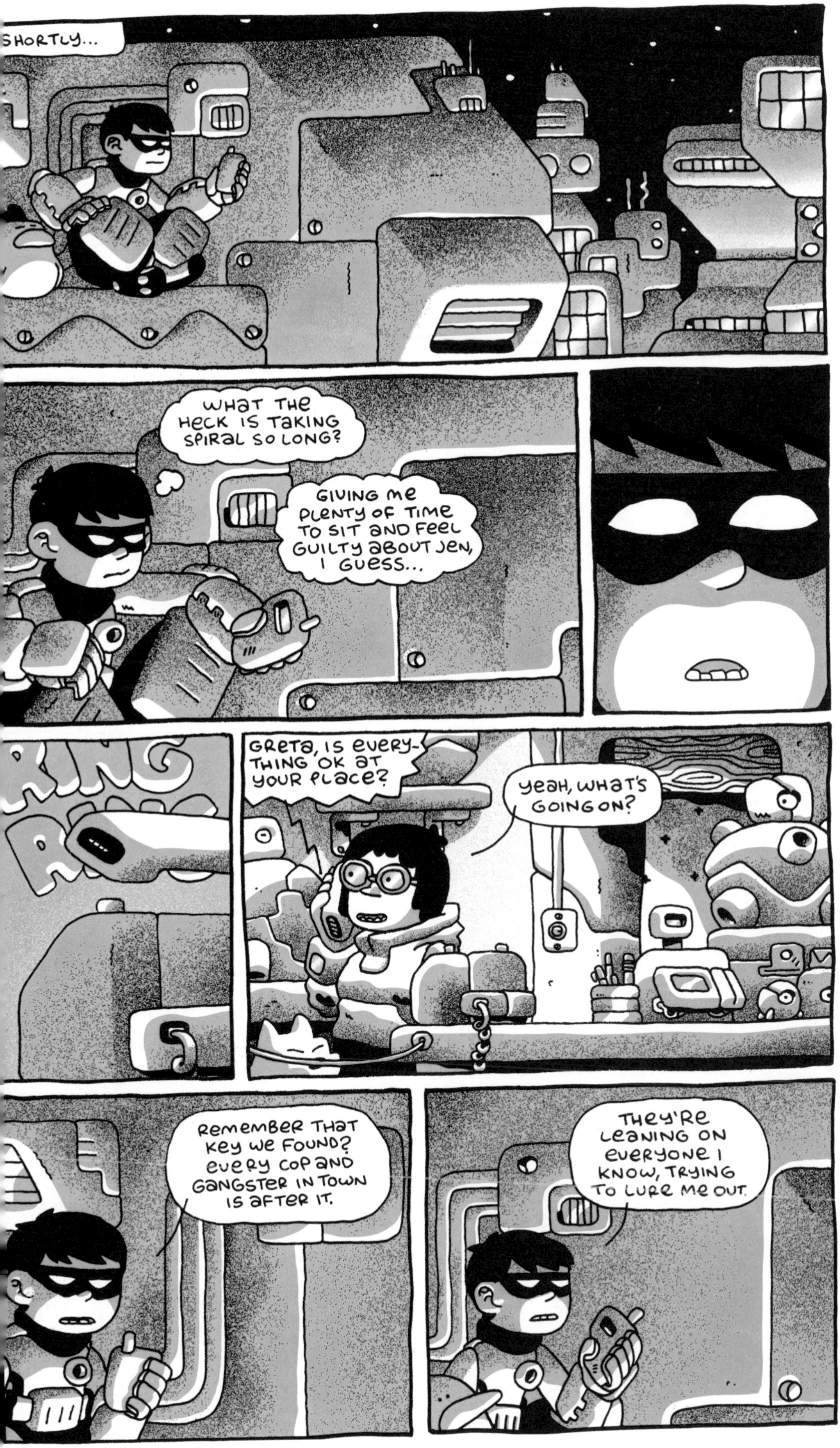

SHORTLY...
WHAT THE HECK IS TAKING SPIRAL SO LONG?
GIVING ME PLENTY OF TIME TO SIT AND FEEL GUILTY ABOUT JEN, I GUESS...
GRETA, IS EVERY-THING OK AT YOUR PLACE?
YEAH, WHAT'S GOING ON?
REMEMBER THAT KEY WE FOUND? EVERY COP AND GANGSTER IN TOWN IS AFTER IT.
THEY'RE LEANING ON EVERYONE I KNOW, TRYING TO LURE ME OUT.

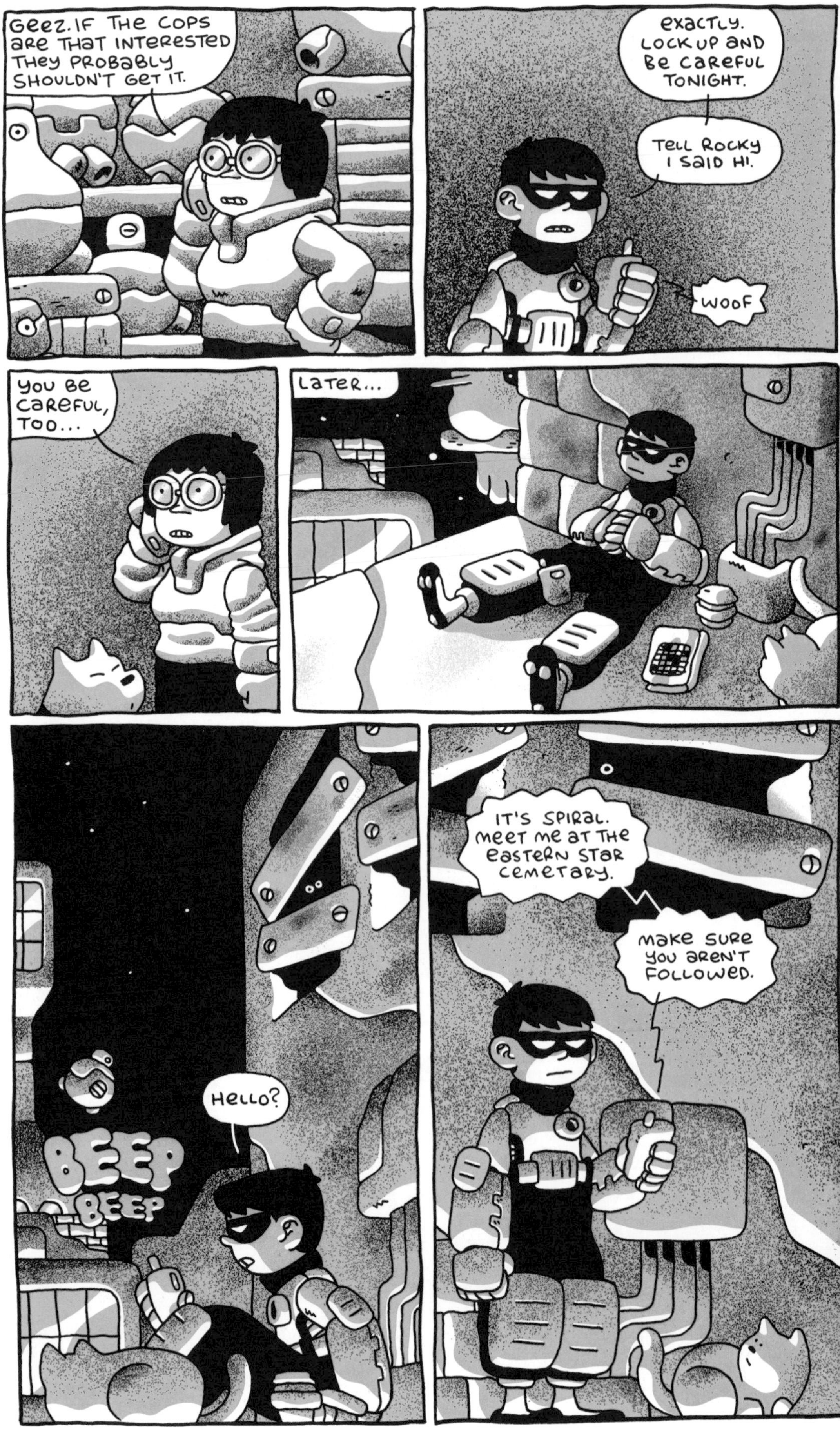
GEEZ. IF THE COPS ARE THAT INTERESTED THEY PROBABLY SHOULDN'T GET IT.
EXACTLY. LOCK UP AND BE CAREFUL TONIGHT.
TELL ROCKY I SAID HI.
WOOF
YOU BE CAREFUL, TOO...
LATER...
BEEP
BEEP
HELLO?
IT'S SPIRAL. MEET ME AT THE EASTERN STAR CEMETARY.
MAKE SURE YOU AREN'T FOLLOWED.

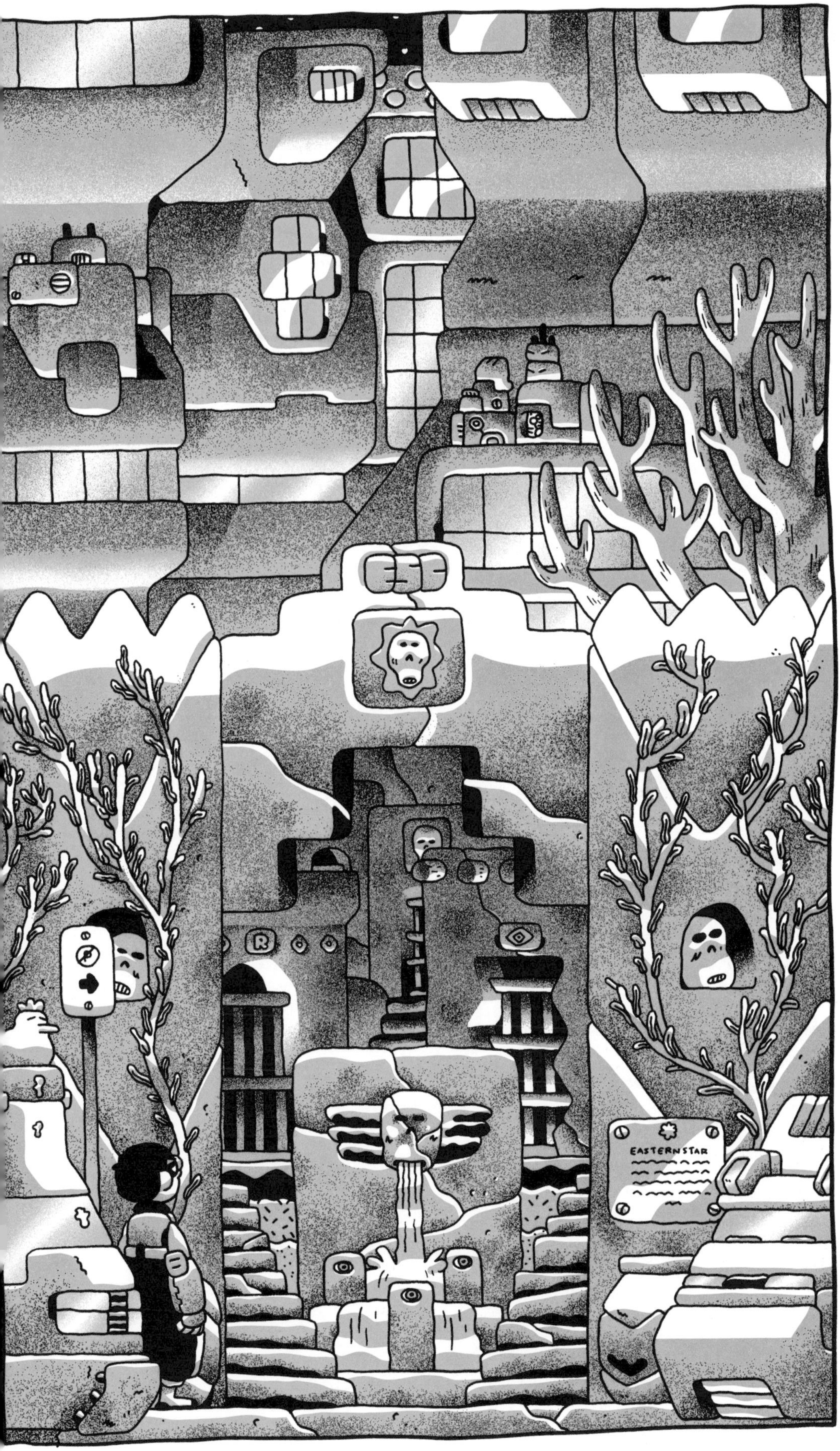
EASTERNSTAR

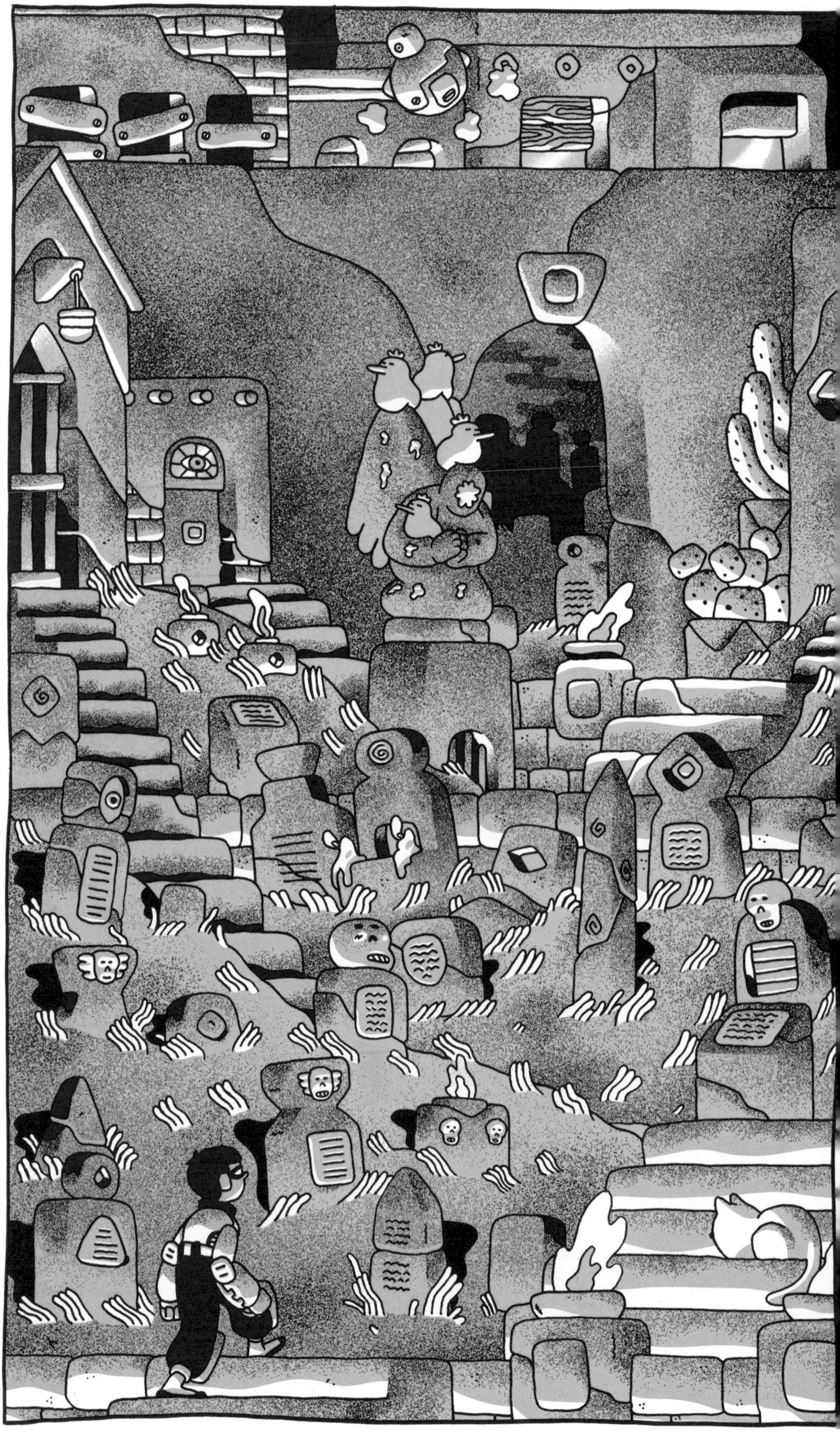

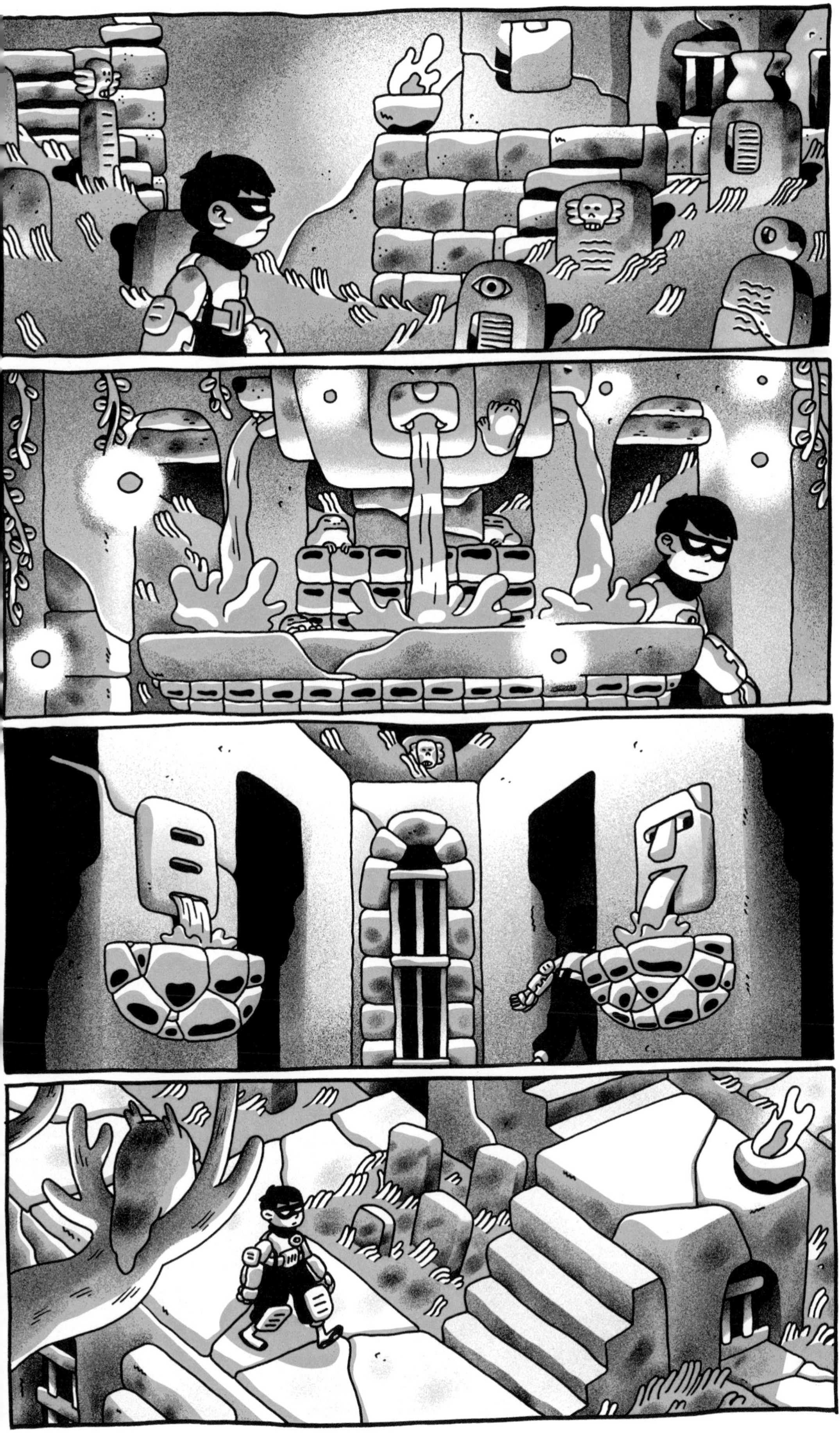

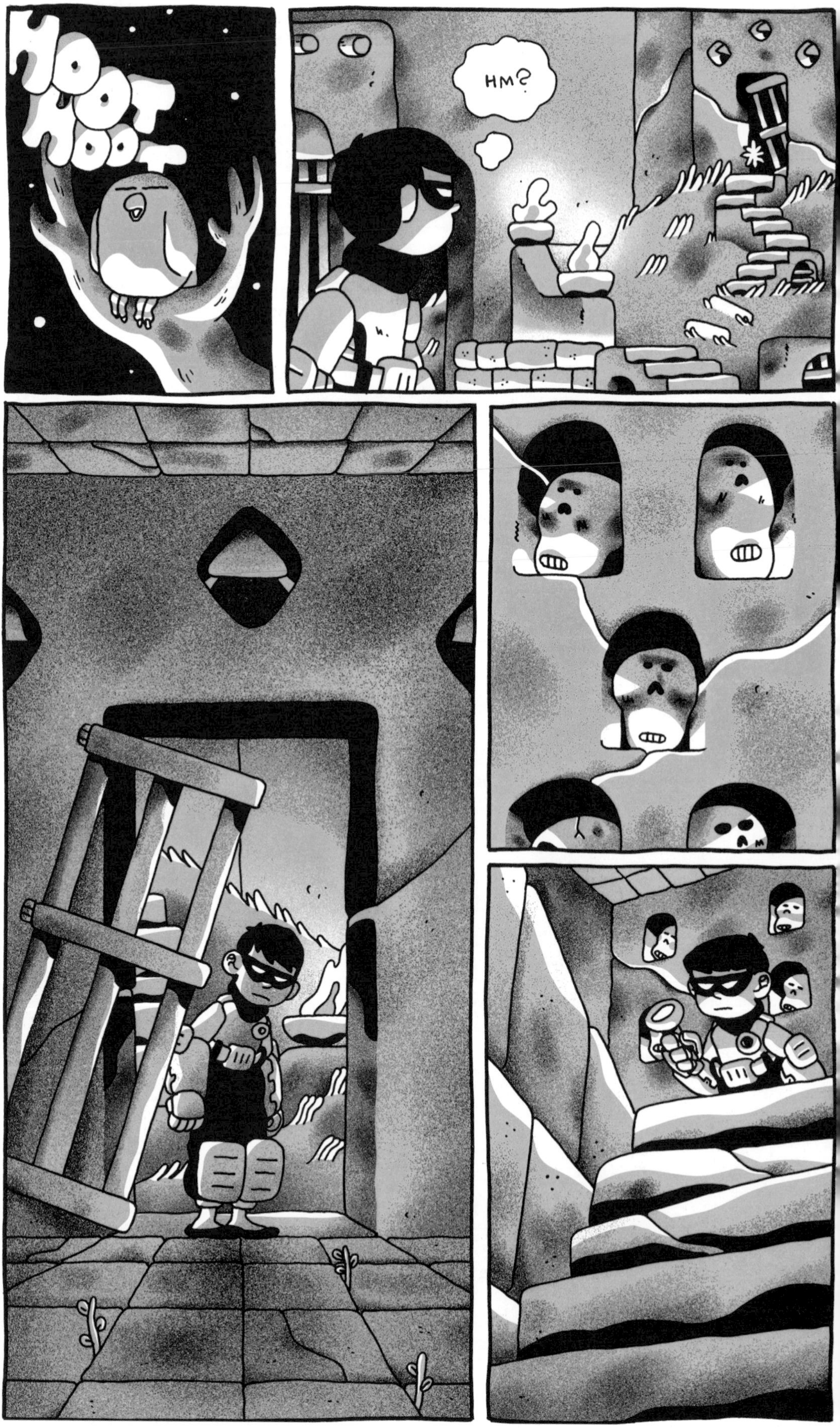
HOOT HOOT HOOT
HM?

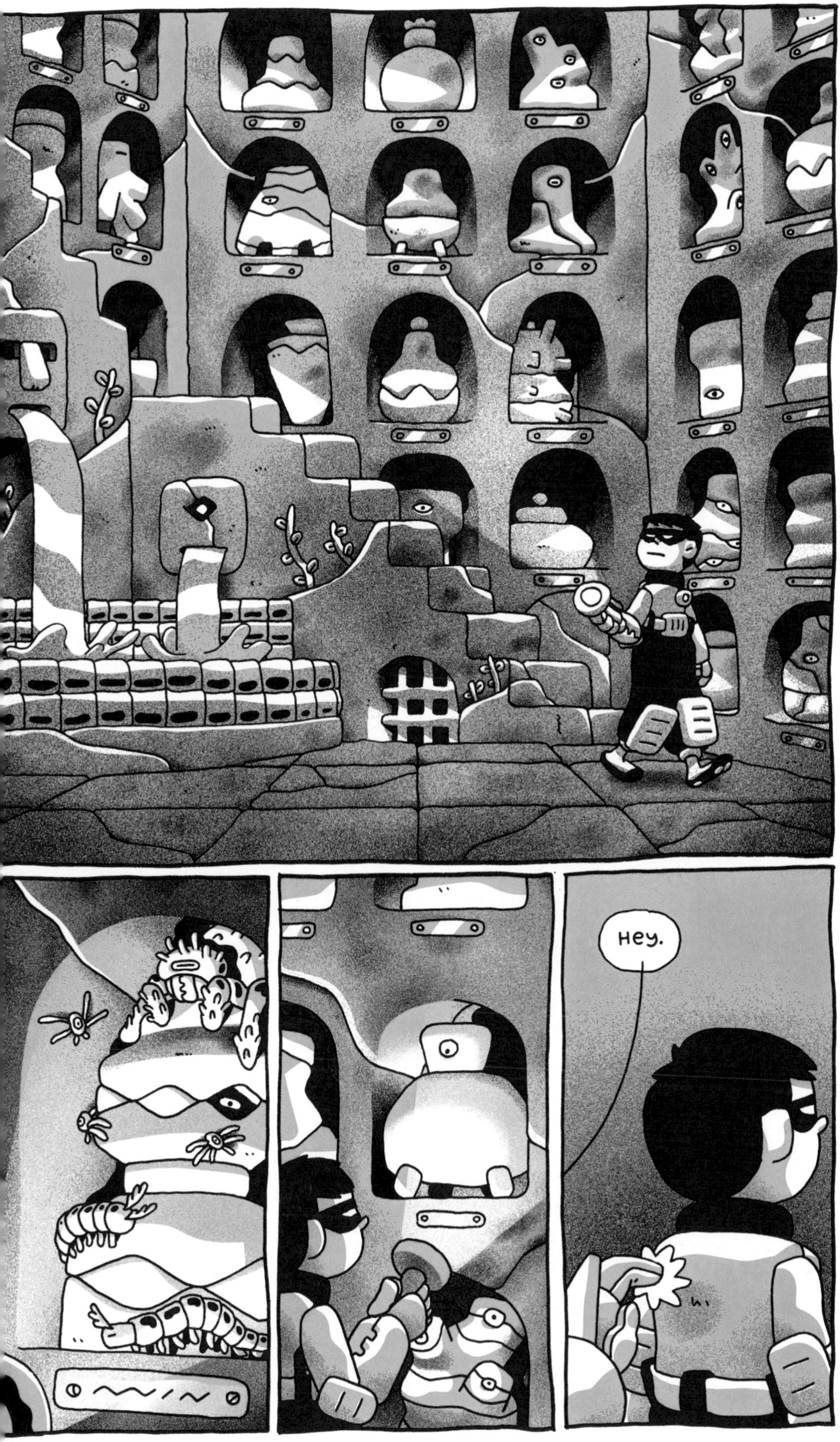
Hey.

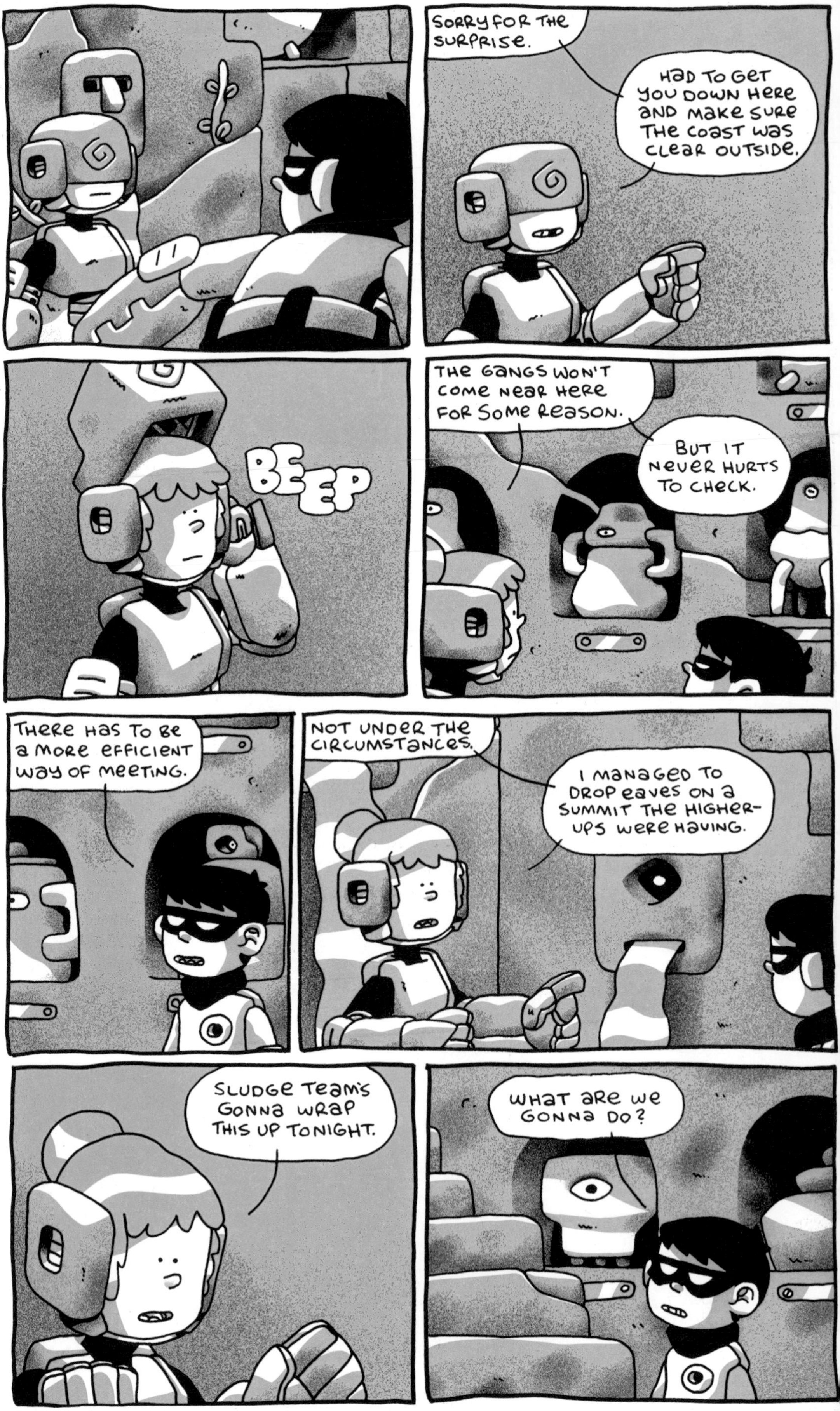
SORRY FOR THE SURPRISE.
HAD TO GET YOU DOWN HERE AND MAKE SURE THE COAST WAS CLEAR OUTSIDE.
BEEP
THE GANGS WON'T COME NEAR HERE FOR SOME REASON.
BUT IT NEVER HURTS TO CHECK.
THERE HAS TO BE A MORE EFFICIENT WAY OF MEETING.
NOT UNDER THE CIRCUMSTANCES.
I MANAGED TO DROP EAVES ON A SUMMIT THE HIGHER-UPS WERE HAVING.
SLUDGE TEAM'S GONNA WRAP THIS UP TONIGHT.
WHAT ARE WE GONNA DO?

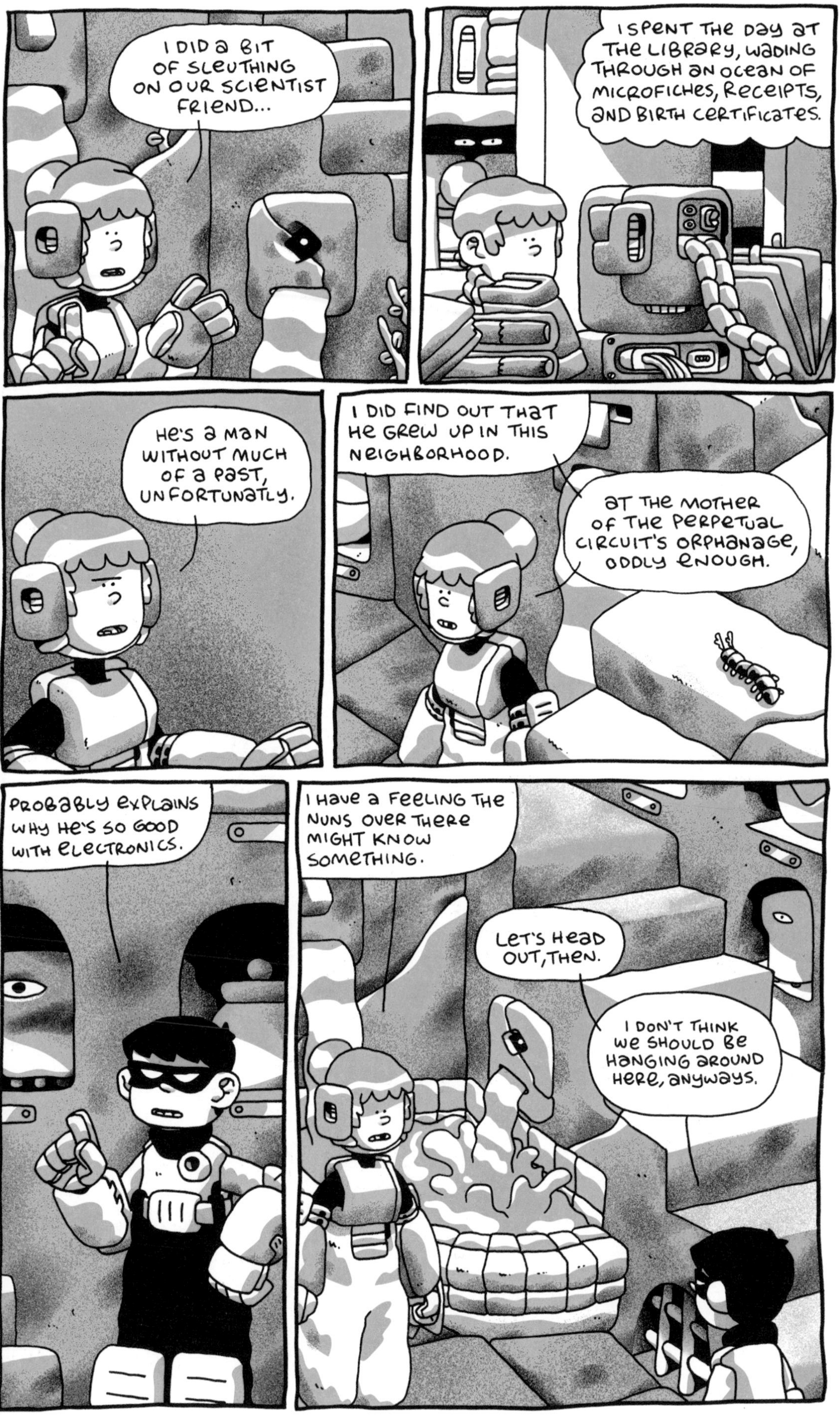
I DID A BIT OF SLEUTHING ON OUR SCIENTIST FRIEND...
I SPENT THE DAY AT THE LIBRARY, WADING THROUGH AN OCEAN OF MICROFICHES, RECEIPTS, AND BIRTH CERTIFICATES.
HE'S A MAN WITHOUT MUCH OF A PAST, UNFORTUNATLY.
I DID FIND OUT THAT HE GREW UP IN THIS NEIGHBORHOOD.
AT THE MOTHER OF THE PERPETUAL CIRCUIT'S ORPHANAGE, ODDLY ENOUGH.
PROBABLY EXPLAINS WHY HE'S SO GOOD WITH ELECTRONICS.
I HAVE A FEELING THE NUNS OVER THERE MIGHT KNOW SOMETHING.
LET'S HEAD OUT, THEN.
I DON'T THINK WE SHOULD BE HANGING AROUND HERE, ANYWAYS.

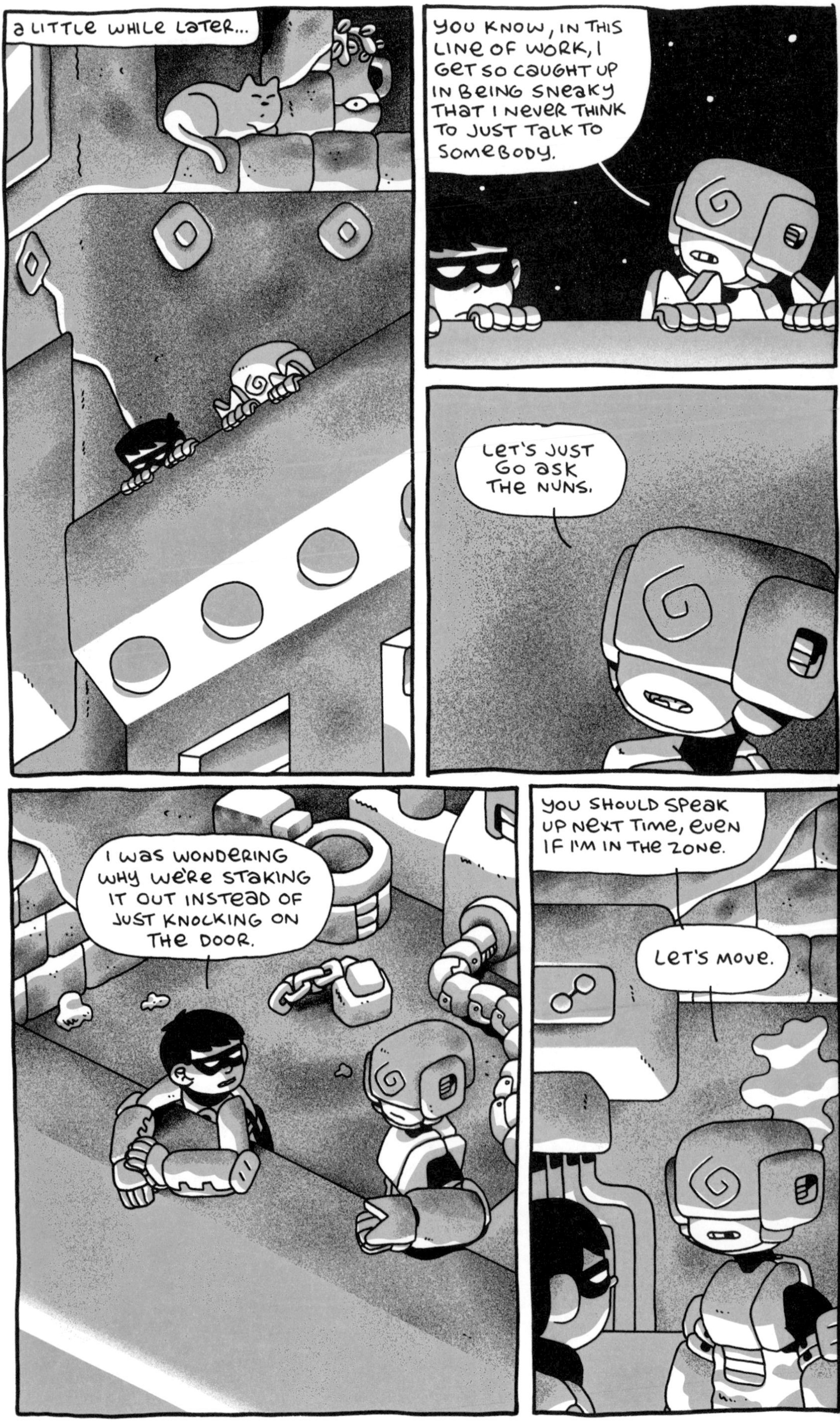
A LITTLE WHILE LATER...
YOU KNOW, IN THIS LINE OF WORK, I GET SO CAUGHT UP IN BEING SNEAKY THAT I NEVER THINK TO JUST TALK TO SOMEBODY.
LET'S JUST GO ASK THE NUNS.
I WAS WONDERING WHY WE'RE STAKING IT OUT INSTEAD OF JUST KNOCKING ON THE DOOR.
YOU SHOULD SPEAK UP NEXT TIME, EVEN IF I'M IN THE ZONE.
LET'S MOVE.

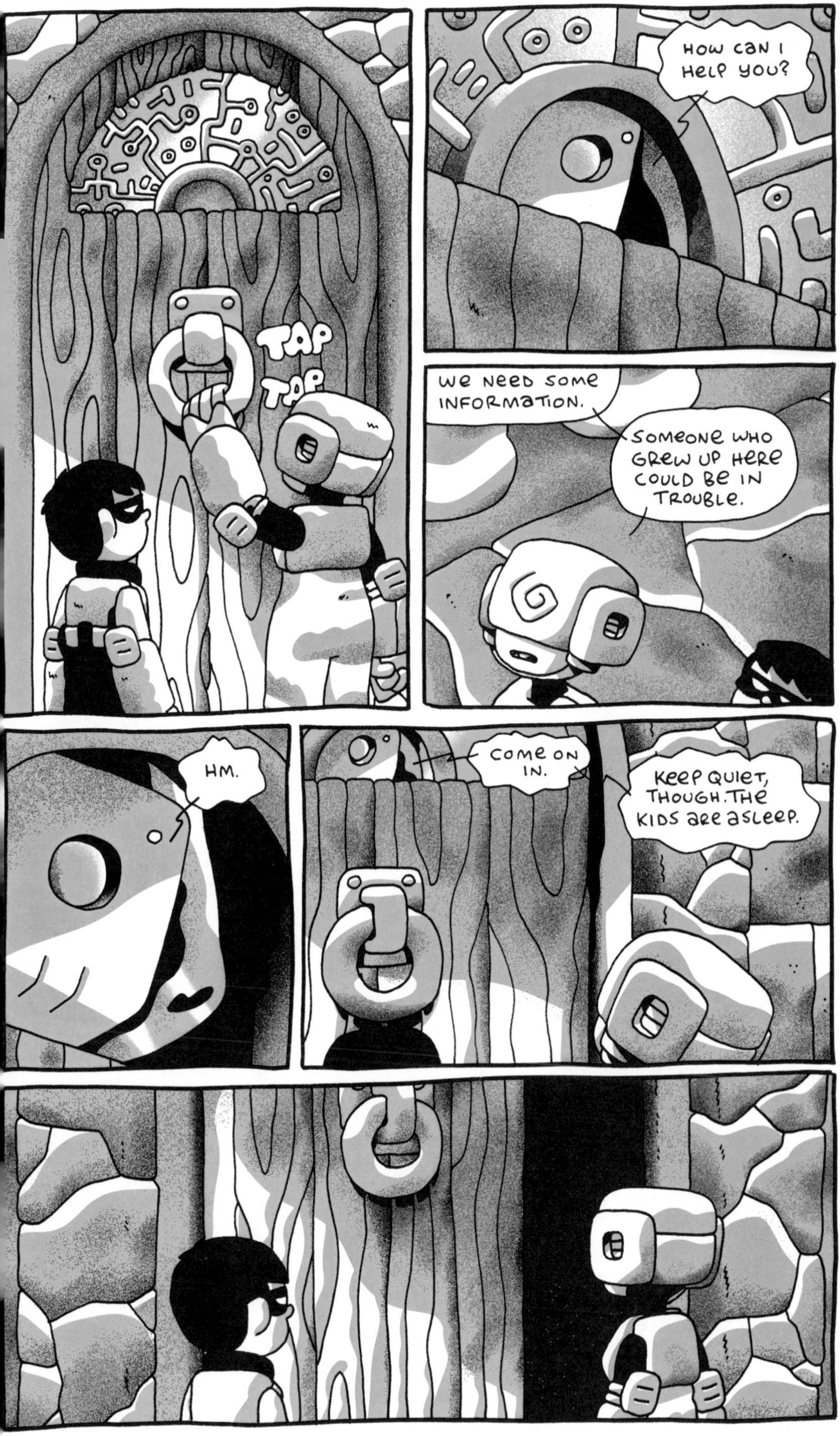
TAP
TAP
HOW CAN I HELP YOU?
WE NEED SOME INFORMATION.
SOMEONE WHO GREW UP HERE COULD BE IN TROUBLE.
HM.
COME ON IN.
KEEP QUIET, THOUGH. THE KIDS ARE ASLEEP.

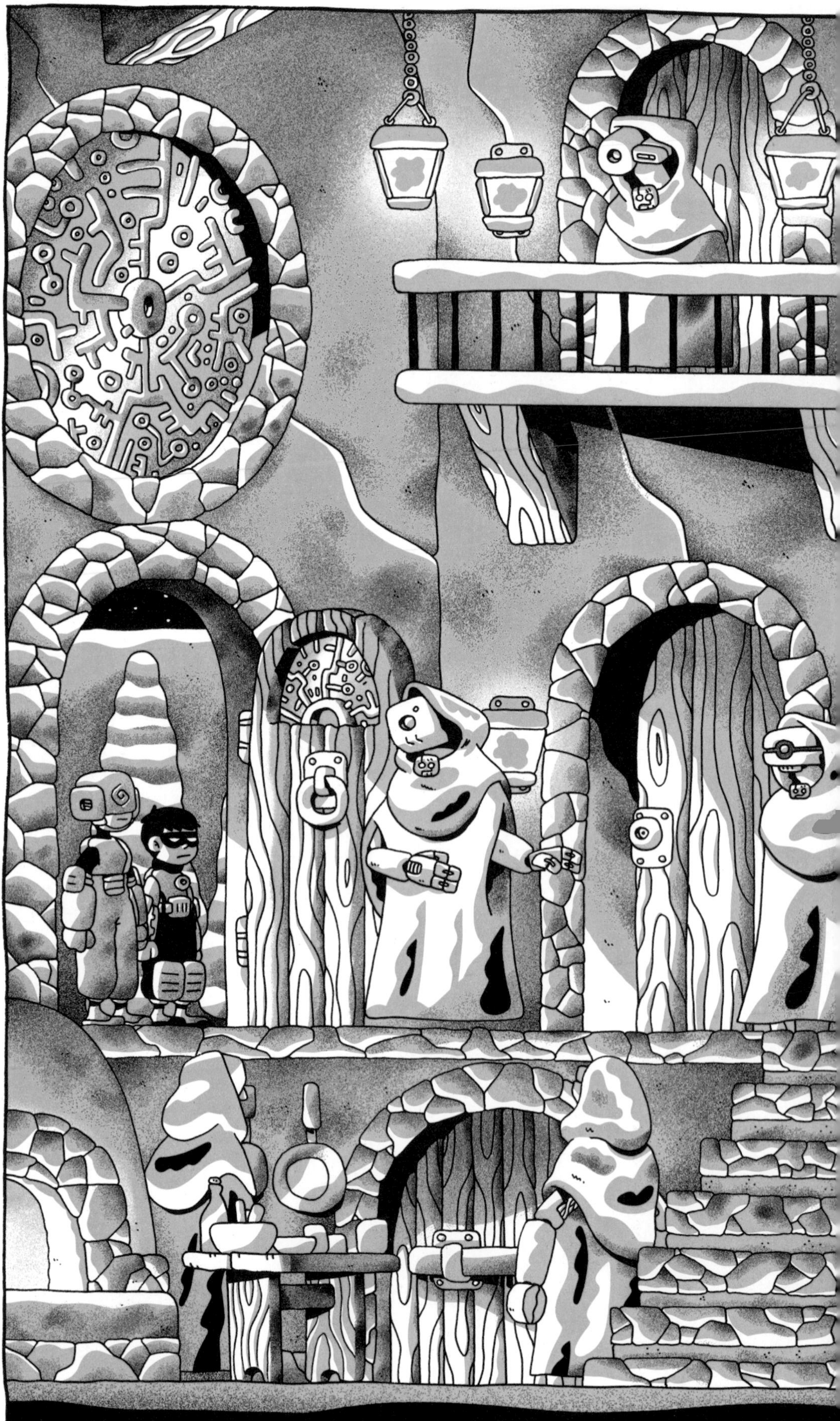

This way, please.

It's Ricky, isn't it.

Afraid so. He's being forced to design weapons for the cops and gangs.

He's managed to jam up their enterprise, so that's why we stopped by.

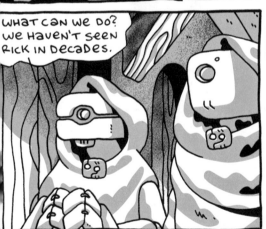

What can we do? We haven't seen Rick in decades.

It's OK, Sister Bernice. I think I've heard about these two.

Anyone who takes a swing at a B.C.P.D. officer is OK in my book.

Oh, well in that case, make yourselves comfortable.

WE'RE HOLDING SOME DOCUMENTS FOR RICKY.

HE WOULDN'T TELL US WHAT THEY WERE.

ONLY THAT WE SHOULD KEEP THEM ON LOCKDOWN.

I'D WAGER IT'S THE WEAPON DESIGNS THE SLUDGE TEAM WAS FORCING HIM TO WORK ON.

I KNOW HE TOLD YOU TO KEEP THEM SAFE...

BUT TORCHING THEM MIGHT BE THE SAFEST BET.

I DON'T KNOW WHAT YOUR SECURITY IS LIKE HERE...

BUT I THINK THE SLUDGE TEAM AND THE COPS ARE GONNA MAKE A FINAL PUSH TO GET THOSE DOCUMENTS TONIGHT.

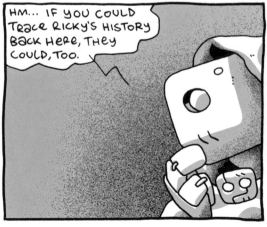

HM... IF YOU COULD TRACE RICKY'S HISTORY BACK HERE, THEY COULD, TOO.

TIME COULD BE TIGHT.

HMM... WHAT DO YOU THINK, SISTER?

RICKY TRUSTED US.

BUT I aLSO KNOW HE WOULDN'T WANT THE COPS TO HaVE EVEN MORE GUNS.

HE MUST'VE THOUGHT THEY'D NEVER TRACE IT BACK HERE...

I aGREE.

LET'S TAKE a TRIP DOWNSTAIRS, SHALL WE?

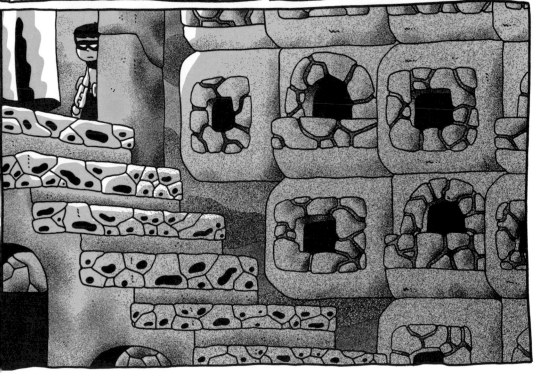

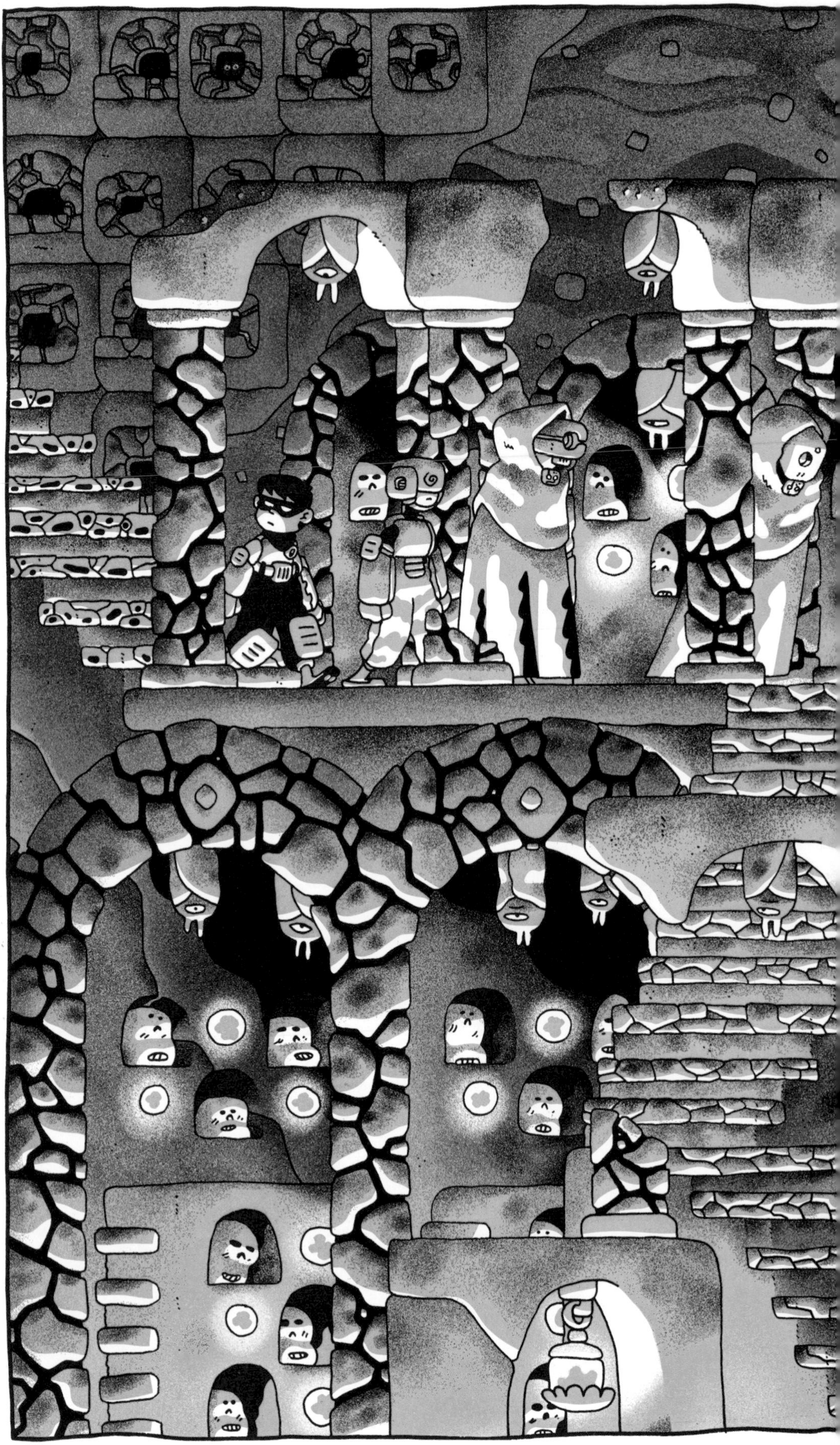

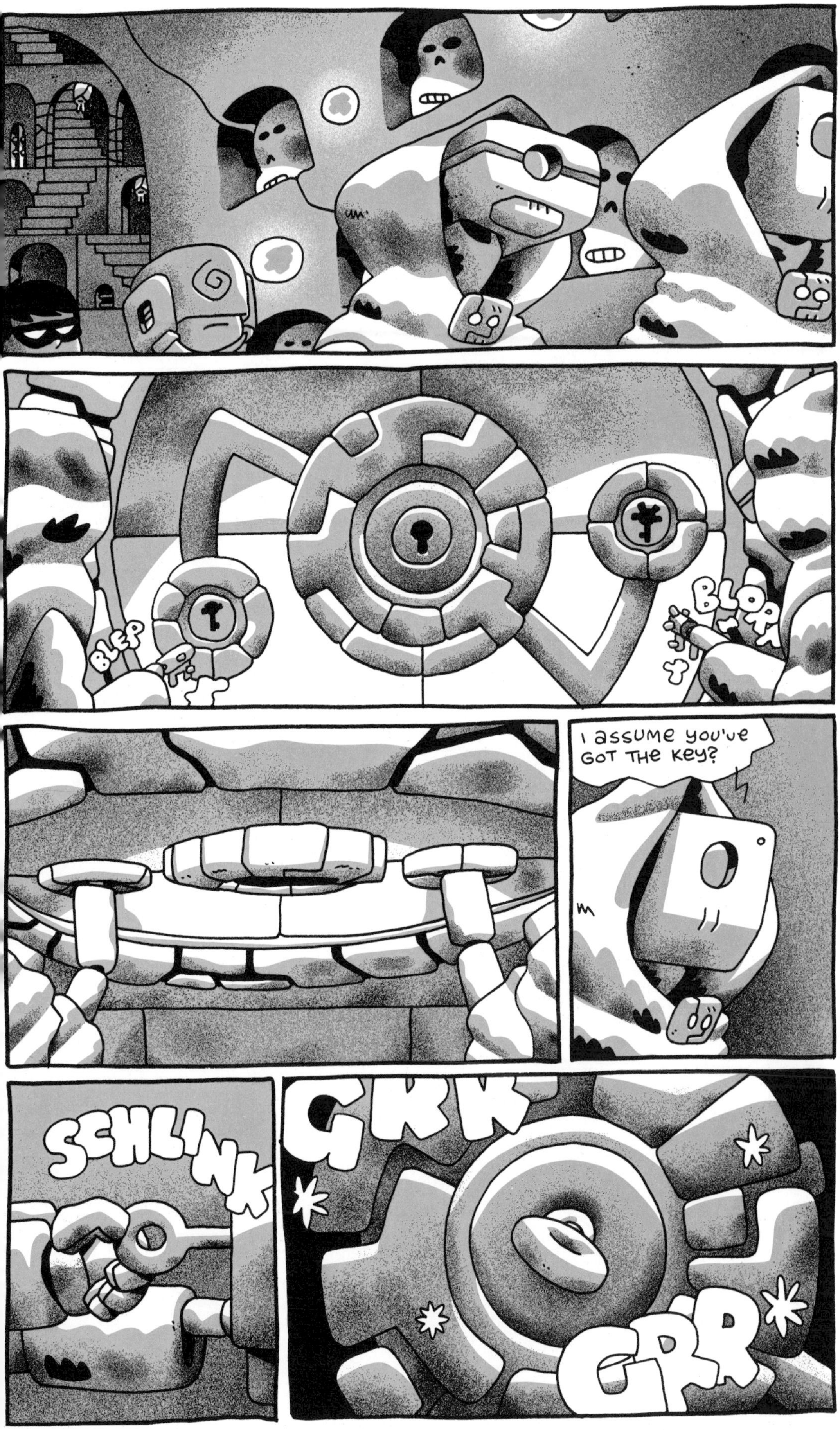
BLEP
BLORP
I ASSUME YOU'VE GOT THE KEY?
SCHLINK
GRK
GRR

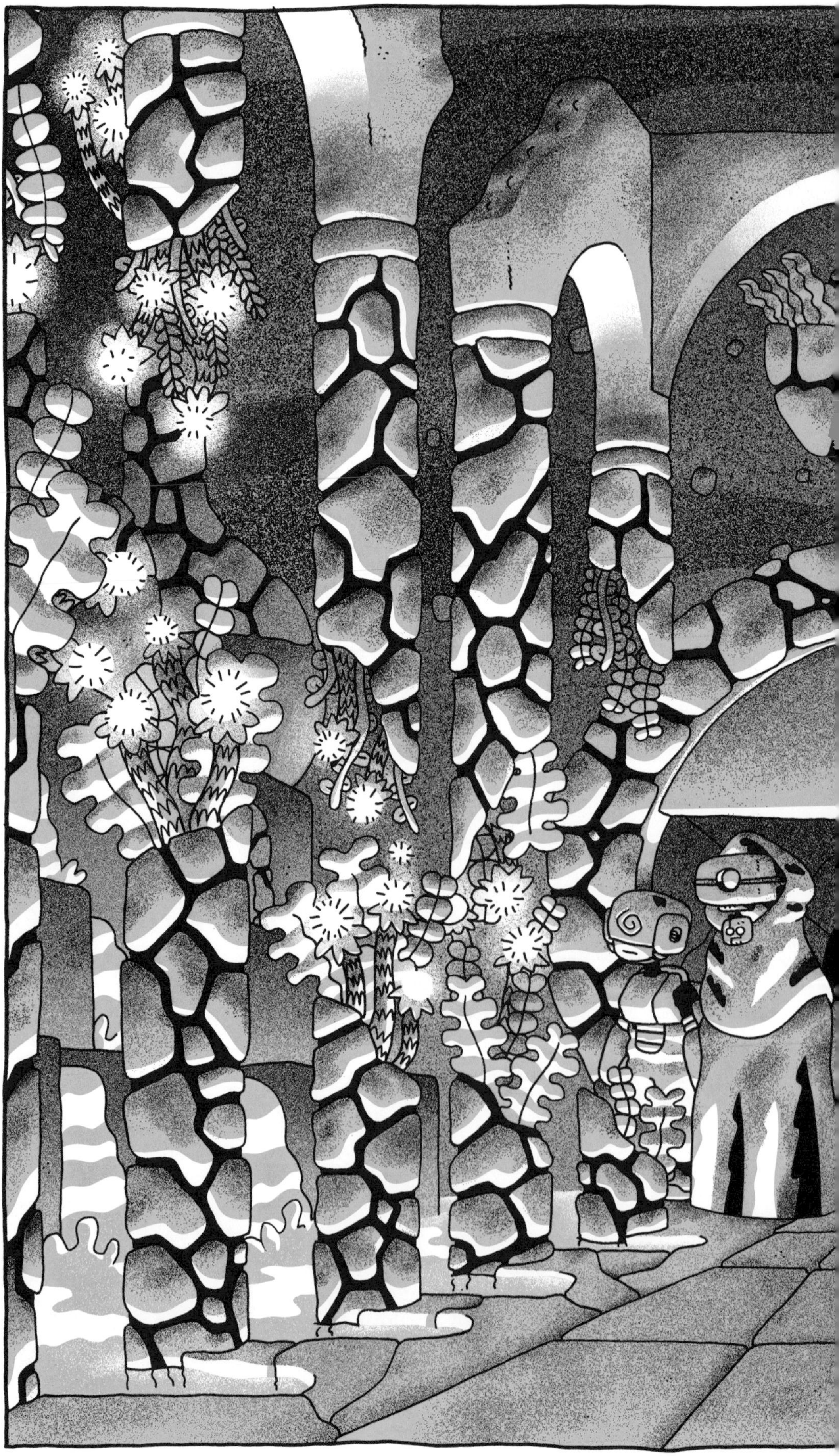

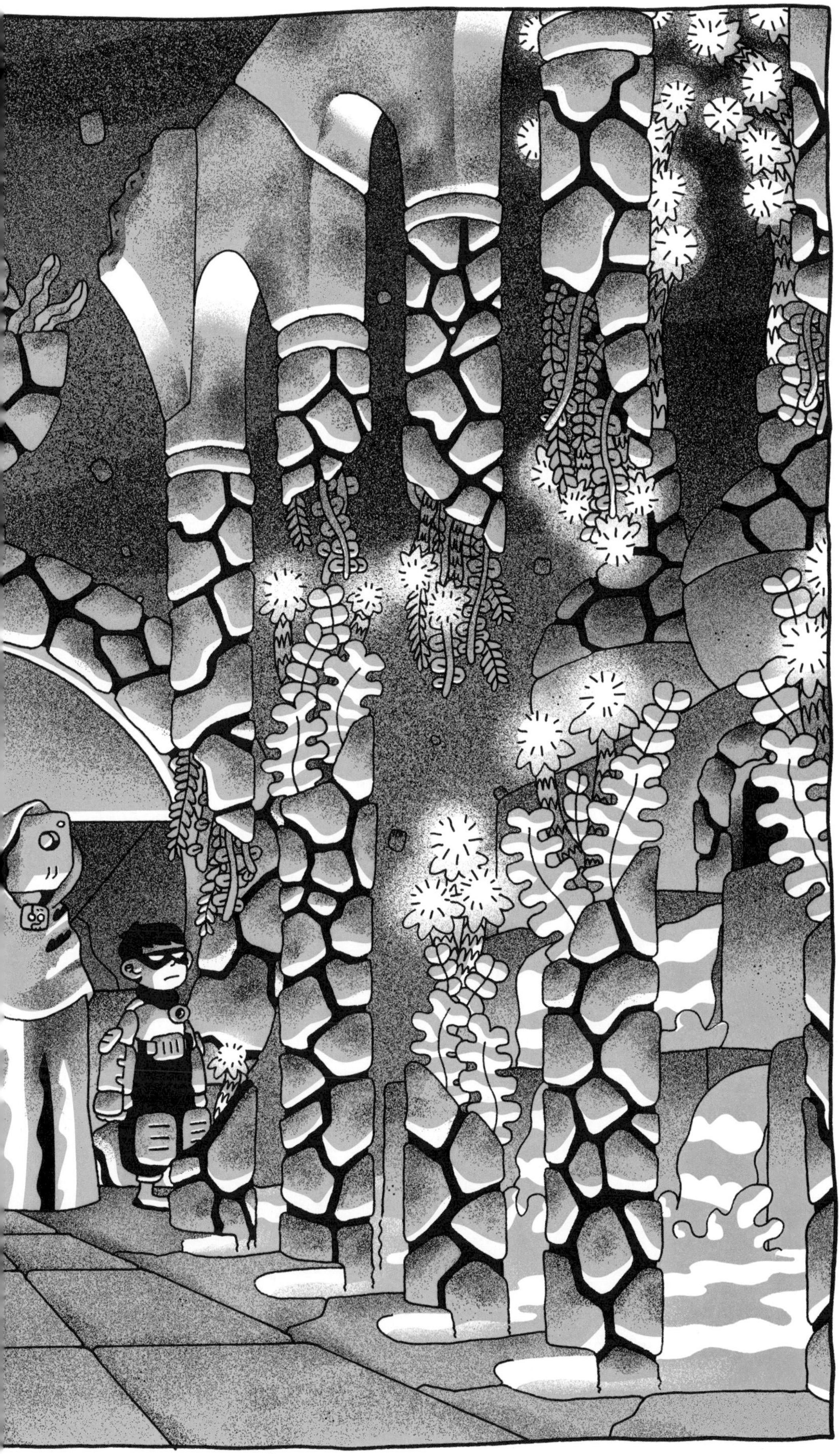

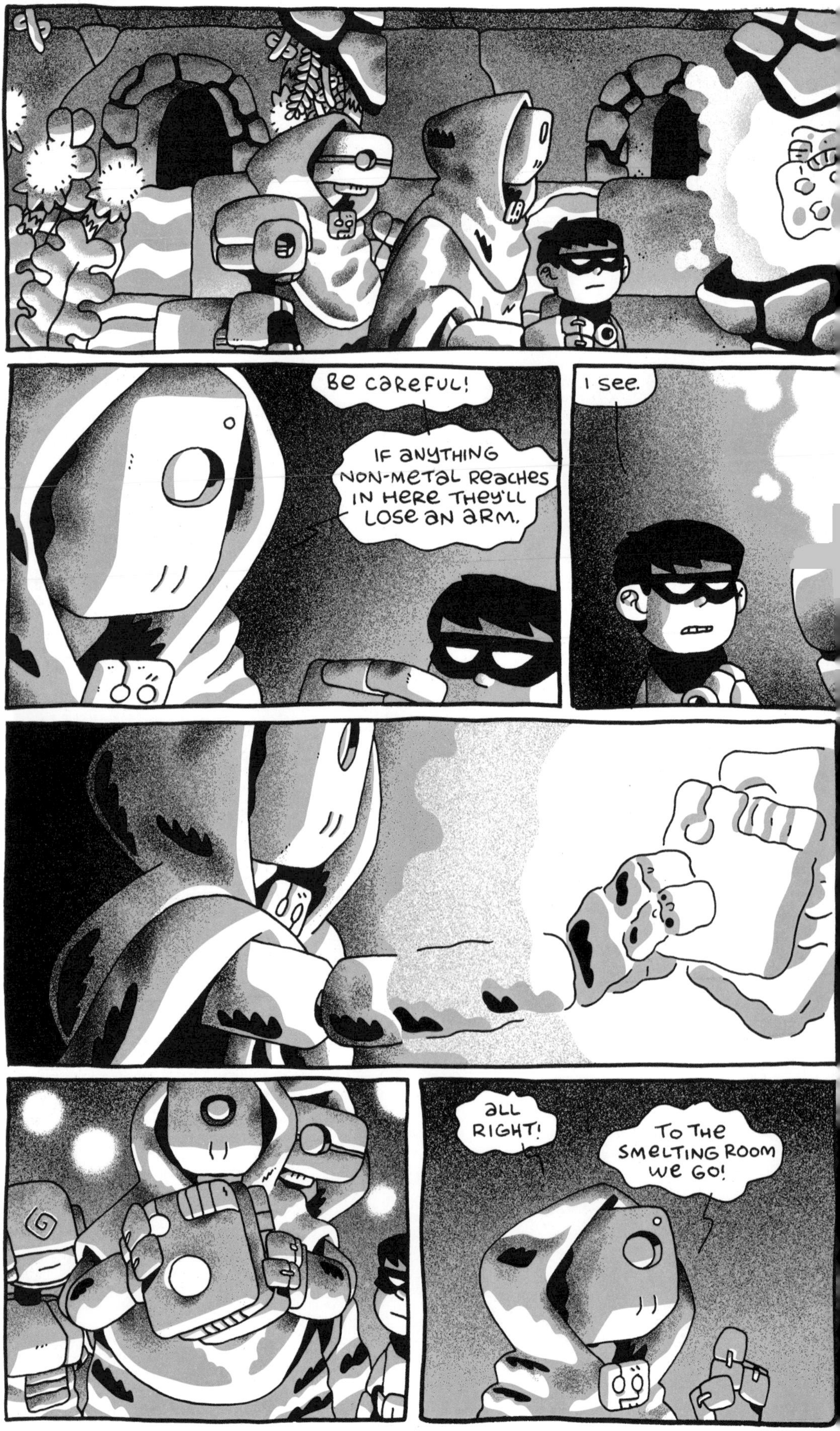

Be careful!
If anything non-metal reaches in here they'll lose an arm.
I see.
All right!
To the smelting room we go!

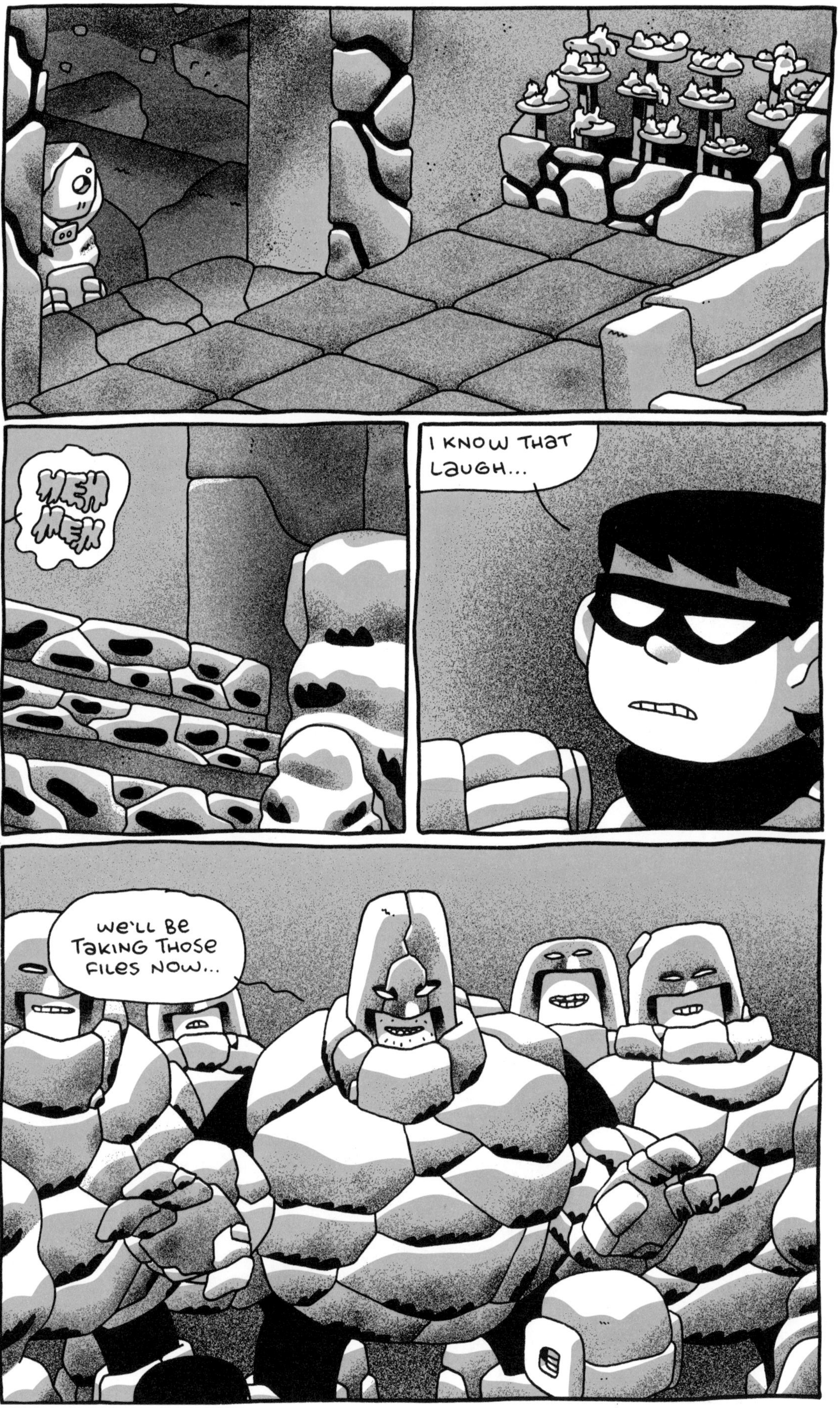

HEH HEH
I KNOW THAT LAUGH...
WE'LL BE TAKING THOSE FILES NOW...

WE FINALLY BEAT THE LOCATION OUT OF OUR OLD PAL.

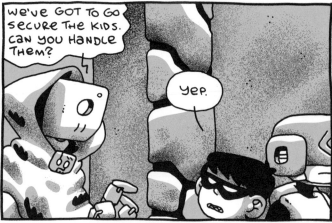

WE'VE GOT TO GO SECURE THE KIDS. CAN YOU HANDLE THEM?

YEP.

I SHOULD THANK YOU FOR GETTING THOSE COPS OUT OF THE WAY.

NOW WE GET TO STOMP YOU AND RECOVER THE GEEZER'S RESEARCH.

SO HAND OVER THE FILES.

FINE. YOU GOT US. WE CAN'T WIN.

HERE YOU GO.

HEY! WHAT ARE YOU DOING?

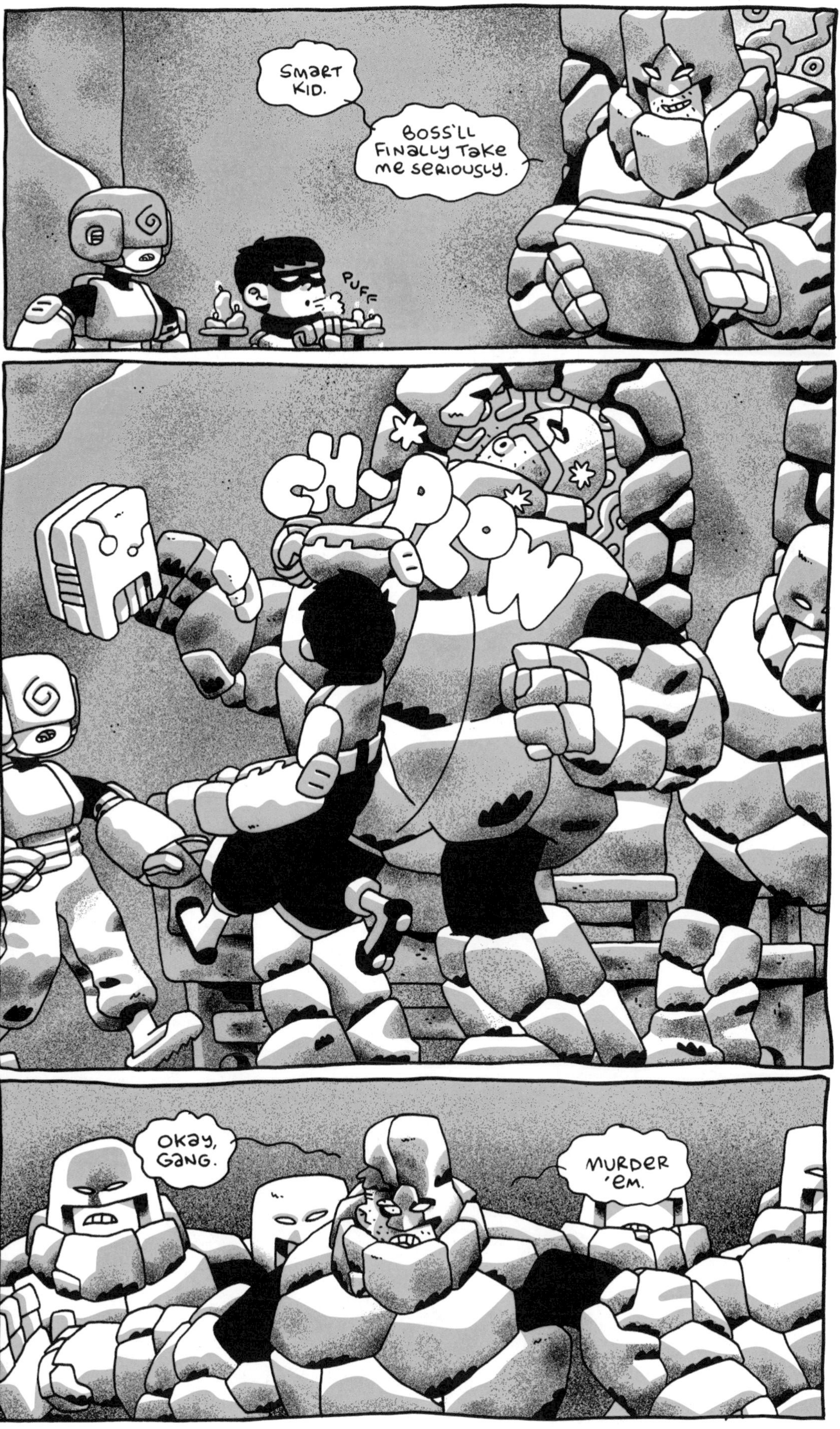
SMART KID.
BOSS'LL FINALLY TAKE ME SERIOUSLY.
PUFF
CH-PLOW
OKAY, GANG.
MURDER 'EM.

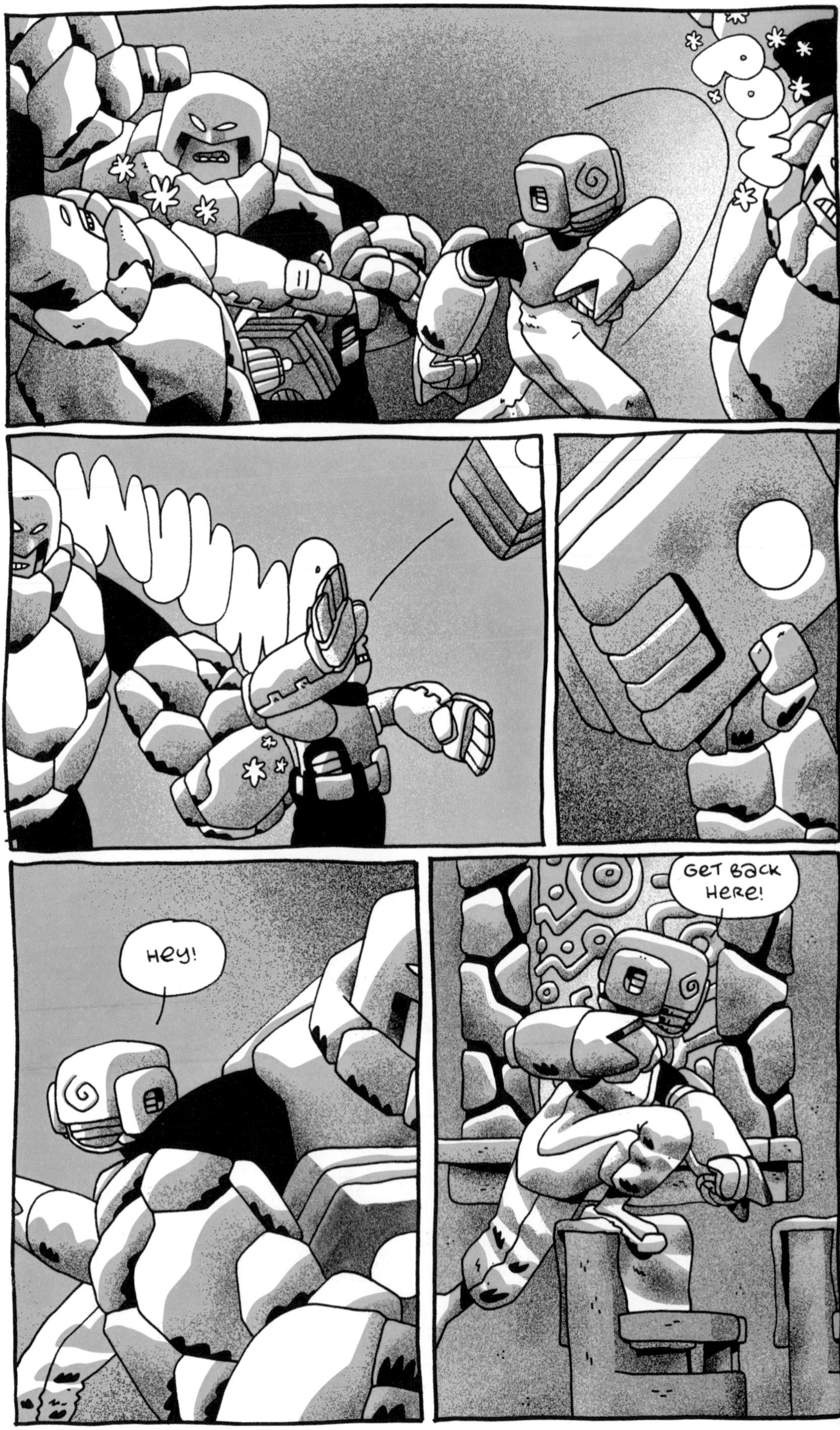
POW
WHUMP
HEY!
GET BACK HERE!

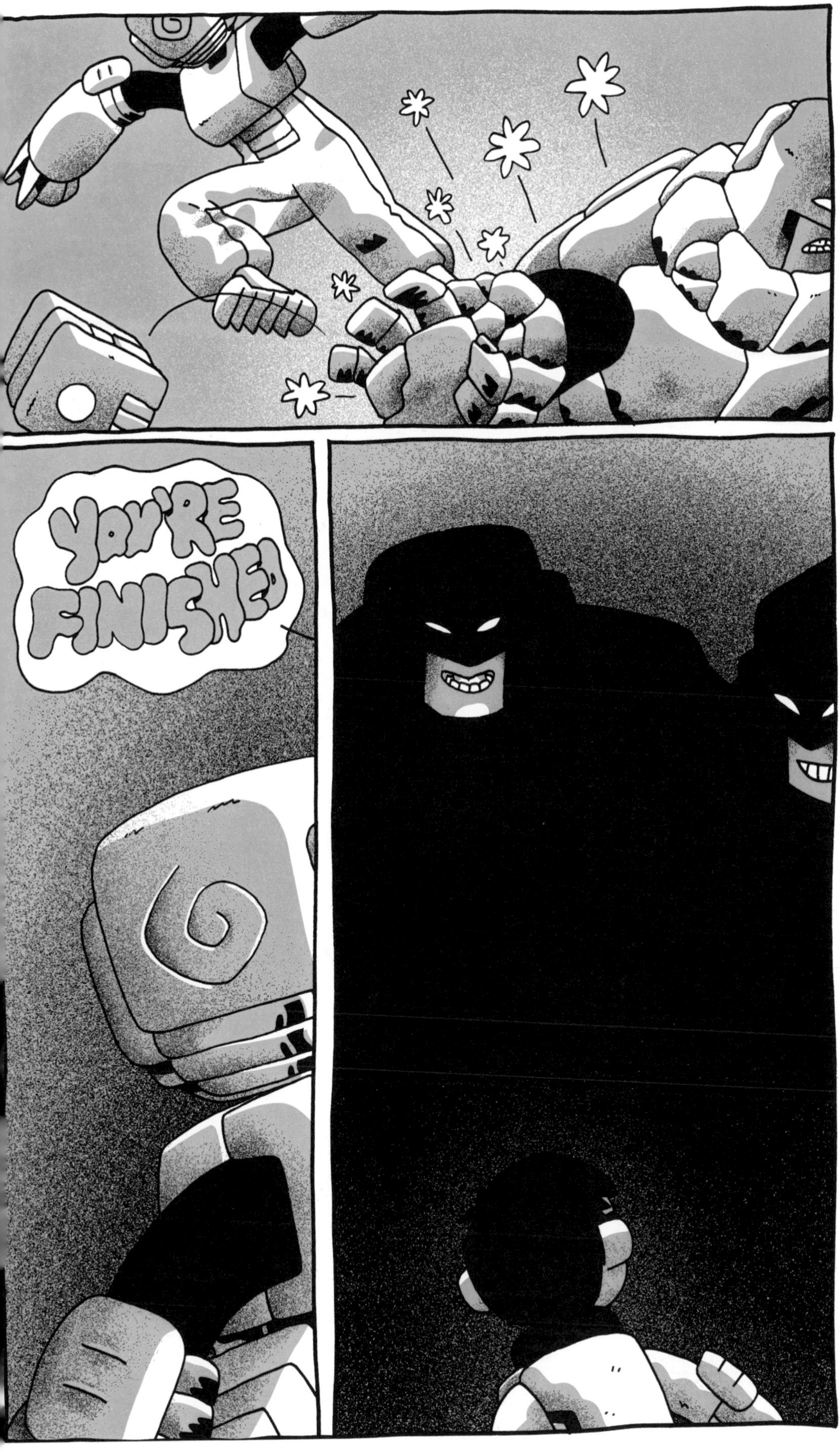
YOU'RE FINISHED

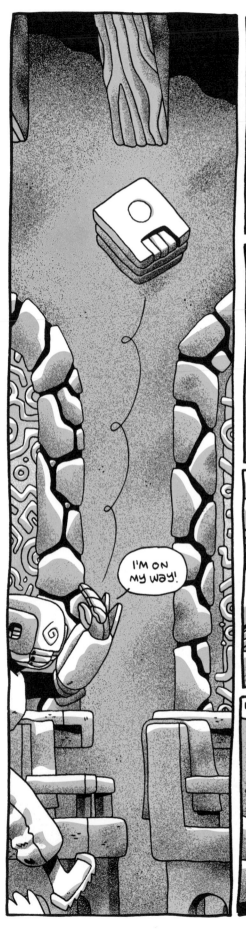

I'M ON MY WAY!

THANKS FOR THE ASSIST.

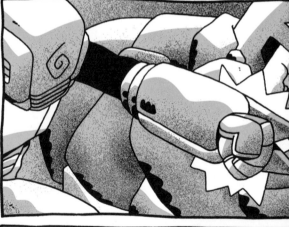

NO PROBLEM.

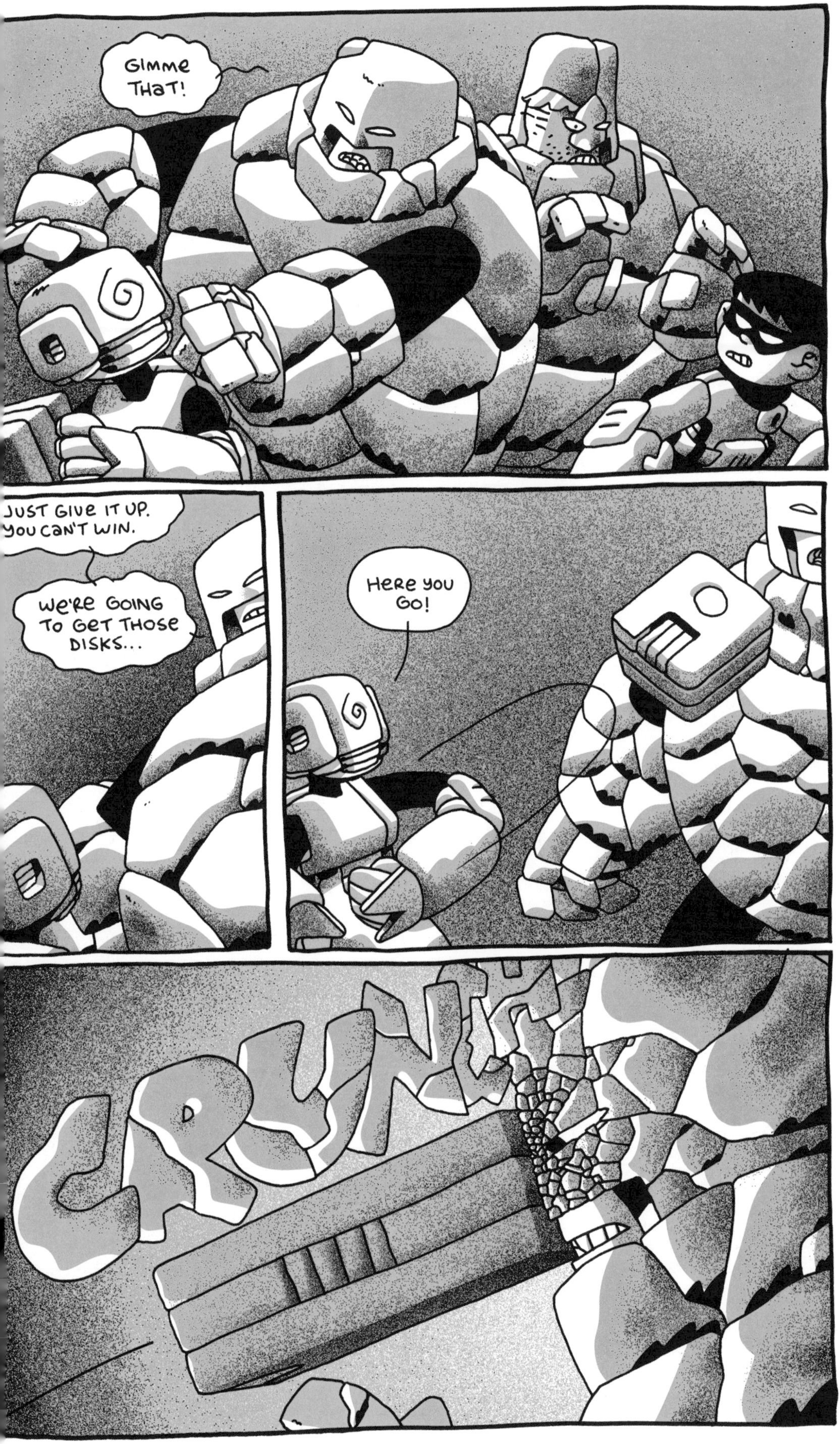
GIMME THAT!
JUST GIVE IT UP. YOU CAN'T WIN.
WE'RE GOING TO GET THOSE DISKS...
HERE YOU GO!
CRUNCH

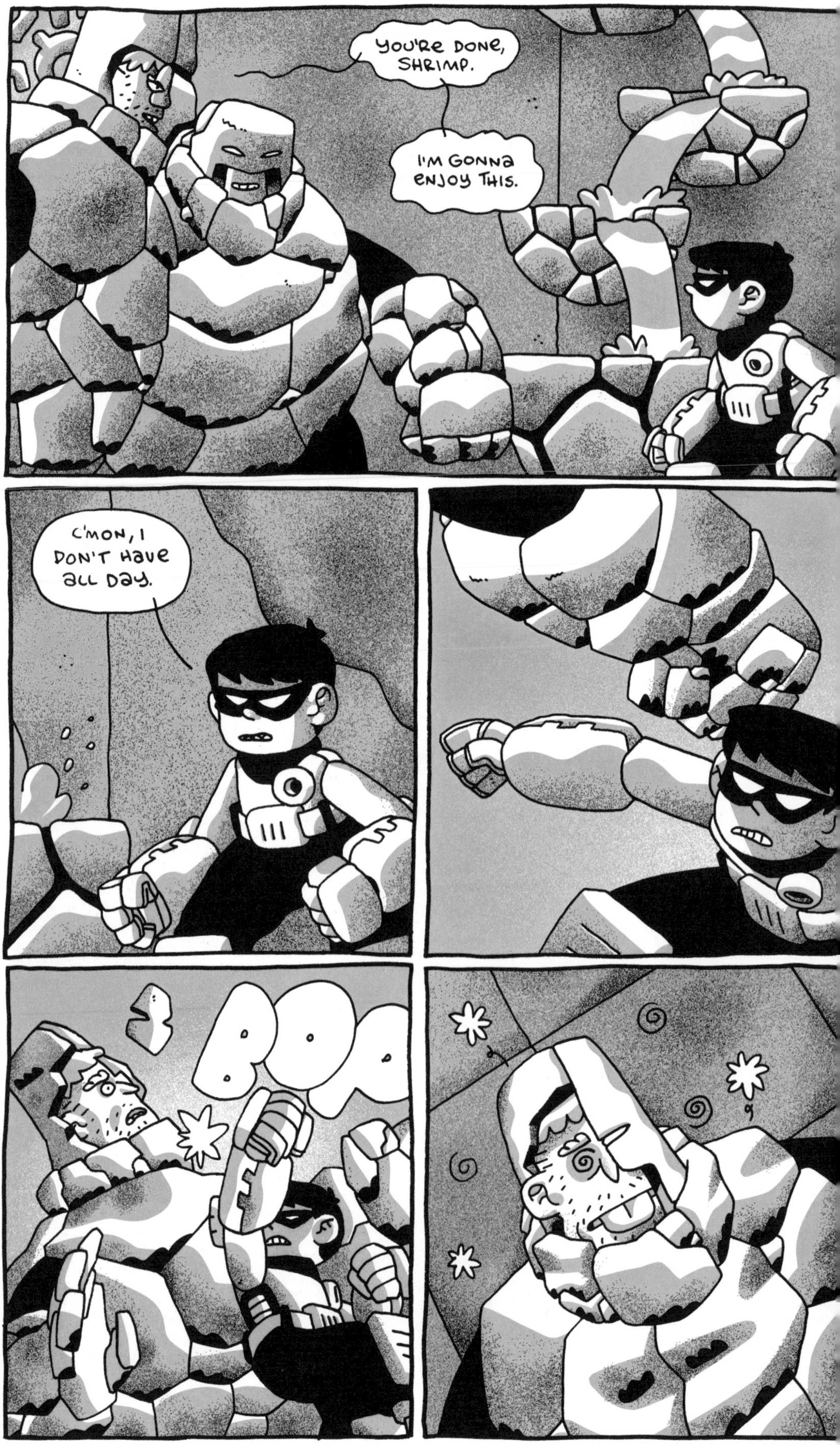

YOU'RE DONE, SHRIMP.
I'M GONNA ENJOY THIS.
C'MON, I DON'T HAVE ALL DAY.
POP

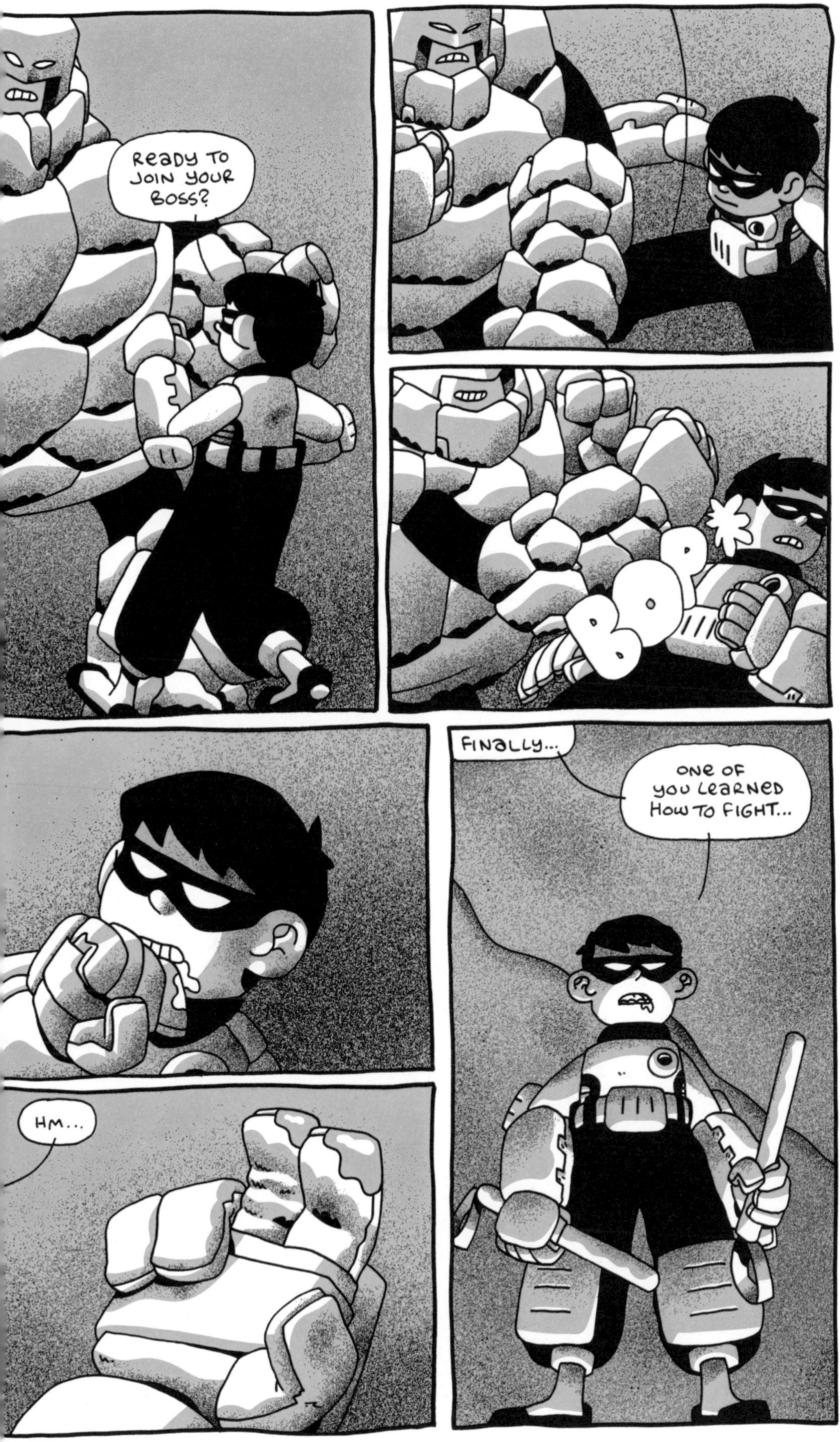
READY TO JOIN YOUR BOSS?
BOP
FINALLY...
ONE OF YOU LEARNED HOW TO FIGHT...
HM...

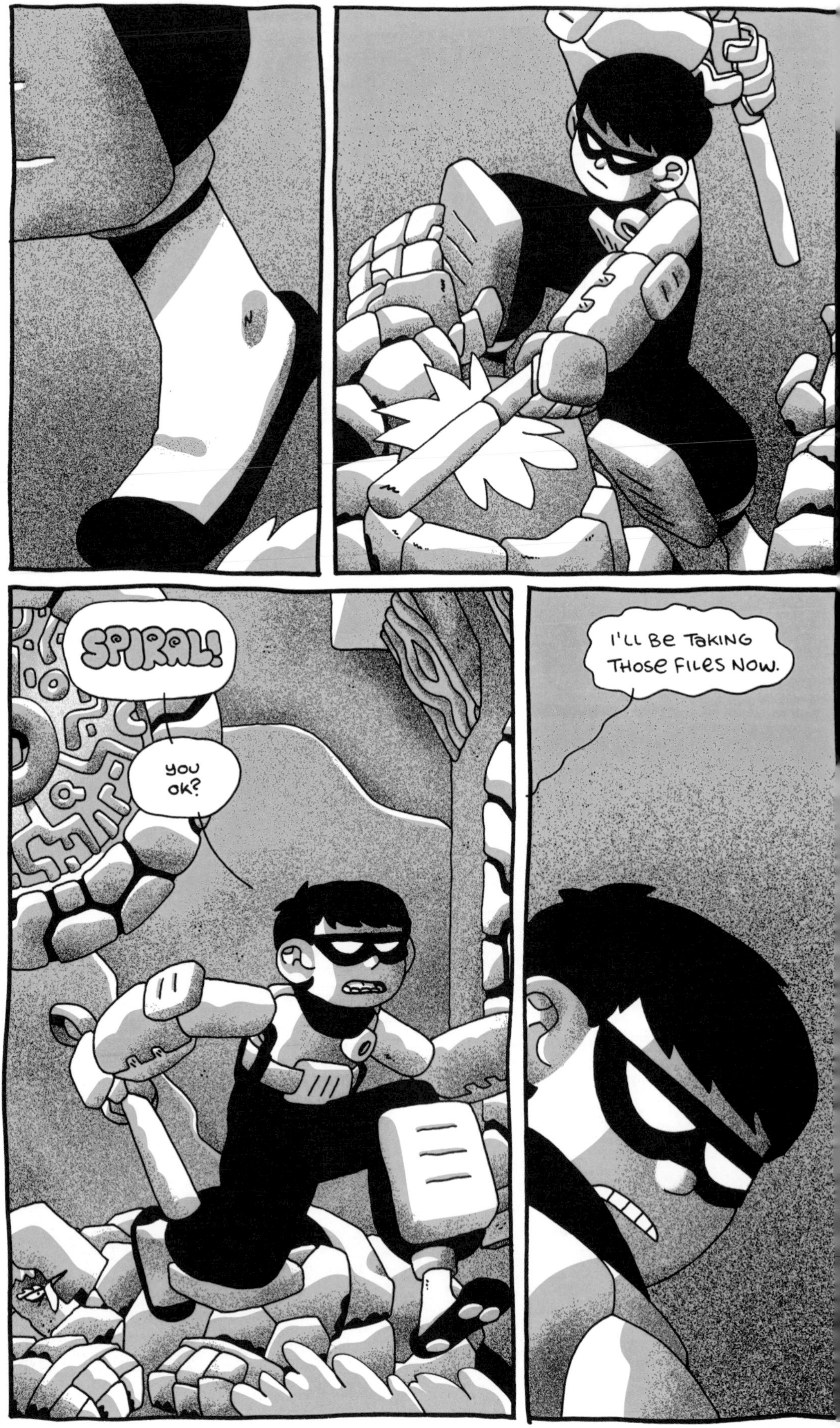
SPIRAL!
YOU OK?
I'LL BE TAKING THOSE FILES NOW.

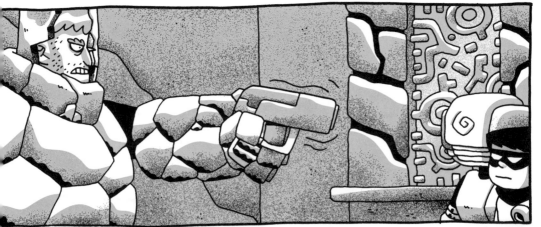

I WANTED TO BEAT YOU AT YOUR OWN GAME...

CLICK

...HUMILIATE YOU LIKE YOU DID TO ME...

BUT I'M JUST GONNA BLOW YOU AWAY AND TAKE THE FILES.

YOUR STOMACH DOESN'T SOUND SO GOOD.

SHUT UP.

GROOGLE

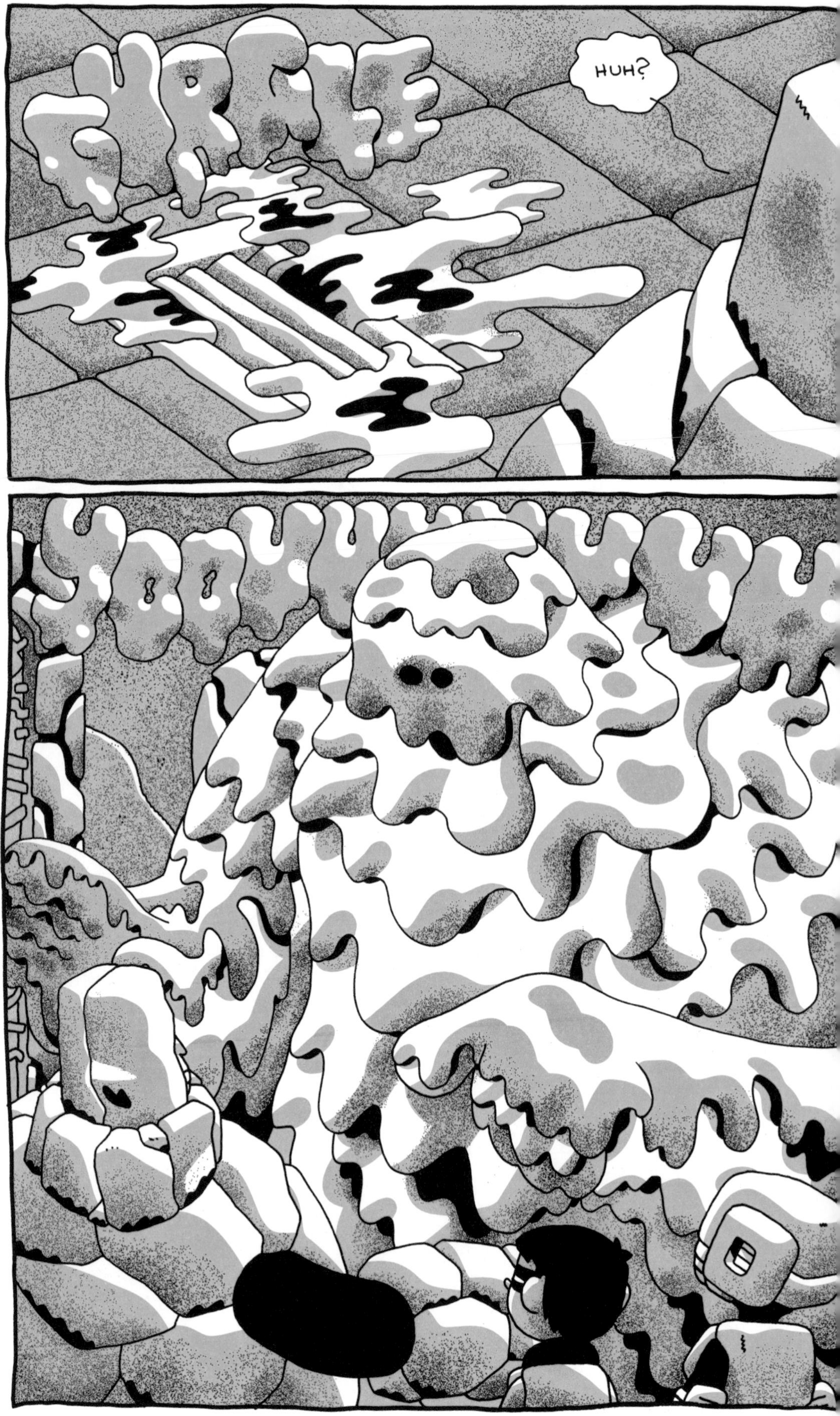
HUH?

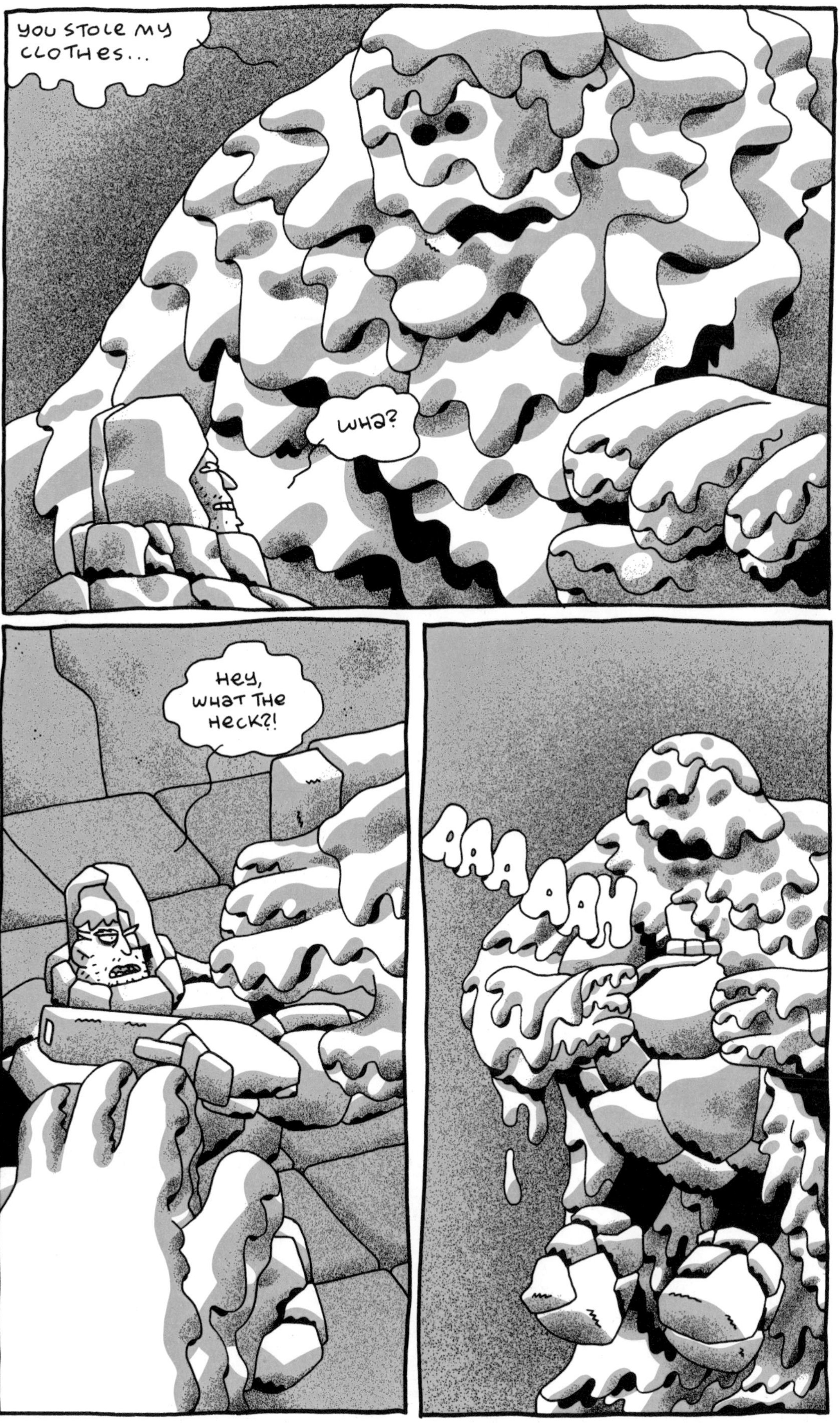
YOU STOLE MY CLOTHES...
WHA?
HEY, WHAT THE HECK?!
AAAAAAH

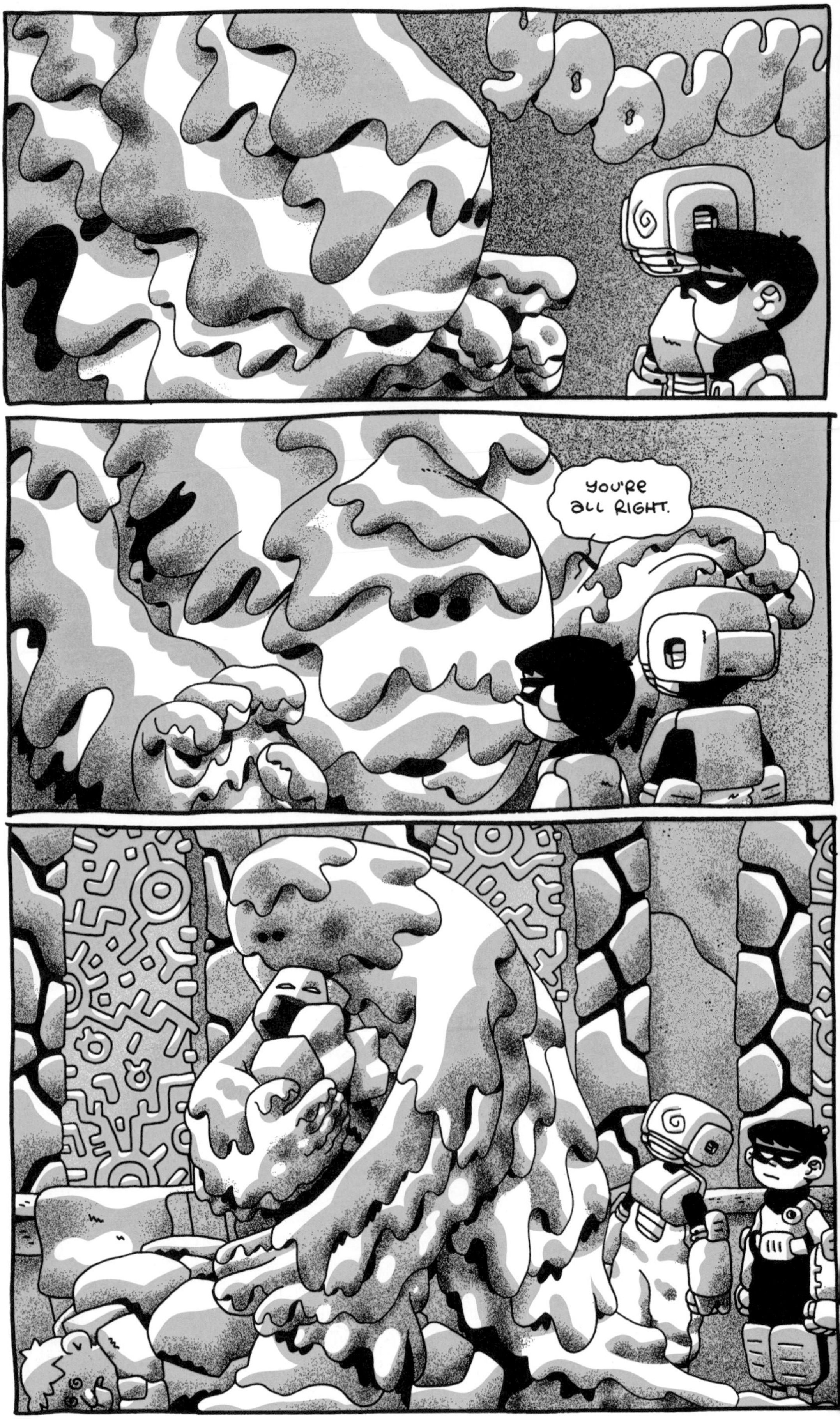
YOU'RE ALL RIGHT.

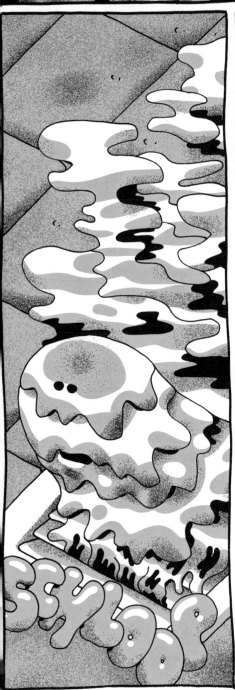

WHA...

WHERE'S MY SUIT?

OH.

UH OH.

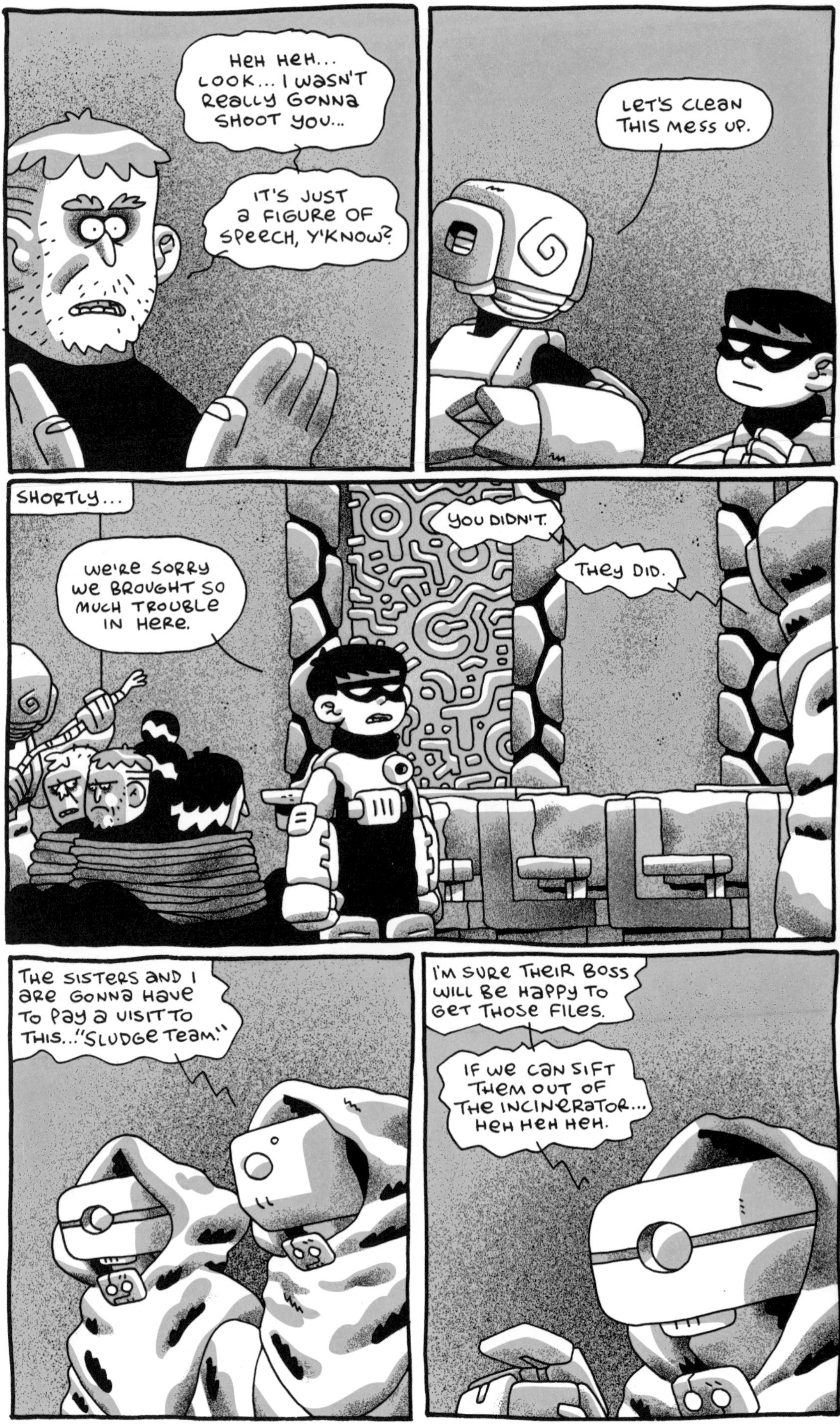
HEH HEH... LOOK... I WASN'T REALLY GONNA SHOOT YOU...
IT'S JUST A FIGURE OF SPEECH, Y'KNOW?
LET'S CLEAN THIS MESS UP.
SHORTLY...
WE'RE SORRY WE BROUGHT SO MUCH TROUBLE IN HERE.
YOU DIDN'T.
THEY DID.
THE SISTERS AND I ARE GONNA HAVE TO PAY A VISIT TO THIS..."SLUDGE TEAM."
I'M SURE THEIR BOSS WILL BE HAPPY TO GET THOSE FILES.
IF WE CAN SIFT THEM OUT OF THE INCINERATOR... HEH HEH HEH.

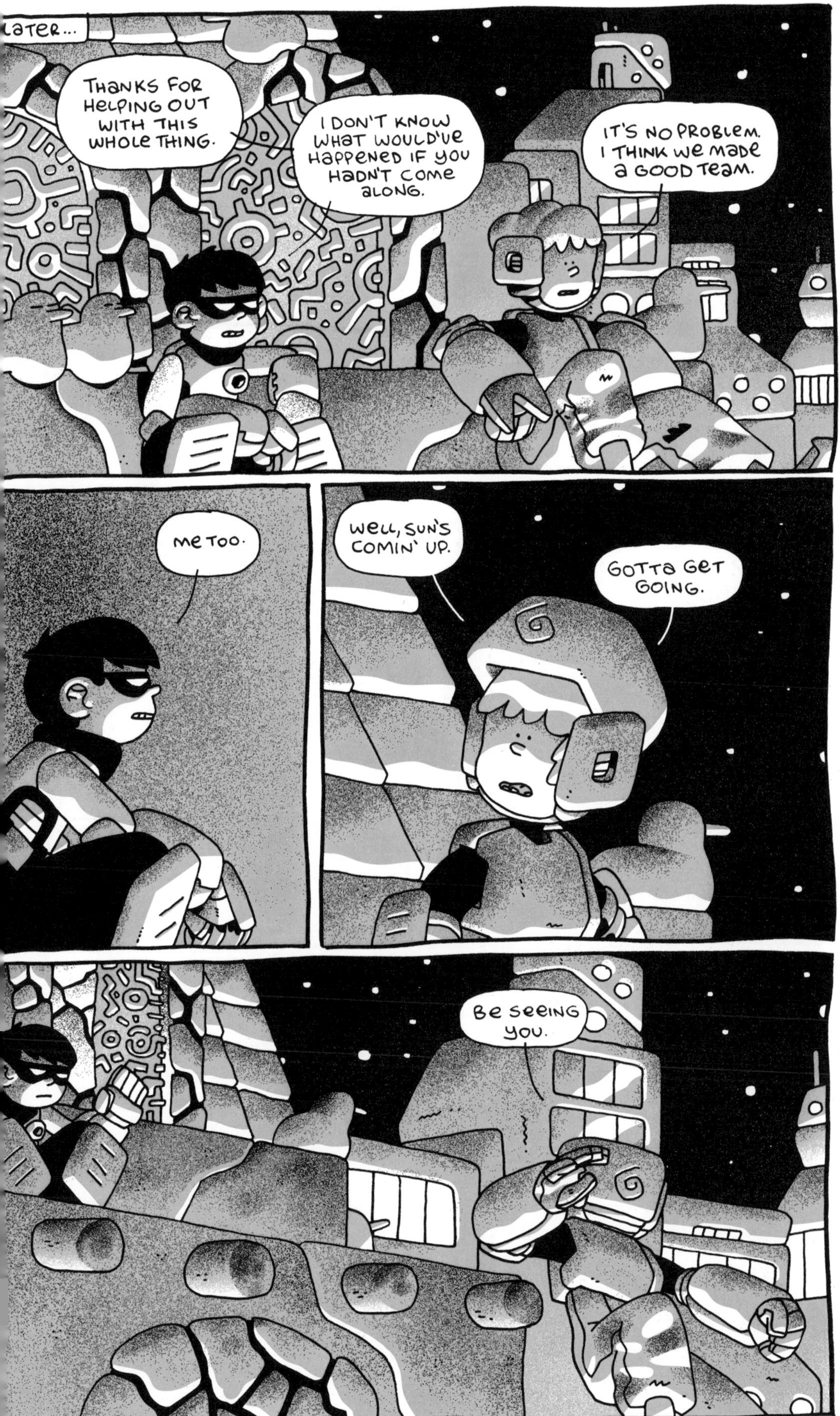
LATER...
THANKS FOR HELPING OUT WITH THIS WHOLE THING.
I DON'T KNOW WHAT WOULD'VE HAPPENED IF YOU HADN'T COME ALONG.
IT'S NO PROBLEM. I THINK WE MADE A GOOD TEAM.
ME TOO.
WELL, SUN'S COMIN' UP.
GOTTA GET GOING.
BE SEEING YOU.

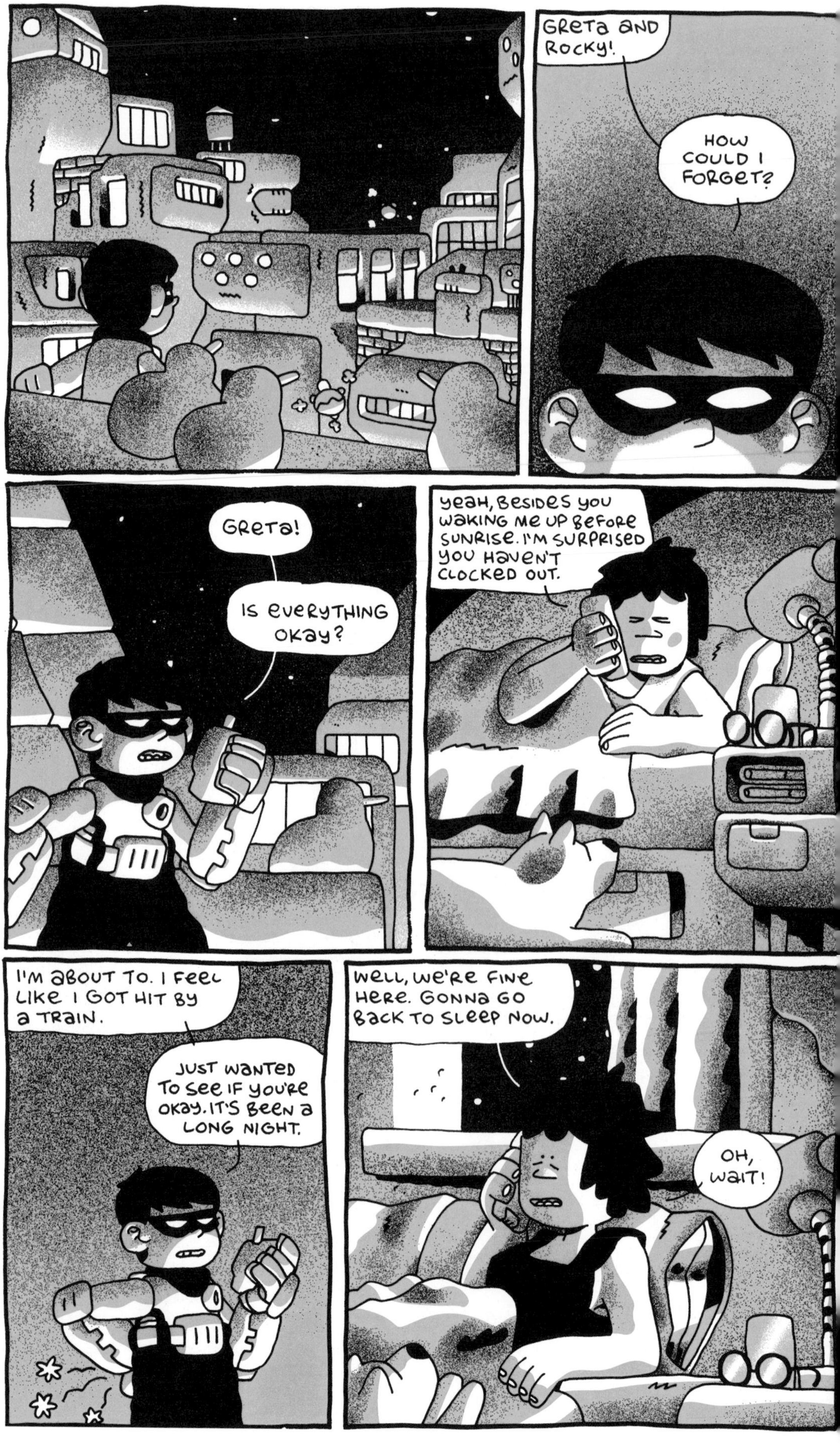
GRETA AND ROCKY!
HOW COULD I FORGET?
GRETA!
IS EVERYTHING OKAY?
YEAH, BESIDES YOU WAKING ME UP BEFORE SUNRISE. I'M SURPRISED YOU HAVEN'T CLOCKED OUT.
I'M ABOUT TO. I FEEL LIKE I GOT HIT BY A TRAIN.
JUST WANTED TO SEE IF YOU'RE OKAY. IT'S BEEN A LONG NIGHT.
WELL, WE'RE FINE HERE. GONNA GO BACK TO SLEEP NOW.
OH, WAIT!

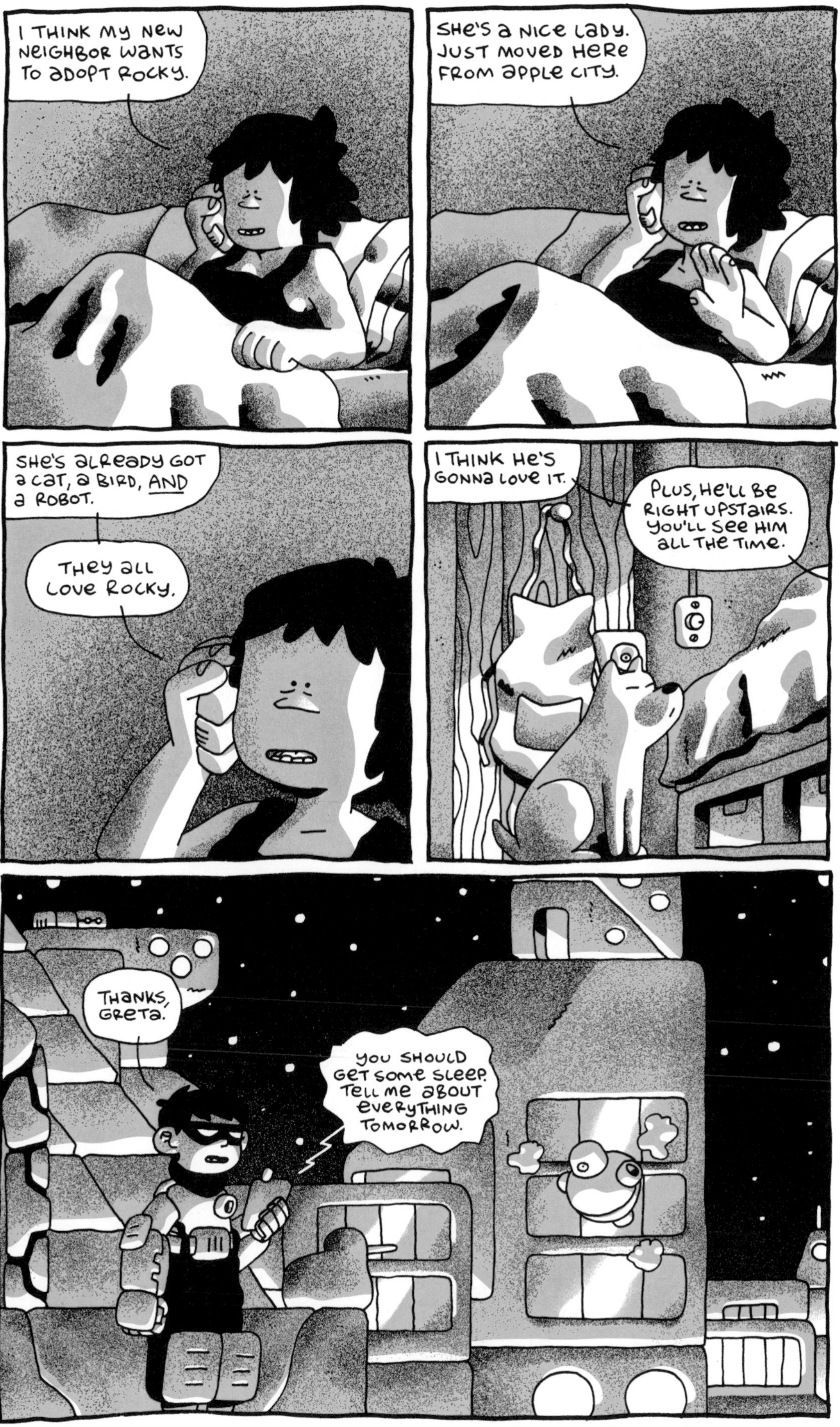

I THINK MY NEW NEIGHBOR WANTS TO ADOPT ROCKY.
SHE'S A NICE LADY. JUST MOVED HERE FROM APPLE CITY.
SHE'S ALREADY GOT A CAT, A BIRD, AND A ROBOT.
THEY ALL LOVE ROCKY.
I THINK HE'S GONNA LOVE IT.
PLUS, HE'LL BE RIGHT UPSTAIRS. YOU'LL SEE HIM ALL THE TIME.
THANKS, GRETA.
YOU SHOULD GET SOME SLEEP. TELL ME ABOUT EVERYTHING TOMORROW.

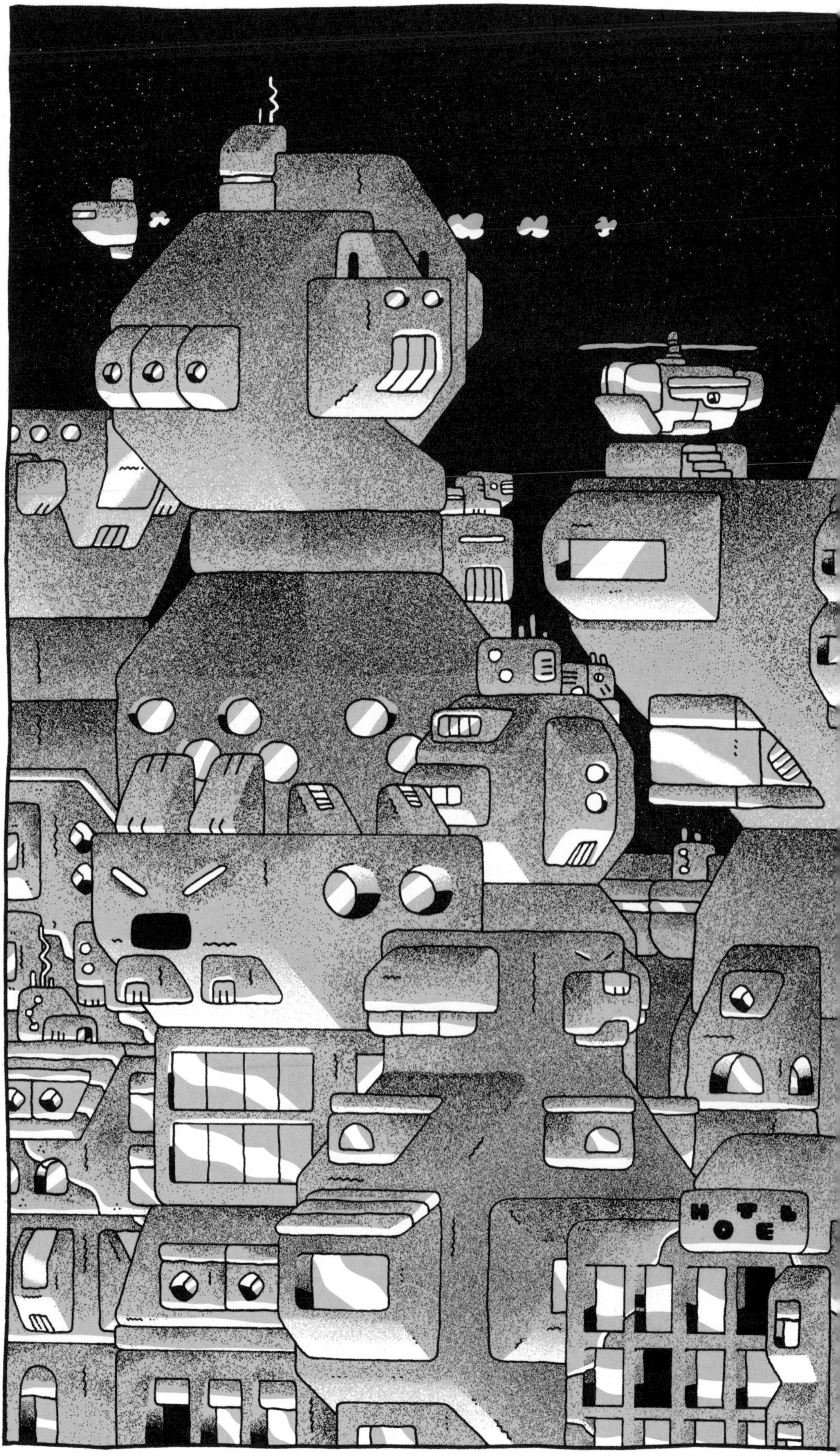
HOTEL

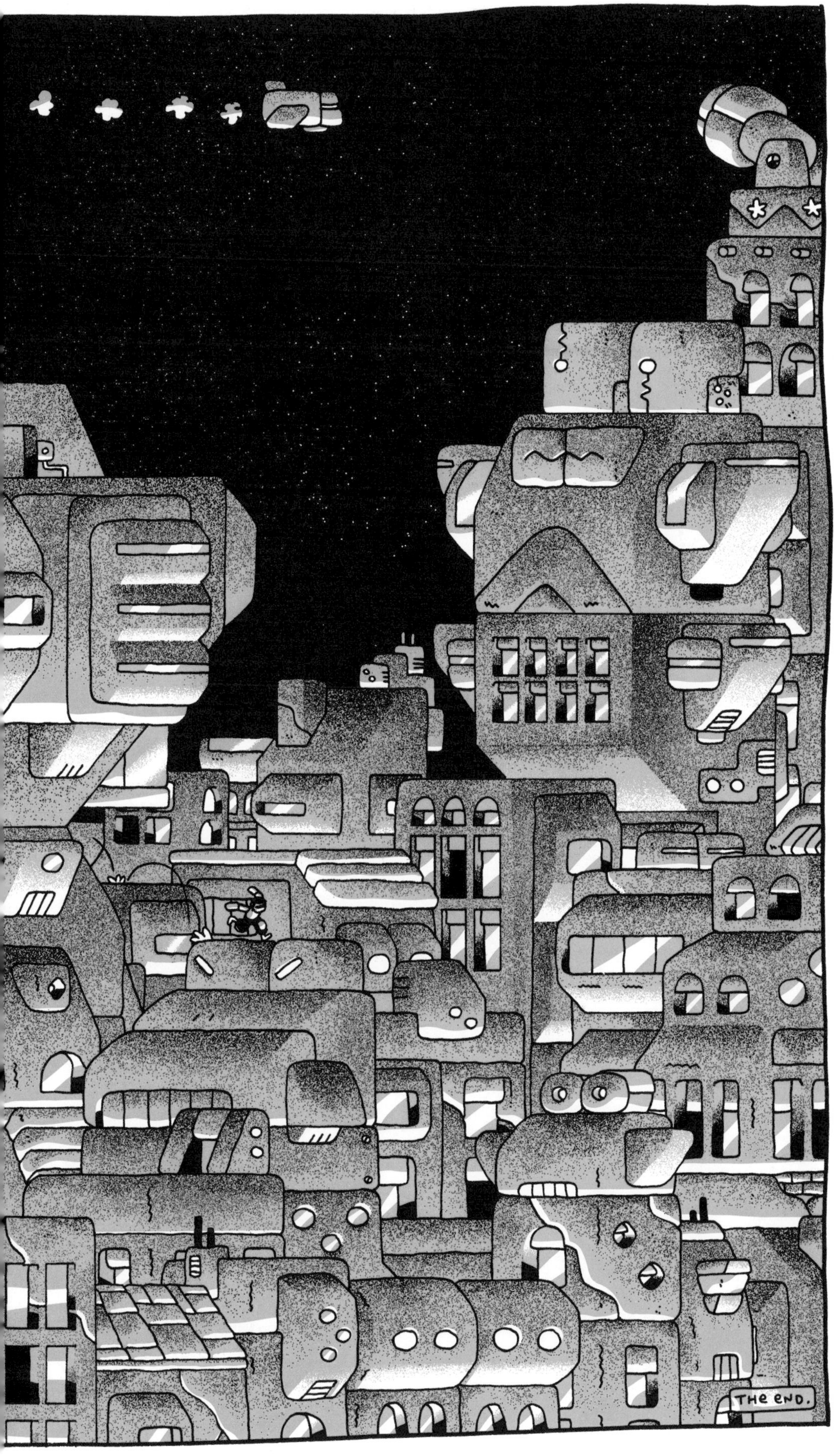
THE END.

**FOR HARPER,
A VERY GOOD FRIEND**

SEE MORE WORK: FREEBENSEARS.COM
CONTACT: BSEARSDESIGN@GMAIL.COM

OTHER BOOKS IN THE PLUSWORLD SERIES:

FOR SEEKING HEAT (2014)

THE SWEEPER (2015)

NIGHT AIR (2016)

VOLCANO TRASH (2017)

THE IDEAL COPY (2018)

THE SWEEPER & THE BAD EGGS (2018)

HOUSE OF THE BLACK SPOT (2019)

PETROLEUM SPIRIT DAZE (2019)